With a steadying breath drawn in slowly, Gwyn felt the panic loosen its vice in her chest. She tried in some way to return that gentle smile and then, at last, her own voice came again. "I beg your patience...I seem to have lost my heart amongst your things."

The words sweetly stole the breath from Llinolae with their honesty. She stepped nearer and took Gwyn's face in her hands, her blue gaze seeming to stare into Gwyn's very soul. "My own heart's a bit lost around you too, my dear Amazon."

Fires of Aggar

by Chris Anne Wolfe

New Victoria Publishers

Published by New Victoria Publishers Inc., a feminist, literary, and cultural organization, PO Box 27, Norwich, VT 05055-0027.

Cover Art and Design by Ginger Brown

First Edition Printed in the U.S.A.
1   2   3   4   5   1998 1997 1996 1995 1994

Library of Congress Cataloging- in-Publication Data
Wolfe, Chris Anne.
    Fires of Aggar / Chris Anne Wolfe.
       p. cm.
    ISBN 0-934678-58-8: $10.95
    I. Title
PS3573 . 0497F57 1994
813' .54--dc 20   94-15388
                                                                 CIP

My thanks go to my friends and family for their loving support, especially to Bonnie N. and Bob G. And I thank the entire crew at New Victoria for their patient faith! I also continue to be incredibly grateful to the City of Hope National Cancer Center where *kindness* seems to be contagious.

But there are two very special women to whom I dedicate this book.

To Dr. Eileen Smith...
>because without you there wouldn't have been
>any more writing nor the opportunity to meet—

Jennifer Anna DiMarco...
>and without you, Jennifer Anna,
>there wouldn't have been such joy.

Prologue

In the long, declining years of the Third Galactic Empire, the Terran Imperialists struggled to defend their interstellar borders against all encroachers. But the greedy ambitions of their own factions ultimately sabotaged the stability of their trade and civilization. Their stranglehold faltered. Intergalactic war broke out. The end became inevitable.

For many, that self-destructive path had always been recognized—the downfall anticipated. Among those wiser peoples were the Council of Ten and *dey Sorormin*. Separated by innumerable light years and by varied resources, the two cultures had none-the-less become intricately entwined. Once, during the height of the Terran Empire's reign, the Council of Ten on Aggar had enlisted the aid of an Amazon from *dey Sorormin* to prevent an intergalactic border war that would have annihilated Aggar's very existence. In exchange for that help, *dey Sorormin*—the Sisterhood—had found themselves gifted with a daughter of Aggar who brought with her the Blue Sight. And as that precious gift of mystical powers spread amongst *dey Sorormin's* descendants, the Sight came to enhance the Sisters' most cherished values of conscience and spirituality.

So when the time of the Terran's imperial demise came, the Council of Ten again sought the aid of *dey Sorormin's* Amazons. The Sisters were angered at the injustice of Aggar's plight. No culture, no people deserved to be thoughtlessly eradicated by the feuds of their neighboring star systems. But Aggar was a metal-poor planet, without the resources or technology to defend itself. Caught in an endless era of steel swords, stone mortar and glass kilns, their world was powerless against the careless whims of galactic politics.

But *dey Sorormin* was not.

In a decision of conscience, a fleet of Amazons left their home world and answered Aggar's need. With them, they brought the technologies and raw materials for their battles...and they brought their families, their livestock, selected seeds and skills as well as their values to Aggar. These Sisters knew that the starry battling would be done only when the invaders succeeded, and the Terran's Empire was destroyed. By that day, interstellar travel would be dangerously limited if possible at all. The Sisters knew they would not be able to return home.

The Council of Ten had known this too. It is why they did what they could to prepare a welcome. As the quiet guides of Aggar's own conscience, the Council had urged the kings and merchants and common folk to embrace these honorable guardians—these Daughters of the Stars. And when the end of the Empire came, stranding the Terrans of the Aggar outpost and the Amazons of *dey Sorormin*, the rulers of both the Northern and Southern continents welcomed the exiles.

The Amazons were the first to accept the kindness, and they began to build their settlement north, in Valley Bay. But the Terrans balked at such patronizing charity. Instead, they clung to their base grounds jealously.

The Amazons respected Aggar's precarious balance of technology and culture, carefully adapting and interacting with other folk while still preserving their own ways of *dey Sorormin* in Valley Bay. The Terrans hoarded their technical skills and resources, shunning the Ramains' Queen's offered assistance, shunning even counsel in matters of farming and lands.

In Valley Bay, the Sisters created their governing circle, much in the fashion of their home world's communities. Seven women were chosen. Six of them varied in skills and wisdom—they formed the Ring. The seventh was selected from among the most talented daughters of the Blue Sight—she became their Ring Binder. Always powerful enough to reach into the stars, always possessing the rarer ability of out-of-time Seeing, the Ring Binder literally bound Valley Bay's settlement to *dey Sorormin's* home world. Stretching across the light years to that distant welcome, the Blue Sighted daughters of Valley Bay and the Blue Sighted daughters of Home kept the ties strong, kept the harmony of *dey Sorormin* alive and well in Valley Bay's descendants.

The Terran encampment was not so blessed. In struggling to refute their isolation, in feigning to assert some sort of independence, they tenaciously held to their imperial ways. As their resources dwindled, they drew more and more upon their technological superiority. Even as they lost the skills to maintain or repair most of their machinery, they relied upon their weaponry to raid and pillage the neighboring trade routes. Eventually, the overland routes from the Southern Continent closed as the merchants chose to sail ships rather than better arm their caravans.

Time passed, and the daughters of *dey Sorormin* became more and more a part of Aggar's soul. Trade and trust grew between the Ring of Valley Bay and the Ramains' Royal Families, as well as with the other folk of Aggar. The Sisters lent the Council of Ten support in those gentle urgings for tolerances, and they lent strength to the Royal Courts against injustices. They opened their hearts and their homes to the women of Aggar, and the settlement of Valley Bay grew richer in its turn.

The Terran Clans found less and less prosperity, however. As the generations passed, they grew only more isolated and sullen in their grievances. Mistrusts grew between the Khirlan District and the Clan folks. Anger spawned hatreds. Isolation spawned fears. Until inevitably, the rising turmoil ignited a fiery violence—and once again, there was need of the Amazons' aid...

Part I
One Shard Called Honor

Chapter One

winged shadow rippled up across the sheer rock of the embankment. The shape veered off, falling from those jagged cliff tops, then reappeared. With a sudden drop, the small winged-cat fell through an air pocket, and briefly she relished the coolness of cleaner scents, until the heat rose to catch and lift her again. The golden tips of her sable fur ruffled in the caress of that ill wind. The eitteh banked to the north away from the escarpment, seeking altitude before circling back.

The new horizon did not offer her much greater solace. The great, gaping holes of the Firecaps spewed in the north, orange bleeding in a mire of swirling black. The volcanic land stretched to infinity, and the winds it sent south were tainted with a sulfurous stench. The air was blistering hot and grubby with ash. There was grit that tasted of carbon and sand. It was not a place fit for human nor beast.

The eitteh whirled to search once again that nearly featureless rock of the embankment. The barrenness was uninviting, and her scrutiny of that faint, upper trail would have been wasted other times. But today she was rewarded in finding the Amazon's small caravan.

A pair of stub-tailed sandwolves, taupe and beige in fur with massive shoulders tapering to slim hips, shambled along well ahead of the horses. Long trained as scouts, the canines moved with their heads hung low and swinging from side to side as they loped along, being cautious of scents that may or may not be found. The shadow of the eitteh passed before them, and they halted, lifting high blunted muzzles of hairless hide. Eyes as clear as the sands of their ancestral Southern Continent reflected a quiet intelligence; they recognized their winged visitor. The smaller of the sandwolves turned and trotted back along the trail while the other continued forward.

The horses behind were plodding along with heads down bent into the winds, and they paid no heed to the sky above nor to the sandwolf returning from the front. There were three mares. Each of them was well-muscled, broad in the chest and square in build, and each was a blood bay of rich ruddy-red with high black stockings to match both mane and tail. They were obviously not simple pack animals, and in fact, even the packs on the leading pair seemed too small and light to be of much consequence.

Instead of canvassed packs, the third mare carried a lone Amazon. Dusty ash had obliterated the color of her long coat-like garments; her hood and scarf were equally as layered with grey. The dozing slouch of her shoulders and the size of her mare belied her true height; but right now there were no raiders to warn off with impressions here. Nothing was ever very exciting—unless of course, darkfall found one still astride a beast and still leagues from the shelters; then it could become all too exciting along these steep paths.

A sudden shriek rent the afternoon stillness. The sandwolves spun, noses to the air—the Amazon wakened, sword half unsheathed. Again came the cry. The haunting echo blew apart, heart-piercing and unsettling in its humanness. But it was only one of the men-cat.

5

Both the sandwolves and Amazon breathed easier as the sword was resheathed. They were in no danger from those mournful beasts. There was no way down from the upper heights onto this trail. Besides, no matter how savage the eitteh males were, one lone men-cat would have had no chance against the larger sandwolves.

The smaller sandwolf waited until the horses finally began to pass her. Then crouching, she darted beneath the last mare's belly to the rider's right—protectively placing herself between her favored human and that fathomless precipice of the trail's edge.

The Amazon pulled the scarf down from her face and leaned over, curious of the sandwolf's appearance. The creature whined, then with a single yap tossed her head up, and the woman's copper gaze went skyward.

The female eitteh was circling again.

With a muttered half-oath, the woman recognized the messenger of Valley Bay. It was no wonder the wailing men-cat had awakened.

With rueful disgust, she glanced at those Firecaps in the north; because of them the air currents were too dangerous for the winged-cat to risk landing on this trail. She twisted behind, looking for bearings, then ahead and confirmed they were indeed near the end of this isolated stretch. Soon, barely shy of two leagues, the path would cut south through this ascending cliff, and a league after that they would drop beyond the scent of sulfur and find the southern Gate House. Whatever was happening, the news would best wait until that hearth was reached.

News—what could be good? It was always a risk sending the winged-cats to any of these ranges during the spring mating season.

Resigned, the Amazon waved the airborne messenger on, then touched her heel to the bay. The sandwolf bounded forward to herd the pack mares along faster, and the small troupe picked up their pace. There had been enough napping. It would be better not to tempt the Fates so soon in this journey; it appeared, there would be enough opportunity for that later.

* * *

Darkfall had not quite reached the southern side of the embankment as the group rounded the high rocks which marked the haven of the Gate House canyon. It wasn't much of a canyon, but it was large enough to corral a good dozen beasts and to support a stone cottage to house as many riders.

The horses livened their steps at the smell of fresh water, and the sandwolves shambled aside to let them pass. The rider swatted at her sleeveless coat and hood, sending up clouds of dust in the twilight and bringing forth the bright copper-bronze color of the fabric with the golden threads and buttons of its quilting. The larger of the sandwolves sneezed, shaking her head with squinting eyes and a huff or two as the dust threatened to engulf her.

Laughter rang clear as the Amazon uncovered herself, pushing her hood back as the youngest sandwolf sneezed again. She shook her hair loose, its copper shade exactly the match of her sparkling eyes. It was an unruly tousle tied back at the nape of her neck, caught in the folds of scarf and hood.

"You would do well to trot a wider circle, Ty," she teased, and the older sandwolf, Ril, expressed her agreement with a drooling, long-toothed grin.

The sound of her voice brought another Sister from the stone hut, a tall figure clad in plainer garments of green and tan. She carried a wooden bucket of grain for the horses, but her empty hand lifted in a friendly greeting. "Mother's blessings, Royal Marshal—"

"Marshal indeed!" taunted the newcomer. "Have I been gone so long, Tawna?"

The horses drew nearer in the dimness, and a sudden smile brightened the other's face. "Gwyn! I didn't recognize you bundled so neat. Come in, *Soroe* ! So late in crossing? You're lucky to have made it—I was sure you must be a lowlander or some Sister returning. What makes you dally or have you done the two days crossing in one!?"

"In truth, I did just that," and the young woman sighed as she stepped down from the stirrup. The saddle creaked and the bay, Cinder, grunted in relief as the girth uncinched for the first time since dawn.

Tawna squinted, her dark eyes shrewd as they took measure of her guest. The lines in Gwyn's faced underlined her fatigue. Between the grit and the apricot gold of her skin, the creases seemed almost to be worked into wood. Gwyn was a Royal Marshal by trade as her bright copper-bronze coat declared; she was *Niachero*—Daughter of the Stars—by birth as her height and tan attested, but she was a young Sister too. Twenty-seven by the reckoning of the ancient home stars or thirteen-and-some by the tenmoons of Aggar, not so very old and not so very young. Yet Tawna noted the weary tightness about her lips and that all-too-knowing squint about her eyes. That sensitive, assessing face should have belonged to someone much older. It wasn't fair, Tawna thought, even without knowing what the duty was this time; Gwyn was too young to be cheated of her own youth. But then *Niachero* were born with that bittersweet brilliance—that stubbornness of ability—to carry what must be carried.

"Has the eitteh arrived?" Gwyn asked abruptly, stripping the red leather saddle from her mare and heaving it onto the corral's stony fence.

"Aye, it was Sable. But she wouldn't wait to take an answer." Tawna felt her throat close with momentary despair. The business must be more serious than she feared, if the eitteh was sent out so quickly after Gwyn's home departure. Then with a sudden shake of her head, Tawna gathered her resolve and opened her arm to hug the taller woman close. Gwyn was *Niachero*, she could take care of herself.

Surprised, Gwyn returned the embrace and looked at her friend questioningly, "*Nehna* ?"

"Rash fool," Tawna muttered, her mouth curling with a strained smile.

"We both," and her eyes glinted with an old teasing.

The sudden strength of Gwyn's mischief broke Tawna's misgivings like a prism does sunlight, and the woman caught her breath.

Gwyn laughed as the bucket of grains was suddenly dropped at her feet. Tawna shook her head, striding away with an exasperated cry, "See to your poor beasts! A single day's crossing? They've been abused enough without waiting for their feed as well!"

* * *

"Do you ever get tired of being alone?" Gwyn murmured, half-lost in her

7

own world, and Tawna smiled gently, brushing the feathery copper from Gwyn's forehead as they lay. Gwyn's attention shifted, returning from that far-away place and worry etched faint furrows between her eyebrows. "How do you manage?"

They were wrapped in a soft spun blanket, the fire in the hearth flickering with a heartwarming glow that echoed the tenderness of the touch they had shared. The small cottage smelled of wood smoke and herbs, far cries from the musty ash of sulfur in those distant heights. It was a good place to find refuge and it reflected the woman's care and welcome. But tonight the Sisters' Gatekeeper was not to be deluded by her dear companion's rhetoric, and Tawna's head shook with a sympathetic smile. "You're missing Selena then?"

A pause, a sigh, and a weary denial closed Gwyn's copper-hued eyes. "I wish it were simply that."

Tawna studied her carefully. "It's almost been a tenmoon-and-a-half, Gwyn."

Eyes opened, blurred with tears. She nodded.

"Has there been no other?"

At Tawna's concern, Gwyn offered a fond smile. "You count yourself so little, *Soroe*?"

"No, but I count myself as your dear friend," Tawna returned solemnly, "not as your heartbound companion."

"Truth," she sighed faintly. "No, there has been no heartbond since Selena."

Tawna nodded, realizing she had always known this. Gwyn was a woman of intense, committed passions. Their time together would have changed, altered from loving rapport to gentle companionship if someone that special had come along. Gwyn was not capable of losing herself in one woman's arms for long, if her heart was entwined with another.

"It takes time to heal," Tawna added belatedly. "What you had with Selena is rare, it will not be easily replaced."

"It will never be replaced," Gwyn corrected hollowly.

"No, but there are as many ways in loving as there are women to love."

"I know that."

"It is a hard thing to remember through death's empty wake."

A slow breath passed her lips, and Gwyn shook her head vaguely, "It is perhaps that I am more frightened of finding...awakening such feelings again, Tawna. The intensities, the depths given with such heartbonds. But still, how do you bear the loneliness?"

"For me it is not lonely," Tawna murmured, the truth of it reflecting in her gentle gaze. "We are different, our needs are different. You are meant to follow passion and bright stars, while I? I'm content to watch the Twin Moons, to sing with my lute, and pray with my poetry. This rocky alcove offers a priestess' seclusion for me, dear Gwyn. It is not lonely. It's merely my home."

Gwyn thought about that, listening to the whispering winds as they stirred through the mountains. For a moment she could almost imagine the stars swirling, dancing in the moons' light beyond that rough hewn roof. Still, it was only a glimpse of what her companion embraced, and she knew again the differences they would never breech.

"I think, it is not only the companionship you are missing," Tawna mused, watching Gwyn's face closely. "Perhaps it is the intimacy of the Blue Sight as well?"

Gwyn laughed with a sudden shout, and her friend grinned with her. "Intimacy? What a delicate word from you, Tawna. Aren't you meaning naked exposure? Sheer lack of privacy? Isn't it always you who maintains that to love a Blue Sight is to drop every barrier to the depths of the soul?"

"Well, perhaps I lack that particular sort of courage. After all, I am not *Niachero*."

No... Gwyn sobered, remembering just how many women were frightened by the very passions that would bind their hearts to another's life. It hurt to remember those who had turned from her own offer because of that fear.

"And...," Tawna reminded her with a teasing smile, "I was not raised with a mother and a sister of the Sight. My hermit-like ways would have been quite lost in that sort of household, don't you think?"

"In truth."

"Also, Selena was gifted with years as well as Sight. You held much to treasure there."

Again Gwyn had to agree.

"Yet why now?" Tawna probed, concern reflected with fond love as she tipped Gwyn's face upward. "What has happened to bring on this soul searching, *Soroe*?"

Gwyn shrugged, growing almost off-handed as she turned to slide her arms about Tawna's smooth shoulders. "I go to escort a Blue Sight. Perhaps the thought has made me nostalgic?"

Tawna felt her lips curl in amusement as Gwyn's soft mouth claimed her. She knew better than to pry, but she wasn't about to object to the delicious distractions either.

* * *

Off in the darkness, Cinder gave an annoyed snort and stomp. Gwyn glanced up from her whittling, squinting to make out the wavering shapes beyond the fire. She could see nothing. A warm muzzle laid itself down across her knee in reassurance, and the Amazon grinned. She gave Ril a fond rub down her furry backbone. "So our bondmate finally returns from her hunt. Think she'll behave herself for a day or two?"

Ril answered with a vague whine of doubt. With her head still in Gwyn's lap, the sandwolf twisted, brows high, as she searched expectantly. Obligingly, Ty padded out of the darkness to join them. Her cold nose bumped lightly against Gwyn's cheek and then Ril's.

"Good Eve to you too, Young Ruffian." Gwyn grunted as the tardy sandwolf flopped to the ground and rolled her weight into her human. With a good-natured chuckle, Gwyn accepted her role in life as a backrest. She gave the great beast a pat on the stomach and a hearty hug. Ty grinned back over a furry shoulder at Gwyn; it was a toothy, comical grin at that upside-down angle. "I'm glad you ate well. I'm even happier to have you safely in camp. But what were you doing to poor Cinder?"

Ty flipped to her belly and cheerfully refused to answer. Panting with feigned ignorance, she stared off into the dark.

"Hm-hmm. Thought so." Ril politely moved her nose as Gwyn resumed working on the small flute. The campfire crackled, and its noise blended easily with the stirring night sounds. A yellow cricket awoke somewhere and soon its chirping had roused the neighbors from their leafy beds. One of the mares shifted her weight, rustling the twigs and such underfoot. Ril moved closer to keep Gwyn's leg warm as a wayward breeze tried to make the spring chill chillier.

But Gwyn's thoughts were on the note *M'Sormee's* eitteh had delivered to the Gate House for her. Her mother had heard from the contacts at the Royal Court and their discreet inquiries had only confirmed Gwyn's suspicions; neither the King nor the Crowned Rule, his daughter, had received any news of the unrest in Khirlan. They were not ignoring the Dracoon's pleas for help, the Royal House was simply unaware of her needs which supported the unsettling probability that there was a traitor among the Dracoon's own scribes. Either that or the Dracoon was downright paranoid, and Gwyn's mother would have Seen something odd if such were the case. But as Gwyn thought back to that evening with *M'Sormee*, she remembered her mother's trust in the Dracoon. No, Bryana had Seen no amarin of madness, only of desperation...

The whitewashed walls of the garden were bathed in orange by the setting sun. The woman's red hair was afire as well, though she was ignorant of its sheening colors. She'd bound it back in a thick braid to stay out of the way as she tended the rose bushes. Her hands were protected by thick gloves, but her movements were efficient and unhindered by either her gloves or her heavy apron. The emerald robes she wore beneath the gardening apron suggested that scrounging around on her knees in the mulch was not her usual pastime.

Shadows began to lengthen. The globe lamps along the walls and paths gradually brightened, subtly fending off the twilight just as the climate control kept the icy ting of the new spring away. Heedless of time, the woman worked on until finally a shadow did intrude. A faint smile creased the corners of her blue eyes, although she never stopped in her task.

"You're working late, *M'Sormee*."

"I started late." She finished to her satisfaction and looked up at the tall, strong figure of her birth daughter. As always Bryana thought how like her Beloved this daughter looked, and as always she felt pride stir for those two Amazons of her family. Like Jes, this daughter possessed the height and strength of their foremothers—like Jes, Gwyn tanned lightly from the sun. The only thing that bespoke of Bryana's own blood was the hair, but even that had become uniquely Gwyn's. A fairer red and finer than Bryana's, it tended to unruliness if the curls worked free from the short braid. That disarray was again more reminiscent of Jes' dark locks.

That infectious, familiar grin challenged her silent assessment. Bryana relented and set aside her trowel. She accepted the offered hand as she went to rise, ruefully conceding how stiff age and gardening had made her this evening.

"I began late because the Ring met overlong this afternoon. Too many concerns for our Sisters who will be returning from the Changlings' Wars. This summer season will not be an easy one for Valley Bay, I fear."

"And as usual they expected the Ring Binder to magically provide all the answers."

Bryana nodded, patient humor sparkling in her eyes. "There is a certain assumption that since the Blue Sight shows me what event is to happen, it must naturally also tell me how to deal with that event."

"Yet it's just the opposite," Gwyn murmured. She gave her mother an arm to lean on as they turned for the house. Despite the creamy smoothness of Bryana's face, her daughter knew how age-worn the seasons as Ring Binder had made this woman.

"It is a worry," Bryana continued almost as if she were speaking to herself. "The Wars have robbed so many of them of limbs, of trust...of hope.

"We spent hours with the n'Shea crones of Home, searching for records and methods of dealing with these battle stresses. I believe our own House n'Shea found some of it useful. I hope so, anyway."

"But it leaves you tired, using your Sight to cross that starry chasm of time and space."

Bryana shrugged. Gwyn place an arm about her mother's shoulders, and a grateful if amused smile appeared. "And who comforts who here?"

Gwyn only hugged her gently. "Then think of me as *Niachero* , not as your eldest."

Bryana laughed beneath her breath. They entered the house, and as Bryana crossed the room to sink gratefully into the depths of the great couch, Gwyn unfolded the slatted doors that separated the house and gardens. She paused to be certain the outer lights were dimming off, then turned to kindle the wood laid in the fireplace.

"You sent for me," Gwyn reminded her mother softly, settling back against the side of the hearth. She watched in silent concern as Bryana wearily shrugged out of the work apron. Not for the first time Gwyn thought that it was fortunate *N'Sormee* would be coming home this summer with the rest of the veterans; Bryana seemed to tire less easily when Jes was near to lend her strength. "Would you like some tea, *M'Sormee* ?"

"No," Bryana raised a brow, irony touching some inner thought which she finally shared. "Do you know how many kettles of tea I've consumed today?"

Gwyn laughed quietly. "We should ask Kimarie to send down a few kegs of her orchard juices. Offer you a change of taste."

"Your little sister has enough to worry about right now. Calving season is beginning for our beasties, remember?"

"Aye—no," Gwyn stretched out her booted feet, with a deliberate slowness to the motion that was not lost on her mother. "I'd forgotten."

"You are treating me—like I'm made of fragile glass."

"Sometimes, perhaps you are."

"Sometimes, perhaps I'm not."

Gwyn acknowledged that with a tip of her head. "I'd never contest your strength."

A rich, soft laugh eased much of the weariness in the older woman. "In some ways, you are very much my daughter. Always the diplomat!"

Eyes widened in mock surprise. "*M'Sormee!* Am I not always your daughter?"

"No." A quite composed, blue gaze fell to Gwyn, though Bryana was careful as always with her Blue Sight not to actually lock glances. "Often you are Jes' own."

"Never!"

They laughed together at that, companionable in the way loving seasons and simple respect had created. Then slowly, the stillness came to wrap about them. Gwyn bent a knee and rested her chin atop it. Hands folded about her ankle and her copper eyes studied her mother. Once more, she prompted. "You sent for me. Was it because of something that happened within the Ring? Or something that comes from our Sisters of the home planet?"

"Neither really. A few days ago I had a visitor. Well, not precisely a visitor—a harmon. And now I find I have need of a Royal Marshal."

That startled Gwyn a bit. There weren't many Blue Sight's talented enough to project their harmon—that ghost image of themselves—across great distances to another, Blue Sight receptor. It was a necessary talent in the Ring Binder who was often the sole link between the Sisters of Aggar and their distant home world, but even the Council Seers were not always so gifted. Curious, Gwyn pressed, "The visitor was from the Council? No? From the Royal Family in their western Palace—or the Prince's northern field camps?"

"From Khirlan."

"Khirlan? The most southeastern district of the Ramains?" Gwyn's chin dropped with a contemplative frown. "I've never heard of any trouble from them. But they have been pretty isolated during the Wars. Being so far south and inland, it's always been more economical for them to provide extra tax monies rather than armed support for the Prince. I don't think they've even got a standing regiment among his northern troops. But then the King and Crowned Rule still endorse the Old Law for border Districts and with the Clan's Plateau being Khirlan's neighboring—the Clan!"

Understanding dawned as the Amazon sat bolt upright. "The Old Law exempted Khirlan from Royal Conscriptions, specifically *because* of the Terran Clan's threat to the Ramains' Realm. They send Churv money instead of sword carriers, because the swords are simply needed *in Khirlan*. Between the continual raids and the occasional invasions of the Clan, the Khirlan folk are in a constant struggle and have always had to maintain an active militia."

"Well apparently...," Bryana amended somberly, "the last few seasons have only seen Khirlan's struggle grow worse."

With a grim frown, Gwyn nodded. She knew all too well what must have happened. "The Clan finally capitalized on the fact that the Prince's troops were occupied on the northern borders. The Clan Leads realized the Royal Family wouldn't be able to send reinforcements and decided to see what they and their fire weapons could gain from it."

"So it would seem."

"*M'Sormee*?" Curiously, Gwyn glanced at her mother. It was odd that Valley Bay's Ring Binder had become involved in this sort of matter. "Who was this visitor?"

"The King's Dracoon of Khirlan."

"She or he?"

"She. Her name is Llinolae."

"She came to you and not to the Crowned Rule? Or even to the Council of Ten? Surely the Council has jurisdiction over the Clan's affairs. We're only

12

interested bystanders."

"Ones which the Clan would prefer did not exist," Bryana concluded succinctly.

"So why does the Dracoon seek you out?"

"It was unintentional."

Her brow creased in a scowl, and Gwyn sat forward in disbelief. "Her Blue Sight erred? That's not possible, surely? Only the Council's own Seers know Valley Bay well enough to find you here in this place. And they would never mistake here for the King's Court."

"Her Blue Gift erred," Bryana returned calmly. "Her Sight—her own, not a Seer's Apprentice stationed within her court."

"There's a Dracoon gifted?" Gwyn had never heard of King nor Council arranging such a thing. "It's certainly a novel idea. I can imagine where it might be useful in foreseeing some of the Clan's antics. But still, *M'Sormee,* you are always reminding us that the Sight's talents lend information rather than knowledge. Having a Dracoon incapable of strategy or deduction is somewhat limiting, isn't it?"

The subtle curve of an almost secretive smile was Bryana's only response. Gwyn recognized that expression. She sighed. Often when her mother saw something of the future that was best left ambiguous, she got that vague, pleased look. It was useless to press further. Instead, Gwyn changed tack, "Who had she been trying to reach, *M'Sormee* ?"

"*Dey Sorormin* of our home world—a Sister n'Shea and one n'Athena."

"Of home?! She's a Sister then?!! How—there's never been a Sister governing as a Ramains' Dracoon!"

"She is not a daughter of Valley Bay, Gwyn. But she has been accepted by both her mentors n'Shea and n'Athena as a foster daughter…she has some claim to us and our help." Bryana let her daughter absorb that for a moment, then elaborated. "My garden with its roses and greens of home is apparently very similar to the garden of her mentor n'Shea. As happens when we grow tired, however, she found she could not See across the stars. So this garden which is so very foreign to Aggar—and my own Blue Sight—drew her here instead."

A wry grin sprouted as Gwyn muttered, "Wager she was shocked to find herself still under blue skies and not beneath lavender."

"She was frightened, a bit."

"Of you? And she with the Sight?" Gwyn was genuinely alarmed. "*M'Sormee,* what were you doing?"

"Snipping the winter roses back…no, it was not my amarin that dismayed her. It was the risk that the Council might learn of her visit. She has asked me not to involve them. I chose to respect her reasons, although she did not explicitly share them."

"Which means she impressed you…and we should trust her." Given her mother's Blue Gift, Gwyn didn't question that decision. "So now, you send for me instead."

"You are a Ramains' Royal Marshal, Daughter, one of the Crowned Rule's emissaries—judge and protector. I had assumed you'd be riding out for duties again this spring…? Ahh, and I See I am right. As a Marshal, I thought…well, it occurred to me that the problems of Khirlan's Dracoon is foremost the Royal Family's business. Clan raiders are threatening the welfare of the Ramains' realm. The people's safety is more important than Council's policies, is it not? Wouldn't it be prudent for a Royal Marshal to investigate?"

"Do you know how well the Crowned Rule has been kept informed of these Clan troubles?"

"Does it matter?" Bryana was not ignorant of the neighboring realm's politics. "When the Crowned is preoccupied, the Marshals tend to the important matters as things arise. Since when do they wait for royal directives?"

"We don't."

"Then you wonder at something else."

For a moment Gwyn considered that uneasy feeling inside, her chin once again atop her knee. Finally her thoughts ushered themselves together, and she found the inconsistencies that teased her.

"You want to know more of this Dracoon Llinolae."

"Yes, I do." Gwyn gave a wry grin. Her mother's Blue Sight was as perceptive as usual. "You say, she wants no involvement of the Council in this? That's fair. They are certainly passive enough with their patient diplomacy to try anyone's nerves—especially when one is dealing with a military threat! And I don't know of *anyone* who'd deny that the Clan and their horde of fire weapons could create a military nightmare! But what I don't understand is how a Blue Sight came to be Dracoon of Khirlan, if the Council wasn't involved? I mean, *M'Sormee* , I intend no disrespect, but you are the Ring Binder and not an appointed official for a reason!"

"Aye," Bryana smiled indulgently. "I See details upon details in the ever-flowing life cycles around us. I bind the Ring of Valley Bay to our home world by traversing the glowing paths of amarin that connect the Blue Sights of Aggar to Home. I read the pieces and share the images, the impressions of life. And rarely can I be objective about those things that I See, because I Feel them in the perceiving. It would make me a very poor leader, in many circumstances. I would forever be biased in favor of the stronger personalities."

"Although that sensitivity makes you an excellent judge of character, it would be a tremendous liability in a leader."

"Ahh...," Bryana nodded, "I understand your uneasiness now. You trust that she is of admirable character, because I can See this in her amarin. But you question the sanity of those who appointed her Dracoon, because of her Sight she could so easily fall prey to bad advice from trusted advisors."

"Yes! *Because* of her Sight—even the most obvious threats could be disguised by passionate, righteous intentions. And yet she was appointed as a District's Dracoon?"

"But she was not appointed, Gwyn. She has always been the Dracoon of Khirlan."

Gwyn tipped her head aside in confusion. Then with a mental shake, she realized that because of the Sight, Bryana was so cognizant of the details of this Dracoon's life that she could not comprehend Gwyn's own lack of knowledge. Gwyn nearly laughed at that. Copper bright eyes returned to Bryana's bemused figure. "All right, *M'Sormee*. If she was not appointed, how did she—with her Blue Sight—become Khirlan's Dracoon?"

"Quite simply, no one knows she has the Blue Sight. Gwyn, this Llinolae holds her title by birth right. Her family has governed the Khirlan District for generations. As the eldest and only child fathered by Mha'del of Khirla, naturally she became the Dracoon when he died. No one had reason to contest it."

"No one had reason? *M'Sormee!* How could no one notice? She has the Blue Sight. Her eyes are blue! Who on Aggar has ever had blue eyes without the Gift?"

"Children of the Clan folk occasionally are blue-eyed, and they have never possessed the Sight, Gwyn. And despite the Clan's self-imposed isolationism of generations, there have been some minglings and marriages throughout Khirlan."

"Some—but it's been a guarded, reluctant mingling at best. And still—the off-spring with that mixed blood have never been blue-eyed without the Sight. *M'Sormee* , you know this!"

Bryana considered that a moment, vaguely realizing she had known of that fact but the young Dracoon's belief had led her to forget the obvious. She smiled at herself in wry amusement, explaining, "The people of Khirla believe differently. Llinolae's mother was a Clan refugee that Mha'del aided and eventually married. When Llinolae was born, no one found it strange that she had her mother's eyes. When she displayed no obvious signs of the Gift, why should those of Khirla's Court have questioned her lack of Sight?"

"Mha'del didn't even know?" Gwyn pressed suspiciously.

"No one knew. To this day, no one outside *dey Sorormin* knows she has the Blue Sight."

"That can't be." Gwyn was genuinely puzzled. "There would have been childhood accidents with illusions from dreams and nightmares? Or was her Clan mother of mixed blood and a Blue Sight herself?"

"No, her mother was not Sighted. Llinolae hid her own Sight—without aid from any other." Bryana shrugged. "She did not wish to leave her family and home to study with strangers at the Council's Keep. She preferred to study with her mentors, n'Shea and n'Athena."

Gwyn was not satisfied. The inconsistency was still glaringly disconcerting to her, and she leaned forward urging her mother to see the anomaly for herself. "She was only a child, *M'Sormee*. The Sight begins to emerge even as a child begins to speak! How could one so young have the skill to hide anything?!"

"No, it was instinctive. It was…she wished to hide, Gwyn. She…," Bryana broke off in frustration, unable to use words to describe such an amarin.

"*M'Sormee* ," Gwyn moved swiftly to her mother's side, clasping her hands and bending to one knee as she forced Bryana to face her. "Show me…please?"

The solution became easy, and the older woman smiled with a gentle gratitude. Then fingers took Gwyn's chin and held her lightly as blue eyes met copper, and gazes locked.

Gwyn shuddered.

Bryana blinked, releasing her immediately.

Gwyn shuddered again, shaking the shock away even as her mother's hand steadied her. She drew a deep breath, only to loosen it with a rush and take another. She rose shakily to take a seat on the couch beside Bryana and forced a crooked grin, "Aye...I understand a little better."

"She has a powerful Gift."

Gwyn nodded, "And powerful motivation."

Bryana agreed. "Even a lesser Gift would have been harnessed instinctually with that..."

"With that sort of desperation?" Gwyn supplied.

Bryana frowned, before cautiously allowing, "In the beginning, perhaps it was a sort of desperation. Yet as she grew, it changed. Perhaps Llinolae was not as desperate as she was desperately *passionate* in her beliefs—in her convictions? She trusted her parents' love and their desire to give her the best by keeping her in Khirla with family."

Convictions? Gwyn thought of that engulfing, consuming sweep of *need* that Bryana's Blue Sight had allowed her to experience. Deep within her, the resounding chord of *Niachero* awoke, and she shivered all over again. There had never been a Blue Sighted *Niachero*—Gwyn's heart went racing at the sheer thought.

She cleared her throat uncomfortably, and glanced at her mother. "Did these mentors she had—the n'Shea and n'Athena—did they ever challenge her choice of hiding?"

"Hmm...I don't know."

Gwyn noticed the idea intrigued Bryana and prompted quickly, "Could you ask them? Perhaps find out a bit more about her abilities and—"

"Jes suggested too that I try and reach them," Bryana interrupted with quiet amusement, knowing she was guilty of being a mother who'd forgotten just how old her daughter had become. "But only after Jes scolded me."

"Oh?"

"Yes , she first reminded me that there are two Marshals in this family. And that you're the one with the experience when it comes to civic, district duties—she's the one with the tarnished battle sword from the north!"

A brief grin flickered across the *Niachero's* face, before "You've already talked to Llinolae's mentors then?"

"No, I could not." Bryana sighed, wearied again by the limitations of her earlier work with the Ring—and now by this. "She is a powerful Blue Sight, Gwyn—perhaps even more so than I. She's been successful in hiding her Gift from the Seers for more than thirteen seasons! She reached our home world using her out-of-time Seeing without anyone's guidance—and she did it as a mere child! To follow her...Gwyn'l, I couldn't even *find her* in Khirla when I went searching. I know she's there! I know her amarin—her harmon! And yet still she can hide from me! Her ability—the scope of her raw talent is—amazing." Bryana finished in a helpless shrug. "Gwyn, I don't know of any Sister who has ever trained a woman like this. I have absolutely no idea who she's been tutored by. That they are n'Shea and n'Athena, I do not doubt—her *Sororian* is too flawless—but there are small oddities in some of her dialect that I can't place with any *Sororian* I know."

"Which means the dialect's either very, very old or not yet used," Gwyn saw the problem finally. "Her out-of-time Seeing allowed her to reach across the stars to *dey Sorormin*, but she's not necessarily speaking with mentors of our time. Is she?"

"Aye...," Bryana agreed. "It's more likely that her mentors are long dead. And counter to our neighbors in the Council's Keep, many of our Blue Sight Sisters do not believe in influencing future generations by documenting visits from out-of-time harmons."

"Understandable," Gwyn nodded at the familiar concept; neither *M'Sormee* nor Selena had ever liked discussing those occasional glimpses of future possibilities. Still, in regards to Llinolae she could have hoped for more...or perhaps not. Gwyn straightened, mentally sorting through all Bryana had told her...and in the end, everything became very simple. Somewhere, sometime on the home world Llinolae had earned the acceptance of two Sisters and she now asked Bryana for help—as an Amazon, Gwyn could not refuse her plea. In this time on Aggar and in their neighboring realm, the Dracoon of Khirla needed help—as a Royal Marshal in the hired service to Ramains' Royalty, Gwyn must answer the Dracoon's call.

Abruptly, she turned back to Bryana. "I've still got two questions."

The older woman nodded for her to continue.

"What, if anything, does the Royal Family know of their Dracoon's plight in Khirlan?"

"Llinolae believes those in Churv ignore her pleas. Initially, she reasoned the Changlings' Wars were responsible for their silence, since so many of the Ramains' resources had to be committed to that defense. Yet now that the Wars are over, she still receives no response.

"Gwyn, I do not understand this! It made no sense to me nor to Jes that the Crowned Rule shouldn't at least send her advisors. You yourself are testimony to the fact that the Royal Marshals are still available—have been available throughout the Wars—to aid and advise in all disputes. It makes no sense."

Gwyn agreed; there was no reason for the King's daughter to isolate Khirlan. Unless...? Gwyn asked abruptly, "Did you think to speak with your Sighted contacts in Churv? Can they tell you if the Royal Family is getting anything from the Khirlan Court? The usual records, their tax monies—anything at all?"

"Yes, I did. Jes had me talk to them. They say, there are regular reports still arriving from Khirlan. There's been no word nor rumor in Churv that Llinolae is in need of any help, though. I've some discrete inquiries being made for us, but it will be a few days before I'll See more."

There was probably nothing more to find in Churv, Gwyn mused. If there was not even a rumor that Khirlan was having difficulty with the Clan, it seemed pretty clear that the reports were being tampered with long before they reached the Royal Family. And that meant Llinolae had a traitor somewhere very close to home—most likely within her Scribes.

"All right," Gwyn drew a deep breath, "that answers my second question—what kind of help does she want? Obviously, she needs to uncover the traitor in Khirla's Court."

"No." Bryana shook her head decisively. "She asks for aid in establishing a new balance with the Clan folk."

"A new balance? A peace treaty?" Gwyn scowled and tipped her head aside. "How does she propose going about that? The Clans haven't acknowledged counsel with anyone in nearly three generations."

"She knows. She is proposing one of two things, either a peaceful exchange of land or resources—"

"It's bad enough to consider *giving* the Clan more territory?"

"Aye, they've taken to burning whole villages with their fire weapons, Gwyn'l. The Clans closed the northeast trade route seasons ago. Since then they've cut deeper west, strangling off nearly all of the northern exchanges. And last summer, they began to harass even the western routes."

"*Mae n'Pour*, it has become bad. Yet if a peaceful exchange can not be negotiated, what does she hope to try?"

"She'll destroy their cache of fire weapons."

Gwyn balked at the enormity of that idea. The most audacious attempts in the past had never even discovered the location of the Clan's armory! Certainly the Council Seers could discern that easily enough, but the Council had always refused to aid in an assault against the Clans. The Council usually refused to aid in any kind of aggressive assault, not just those against the Clan. Instead, the Council kept gently suggesting to the Clan folk that they melt down their alloys and use it for more prosperous trade ventures. But culturally, those fire weapons had become a symbol to the Clan folk of their strength and off-worlder heritage. A symbol of bullies—Gwyn thought grimly—a *symbol* that their mounted warriors had come perpetually to abuse in pillage and plunder.

"It would not be an easy task," Bryana observed quietly.

"But it's one Jes has agreed to...as do I," Gwyn returned. "The northern folk didn't deserve the Changlings' attack, and the people of Khirlan do not deserve the Clan's renewed abuses. No, if there is no success in arranging a peaceful balance, then perhaps it is time the Clan forfeit their precious horde."

"So you will ride to join Jes in Gronday?"

"And then south with her to Khirlan." Bryana nodded as her eldest stood, and Gwyn brushed a kiss of farewell along her mother's brow. "I must tend to packing."

"I know," Bryana smiled with a gentle amusement that tempered the rising amarin of her melancholy. "You have the same shimmer of excitement and tension Jes so held in her youth. This season has been an overly long winter in Valley Bay for you, hasn't it?"

Gwyn flushed a faint brown in admission. But her mother had taken no offense in the truth, and they had parted with that gentle understanding.

Gwyn came out of her memories with a crooked smile and a chuckle. Ril's head lifted in a curious query, and Gwyn admitted, "She always knows, doesn't she?"

The sandwolves tilted their heads, attentive and encouraging.

"Bryana—she'd noticed how restless I'd become. We all three had. I hadn't quite realized it yet, but I'd been looking forward to getting out of Valley Bay. I've missed the woods, the travel...."

Ril whined and nuzzled under Gwyn's arm. Her human gave her a hug, amending gently, "And our time alone together, *Dumauz*."

Ty turned about, pushing into Gwyn's lap from the other side. The knife and wood were set aside as she was welcomed into the embrace.

"Aye, it's been a long, quiet wintering for all of us...a nice respite. But much too quiet and I get to feeling rather useless. Our skills are better suited to helping these outside folk than *dey Sorormin*, it would seem."

In response, Ril sniffed; Gwyn was threatening to become much too serious, much too early in this trip. Ril exchanged a glance with Ty—they'd stop that! The two sandwolves suddenly clambered into Gwyn's lap, their wet tongues in her face. Laughing, she went over backwards beneath their furry heap.

Chapter Two

Ril sneezed with a shake of her head, and the fur at her ruff stood up in little, wet spikes. The silver-green leaves of the drooping trees drenched her again as she pushed through the underbrush, and the dense fur at the crown of her head shed the water, sending trickling streams down across the mud-brown of her face hide. The tips of her small, pointed ears sagged amidst her coarse curls, and her pads made sucking plops as they plowed through the road's mire.

This was not the sort of weather to be dragging one's packmates about in, Gwyn thought with a twinge of conscience as she watched her beloved friend trudge along. The two mares on lead behind them didn't look very happy either. A vagrant breeze stole in past her cloak and Gwyn shivered, correcting her opinion to include herself. This was not the sort of weather anyone should be trudging about in.

She sighed and the saddle creaked as she shifted. Of all the things the ancient Founding Mothers had blessed the Niachero with, the one thing Gwyn did not appreciate was this ultra-sensitivity to cold and damp. It was enough to make one retire from travel permanently. At the moment, it was not an option—which left them all wet and plodding on towards the Marshals' lodgings in the Gronday Traders' Guild.

The passing thought of the Guild brightened her spirits considerably. This was the last day on the road to Gronday, and the Guild's Inn had never scrimped on hot food, hot water nor blazing logs.

Ril sneezed again, and Gwyn clucked her tongue softly in sympathy. The sandwolf lifted a woefully grateful expression at Gwyn's support and sneezed once more.

"*Dumauz*—I hope you're not catching ill?"

The animal shook her head adamantly, but Gwyn could not tell if it was in response to the words or to the latest tree-shed of water.

At least it wasn't actually raining anymore. The spring downpour had been brief, even if overly enthusiastic. Gwyn was only pleased that they weren't being forced to weather a full-seeded thunderstorm.

Ty bounded up the road, panting from the uphill grade and the clinging pull of the poor footing. The sandwolf's head dropped low, her massive shoulders heaving with gasps for air, and Ril trotted forward in concern. With a shudder ,the larger wolf pulled herself together and tossed her tongue back into her mouth before turning. She whined as she pointed down the road.

There was need of help below, Gwyn realized with a jolt, and disbelief that any other would risk this slippery mud was usurped by a sudden thought for the river's gorge. Gwyn unlashed the tether lines and dropped them. "Ty, rest and bring the horses on. Ril—show me where!"

The sandwolves paused, passing wordless knowledge between them, and then Ril darted forward. Gwyn clamped her heels to Cinder's flanks and prayed the footing would hold.

The foliage broke and the wind whipped at them from the canyon below.

A rough stone wall lined the muddy trek as the road leveled and followed the river's gorge. Gwyn felt the barest relief as her gaze found no sign of damage in that wall. The roar of the Suiri River echoed high with the wind. She urged Cinder on towards the mountain crevice that bent the road sharply north, but the bay had to slow some to keep her footing. As they rounded the bend, a gasp caught in Gwyn's throat at the sight of the bridge below. Along the mountainside the road twisted and turned, dropping some fifty feet to where the wooden scaffolding of the bridge spanned the gorge. Upon the side of that bridge, a wagon hung. The rear axle was clinging tenaciously to the side of the structure, the right back wheel was shattered and dangled as the team of horses shied, threatening to slide and slip back even further.

There was the steady voice of a man calling, his low pitch trying to cut through the distorted eddies of the wind—trying to stay calm. Then above it all, the answering wail of a child came. Gwyn felt her heart stop as she made out a small, bundled figure in the rear of the wagon.

As quickly as she dared, she guided Cinder down. Below, the harnessed horses screeched a shrill sound of fear that rang through the gorge cliffs.

"Ril!" Gwyn called sharply. Shamed, the sandwolf retreated from the foot of the bridge, belatedly remembering the wagon's team was not from Valley Bay and would be terrified by a sandwolf.

Gwyn snatched both rope and sword from her gear and left Cinder with Ril. Shedding her cloak and the bulky copper coat as she moved, Gwyn felt her feet slide in each step. The wooden boards were slick, and it was suddenly very easy to see what had happened.

With an agonizing creak the wood of axle and bridge strained. The wagon shifted again, then steadied. The left front wheel was nearly thigh high off the bridge. The draft team had grown calmer, but there was no decent footing for their strength to be used.

"Marshal!" the burly man at the horses' heads shouted his greetings in relief.

Gwyn stowed her discards in the wagon seat, already tying the rope about her waist.

"My daughter is not nearly five seasons. She's caught below in the wagon box, but each time she goes to climb the load shifts and the horses lose another handspan of footing."

"I can see why." Gwyn grimly took up her sword again. A step or two shy from the edge she paused, eyeing the broken railings with dislike. She would not trust her life to those severed timbers. With a deep scowl she planted her feet firmly and concentrated. From the hilt of her sword a warmth began to seep through her gloves as she stood poised, blade pointing down. The lifestone embedded in the hilt gathered its energies as she gathered her strength, and with a cry she drove blue flashing steel into the very depths of the bridge. The weapon sank to its hilt guard. With a gasp, Gwyn tore her hands from the grip, and then she hurried to secure the rope's end to the hilt.

She thought again how much she hated the cold as she slipped over the side into that icy wind.

Carefully, trying to carry as much weight on the rope in her hand as possible, Gwyn inched along the underside of the wagon. Its massive weight shifted above her, and she felt her heart pound. There was very little comfort in realizing how heavy the thing over her head actually was.

The child was a leggy girl of four-and-more tenmoons who was obviously finding courage that she'd never known she possessed. Her skin had darkened to the velvet-black tones of the furs beneath her, and her hands were bleeding where they clenched the thin ropes that tied in the wagon's load. But her face was tear-stained, and there was a visible trembling to those small limbs that warned Gwyn of expiring strength.

"Are you all right, Min'l?" Gwyn called, smiling cheerfully as she looked up from beneath the edge of the wagon.

The girl nodded, her twin braids bobbing. But her lips were bloody from biting them in fear.

"I'm Gwyn," she continued, struggling a bit to work her way lower and still keep the rope tightly wound around her one hand. "Do you have a name? Or does everyone call you Min'l?"

The teasing almost roused a smile from the child. "Mak'inzi. They call me Inzi sometimes."

"And what would you like me to call you?" Providing anyone calls either of us anything again, Gwyn thought. A piece of the shattered corner of the wagon box broke in her grasp and she almost lost all hold. The wagon shifted under her frantic fumbling, and then reluctantly it settled. She heaved on the rope in a little jump upwards and gasped, thinking her shoulder was going to tear in two, but she managed to loop the line around her wrist one more time. Gwyn swallowed hard and forced her attention back to the child; somehow she had to edge the girl's mind away from the panic. "So, what should I call you? Or would you rather I called you Min until we've have a proper sort of introduction?"

Her efforts won a real smile, if only a fleeting one. "Mak'inzi is good, Amazon."

"Now, now," Gwyn threw her a warming smile, "I said Gwyn. After all, if you grant me the privilege of your given name, why shouldn't I do the same for you, hmm?"

The wind tore at her feet as the river roared, and the wood above cringed, squeaking. They both held their breaths, glancing at the bridge overhead. They looked to one another. Gwyn shared a rueful grin from her place below and admitted, "Not much room for formalities, you could say."

Mak'inzi nodded, bravely plastering a smile over her fears.

"Now then," Gwyn quickly rechecked her position, assuring herself of some stability for a second or two. "I need your help here."

Again the girl nodded, her dark eyes glued to Gwyn's face.

"I need you to work yourself back down to me. Yes—that's good Mak'inzi, like that."

Slowly the child lowered herself, teeth biting her lower lip again as the cuts in her hands began to open. Somehow she managed to avoid Gwyn's face with her feet and finally, hesitantly she dropped her hips free.

"Good. You're doing well, Mak'inzi." Gwyn wished she had more than two hands as she hung there spread-eagled between the rope and wagon. It was a useless wish though, so she tried to make her voice sound encouraging. "Now you need to let go with one hand and turn around to grab my neck."

"But you're behind me!" Mak'inzi's voice almost slipped into a whine, but she caught it and struggled, "I mean...Gwyn...how do I do that?"

Gwyn inched along the wagon a little and pressed herself into Mak'inzi's dangling legs. "Can you feel me here?"

Mak'inzi nodded and gulped, "Yes."

"Do you think you can guess where my head is?"

"I...?"

"Here," Gwyn butted the girl's waist gently with her forehead, "I'm here."

"Yes...yes, I can I think."

"Good girl. Let's give it a try."

Abruptly, the child twisted and let go with both hands at the same time, snatching for Gwyn's neck as she fell. The wagon bounced at the drastic weight change; the rope nearly pulled Gwyn's arm from its socket, and suddenly her grip was gone. Gwyn grabbed for Mak'inzi as they fell. The rope snapped between them and smacked the girl's chin hard, yet Gwyn held her despite that instinctive pull-away. The wind caught them and sent them twirling as they swayed, but the knots on neither sword nor waist would yield.

Gwyn took a steadying breath, thanked the Goddess Mother for Her watchful eye, and shifted Mak'inzi up a bit so that the girl could get a better hold about Gwyn's neck.

"Mak'inzi...you all right, Min'l?" The child nodded with a tiny little jerk, eyes squeezed shut tight. Gwyn's voice gentled as she prodded, "Can you get your legs around me now? Aye, good girl."

Finally, with a heartfelt sigh, Gwyn could get to the rope with both hands. She pulled them up hand-over-hand as the echoing canyon winds whipped about them, defying her to ascend. But the sway and tug of those eddies were useless against a *Niachero's* strength, and Gwyn gained the bridge within a few fleeting moments.

Mak'inzi proved again that she was a girl of sense as she managed to loosen her death grip on her rescuer and pull herself up over the edge before offering a hand back to Gwyn. The older woman hid her amusement and declined the aid, joining her quickly.

"By the Mother's Hand—I thank you!" the father cried and Mak'inzi scampered forward, ducking under the horses to grab the burly giant around his waist.

The man spared her a trembling moment, and Gwyn felt a warmth grow at seeing the bond the two shared. Then he turned brusquely to the chaffing horses. The great beasts shied again, their mouths frothing around the bone bites, and the wagon bounced with their nervous prance.

"Loosen the bolt there, girl!" Her father grabbed the second horse by the halter again.

"But our furs! Papa! It's our whole winter's work!"

"Do as I say, Inzi! No cargo's worth the beasts or our lives."

"Tad!" Gwyn moved forward, untying herself from the rope. "A whole winter's trappings? Can you afford to be so generous to the Fates?"

He hesitated, gnawing on his lower lip. He was tempted. With a cautious inquiry he nodded, "Nay, Amazon. Is there a way you see different?"

"Can your daughter handle the horses?"

"Well enough."

"Good. It will take the three of us—with Mak'inzi at their lead, your weight on this up-lifted wheel's corner and mine pushing from 'round the back there. The thing should come clear."

He eyed the dangling back wheel shard and then the tall woman again. "You're willing to risk life and limb for a stack of pelts? One slip and the whole thing will be pushing you over first."

"It's not a mere stack. It's your livelihood. And I will."

She had him with that. He nodded, handing the horses over to his daughter. "Tell me again."

Gwyn pointed and together they grasped the suspended wagon wheel. She had been nearly right in her guess; his weight was enough to tip the wagon to a more even keel. She left him, throwing Mak'inzi an encouraging smile as she passed. Carefully she approached the broken railings along the wagon's back. The timbers were holding more securely on this side of the load, and in fact it was their solid stubbornness that had held the wagon from crashing through in the beginning. She wedged herself between the wagon and the jutting beam; she grunted with satisfaction as her toes pressed the beam and found there was still no give. She heaved, her back to the wagonbed. It shifted with a bang as the front wheel hit the bridge.

The horses neighed, but the girl held them steady and soothed them with a low voice. Without loosening her hold Gwyn flexed her fingers slightly, seeking a better grip.

"On your word, Marshal!" the father called.

"Ready, say—now!" and together they all moved.

Mak'inzi urged and the horses strained forward as the father roared, his powerful frame bulging as he pulled. Gwyn ground her teeth shut, lifting with all her might. Her skin flushed dark as her power gathered. Sheer will kept her footing as inches were gained and the slick wood threatened to let her boots skid. The thing creaked forward, scraping with the sanding, harsh sound of wood splintering wood. Gwyn sucked the air in with growing anger.

This was not a battle those sadistic Fates would win! With a snarl she found the strength of her ancient mothers and the wagon lifted clear of that clawing edge. The horses leapt forward at the sudden release, and Gwyn fell in a heap as the resistance jerked away. She tucked and rolled into the bridge railing. The jagged points of shattered hub and axle nearly caught her as they bounced high. With a bang the wagon corner smashed down into the bridge again.

"Halt them!" the father bellowed.

Wet wood skittered the frame sideways even as it was dragged forward. With a protesting half-rear by one, the draft horses drew to a stop. Mak'inzi held them, nearly pulled from the planks by their dancing, but she did hold them—and the wagon did not crash into the railings again.

"Marshal—Amazon! Are you hurt?!" The man hurried forward to help Gwyn as she struggled up.

"Not the least," she grinned, wiping the dampness from her ruddy red breeches the best that she could. "Merely very wet."

24

He stared at her for a moment in wide-eyed disbelief. Then a hearty shout of laughter exploded. His great arms wrapped about her waist and lifted her in a joyous hug.

Too startled to protest, Gwyn was dropped just as suddenly back to her own feet and was left facing him. A laugh won its way clear, and she bent at the knees, lifting him high in a returning embrace.

"No disrespect, Amazon!" he protested, and she set him back down to find him still laughing, but there were tears in his eyes as well. "By oath, no disrespect!"

"None taken, Tad," she assured him, clasping his brawny forearms as he offered both hands, palms up, in belated greeting. "There is reason to celebrate!"

"The name's Olan, please! Formalities are beyond us now, I think. My daughter, my season's profits...I owe you much."

"I am as grateful to you, Olan. It is not often I have the opportunity to lend my sword without drawing blood. I savor the chance when I may."

Mak'inzi came to join them and he squatted low, pulling his child into his arms once more. A husky note crept into his voice as Olan asserted, "It is not enough."

"It is, Olan. I am a Marshal, King's Protector of Travelers. I'm only doing what the Royal Family and Guilds expect me to do."

"No," Mak'inzi interrupted, as solemn as only a child of four tenmoons could be. She left her father to come stand before Gwyn. "You helped because you are an Amazon, because you honor life. Just as the legends say your Mothers honored life so much that they came to Aggar's aid even though it meant exile from your home world. You are a Royal Marshal because you're an Amazon, not a rescuer because you're a Marshal. And every friend of Council and King knows that truth."

Chapter Three

The Marshals' Commons entrance was a single door in the length of a long corridor amidst a maze of grey stone hallways that comprised the Trader's Guild Hall and Inn. The only thing that marked this entrance as welcomingly different from others was the placket of copper-red cloth webbed with bronze string, the colors of the Royal Marshals—and it was a *very* welcoming difference.

Within, the commons was warm with three blazing hearths and an endless supply of meats and mead. The temperature was high to ease the stiffened muscles of hard ridden leagues and the aching scars of sword wounds. The food was plentiful and the hours unnumbered, because those guarding the caravans ended journeys at odd hours and often began new assignments before the old had even seen its cargo unpacked. The mood was always welcoming, enticing with stories from boisterous veterans of hapless bullies and with the sweet singing of traveling troubadours. It was also the sole place in Gronday where the eitteh and sandwolves of the Marshals' crews were as welcome as a pillowfriend. It was a place that many wintered, and a place many called home.

Gwyn paused in the doorway, allowing her four-legged friends to push in around her. They had all been to the baths and settled their gear in the lodging rooms. The mud-splattered coats of the sandwolves had been washed and brushed, the gleaming ripples of lighter beige-grey on taupe were well marked once more, and Ril had ceased her sneezing while Ty was again thinking only of food. Gwyn too had become equally presentable in her soft breeches and laced jerkin of ruddy-brown; the soaking, travel-worn garments had been left at the laundry. Even her fiery red hair had been drawn back and, in the traditional guard-style, had been woven again into a short braid.

Gwyn drew her attention from the milling crowd as Ty gently tugged on her tunic's sleeve. She bent low, staring across the smoky commons from the vantage point of her packmates, and a crooked smile grew on her face. "I did promise you stewed meats, didn't I?"

Ril added her own panting grin to their plea.

"Fair enough." Gwyn pulled at the leather throng about her neck, drawing the green glass Marshal tags from beneath her shirt. Ty gingerly took the leather in mouth, but Gwyn's fingers held the tags for a moment longer as she warned, "Don't feast us beyond saddle and bow!"

Ty had the good grace to look guilty.

Gwyn grinned, "Off with you—"

Ril hung back for a moment, a questioning lift to her hairless brows.

"To find Jes," Gwyn reminded her.

The sandwolf butted her human's thigh lightly and padded off for the kitchens.

Jes was not a difficult woman to find, if one knew where to search. She was in the small alcove of the Minstrel's Hearth, and the singers were gently plucking their strings, voices quiet as they contentedly blended their instruments' harmonies. Alone and content, Jes sat with her back to the noise and smoke of the open commons. Her feet were propped high on her table's edge, and her dark, graying hair was as short-braided as any other's.

In the farther corners, there were a few Amazons scattered among the Marshals, and one of these Sisters smiled as Gwyn appeared in the wooden archway. "Behind, Jes!"

Without turning Jes raised a hand above her head, palm upward in greetings. "I heard of your escapades in the gorge."

Gwyn laughed, joy and precious love binding her heart as she ignored the hand and hugged the woman from behind.

"Ahh careful, child!" the low timbre warned, and Gwyn was suddenly aware of the right arm that was bound tightly in its sling.

"*N'Sormee* ?!" She knelt, facing her mother as concern flashed in her copper eyes. "Your messages said nothing of injury! What happened?"

Jes' fingers hushed her daughter's lips as she offered a soft, reassuring smile. Her dark gaze sparkled with familiar mischief and Gwyn felt her anxiety ease. Gwyn pressed a kiss into the callused palm, rising to draw a seat near.

"I'm fine," Jes murmured. "It was a clean break and due solely to my own foolishness."

"Which was?" her daughter challenged, elbows on knees as she leant forward.

"I slipped stepping out of the baths."

Gwyn found them both laughing.

"I'm a rickety old bucket of bones! What else is there to say?" And then the humor died to be replaced with a deep warmth. "It's good to see you again, Gwyn'l."

Their hands grasped together tightly, and Gwyn nodded. "It's been a long winter without you, *N'Sormee*."

"Aye," Jes brushed the tousled red hair from her daughter's eyes, "it has been so very long. How is Bryana? And your sister, Kima?"

"*M'Sormee* sends her love. And Kimarie too, I imagine, although I didn't have time to see her before I left." Awkwardly, Gwyn looked down as her hand withdrew from her mother's.

"You hesitate?" Jes' murmur was one of quiet encouragement.

Gwyn forced a smile, blinking aside an unexpected tear. "You've been missed."

Jes nodded solemnly. "You all were sorely missed as well. I'm too old to be wintering away. You do know it was not my intention?"

Gwyn nodded. "It was necessary. We knew that. But the Changlings' Wars are over at last!"

"For now."

"That's what truly matters."

"No," Jes corrected quietly. "What matters is that you are all still there to come home to."

"We are."

"Are you hungry?" Jes asked suddenly. She waved towards the table and for the first time Gwyn noticed the steaming platters of food. "They brought word when you arrived. I figured you'd be hungry—and cold! The mead's been warmed. Which reminds me, two souls seem to be suspiciously absent?"

Gwyn grinned, helping herself to cup and plate. "Ty's stomach couldn't wait. They're off in the kitchens somewhere."

"I thought she'd outgrow that monstrous appetite of hers?"

Gwyn laughed, "If anything, she's eating twice what she did as an adolescent."

"Has she filled out any since I saw her last?"

"Not a bit. She's as lean and leathery as ever. But she seems blessed with a boundless energy, so she's still fending for herself mostly, even on our longer trips."

"And Ril? Is she still her sedate, observant self?"

"The very same. You'd think she was a matronly twenty-four seasons instead of four."

"Whereas Ty you'd swear was a pup?"

"You'd certainly never think of them as sibs. Although," Gwyn's smile softened with a fondness, "to be fair, Ril has a wonderful sense of humor and Ty is actually very responsible when needed. They truly both believe the three of us can handle anything that comes along. To Ril that means she can settle back and relax, be content to watch things unfolding. Ty takes it as permission to play while she has the chance."

Jes thoughtfully eyed the round berry in her hand. "Where does that leave you?"

"In the middle?" With a pause, Gwyn considered the question more closely. She shrugged suddenly and sat back in her chair. "Ril's calm is—well, there are times I'd swear she was a Blue Sight projecting that infectious quietness. She helps to center me when I grow too gloomy or anxious. Then there's Ty playing the clown, keeping me laughing even in a drenched campsite. Both help to keep my head clear enough to keep the three of us out of trouble."

"So you don't regret the seasons of growing and training? The responsibilities I imposed by imprinting them to you?"

Gwyn shook her head adamantly. "They're family. We make a good pack. I'd not trade them for a dozen eitteh, Jes."

"Well, Khirlan probably has more experience with sandwolves than with winged-cats anyway. It was once quite a traders' city, being on that old route up from the Southern Continent."

"Hah!" A strange voice intruded with a mocking shout. "Do you seriously think that matters? I tell you! No one on this wooded continent has experience with sandwolves save those fortunate enough to be part of a pack!"

They both looked around to find a spry, skinny little figure of a woman dressed in the flamboyant, bloused tunic and yellow jerkin of the tinker-trade's costume. Her bony cast of features clearly declared she was from the Southern Desert Peoples, and the crinkles beside her honey-brown eyes attested to an exceptionally good-natured disposition. She leaned over the back of their vacant chair in a leisurely fashion, all the while staring expectantly at Jes. Gwyn watched in fascination as those smiling, thin lips fairly danced with some amusement, and then Jes let out a shriek of recognition, pulling the newcomer close in a welcoming hug.

"Sparrow? By the Mother's Own Hand! With your hair grown out and in full troubadour colors no less! What are you doing in Gronday?! Oh...here,

Gwyn'l, this is Brit's companion and love, Shel n'Sappho."

"Actually, everyone calls me Sparrow these days," the woman asserted, grasping Gwyn's palms across the table. "And I'm guessing you to be Jes' oldest and the Royal Marshal, Gwyn n'Athena?"

"That I am," Gwyn confessed readily, liking the faint musical lilt of the Desert folks' accent.

"I knew it!" Sparrow spun the chair about and straddled it with a bounce. "You've got that red-fire hair of Bryana's youth."

Gwyn's brow lifted in surprise—Valley Bay wasn't that small! "You've met *M'Sormee?*"

"Once or twice eons ago, at the Keep. I was with the Council before I joined Brit."

The oddity registered then and, frowning slightly, Gwyn tipped her head aside. "You said to call you *sparrow?*"

Mirth creased the corners of her eyes again, and the woman bobbed a nod. "Brit's responsible for it. Shortly after we joined, she dubbed me Sparrowhawk for some reason— after some ancient people's bird. I don't even think the thing was one of Aggar's."

Jes' low chuckle erupted. "Brit always told me the creature was known for speed, agility and quick-wits, despite its petite size."

The other pulled a face at her and confided in Gwyn, "A backhanded compliment, if ever I heard one."

"But it stuck, spindly frame and all," Jes said, grinning without shame. "Eventually it got shortened to plain Sparrow—"

"Sparrowhawk is rather a mouthful." Sparrow winked at Gwyn.

"And today—few think to call you Shel anymore."

"Not even my old Council mentors." A wistful, woebegone sigh and a roll of her eyes mourned the loss dramatically.

"Enough!" Jes gave a wave of her good hand, "Why are you here? And where's that pompous old healer of yours?"

"Brit? Oh, she'll be along in a day or so. Ran into difficulties with the ice and mud south of Colmar and nearly lost a wheel. We managed to limp along to Crossroads' wagon works, but then she sent me on ahead to corral you into waiting for her."

"Me?" Jes raised a brow in puzzlement. "What have I done to bring you two out of Rotava before the Black River even thaws?"

Sparrow shrugged, then pointed at the food and at Jes' tacit consent helped herself to a stray piece of roast lexion. She nibbled on the fowl, eyeing both Sisters for a long moment, before she shrugged again. "Don't know."

"Ah-huh," Jes accepted agreeably, and Gwyn stifled a laugh as *N'Sormee* continued with, "The two of you merely missed my sober face so much that you dragged out those ole plow horses and that rickety, rotting ole tinkers' wagon— through more than a ten-day of mud and muck, mind you—just so you could join me by the Minstrel's Hearth. Right. And men-cats have wings now.

"I repeat, Sparrow, why are you here?"

"I don't know," Sparrow returned blandly, then her smile brightened quickly. "Honestly, Jes, I've barely a clue. We got a message that you might need help. The fellow said you were here and that we should hurry or we'd miss you. But there was nothing about the whys or wherefores. Still, you know the Council. Rarely tells you half of what you need to know." She popped another morsel in her mouth with more apparent interest in the food than the words.

Gwyn scowled, unconsciously mirroring the expression on Jes' face as her mother asked, "What's become so serious that the Council tries to take advantage of their past ties to you?"

Sparrow lifted a shoulder, busily sopping up some of the platter's gravy with a piece of bread. "Brit's got the same questions, yet you know how often those elderly Mistresses and Masters are right about trouble coming—"

"I know!" Jes snapped, cutting short the flippancy. "But what did they say to get Brit to agree this round?"

Sparrow met Jes' gaze steadily, all jesting gone from her manner now. "They said that you two needed help. They didn't need to say anything else. You know that."

"Forgive me," Jes sighed, her frustration fading to sheer weariness. "You're right. Brit would walk the Firecaps naked if it meant aiding a Sister, even one she didn't know."

"We all would," Sparrow amended quietly.

"We should have expected the Council to take notice eventually," Gwyn murmured, eyes downcast as Jes looked at her sharply. Her mother stared hard a second, then saw the reason in what Gwyn was saying. Gwyn's copper glance lifted finally and a crooked smile teased a semblance of better humor from Jes. "It's only fair play, N'Sormee. Our Ring's Sighted members keep abreast of the Council's doings, why shouldn't we assume the Council's Seers are following us as well?"

"I'd just hoped they'd be a little slower in interfering this time." But Jes was smiling again.

"Well, they are interfering," Sparrow piped up as she stole another bite of lexion. "Not very forcefully, though. As usual. All you have to say is 'no thank you' and Brit and I will leave you be. The Council knows that as well as either of you, so I shouldn't think they're very concerned about...." She broke off and grinned at the irony of the fact that she didn't even know what the trouble was. "About whatever it is."

"Ahh...," Jes interjected quietly, "perhaps this should all wait until we're somewhere a little more private?"

"It should wait until Brit arrives," Sparrow declared matter-of-factly, inspecting the berries in the fruit bowl. Her sandy eyes suddenly jumped to Gwyn, and a mischievous glint sparkled as she recognized the younger woman's obvious surprise. "I admit it. I have absolutely no curiosity whatsoever. Never have, probably never will. I leave that to Brit. As long as she lets me tag along for the exciting parts, I'm perfectly content to let her choose our battles. But that's a prerequisite of my trade—patience."

Gwyn was only more confused, and Jes scowled at the slight woman with, "Spare her the riddles, Sparrowhawk. You know no one's told her."

"I'm sorry." Sparrow planted an elbow on the table, shaking down the long sleeve of her blouse to display the blond leather wristband she wore. Her voice dropped low as she explained, "I'm more to Brit than the love-of-her-life, Gwyn. I'm her Shadow."

"Bonded by lifestone?" Gwyn nearly gasped, still amazed that any of *dey Sorormin* ever submitted to such a merging.

The other nodded unconcerned, pulling her sleeve back over the band again. "I was only adopted into *dey Sorormin* after our march across the ice plains."

"The Exile's Trek?" Stunned again, Gwyn's breath caught. "The Council sent you to help Brit with that desperate venture? After the Changlings had poisoned Maltar's eastern water range, wasn't it?"

"You've heard of it then."

"Who hasn't," Jes muttered darkly.

Gwyn found herself staring at this small, wiry woman with an added measure of respect. "They say, there were a hundred lost to frostbite and exhaustion, while you saw nearly six times that many to safety."

Pain shadowed those honey-brown eyes as Sparrow remembered not the numbers, but the faces of each one on that despairing trek. Jes placed a hand over Sparrow's small one, gently pulling her back from those tragic memories. "What is done, is done. But the Council was right in sending you then, and to us now. With this arm I can't make this southern journey, and Gwyn shouldn't make it alone, packmates or no. If you and Brit could see your way to help her...well, there are answers needed or more lives may be lost."

"Southern?" Dread echoed in that almost child-like voice of anxiety. "My Desert Folks?"

"No, none of them are concerned," Gwyn reassured quickly, and she offered a warm smile of apology for the misunderstanding.

"But south?" The pieces leapt into place, and Sparrow felt that something even worse had come. "South where the Clan raids?"

Gwyn's grimness answered her. Jes only stared at the remains left on the table. Sparrow forced a cheerless laugh. "First I exchange the Southern Deserts for the Northern Ice, now the Changlings' Plateau for the Clan's Plateau. My life is becoming terribly repetitious, isn't it?"

Jes looked at her, puzzled.

"Leaving one wasteland for another, I mean—not a pretty challenge."

"No," Gwyn agreed, thinking now of the lives desolated by the Clan's raiders and their fire weapons...with aid from some Court traitor. "No, it won't be a pretty challenge at all."

* * *

"I'm down here on the left," Jes pointed as Gwyn and the sandwolves followed her into yet another hallway of the Guild's endless maze. "I admit, I've indulged myself a bit this wintering. I've had someone in to start the fire early and to tidy-up regularly. But since I cracked my arm, it's been a necessary help."

The tell-tale clack of the sandwolves' nails paused beside the closed door as they both warily sniffed about the threshold. The two women joined them, and Ty grinned up at her human, offering reassurance that no one seemed to be within. But as Jes undid the ashwood lock, they pushed through first.

Jes smiled a little dryly, slanting a glance at her daughter as she shut the door behind them all. "Gotten to be a cautious lot, have they?"

Somewhat surprised, Gwyn drew herself back from her musings and darted a quick look to her packmates. She smiled then with fondness, completely missing her mother's intended irony. Ril was perched on her hind legs, a forepaw gingerly balancing her against the bedside table so that she could get the scents from the shuttered windows beyond. Ty had planted herself in a nervous crouch against the door, eyes flicking between Ril and the curtained-off closet. Ril finished her inspection of the window only to proceed to the closet to nose aside the curtain and satisfy herself that nothing lurked there either. At that point, Ty finally relaxed enough to lie down. But her massive bulk rested against the door and assured them of no unannounced entries.

"*N'Sormee*, you once told me never to trust any place as safe if I was beyond the Gate House of Valley Bay." Gwyn nodded to her packmates. "They too were listening that night. And in some things their memories are much better than mine."

"Yet they left you alone in the commons?" Jes quipped. She sprawled out on the chair and footstool that sat before the hearth and its blazing fire. "Or do they think there's safety in sheer numbers?"

"Something like that. After all, with so many Marshals in one place, how could there help but be a few honest ones about?"

Jes laughed obligingly. Gwyn brought another chair near enough to share the footstool, while Ril curled up on the hearth.

"Are you sure you don't need help getting set for bed?" Gwyn prodded with concern. She'd noticed the slight flush that browned her mother's skin.

"I'm fine. Merely tired, Gwyn'l, and perhaps somewhat overexcited. It has been such a long time since I've seen any of you."

"Which is all the more reason to rest."

"*Coramee*, enough!"

Chagrined, Gwyn gave in with a gracious wave. "Do tell Bryana I tried."

"I will," Jes assured her. "But I've got a healer's apprentice for all that. She stops by first thing in the morning and last thing at night. If you want to worry, worry about Sparrow and all that restless tossing and turning she'll be doing tonight so far from her shadowmate. Or better yet, worry about Khirlan!"

The last comment sobered Gwyn all too quickly. Dejectedly her head went back against the embroidered cushion, and she turned a sightless stare towards the dim corners beyond the hearthside. After a moment she sighed. "Should I really wait for Brit, do you think?"

Startled, Jes glanced at her daughter. But Gwyn was still gazing at nothing. "Why do you ask?"

"She's still working under the guise of the tinker-trades. The wagon and draft horses will slow us. The bartering at each village will detain us even more often. Instead of several ten-days, this will turn into more than a monarc of travel. It's already late spring that far south. It'll be summer there by the time we arrive in Khirla."

"You're concerned that the Clan will be controlling even more of the travel routes by then?"

"Closing them down—by the sound of it."

"Still…you said you're convinced there's a traitor within the court itself."

"You're saying I'm wrong?" Gwyn snapped back in irritation.

"No," Jes amended softly. "I think you're right. That's why I'm also thinking you need Brit and Sparrow to help you with this."

"Aye—as a Royal Marshal I'm too public a figure. I won't hear half of what Brit will."

"And Sparrow is quite adept at stealth-and-theft, Gwyn. I've seen her sneak into a Changlings' camp and come out again with enough flint to replenish a whole patrol with fire kits and arrowheads. And she claims she's even better in an urban setting—more shadows to blend in with, I guess." Gwyn ruefully acknowledged her mother's attempt at humor, but Jes saw she was far from convinced. "Gwyn'l, could you find such a traitor alone?"

Ril's head came up sharply, lips curling in a silent snarl. Ty's objection was more audible; an angry growl rose from her place at the door.

"Hush! Both of you," Gwyn ordered. Yet she was more annoyed at herself and her personal limitations, so her voice gentled as she explained to her friends, "I'll be in the Dracoon's Court alone. Neither of you are very patient with human intrigues, and you know it." Then to Jes, "And no, alone I will not find this basker jackal. Which would mean any party the Dracoon and I left the City with would be in danger of discovery—and ambush!—long before we gained any chance to negotiate anything!"

"Aye, but if your presence as Marshal were prominent enough, you'd certainly draw the attention away from simple troubadours and healers. Brit would be able to move about more freely, especially with Sparrow beside her. Sparrow's obviously Southern blood will only reassure everyone that they really are on their way to the Desert Folk. And certainly, traveling with a Royal Marshal through Clan-infested areas has visible merit. Few would even question your arrival with them."

"It would be better for us not to arrive together at all."

"Then separate before you reach Khirla City. But Gwyn, remember in Khirlan—even before we knew of the worsening times—travelers have always been endangered by the Clan raiders. And none of you will do the Dracoon any good, if you never reach her."

Gwyn sighed again, conceding the point. Besides, no matter how clever a Marshal could be—one person could only do so much. In another situation, she might have been able to offer a new perspective to alter the strategy in some useful way...and indeed usually that was a Marshal's most effective role, to advise and reorganize. But with a traitor hidden among the trusted people, there was no way to successfully deploy any new tactic because it would be shared and countered immediately.

It left her with little she could do alone...for now. Gwyn shook her head at herself, a cheerless smile twisting her lips. "I do so hate intrigue and deception. Give me a rabid buntsow or a contaminated water well any day. Those are tangible puzzles that I can work through. But liars—the ambitious ones, not the sort who do it from shame or embarrassment, but the clever, self-serving deceivers—they're my undoing. I lose patience with them."

"Take care in your wishing, *Coramee*."

Puzzled at the warning, Gwyn glanced at Jes.

"Unveiling a Court traitor is often easily done when outsiders arrive and view the obvious with new eyes. Motivating an enemy to join you at the negotiating tables, however, won't be nearly so simple."

"Aye...," Gwyn dropped her gaze back to the fire, and the leaping flames of orange and yellow stirred memories of another flame licking out in destruction. Only once had she ever seen a Clan's fire weapon at work, and the white-hot flicker of its tongue had torched the warehouse with a single kiss. Aye—Jes was right—a Court Traitor could be the least of their worries.

Chapter Four

Gronday's Market Square was a boisterous mayhem of tented stalls and jostling shoulders. The clatter of wooden crates, the clink of glass coins, and the colorful banners of the sellers all blended well with the scolding and laughing tones of the busy folk. Children raced through the crowds, shrieking the mysterious battle cries of their play. Vendors shouted the bargains of their wares. It was all very lively and all perfectly matched to Sparrowhawk's taste. She'd been brought up in such bedlam until she'd left the Desert Folk to seek out the Council, and if she'd not passed muster as a Shadow Trainee, she probably would have settled quite happily into the tinker-trade's life on her own. As it was, she had no doubts that the Mother's Hand had matched her to Brit and in so doing, returned her to the merchant's life.

Today the mood about her was more festive than usual. Not only was it monarc's end and so nearly every local trade had freshly stocked its booths, but the first flatboats from Rotava had finally arrived with their riches. It meant that the rivers had thawed from Gronday to the sea, and with the Plateau Treaty between Changling and Human holding, it was clear that the northern goods and ports were ready to service the inland cities again.

A great piping of steam blew the clock whistle and Sparrow, with a fair number of others, stopped to look up. The Great Clock housed in the Traders' Guild Tower rose above the south side of the Square. The high-pitched whistle keened again, and Sparrow felt the excitement of the visitors around her; the Clock Keeper's little sundial and sexton had declared mid-day was arriving, and the Keeper had launched the steam-powered show. Sparrow felt her breath catch as the third piercing call to attention sang out; the only other time she'd been in Gronday the clockworks had been shut down for repairs.

The carved, lattice hands for monarc, day and tenmoon swung in complete circles, while on the largest of the clock faces the ivory point moved from its quarter-day pose to the half, and the pipe organ began. Wooden dolls popped up with the music as the steepled little roofs of each pipe turned into a cone hat blown loose. Children, prippers and baby birds danced up at the high notes. Burros brayed lower while horses whinnied tenor. Grumpy drunks and sour soldiers rose with the bass. And the whole crowd of them fluttered merrily in concert.

It was over all too quickly for Sparrow, and she promised herself to be back tomorrow, if at all possible. She rued that she had missed it the past two days here, but then the fact that it was mid-day reminded her of her stomach's emptiness. As usual, she was hungry; it was even worse given her separation from Brit. However, food was never scarce at Market. The only true difficulty here was deciding what one wanted to eat.

A pair of slender fellows wandered past her, bumping into her and apologizing politely before dreamily returning their attentions to each other. Sparrow grinned. They were certainly love-sick enough for one another, but it was the pastie they were sharing that caught her attention. A wonderful, flaky little pastry pouch—one tucked full of meat and gravy with spuds and vegetable bits—was just what she was looking for.

The larger awnings of the kitchen tents and tables were on the north side of the Square, and Sparrow headed there. Although she could have gotten brazed and skewered stuffs, sweets or an endless variety of other goodies in any aisle, the kitchen tents would be the only place authorized for use of the heavier ceramic ovens. And it took ovens and fire pits for pasties and stews. She wasn't disappointed. The scents wafting back over the shoulders of those waiting promised varieties of fowl, meat and fish as well as hot pastries and breads.

Sparrow took her place in line, absently studying the Palace walls that lay just across the lane. As impressive as the Guild's painted clock was, the Dracoons of Gronday had done their best to surpass the clock with their Palace. Instead of bright paints and merry pipes, the facade of the Palace walls were sculpted in rich panels of almond stone. Epics of the Ramains' royal houses, figures of the Council and Keep, market days, weddings, almost every joyous occasion of the Ramains' folklore was to be seen. She tipped her head back, squinting against the bright blueness of the spring sky, and wished she were that bird Brit had named her for. In the upper balconies was a panel barely visible from here. Her view was worse for her short height and the shadows of those nudging around her. But none-the-less she knew the carving well. It showed the Treaty Table at the Council's Keep and the signing of the agreements between Queen, Council, and Amazons which had created the Valley Bay settlement. Someone asked her to move ahead, and reluctantly she left off her scrutiny; the panel was best seen at night anyway, when the upper torches were lit and the Market Square had been cleared of stalls.

Finally, with a pair of pasties in hand and a small gourd of warmed cider at her hip, Sparrow returned to her original task. Brit would be arriving late in the afternoon and she'd rightly be annoyed if Sparrow had left this particular errand undone. Her shadowmate seldom got along with herbalists—most healers didn't; the idea of profiting from someone's illness was too gruesome for their ethics. But in this northern area, no one else was likely to have a dried supply of the Southern Continent's medicinal flora—at least no one likely to sell a share of it.

A youngster darted by. Sparrow's eye caught the bright orange kerchief tied to the upper arm that designated the child as a City Runner, an orphan contracted for messenger service. Sparrow sighed sadly for a moment over memories of her own childhood. This decided her on another detour, and she refrained from starting in on the second pastie. There was another who would probably need it more.

She wove her way to the west corner of the Square. Near the public fountain she found what she sought, the Corner Crier.

An older woman, joints swollen by the betrayals of poor health and poverty, sat upon a bare wooden bench. Her posture was upright and stiff with pride, despite the overly-mended dress and breeches she wore. There was a stack of blank parchments, an ink well, and several quills laid out carefully on the bench alongside of her. At her feet a small model of the city was set. A coin box for donations sat next to that.

She was not a beggar, though she was undoubtedly penniless. Her family had probably been lost to fire or disease—or as was more common in Maltar or the cities further north, the losses might have been due to the Wars. Gronday was affluent enough to have a workhouse, however, and those like this woman who proved most trustworthy were often contracted as Corner Criers. The city model was an aid for strangers who stopped to ask her for directions, or for more familiar travelers who needed to know where some trade house had relocated. Often parcels would be left in a Crier's keeping as well and collected for deliveries by the City Runners. The Runners frequently stopped by the corner stations to collect notes and those parcels for delivery. It wasn't a bad system; it ensured easy contacts between city dwellers and useful work for those stranded in life without provisions. It also ensured that the youngsters would acquire some education and that the elders would have some healers' care. But Sparrow knew from personal experience that the system seldom substituted much for the shattered losses that had created the desperation in the first place.

The old woman pushed herself to her feet with a determined disregard for the aches in her body, although the pain made her motions awkward and jerky. She smoothed down her skirt and managed a formal bow to Sparrow, then waited in silence for the patron to speak first.

Sparrow waited quietly herself until with a nervous glance, the woman risked looking her full in the face. She smiled at the Crier and offered a little bow of respect. "I am Sparrowhawk."

The woman acknowledged that with a bob of a nod, her lips moving silently as she memorized the strange name.

"Has there been word of another tinker-trade seeking me?"

"No Min. But the last news was sent 'round at quarter-day. Mid-day missives are still being gathered."

Well, she hadn't expected Brit to be early. Sparrow turned to business instead. "Where might I find the stall of the herbalist Iseul?"

The old woman pointed down the aisle behind them. "All the herbalists are at the end there and two rows left. Are you searching for medicines or for Iseul herself, Min?"

Sparrow blinked, pleasantly surprised that the old woman was no longer afraid of her. Asking a question of strangers was often considered prying in Gronday, and a Crier could seldom risk such a gesture even if it would save the patron legwork to know more details. "Actually, both. Iseul, I understand, usually has a cache of rarer stuffs, but I need to buy enough to restock my barter supplies."

"Then not for your personal use, but for your wagon?"

"Aye, for my business." The bright saffron yellows of Sparrow's vest and boots over those dark oranges of bloused trousers and tunic could not possibly have belonged to anyone but a traveling merchant. "Should I be looking elsewhere than with Iseul?"

"No Min, you've the name of the best. The House of Iseul still sponsors a booth here in the Square. But it sells bits and handfuls of most things and not the quantities you describe. For that, it would be best to see the clerks at the Trade House proper."

"All right," Sparrow agreed readily. "Where is this House?"

"Not far—along here." The old woman stooped over the city model, pointing with a stick that had been resting against the backside of her bench. "See the alley just between this Market Square and the court for the Beast Sellers?"

"Aye, I know the street. Off the sou-west corner. Mostly has weavers and clothiers, doesn't it?"

"The one and same." The woman actually smiled, and Sparrow grinned right back. Then the young woman remembered the payment, and she straightened to unlash the gourd from her sash, asking, "Would you take a meal or prefer coin?"

"Oh...the pastie would be fine, Min." The old woman's eyes watered with near tears. The workhouses supplied gruel for breakfast and fish stews for eventide, but mid-day was never more than the two wedges of bread they took out with them to their contracts. And the pastie Sparrow presented her with was more meat than she'd see in most ten-days.

"The cider too?" she breathed in astonishment, fumbling a bit from her hands shaking so.

"It's for remembering a message also," Sparrow explained, her voice and face carefully set matter-of-fact so that there would be no stint of 'charitable pity' to demean the other's pride. "Should any come searching for the Tinker-trade Sparrowhawk, have them know I first went to the House of Iseul and then returned to the Guild's lodging."

"Aye Min," the woman bowed again, "and you left here at mid-day."

"Good enough. My thanks to you, Min."

"My thanks to you, Tinker-trade."

And I wish I could do at least as much every day for you and all your hearth-kin, Sparrow admitted to herself. But it wasn't an option, so she kept calm and set aside the old hauntings. She did what she could when she could; as Brit always told her, it would have to be enough. She missed the understanding embrace that always accompanied that rhetoric though. One of the reasons she loved Brit, she realized, was their shared regret for the fact that they could probably never really do enough—no matter what words they denied it with.

Goddess Mother, I miss the old tyrant. And it's not just the bond of the lifestone! It's herself that I miss. Sparrow sniffled and wiped the sudden mist from her eyes. Brit would tease her no end if she guessed how maudlin Sparrow had let herself get.

Oh, but what sweet teasing it would be!

At the corner of the side street there was an open air Hood'n'Cloak shop with a black-backed glass in front. Sparrow took a quick stop to check her reflection and dry the hint of teary streaks from her face. She moved on, pulling the clip from her hair and neatly gathering up the mohair-like strands with a twist before securing it again. The light brown stuff was usually quite manageable and really hadn't needed the fussing, but she was suddenly edgy. She frowned at herself and decided a little irritability would probably help in the bartering, then pushed through the swinging doors of Iseul's establishment; she hoped the clerks were in a mood for dealing.

Some time later Sparrow emerged from the Trade House with a distinct dissatisfaction that puzzled her thoroughly. She'd gotten everything they'd needed, delivery on the morrow to the Guild stables without extra charge, and reasonably good prices even on the rarer mustard oils.

A bright bit of brocade with a braided trim distracted her then and took her to the cloth racks across the street. The material put her in mind of a wedding cape for some groom, and she wondered if they had room for any more bolts of fabrics. They'd be south before mid-summer, plenty of time for tailors to use it for the harvest weddings. She toyed with the thought, eyeing a few other designs as well. Absently her fingers strayed to the wristband beneath her left sleeve and tugged at it to ease the ache.

Ache? Her attention shifted abruptly.

Sparrow flexed her wrist experimentally, but there was no restriction; nothing was laced too tightly. Yet the dull throbbing was unmistakable.

Which meant only one thing! She looked to the sun in confusion. The day was still nowhere near three-quarters, let alone eventide. It couldn't possibly be Brit? But she knew it was; the lifestone embedded in her wrist was insistently prodding—it *was* Brit. Somehow it was Brit!

And close—not merely in the city or settling into the Guild's Inn at the far end of the Square, but here. Near.

Sparrow jumped up to the top of the weaving shop steps, craning her neck to see over the racks of fabrics and people's heads. She half-expected the woman to be at Iseul's own doors, but there was no sign of that familiar face. She concentrated a moment, letting the pull of the lifestone give her a direction. Surprisingly, it drew her further south towards the Beast Sellers' court. Then she grinned suddenly, remembering the new harness pieces Brit had hoped to find in Crossroads. If she hadn't been able to get the pieces though…well, some of the best leather work shops in Gronday were along the Sellers' court and doubtless would draw Brit here on that errand.

Sure enough, the pull of the small stone led Sparrow through the penned maze of livestock to the Guild's favored leather shop. And in the midst of yokes and saddles and piled leather riggings, the stoic bulk of Brit n'Minona stood arguing with a crafter. Sparrow smiled and sat herself down on a railing between two shining saddles. Content just to watch, she felt a warm glow rising inside. There was no doubt about it—she loved this woman.

Brit stood there ranting, hands on broad hips, feet planted wide, and fairly shouted at the burly male who towered over her. She railed at him with all the spirit of a true Amazon, despite the fact that she wasn't anywhere near as tall as any *Niachero*. In fact, for all her bulk Brit wasn't any taller than an average woman of the Ramains. That placed her a good head shorter than this fellow, although Sparrow only came to Brit's own shoulder's height. Brit was a strong woman and a big one though…"nearly as broad across as I am up," she was fond of saying. But unlike most tinker-trades, Brit wasn't dressed at all flamboyantly. Her knee-length dress was belted and slit at the sides for easy movement, and her trousers were comfortably tucked into low boots. She was a collection of muted grays and browns, the traditional healer's colors, which was good for advertising that added specialty of their business.

Sparrow chuckled as the crafter raised placating hands of submission, pleading something or other to gain any calm. Sparrow would bet her life that the man had seen the healer's garb and figured a modest temper with a modest aptitude for bartering. To his chagrin he'd obviously discovered all healers weren't so meek when overcharged.

"Not at quarter-day!" Brit snapped all the louder as the man retreated into the shop. "Deliver the lot *first* thing!" She came away still grumbling and pulled up short at the sound of applause. A broad grin met her as Sparrow sat there clapping gleefully. "*Ti Mae!* My word—come here, Love!"

Laughing, Sparrow bounded into Brit's arms. The hoots and whistles of well-meaning apprentices were staunchly ignored as she claimed both a hug and warm kiss.

"Oh *Soroi*—I've missed you, Sparrow dear."

"Mutual, I assure you."

"When they said you were out, I figured to finish with this mess then be freed for the rest of...let me see you proper." The older woman paused a moment, appraising the shadowy bruises and faint caramel flush that attested to her shadowmate's exhaustion. But the smug confidence beamed through the weariness and satisfied her too; they'd not been apart too long.

"Do I pass muster?"

"Certainly do." Brit tucked Sparrow in under an arm and started them off towards the Square. "Now, I went without mid-day, so let's find me something to eat on the way to bed!"

* * *

"Brit! You look—"

"I know, I know!" She waved Gwyn's nonsense aside. "The brown in the hair's gotten more gray. And aye, I still wear it too bristly short. Not to mention, the waist has gotten fatter and the old voice gruffer."

Gwyn raised a brow in rueful humor. "I was about to say you look in rare good form, but I get the feeling you're not in the mood for compliments—no matter how true they may be."

The older woman growled and wrapped Gwyn up in a big hug. "I should know better than to spar words with you, Young Gwyn'l! Not you! The eldest daughter of our Ring Binder."

"A diplomat you mean?! Oh Brit, please! Insults so early? We haven't even left Gronday yet! And your hair's not so short in back. You've still got a respectable bit of a tail there." Gwyn tugged on the tiny braid playfully. "Even if it isn't any bigger than my little finger!"

"Well I like it that way!" Sparrow chimed in, shooing Gwyn's fingers away and gently stroking Brit's braid back into place. Her lover smiled at her, knowing it was only a ruse to caress that tender place on the nape of her neck.

"So sit—sit! Here I am being a rude host." Gwyn's room was a reflection of Jes' own, the standard among the Marshals' lodgings at the Guild. And she pulled the two chairs away from the table, nearer to the fire. "Have you had eventide yet?"

"Aye an' then some." As Brit hunkered down into her seat, she glanced at Sparrow to share a mischievous smile.

"No, I'm fine where I am Gwyn," Sparrow spoke up suddenly, seeing the Amazon was about to settle for the flagstones by the hearth.

"You're certain?"

Sparrow nodded quickly as she wrapped her arms around Brit from behind. Half-teasingly she grinned and strengthened her hug for a brief moment. "This is the only time I can reach her properly." At Gwyn's continued hesitation, she added, "I'm Shadow, Gwyn'l. Remember? After a separation, the physical contact helps. I need it."

"How do you...?" Gwyn bit off the words with a faint blush and finally took possession of the chair. "Forgive me. I hadn't meant to pry."

"Bright Heavens, woman! It's all right to ask!" Brit leaned forward to pat her hand lightly. "Why you an' Kimarie are good as my own nieces, with Jes always feeling like my sib. Go ahead and ask."

"Well, it's just that I was surprised you'd sent Sparrow on ahead like you did. Everything I've heard suggested it was pretty impossible for shadowmates to be separated?"

"For more than a ten-day? Undeniably is. I'd be dead for certain," Sparrow amended. "But it's not bad for short stints. I do get tired and restless after a few days—"

"And those nasty bruises of exhaustion start appearing under your eyes," Brit grumbled. Gwyn noticed then, she'd not really seen Sparrow without that faint caramel undertone of exertion before tonight.

"But we've had a lot of practice at it—being apart, I mean. And I barely notice the strain these days. Until I see her!" Sparrow smiled at Brit once again, and Gwyn saw much more than simple relief in that glance. "It's almost worth the separation just to feel so intoxicated."

"That's not all the stone's bonding, I hope," Brit huffed.

Sparrow hugged her fiercely, muttering, "Don't be a fool—you know it isn't."

"But I do so like to hear you say it," her partner chuckled and flushed a deep brown with pleasure.

"Even I as an outsider can see that it isn't," Gwyn inserted gently. She watched her old mentor with a fondness that was fast growing to include this young Sparrowhawk. "I'm finding it hard to imagine you've only been together a season or so."

"Almost two now," Brit corrected. "Come end of summer, it'll be two."

"And the lifestone does help with some of it," Sparrow shrugged. "Major arguments get sorted out, no matter what. It's simply a given."

Brit offered a rather bashful admission then, "You know my temper—it's no small thing to know she'll be there in the morning despite my cold ire."

"You just needed the security of commitment," Sparrow assured her. "I rarely see that icy shoulder anymore."

"Whatever it is," Gwyn grinned at Brit, "it seems to suit you—both of you."

Brit squeezed Sparrow's wrist with a sigh, that strong clasp of arms still wrapped around her. Then reality asserted itself, and she looked at Gwyn pointedly. "So, what's this mess with the Clan that the Council shouldn't know about?"

Gwyn told them succinctly of everything, including Jes' reasons for their joining in the escapade. Yet Brit surprised her when she was through, because the first thing the woman remarked on was the Dracoon's Sight and not the Clan.

"A Blue Gift strong enough to reach our home world? Aye, I can see where that explains her reluctance to involve the Council as well as her initial discomfort with Bryana."

"How so, Love?" Sparrow prompted.

"The agreement between us and the Council specifically states that no Blue Sight outside our Sisterhood will violate the privacy of our home world. Anyone wishing to speak with *dey Sorormin* at Home must first petition the Valley Bay for permission, and the contact must be supervised by the Ring Binder. It would seem that this Llinolae somehow stumbled onto a friend, despite the ban. Still I doubt she did it deliberately, given that Bryana trusts her. Any sort of deceptive personality would certainly have found it difficult to gain your mother's confidence, Gwyn'l."

"It would explain why this Dracoon is avoiding the Council instead of asking them for help," Sparrow saw. "They get terribly angry at anyone who breaks pact with Valley Bay."

"Good friendships do have a way of ignoring boundaries, though," Gwyn remarked. "Seeing her mentors, n'Shea and n'Athena, accepted her as a fosterling, I find no cause for any of the Council to start wielding judgments. It's a concern for *dey Sorormin*—not for the Keep!"

"Absolutely," Brit nodded. "I'd wager most Sisters would agree."

"Still, it would be best not to actually *tell* the Council. At least, not at this point," Sparrow warned. "You know how they are about setting new precedents. They get very stodgy about some things."

"Then we proceed as Royal Marshals," Brit declared amiably. "Both Gwyn and I are official enough, even though I'll never look it. And you—"

Sparrow laughed, "I know. I'm the perpetual Marshal's apprentice!"

"Just as far as the Royal House is concerned," Brit amended, then glanced again to Gwyn. "But I do agree with Jes. In Khirla it might be best to work independently. We two will stay in character as tinker-trades, while you distract the Court as the confident, yet ineffective, Marshal-at-hand."

"And the sandwolves?" Sparrow prompted.

"Best to wait and see, but they might do us the most good outside the city gates."

"You mean as spies watching for suspicious Palace couriers?" Sparrow elaborated shrewdly.

"Precisely." Brit grinned, then suddenly realized she hadn't seen so much as a furry paw since arriving. And the bed was set too low to hide such monsters beneath it. "Speaking of your motley crew, Gwyn, where'd they get to?"

"Jes took them to Market with her. I think they were hoping for a treat."

Brit's laughter broke with a shout. "While she's hoping to intimidate the barters!"

* * *

"Now you have everything—absolutely certain?"

In the Guild Stables, Gwyn looked up from tightly cinching Cinder's girth, a wry lift to her eyebrow.

"All right," Jes sighed. It was rather late in the day for travelers to be leaving, but Gwyn's small group would easily catch Brit and Sparrow by darkfall. "So you've remembered everything, but whatever you've forgotten."

"Minus whatever you remembered for me."

"Most of which you discarded again."

"Only because I'm not riding into war, *N'Sormee.*" Gwyn draped an arm over Cinder's withers as she faced her mother. Then she grunted at the unexpected weight as Ty promptly took advantage of her stillness and leaned a shoulder into her thigh.

"You very well might be, with the Clan involved, Gwyn'l."

"No," Gwyn tempered, frowning. "I'll accept a skirmish or two, but I'm not about to tackle an entire campaign with only two Amazons and a pair of sandwolves behind me. If things have deteriorated that badly, we'll get out. And with the Dracoon's consent or without, I'll bring both the Council and Crowned Rule into this."

"Sound judgment." Jes eyed her eldest with approval. "You've grown much in the last tenmoon-and-more."

"Aye," Gwyn stirred uncomfortably and gave Ty's ears a rub. "Well, I had good teachers somewhere along the line."

"Brit and myself? Unlikely," Jes scoffed. A tender glance met hers, and the elder relented. "Perhaps we didn't do so poorly, after all."

"Nehna?" Gwyn straightened and nudged Ty off of her foot. "Have you any last words of advice?"

"Oh, two things." Jes drew a parcel from inside her sling.

"What are these?" Gwyn opened the beige cloth curiously. "Vambraces?"

"Look more closely."

The amber-brown leathers were long sheaths that would wrap about not only a wrist but also a forearm. In the design, there were exquisite etchings of entwining vines alternating with finger-wide strips of raised smoothness, and a brown-ivory bracelet was bound near each wrist cuff. Then Gwyn did look more closely, and at the inner seam where each tied, the raised smoothness sheathed a taper-thin knife. Its bone-knob hilt was fitted seamlessly into the cuff ring.

"They're even of steel—the blades I mean. I had the smithy replace the glass-edged ones with metal reforged from some of my special arrows. I reasoned I'd not be needing the arrows as much as you might need these."

"Aye," Gwyn returned, appreciative of the forethought. "In Court, there are always places where swords aren't permitted."

"Certain courtiers would probably prefer you to be with nothing. But if there really is a traitor in there, you'd best be prepared for unpleasantness."

"Thank you."

"Then the other thing," Jes continued, producing a small oblong piece of soft wood with a hole in its center. "At practice yesterday, I heard a faint shing when you drew your sword. You've probably worn through to the stone rim on a corner of your sheath ring."

"I heard it too." Gwyn pocketed the thing gratefully. "I was going to ask Brit if she had any in her stock."

"I know she's got the tools to help fit that one in place."

"No doubt. So?"

"So," Jes drew a deep breath, hating the words, "we find ourselves parting ways once again."

"We do seem to do it more often than not."

Jes responded with a warm hug and both lingered a moment more, before Gwyn pressed, "You're leaving for Valley Bay soon. Aren't you?"

Her mother nodded with reassurance. "Since you've arrived, I've realized how badly I've been missing you all. I almost suspect myself of breaking this arm semi-purposely."

"As an excuse to go home?"

Jes shrugged, a little sheepish of that truth. "Extremist and foolish."

"But for the best of reasons." Gwyn stared at her steadily. "It's important for Bryana too, *N'Sormee*. She's grown tired without you, especially in this last wintering."

"Then it hasn't merely been the haze of her harmon shimmering that I noticed?" Jes sighed. "When she last reached me here through Kyra's Sight, I thought she seemed...well, less than herself. I'd...I'd hoped it was only the strain of reaching me through Kyra here, since Kyra's Blue Sight has no out-of-time Gift and I know that can make the harmon's traveling more difficult."

"No, it is more than simple weariness for her...," Gwyn smiled gently, "and for you."

"Aye—loneliness far outstretches duties and achievements, Gwyn'l. Remember that, should you ever be forced into a choice between roving and loving."

"Forced as you were into *no* choice? There would never have been a Plateau Treaty without you, *N'Sormee*. The Changlings' Wars would still be waging, if you had left them."

Jes denied that wearily. "There is always someone else capable of taking my place—or your place, Love. Someone would have managed something, if I'd been elsewhere."

"I don't believe in that 'always,'" Gwyn refuted. "Neither do you. Or you wouldn't have stayed."

Her mother's good shoulder shrugged in a helpless gesture. "We *Niachero* are a stubborn lot—too egotistical for our own good."

Gwyn knew only too well the ironic truth of that. She shook their melancholy aside—her troupe needed to be moving. Taking her mother's hand, she straightened and smiled gently. "May the Goddess walk beside you, *N'Sormee. Quita z'Kau. Ann?*"

Jes nodded in reassurance. "May Her Winds ride with you *ti mae Coramee*."

The two sandwolves reappeared from the shadows as Gwyn stepped up into her saddle. "Give my best to both Kimarie and Bryana."

"You know I will."

Chapter Five

Clear laughter sang through the forest's coolness, and Gwyn pulled up her mount for a moment. Brit's gravelly voice wove into Sparrow's mirth, and Gwyn realized the older woman must be spinning a new tale or something. The squeak of leather harness and the wagon's creaking grew audible. Gwyn's heels tapped her horse's flanks and they trotted forward toward the sounds. The pitch of voices quieted to a more serious murmur, and Gwyn decided abruptly on a more parallel route. She clicked her teeth and tongue in a pripper-like noise and the sandwolves ahead looked back at her, then quickly shifted directions to follow her. Gwyn knew her Sisters got precious little time alone on this journey, and she was loathe to invade their privacy yet again.

The mumble of conversation drifted on, mixing pleasantly with the rustle and chatter of the forest. The rhythmic beat of hooves beneath her was more felt than heard, and Gwyn had to admit that Calypso was much better suited to the woods than her favored mount, Cinder—though her third bay, Nia, was even more placid than Calypso. Still, Gwyn knew Cinder was her favorite because like Gwyn, the horse often enjoyed the challenge of a direct confrontation. Unfortunately, Cinder was a bit over-eager at times in taking the initiative and in their younger days it had led to occasional trouble.

But then risk wasn't always a thing to be avoided.

She heard laughter again, this time Brit's. Gwyn felt a wry smile on her own lips. She had wondered why this trip seemed so strange to her, until she realized how much she was feeling like an intruder.

It certainly wasn't coming from her companions. Neither Brit nor Sparrow had done anything to make Gwyn less welcomed in their company. They had even offered to let her take the upper berth in the wagon rather than tent out with her packmates. No, it was her own envy that was making her feel awkward.

Awkwardly lonely and isolated, Gwyn thought with irony. True, Brit had intermittently been part of her life since Gwyn's birth, and the older woman had been her teacher-spy during Gwyn's brief stint in the Wars. That pairing had been a good many tenmoons back, however, and since then Gwyn had ridden a great number of lone missions and commanded a fair lot of Dracoon patrols. The problem was, these last seasons she had been alone, and now she found herself envious of Brit and Sparrow's rapport.

And it was spring, Gwyn dourly reminded herself. A time for lovers, for adventures; a time for the awareness of what one lacked—such as Selena. No, it wasn't that simple. Gwyn remembered the woman standing beside the ship rail and watching the sails flutter on their slack lines above her, that silver hair gleaming under the early sun until she turned about at some order from midship and was called off to her navigator duties. For some time now, the memories no longer brought pain with them, yet there was a longing to fill that void. No one could ever be Selena, but that didn't mean there should never be another love again.

With a vague start, Gwyn realized what was happening to her—that shell about her heart was dissolving. Perhaps seeing Brit and Sparrow's obvious devotion had been the final stroke, but it must have been happening slowly for a while. The exchange she'd had with Tawna came to mind, and Gwyn found that her fears of risk had ebbed. That was what Brit and Sparrow had given to her—a tangible reminder that the loving could be so strong and so special—a reminder that the emptiness of being alone could be as much of a physical ache as the emptiness of a loss.

Ty suddenly gave a loud sniff and swung back to the right. She buried her nose in the leafy mulch and froze. Calypso amiably circled around the sandwolf and kept going.

"Come on, girl," Gwyn murmured. She patted the gutted bulk of the bray-goat that was lashed to the back of the saddle. "We've more than enough meat for today."

Ty snuffed, shaking the debris from her muzzle, then promptly began searching the ground for a trail.

Gwyn frowned as Ril loped back to join Ty's anxious weaving. Calypso agreeably halted and watched as Gwyn too began to scan the twig and leaf blanket of the woods' floor. Gwyn nibbled her lip in puzzlement and twisted quick to watch both of the sandwolves bound towards the road. They stopped short as their two trails intersected and some wordless communication passed between their bright eyes, before urgent gazes lifted to Gwyn.

"People? Find me something I can read, *Dumauzen*," Gwyn encouraged softly, already wary of who else might be near to hear.

The pair backtracked. Gwyn pulled Calypso around, careful to keep the mare away from the area her bondmates were working over. She had no desire to confuse an already difficult trail. "How recent was it made?"

Ril paused, glancing up expectantly. Gwyn's chin jutted towards the unseen track. "Is it yesterday's?"

Black gums showed with her soundless snarl of negation.

"Today's then?" Ril shook her head with a dip, like some silent canine sneeze, and Gwyn felt her stomach tighten apprehensively. "Since this morning's rain?"

Again Ril confirmed her suspicion, and Gwyn sent her back to searching with a curt nod. Most likely, Gwyn reasoned, it would be others hunting just as she had been doing. But the nape of her neck prickled, and she had lived through a good many would-be ambushes from thieves by being cautious. It was not a habit that she intended to put aside quite yet.

Ty rumbled low, bringing Gwyn nearer to see what she'd found. The imprints were fairly deep between the waterlogged little dip and the mud beneath the decaying leaves. The scuffs along the base of the tree weren't nearly so clear, but they were there. At least two horses had been through, one with a chip on the outside of a back hoof. That meant, perhaps, one with a heavy pack and one with a rider. Or worse, two riders with a middling amount of gear each. She looked up to find Ril patiently waiting to show her something else. She guided Calypso around the trees, still careful not to disturb the tracks. Three, she saw then. This last print was obviously too large to match the mounts that had made the others, but its depth wasn't indicative of a heavier load for all its heavier size. That strongly suggested three riders and no pack animal among them. It also suggested they were either very lousy hunters or they hadn't been hunting forest game; something large enough to feed the three of them comfortably—like the braygoat she'd taken—would have made the horse which carried it make much deeper prints than any of these.

"I don't like this," Gwyn muttered. "Now tell me what I already know. They were headed for the road and not away, no doubling back into the woods for some camp or other?"

Ril and Ty bolted in different directions to check for such meanderings. Gwyn grimly turned Calypso towards the road and the wagon. It suddenly seemed like a better idea not to leave the two of her Sisters so overtly unarmed. In truth they could fend off a small band of three quite competently, but the presence of a Royal Marshal might discourage raiders from rashly discovering that the obvious often hid the unexpected. Besides, even the best of fighters had off-days, and she didn't want to gamble that Brit or Sparrow might be due for one.

* * *

The square bulk of the tinker-trade wagon was a mere silhouette beyond the light cast by their fire. Ril's snoozing figure was curled comfortably on the roof of the wagon; her bed was made of grain sacks and fabric bolts that were snugly packed beneath a waterproof tarp. The sandwolf was barely visible amidst the other lumpish shapes, and if anything did manage to get past Ty's circling sentry, Ril would undoubtedly become an unwanted surprise to any intruder.

"It doesn't figure," Brit mumbled, joining Sparrow and Gwyn at the fire. The canvas and wood of the folding stool creaked as the woman's heavy frame settled into it. "These three riders have been weaving in and out of the woods, back and forth across the road, for the last two days. They aren't making any better time than us with the wagon and drays. They're barely a full-day ahead of us now. My guess is, we'll meet them come Bratler's Hoe at the very latest."

"They're obviously looking for something…or someone." Sparrow idly tapped a stone in the fire ring with a stick. Lips pursed as she concentrated on their little puzzle. She shrugged and shifted some in her cross-legged seat on the ground, easing a muscle. "What do you think of these strange hunters, *Niachero*?"

"What I think?" Gwyn's brow lifted, though her eyes and hands remained steadily engaged in her whittling task. The thin pipe was beginning to actually look like a musical instrument, but only barely. "I think that they are indeed hunters. And I think they are searching for something very particular. What that something is, however, I haven't a hint."

Sparrow said nothing for a long moment, then offered, "Could they have something to do with Khirlan's troubles?"

"I'd thought of it." Brit laced her fingers together as she leaned forward, elbows to knees. "We're certainly close enough to the district divisions for something to crop up."

"A ten-day from the boundary?" Gwyn considered that. It left her unconvinced. "South of Bratler's Hoe, perhaps. It's a fair ways between Hoe and that tiny settlement at Millers Crossing. Tinker-trades, lone travelers…Fates' Jest! A middling sized caravan could disappear in that forested stretch and no one would ever be the wiser. Especially if someone at Millers was part and parcel to the schemes. It's a full ten-day to the next village along the westerly trail, and at least as far to the first marked settlement, if you cross over into Khirlan."

Brit nodded vaguely. "Then again, maybe they're out scouting for brigands themselves."

"A locally organized patrol?" Sparrow didn't like the sound of that. "What's so precious that they've got to send guards way out here?"

"Maybe...?" Brit frowned, giving the idea time to focus in her mind.

Gwyn was ahead of her already. "Could it be the Clan's started to push this far north? If so, then scouts would be out watching for more serious trouble than the usual brigands are likely to give."

"Possibly," Brit's frown deepened into a scowl. "Or maybe these three are from the Clan themselves?"

"You're suggesting that they're trailing a few days behind that mead and fur shipment up ahead of us?" Gwyn shrugged. "That would mean they're waiting for the isolated stretch beyond Bratler's Hoe before attacking."

"And that they'll be joined by others shortly." Sparrow shut her eyes and shook her head in disgust. "How did *dey Sorormin* ever manage their home world treaties with Terran-sorts?"

"I'll tell you some day," Brit chuckled, grey eyes dancing. "But I warn you, the story of the Founding is quite a long one."

"I'll wager it was—long and painful, most likely."

Brit confirmed it with a nod.

"There's something we haven't considered about these hunters." Gwyn returned the others' attention to their original issue, only faintly aware that her Sisters had strayed from the topic. "If these could be Clan raiders, couldn't they also be Clan spies sent searching for us? Or at least, for me?"

"You mean, someone at the Dracoon's court found out she'd spoken to Bryana and sent word to intercept a Marshal?"

"If the Dracoon has been in contact with *M'Sormee* again, it would be possible? Wouldn't it?"

"Certainly," both Sparrow and Brit agreed in unison.

"However," Brit continued quietly, "it's unlikely that Bryana would have said anything specifically about you being a Marshal. She knew of your suspicions regarding a traitor in the Court, didn't she?"

"Still...," Gwyn caught Brit's gaze across the fire.

"Aye," the older woman agreed, "we ought to make some discreet inquiries when we overnight in Hoe."

"We should take a few precautions in our travel story as well," Gwyn amended. "At least, if they're expecting one or two meddlesome officials we shouldn't encourage them in assuming either you or Sparrow have anything but the most superficial associations with me."

"Aye, I'd near forgotten that Bryana expected Jes to come with you. Seems easy enough, though," Brit glanced to Sparrow for confirmation. "If anybody in Hoe starts asking, we'll just say we expect to part company with you before Millers Crossing—at the west bend. Then if these trackers are after a Royal Marshal, we'll see them show up beyond Millers, and fairly quick too, I'd wager. But if they're mere thieves after the tinker-trade goods, they'll be waiting forever on the wrong road altogether."

"Ought to work," Sparrow agreed.

Ought to, Gwyn mused. But that prickly sensation on the back of her neck just wouldn't go away.

* * *

Bratler's Hoe was half-a-day ahead and that had them all longing for a welcomed break in the monotony of travel. Not that the place was much to look forward to in and of itself. Bratler's Hoe was a sleepy little village of moss thatch and varnished wood. It's sole infamy, as far as the rest of the Gronday Guild district was concerned, was its custom of hoe farming. The technique proffered the use of hoes and rarely plows, hence its name, but it was a necessity this far south in the Ramains' Great Forest. Here, silverpines had gradually given way to the more ancient honeywoods, and the root of a small honeywood easily out-sized a human limb. This leant very little encouragement to anyone thinking of clearing land for a field. The fact that once the towering gold-and-red barked giants were felled, the top soil washed out within a season or two also bode ill for plow farmers. So the people had adapted. The locals had taken up the hoe farming customs of the Khirlan district—they planted patches of compatible, shade-dwelling crops beneath the forest canopy—their harvests cradled sometimes within the very roots of the honeywoods. After so many generations of experimenting, they had managed to evolve their agriculture into a fine art and their farms into relatively successful ventures.

Brit pointed out that the honeywoods were probably quite satisfied as well. The crops were generally compatible, because they added the nutrients the honeywoods depleted while thriving on those the honeywoods produced.

Seeing the girth of those mammoth tree trunks, some of which could have comfortably housed the tinker-trade wagon whole, Gwyn had no trouble believing Brit. The symbiotic relationship between crops and trees had obviously not hindered the ancients' growth by much.

"Always fascinates me," Sparrow murmured, and Gwyn glanced up at her. Sparrow was stretched out on her back atop the wagon's roof. Arms folded behind her head and one leg dangling across an upraised knee, she looked surprisingly comfortable despite the jostling jolts of the wagon's pitch. "You've got so many different kinds of land in the north."

"The Desert Peoples don't?"

"Oh to some extent, but nothing like this. We've got a few oasis cities on the coasts, a few herding villages in the mountain brush, and one or two wonderful—and religiously pampered—spots where our shipwoods grow. On the whole, we've got coastal strips of barely arable land and then the central plains of rolling dunes. We don't have the plateau countries like the Changlings and the Clan both have. And the only snow ever seen is on the Icy Tips, way off the south reef. But no one lives there. Those islands are even less hospitable than the Maltar Ice Plains!"

"Excuse me—" Brit called back over a shoulder from the lower height of the driver's seat. "The Changlings did away with the last of the Maltar's reigning families. Remember?"

"Picky-picky," Sparrow clucked. "Treaty's not even a season old, and you're expecting me to remember new names already!"

49

"That I do," Brit returned, serious in tone. Her face, however, which her companions could not see, held a broad grin. "And since we're being 'picky,' let me also remind you that nearly a third of those Ice Plains are actually part of the Changlings' lands now."

"If you care to call frozen water and stone 'land.' That frostbitten, Fate cursed—"

"Temper, temper," Brit tisked, twisting about to grin at Sparrow.

Gwyn laughed from her seat upon Nia.

"And just what is she chortling about?" Sparrow asked in feigned outrage.

Her partner shrugged elaborately, and in an overly casual manner turned back to her driving. Then abruptly Brit stiffened. "Gwyn'l—is Ty the one with the tattered ear?"

"Yes."

Gwyn brought Nia forward as Brit nodded down the road. "She's circling in kind of early, isn't she?"

"She certainly is." Nia jumped into an easy canter, and Gwyn went to meet her packmate.

Ty cast a quick glance up to Gwyn and the woman reined in to a halt. The sandwolf whined a soft note, ears back and eyes worried, but she trotted past the horse on towards the wagon. Her fretful demeanor urged Gwyn not to venture further down the road yet.

"We've got company coming," Gwyn announced flatly as Brit came abreast of her. "Someone suspicious enough to worry about."

"Our weaving hunters perhaps?" Brit prompted.

Gwyn shot a look at Ty to find that sneeze-like nod confirming Brit's guess.

"So we stop and stand? Or keep moving?" Sparrow asked, more attentive to Gwyn than to the crossbow spring she was setting with hands and knee.

"Moving," Brit answered quick. At Gwyn's nod to continue, she suggested, "At least until we know what they want. But not you. After two days of sun, this road's hard packed enough to make the prints vague—leastwise too vague to easily mark the time of their making. Take Nia and Ty and disappear for a bit. Leave us to the questions, if there are any. Just stay near enough to help, should we need it."

There was sense in that, Gwyn saw. A Royal Marshal could often soothe tempers by her mere presence; she could also escalate tensions unwittingly with the mantle of her authority, if a stranger's deeds smacked of illegality.

Sparrow sent her a grin, tucking the crossbow and an unsheathed sword into the lumps around her. Brit gave her a wink and saluted with the black coils of her flint-tipped whip. Gwyn chided herself; these two could take care of themselves. "Come on, Ty...ease back."

The wagon pulled ahead as Nia turned her trot into a high stepping prance that would leave similar hoof prints without telling a tracker of her slowed pace. To anyone but a master of mentors, Gwyn knew there would be nothing unusual to the prints. She hoped it would suggest her horse had been inadvertently parallel to the wagon, but not necessarily accompanying it. To that end she was also careful to cut left into the woods to leave the wagon tracks undisturbed on the right. Ty followed, leaving even less of a trail behind.

Ril met them quickly, warning them of the arrival of the hunters, and Nia shifted into a quiet gait, barely bending a twig under hoof. The ruddy red and black of Nia's hide blended with the honeywood trees as easily as did the gold and reds of Gwyn's Marshal garb. The dull beige of the sandwolves melded into patches of stonemoss. The small band fairly disappeared into the dappled shadows altogether.

In the end, very little seemed to come of the encounter. Two of the riders appeared; Ty went scouting for the third. Gwyn hovered in the forest frustrated by the fact that the voices were too muted to hear well. Ty reappeared at Gwyn's stirrup a split second before the third fellow appeared on a huge, brown gelding. It was disconcerting to see him coming down the road from behind. He greeted his partners, eyes shifting warily along Gwyn's side of the woods, and even from her obscured vantage point, she realized he knew she and Nia were somewhere about.

Her body tensed, fingers toying with her sword's hilt. He made some comment about the two bays on the lead rope behind the wagon, and Gwyn held her breath. Brit hadn't missed his nervousness though. The older woman readily confirmed what he already knew, then seemed to embellish it with something or other and a wave at the forest. The trio laughed, made their farewells, and rode off towards Bratler's Hoe.

Gwyn kept Nia to the trees for another full league and sent her packmates on after the strangers as a precaution. They'd all been sword carriers with fairly worn, but well-fitted clothing and gear. That in itself wasn't unusual. The mustering out of the Ramains' troops had begun earlier in the spring, and they easily could fit that sort of description. What was odd was the fact that they'd all been men—bearded men, in fact—and none of them had seemed attached to another. The personal space between their horses had seemed further apart than most, and certainly it had not hinted at any intimate familiarity. In a generation whose sword carriers had known so much of war, it was more typical to find comrades-in-arms staying together because they had become lovers, especially after leaving a company. It was so common in fact, that Gwyn found herself decidedly uneasy with their obvious deviance from the practice.

That, and they were bearded. An old custom it might be, but the Ramains' men persisted in the style of clean shaven faces. It was an intentional attempt to foster trust, applauded by both the Royal Families and by the Council of Ten. A clean shaven face meant a man's expressions of peaceful tidings were plainly visible for all to see. To break with the custom was doubly taboo for travelers, because they had so much contact with strangers.

In truth, this trio had been a strange lot.

The Amazon frowned, half-imagining an odd stench to their very scent. It was almost as if she were one of the sandwolves. She dismissed the illusion as fanciful, but the Fates' corruptible presence was unmistakable. These men were not the simple travelers they alluded to be. Her copper eyes narrowed with stony resolve. She knew a predator when she met one, and she had no wish to become easy prey.

* * *

The Inn's stable wasn't very large, and it was very dimly lit. It got worse as twilight deepened, and Gwyn hurried to finish with the horses. After this after-

51

noon's encounter, none of the Sisters had wanted to leave the tending of their beasts to strangers, and Gwyn had offered to care for the wagon's drays as well as her own three, knowing that Brit and Sparrow would be kept busy with customers demanding both news and goods. They were, after all, the first pair of merchants through from the northern areas since the Wars' ending. Their popularity was also enhanced by the wares they had brought. Many of these folks had never seen a wagon out of Rotava and the far northwest; their parents had not yet been born when the last traders had come south with such goods.

Ril and Ty sulked near their human, moving in-and-out of the bays' stalls and scaring the young stable hand brown with tremors as they became acquainted with things. They would be spending the night here, more as guardians of gear and wagon than as unwelcomed Inn guests. Neither of them relished being separated from Gwyn, but she would be with other Sisters so they had grudgingly agreed to remain below.

From the corner of her eye, Gwyn glimpsed upright movement in the court. She clapped the curry combs together, ostentatiously cleaning them for the sake of anyone watching, then picked up a pail and went to fetch the drays' water. The excuse took her out to the center of the cobblestone court. She hooked the bucket to the pump head and saw a man where she'd expected to— near the corral beyond the barn's side, where the burros and nags were overnighting. It was a corner already sheltered in darkness, perfect for a watcher. But she was surprised by the flashing glint of glass coin and that tell-tale clink of money exchanging hands. She bent over her task, puzzled, but as she straightened to take the water back into the stables, she noted the two figures seemed oblivious of her. They moved, separating at the corral's end. She ducked inside, found no sign of the stable hand and flattened herself against the wall to peer out again. The two figures were both returning to the commons, but one was going through the kitchens instead of the side door. As they each passed beneath the globe lantern, she saw more of their features. The bearded stranger she recognized as the rider of that big brown, the other was a local. Neither carried anything overtly. So what exactly had the bearded one been buying?

The commons held the welcoming, noisy bunch that Sparrow was accustomed to finding in taverns most anywhere. The smoke from pipes was thick, but the cubbyholes in the corners of the ceiling drew it upwards remarkably well. The scents of meats and soups were a bit odd, in an exotic way; most of the seasonings were fairly new to her. The clothing seemed vaguely unfamiliar, and she finally realized she wasn't used to seeing such plain garb on town folk. Tunics here were almost universally made of undyed homespun. Loose jackets of oilcloth were favored over quilted jerkins or vests, but like the trousers, the colors were mostly made of red-browns or stonemoss grays.

It did explain why the few bolts of fabric which Brit had unfurled had sold so quickly. Doubtless their entire stock of material would have been bought out, if they'd wished it. She should have gotten that wedding lace in Gronday.

Her patrons across the table shifted on the bench, still murmuring to one another about the merits of the knives laid out before them. She politely hid a smile behind a cough as she saw them again speculating on this new technique of the resin-glass melt. Those knives were decidedly odd compared to the traditional, kiln-fired blackglass or the expensive steel bladed types. The melt had been created in the glassworks at Black Falls and expanded on a Changling trick for making flintless arrows. By adding blackpine resin to the sands in making the glass, a peculiar translucent-amber shaft could be formed. The edges were then tapered with clearer glass to allow a crystal sharp blade to be honed later. The results produced a resilient knife that could be dropped carelessly and not shatter, yet it cost less than a third of that rarer steel sort. It was also extremely lightweight, was flexible enough to strip along bones when skinning, and sturdy enough to carve hardwood.

It's only drawback that Sparrow could see was the funny oily feeling it had. But she'd found a little leather wrapped about a handle replaced that eerie sensation with a more familiar grip.

She idly smoothed a wrinkle from the corner of the gray shammy beneath her display. It was a small selection she was offering them, less than a dozen, but she had always believed in selling tools she trusted. If it wasn't something she'd be comfortable using herself, Sparrow wasn't about to ask another to buy it. Brit had seemed amused at first by her adamant assertions, and it had taken Sparrow nearly a tenmoon to recognize that Brit's smile hid a tacit approval as well.

We really were matched by more than the Council, Sparrow thought for the thousandth-some time. Her gaze swept around to Brit's place across the room. The soft smile on her lips went cold. The foursome surrounding that center table held no resemblance to the healers that had last been there. Without thinking, Sparrow reached to roll the knives into the shammy as the fellow nearest Brit—no, it was a woman; she was too short for a male—grabbed a fistful of fabric and hauled Brit to her feet.

"Wait a bit…," the sturdy, young woman laid a hand across Sparrow's. Startled, Sparrow jerked about, eyes wide and uncomprehending. "We are serious about buying, just—"

A quick smile leapt forth and Sparrow suggested, "Sleep on it, Min. We're here for all of tomorrow."

The brawny male next to the woman, a brother most likely given that square jawed resemblance, scowled at the dismissal. His sister elbowed his ribs to silence his protest, though, as she noted the anxiety in both Sparrow's darkening skin tones and that searching glance to the far table. The woman nodded his attention to Brit's cheerless party.

"Skinner's daughter and boys," he grunted.

Sparrow tucked the bundled knives into her vest. "You know those four?"

"Aye." He obviously didn't like them. His sister too was nodding in somber displeasure as he explained, "They're not the kind to name friends."

"Trouble wanting to happen," the woman amended succinctly.

Concern doubled as Sparrow stood, but she hesitated. Few of the clamoring folk in the commons had noticed anything amiss, and Gwyn was still absent. Sparrow felt her toes tense impatiently even as she forced herself to stand still. This was not a place to force a confrontation. It was just late enough that sufficient ale had been downed to blur judgments, yet too little had been drunk to dull tempers. If she called their challenging bluff, there'd like as not be a brawl erupting. And a free-for-all wouldn't spare Brit by much.

"Ruffians, the whole family," the young man muttered behind her. "All of 'em want their fun at others' cost."

His sister snorted in disgust. "Bile sort of entertainment, if you ask me."

"Entertainment?" Sparrow repeated in distraction. Then suddenly the solution came, and with a bound she mounted the table, shouting, "Entertainment?!"

The commons rumbled in bewildered surprise, and even the Skinner's kin half-turned to her.

"Entertainment!" she cried, with arms flinging wide and the great hearth fire blazing behind her. "This fellow here asked me for entertainment! Anyone else I hear?"

A hearty roar and round of applause met her. She caught Brit's eye as the bully released her; it was working. Sparrow turned slowly for the crowd, arms still held wide, her brows lifted high with an exaggerated expression that was half-questioning, half-expectant. The people encouraged her more then, banging on tables and whistling. The artful stance, the bright yellow-orange garb—her entire demeanor promised a troubadour's style in any performance, and as in most small towns, they relished that scarce prize.

"A tale of comedy or woe? One of truth or perchance? I know!" The crowd hushed as she dropped to a crouch and spun on her toes, eyes sparkling and darting to each face about. "A little of each, with something to teach!"

Benches and chairs scraped, dozens of feet shuffling as patrons and help alike sought seats. Those that couldn't find chairs took up places along the walls. The four around Brit were sullenly forced to move aside as it became apparent that everyone would soon be aware of their threatening intentions, and no one was going to be sympathetic to any of their insults if it interfered with a show. But they were slow in coming to this conclusion, and Brit who had dropped into her seat at the first sign of distraction was securely surrounded by other patrons, and so the four were left to find space elsewhere.

Now if only Gwyn would get her sword and fancy copper clothes in here, Sparrow fretted. No one but a Royal Marshal could enter a commons without surrendering their sword arms to the innkeeper. And at the moment, an armed Marshal would be a most welcomed deterrent. Sparrow glanced at her lover again, seeing Brit wisely keeping her face blank as the Skinner's kin left. But those eyes gleamed knowingly at Sparrow, and the young woman's enticing smile was suddenly even brighter for all her audience.

Her hand lifted. A hush fell, and Sparrow let it fill the room. Then in a low, clear voice she began.

"It was night, a single moon—stillness black...."

Heads bobbed, all knowing the frightening legends of those infrequent eves when only one of the Twin Moons appeared in the heavens.

"...When above the skies trembled. The Fates loos'd
Their curse! Bright and fiery, bold as a star,
This thing descended to the Queen's own yard!

"It burst silent flame! Silent roar burning!
Quick turned, the Mother's Hand muted the fires.
But the Jesting Fates mocked, feeling clever
As smoke slowly parted to show the Queen."

Sparrow came down from the table, hands gesturing wide as she began to walk among them.

"Upon the ruins lay her bent body,
And yet, the Queen's death was far from complete.
For the woman's harmon had been shattered
Into three shards—Soul shards, naked and torn.

"One shard called Honor, the Fates discarded.
The careless one was Curiosity.
The Jesters planned later to lure her near.
Oh, but the third was incarnate of needs!"

She leapt upon Brit's tabletop and continued,

"The Fates quick claimed her—Named her! Shameless Lust!
And the Cellars' thought they'd tied the Mother's
Hand in calling Lust away. They knew that
The Mother would not force re-unity.

"The Mother gave scant heed to those wry Fates.
Instead she called each shard, 'Daughter.' She spoke
First with Honor, tempering with fact: Both
Sisters were once part of Honor's own self."

Sparrow skipped lightly across to another's table.

"With the idleness, Curiosity,
The Mother took a firmer Hand. She showed
The Daughter what the futures blend, when bold
Deeds and power proceed too thoughtlessly.

"Then She sent these Daughters gently wooing
After Lust, with patient respect—and trust.
The Fates screeched out! Protesting in their rage!
But the Mother intervened to still them."

Sparrow dropped to the floor, walking through the patrons again. She smiled inwardly to see Gwyn's tall figure behind those in the kitchen's door, and full circle complete, Sparrow mounted the hearth's table again.

"It had come time for the Daughters' own say.
Honor shunned righteousness, chose compassion.

55

Curiosity joined her Sisters' hands,
Grasping finally—how questions counsel all.

"And Lust—defiant would-be-kin of Fates!
Lust took and turned Fates' wiles about. She'd learned
Joys of giving, joys that sprang not from greed,
'Til she acquired the gentler name—Desire.

"The Mother smiled at these Lessons, proud to
See Her three once-shattered shards uniting.
They formed yet a stronger whole than before.
And so despite the Fates, their Soul claimed peace and soared."

Her lifted hand swung down to her waist, and in a elegant motion Sparrow gave them a formal bow from the hip, left leg extending back. Her audience leapt to approve with hands clapping and feet stomping in rowdy glee. Sparrow grinned and caught Gwyn's eye as the *Niachero* started across the room for Brit. Gwyn sent her a wink, joining in the applause as she went. Sparrow turned and bowed low again as patrons began tossing their glass coins atop the table— covertly she searched for the Skinner's kin. She noted that Gwyn was bending to whisper something to Brit, but a sudden movement snapped her attention towards the front door. The sister and three brothers were slipping away quickly. Sparrow hopped down from her tabletop, wondering if their departure meant good fortune or not.

She glanced again at Gwyn to find the Amazon grimly watching something beyond Sparrow's shoulder. Then suddenly a cheerful patron was demanding of Sparrow, "You said the tale was to teach?"

Sparrow blinked, then found the thin, old man who raised the tankard of ale to identify himself. He prodded, "Who were these Daughters?"

Another across the room raised her mug and hollered back, "Why us folks, of course! What are you, daft?"

"I'd say Honor was the Council—that right?" A third farmer stood, hitching his belt up with a thumb.

Sparrow raised a crooked grin and gave them all an elaborate shrug, only turning to sweep up the money on the table planks.

"Nah—the Council's Curiosity," the first old man spat.

"Then Honor's the Amazons maybe? You're a Sister, aren't you?" the brawny brother interjected from behind her, and Sparrow nodded, raising her hand to wiggle the signet ring of white stone on her finger. "So Honor's the Amazons. Has to be."

"Which is right?" And the cry was echoed as they urged her to speak. But Sparrow simply smiled and shook her head, palms upraised against their questions. Good-naturedly they prompted her a bit more but left off as she joined Gwyn and Brit. After all, a troubadour's job was to entertain, not interpret.

"I don't quite understand it," Sparrow spoke quietly as she slid into the seat facing her friends. "Those four were grumpily standing there, and then they simply left!"

Gwyn pointed a chin at that far wall behind Sparrow. "Our three hunters departed through the side door just as quickly."

"Seems they all got what they wanted," Brit returned flatly.

Sparrow half smiled. "I should have known you'd piece something together."

Her lover's dark eyes softened fondly. "That was quite a performance. Thank you."

"You're most welcome. I always do think best on my feet." A pregnant pause hovered in the air, and then exasperated Sparrow's hand whirled forward. "*Nehna?!*"

Brit frowned abruptly. "Don't understand quite why they want to know, but it's Gwyn's face they were after."

"Me...what makes you certain?"

"First, they made such a fuss on the road about Cinder and Calypso. Started by feigning interest in buying a matched pair, then..."

"That ended when the third fellow rode in, talking about Gwyn's tracks," Sparrow finished.

"Thought it was strange he was such a good tracker. Still, with the Wars.... Anyway, when I admitted in a vague sort of way that you were out hunting and that we really didn't expect to meet you before Bratler's Hoe again, they seemed satisfied enough."

"Until they arrive here and promptly hire the local brigands to intimidate you." Gwyn mulled that over, then saw Brit's point. "Aye, they did want to be sure of me. They assumed that by threatening you or Sparrow, I'd eventually appear to help."

"Probably suspected our companion to be a Royal Marshal before they ever heard you were in the town, though they'd have wanted to be certain. One of the pair this afternoon made the observation that Cinder and Calypso were fine enough to belong to a Marshal."

Sparrow gave a scoffing grunt. "Fool habit you Marshals have, traveling around on matched mounts all the time."

"Not all the time," Brit teased, reminding them of her own status as a Marshal and how nicely she stayed hidden by driving the wagon.

"Most of us are conspicuous enough," Gwyn agreed absently. "It has advantages as well."

"Not today, it doesn't."

Brit ignored that sour remark. "Did either of you notice that an inordinate number of people seem interested in our next destination?"

Gwyn hadn't, but wasn't surprised. "Only the stable hand asked me. I couldn't tell if it was anything more than the usual curiosity youngsters have for travelers."

"I'd begun to suspect it was rather more myself," Sparrow admitted.

"Well, it seems my four brawny oxen weren't the only ones paid for a little conspiracy tonight." Brit sighed. "I guess, it remains to be seen if they're wanting to follow the tinker-trades or the Marshal."

Neither Sparrow nor Gwyn had an answer for that yet. The three of them resigned themselves to the fact that it was going to be a very long trip to the fork above Millers Crossing.

Chapter Six

Now this is turning into the sort of traveling I like," Brit declared smugly. The long reins slapped an amiable reminder at the butter-blond drays and their ears flicked back as they plodded on.

"What sort is that?" Gwyn asked, only half-attending to her Sister and more concerned with the mysterious creak developing somewhere in her saddle.

"Sunny and rainless with lots of shade." A pothole rocked the wagon precariously, and Brit's broad form swayed with the seat, quite unperturbed. "And—I might also add—totally uneventful."

Gwyn spared her a brief grin. "Thought you were expecting it to storm tonight?"

"Nearly rainless then—ah, laugh at me!"

"No, never." Gwyn twisted to peer behind the cantle of her saddle. The creak seemed to come from beneath the bedroll and saddlebags.

"Aye, I'm old and stodgy. Set in my ways, if you like. Tussles with brigands and bullies are not the glorious delights they once were."

A disbelieving snort from Gwyn belied that anyone sane ever found such encounters 'delights,' and Brit chuckled in that deep, low way she had which made Gwyn join her.

"All right!" Gwyn finally abandoned her useless inspection of the red leather. "I admit it. Your plot worked. Those three went west chasing the rumors of the tinker-trades, just as you'd hoped." A loud bang from the cabin's back door marked Sparrow's approach. "I'm grateful for your experience, foresight and intuition. And I am most humbly grateful to be the recipient of said wisdom."

"Whose wisdom?" Sparrow inquired, dropping lightly down from the rooftop to the wagon seat.

"My own." Brit looked at her askance. "What are you dressed for, Woman?"

"Wisdom about what?" Sparrow countered.

"About setting those three off our tails," Gwyn supplied wryly.

"We're only four days south of Millers Crossing," Sparrow observed. "Little early to be handing out laurels, isn't it?"

"Be respectful of your elder, child," Brit groused and demanded again, "Why are you in those damned blacks?"

"You're not old enough to be my elder," Sparrow quipped and planted a quick kiss on her lover's mouth before another protest got uttered. The retort to that blatant lie turned into a rebuking frown that Sparrow merely grinned at. Then she snatched the reins from Brit, looped them about the foot rail, and deftly hopped forward to straddle the big dray on the left.

"Sparrow!" Brit roared.

Unconcerned, the small woman planted her palms flat, swung her legs back and clear into a perfect arch upwards—bare toes even pointed. Then gracefully she righted into a stand. Gwyn stared in awed surprise; the drays

58

simply perked their ears attentively, clearly accustomed to such antics.

"For someone anxious about ambushes, you're certainly prepared," Brit snapped out. Her hands flexed into fists to keep from grabbing at those reins and distracting the horses.

"Tsk-tsk." Sparrow turned 'round, stance splayed and a foot centered on each mare's back. "Please take heed, Love, of the crossbow directly behind you on the roof. It's cocked with two bolts, and the safety latch is in place."

Gwyn noted the woman didn't mention the two daggers sheathed to her upper arms nor the long knife on her belt. However, the weapons didn't make Sparrow look anything like a soldier. Instead she looked the image of the small, lean acrobat—which her every motion declared was no illusion. She wore a sleeveless top and snug leggings made of black knit, her fawn hair had been braided high in an arching strand that dusted her shoulders with its end, and her hands were wrapped in fingerless, leather grips.

"This is not the time nor the place! Sparrowhawk—please!"

"I need the practice, if I'm going to keep in shape for Khirla." Sparrow blithely turned a sidewise handstand on the right mare into a back walk-over to stand up on the left dray.

Gwyn felt her heart leap to her throat as Sparrow abruptly reversed, somersaulting backwards to the right again.

"Sparrow—*Soroi!* The horses are pulling!"

She smiled at Brit tenderly, pausing to adjust her palm gloves as her body moved in easy rhythm with the mare. "I don't weigh so much that they ever mind me, and you know it."

"It's dangerous enough in light harness," Brit persisted, pleading in a tone Gwyn had never heard from Brit. "With this damned cart they'll run right over—"

"When do you see me fall?"

"Plenty!"

"I mean, what am I doing?" Sparrow's gentle tone lost none of its firmness. "Always—I'm in light harness, attempting a new maneuver. I don't do foolish things in performances nor in practice, and I don't intend to start now." Sparrow glanced at Gwyn with a crooked grin, adding, "I'm not quite that adventuresome; you see."

Gwyn didn't see at all as the other woman proceeded to work through a series of stretches, splits, handstands, and tumbles. She did notice that Cinder had to move a little faster as the dray team quickened their gait; the harnessed mares seemed to enjoy the challenge, stepping higher and matching paces proudly.

"No side hangs!" Brit shrieked.

The shrill note of genuine terror stayed Sparrow in mid-move. Fondly, she shook her head but moved on as requested.

"She hasn't got proper tack for hanging over," Brit muttered to Gwyn. Brit still seemed to be shaking though, and her skin tones deepened as she continued to fret. Yet when Sparrow finally took pity and finished, jumping lightly back to the wagon seat with a pleased breathlessness, Gwyn found that her own nerves had flushed the gold of her tan brown and that her heart was thumping nearly as fast as Brit's must be.

Sparrow studied the two of them with exasperated amusement as she pulled off her gloves. Her color too had darkened from the exertion, but the warm, healthy glow lacked the pinched look of anxiety that Brit wore. She reached around to retrieve a towel from beside her crossbow and wiped off the sweat that blurred her vision. Gwyn had to admit, she seemed pleased with herself and wasn't in the least deterred by Brit's frayed composure. Sparrow draped the towel around her neck and picked up the reins, clucking and praising the two drays ahead.

Gwyn looked at Brit in confusion. Her old friend seemed to be concentrating on breathing, but there was no sign of chastising tension between the two. Gwyn began to suspect this was something Brit had learned to accept as typical of her shadowmate—or at least had agreed to try to accept.

"Your saddle's got an awful squeak to it, Gwyn'l." The *Niachero* blinked with a start, and Sparrow smiled at her. "That wasn't there a ten-day back. Is something coming unglued?"

With a little effort, Gwyn swallowed her bemusement and nodded. "With all the rain we had before Bratler's Hoe, I expect something got through the oil and started to mildew."

"We carry tack tools and glue you can use. And I'm pretty good with stitching, if you want some help."

"I'd appreciate it. I'm pretty poor at it myself."

"Certainly, though the glue will take a few days to set."

Gwyn shrugged. "I can haul out my extra saddle from the things you carry for me."

"I admit I wondered some, when I helped pack it. But I guess I just found out why you travel with two. Something happens with the first, you've got a spare."

"There is more to it than that, you know. Just like our individual mounts are always color-matched. Part of it's because duplication means we can get separated from luggage and still have the necessities for ride and chase. Part of it is that we can seem to be in two places at once, by acquiring an accomplice and then dressing them—and mounting them—identically. But most importantly, we often need speed for our tasks. Sometimes for one of us alone, sometimes for us and a partner of some sort. My experience has been that when I find myself partnered, it's usually under duress and with very short notice. That dilemma seems to be fairly widespread among other Marshals too. So, when possible we count on supplying them with a mount good enough to keep up and with equipment to leave in a rush."

"Hence three mounts?" Sparrow pressed. "Two for riding and one for pack?"

"That and three also help when traveling fast. I can switch off with each of them. By splitting packs for light weights between two and myself on the third, and then rotating between them all, I can travel further and faster than nearly anybody I might be trailing."

"Or fleeing?"

"Especially important then."

"It makes sense," Sparrow reflected. "The nomadic folks I grew up with used to do something similar with their sled teams."

"That would be with dustbears?"

"Yes!" Sparrow was impressed, not too many remembered the Desert Peoples didn't migrate with horse and harness. "You've seen them?"

Regretfully Gwyn admitted, "No, I've never been even this far south before."

"Ah—well they're not very memorable, actually. They're these lumbering, docile dunes of webbed paws and curly, dusty toned hair. But they don't mind the sun's heat much nor the midnight chills, and they can go seemingly forever without water. Though they'll drink a well dry when they finally get the chance."

Gwyn couldn't resist asking, "Do they partner acrobats as sociably as your two drays?"

Brit grunted and abruptly came out of her daze long enough to snatch back the reins. Sparrow merely laughed, and Brit lapsed into those sullen thoughts again as Sparrow returned to Gwyn. "No, dustbears don't stand any higher than most sandwolves. They're strong, but they're not built to dance on."

"Then where did you learn—that?"

"We had horses, don't misunderstand me! However, it's not very effective to pull a village of equipment and belongings across sand or wasteland grit by hoof. We save our horses for less tortuous endeavors."

"Racing, you mean?" Gwyn teased.

"I see we're infamous for it even in Valley Bay!" Sparrow shrugged with a chuckle. "Still, for what I do? Most of the children in my tribe could do as much; it was a point of honor, you might say. At festival gatherings, racing was certainly popular, yet it wasn't nearly as well attended as our show rings. Everything is much less formal and there's no 'winning' or 'losing' in that sense. But there was definitely competition for daring and style."

"So you learned it in the South, and now use it in your travels?"

"Now—yes," Sparrow's voice sobered to a quiet note. "There was a time when I had to perform or I wasn't allowed to eat."

"*Vara Dumauz!*" Gwyn bit her lip at her insensitivity, and quickly—gently—amended, "I'm sorry, Sparrowhawk. I don't mean to pry nor draw forth unpleasant memories."

"It's all right, *Niachero*. It was a long time ago." Sparrow found a sad hint of a smile. "When I came north to seek the Council's training, I came by ship with my uncle. We were bound for the capital Churv and then inland to the Council's Keep. There was a storm, most of the crew and passengers were lost. A merchant guard and I managed to make the shore, and then it took us a long while to reach Churv. I was what age? Barely four seasons, I think. I'm not certain because it did take us so long, and she—the guard I was with—was fevered when we finally did arrive. She died shortly after that and I went to the workhouse.

"Once there...well, I was scared, and I didn't speak the language at first. Amidst all the shuffle, everyone assumed I was orphaned. By the time I understood what was going on around me, it was too late to get anyone to believe I was anything other than a sword carrier's brat. So I did odd jobs, was City Runner for a while, then apprenticed out to a traveling show on their way to the soldiers' camps. They were the ones I performed with, and frequently, I didn't eat. But they went north by way of Rotava which turned out to be very lucky for me, because a pair from the Council's Keep spotted me, recognized my acrobatics as the style of the Southern Continent, and had the presence of mind to remember a child fitting my description had been lost journeying to the Keep. I went back with them. It's not all that unusual a story, I'm afraid."

Brit reached out a rein-callused hand and covered both of Sparrow's. Gwyn glanced up and saw Brit was blinking at tears as she determinedly kept her gaze forward.

"It must have been hard." Beneath her breath, Gwyn sighed. Those words were so inadequate.

"We've all known things that were hard," Sparrow reminded her softly. "It either breaks you or makes you stronger and maybe...a little wiser? I like to think the latter was my case."

Gwyn remembered the days and monarcs following that awful eve when Selena didn't come home. And suddenly she knew how to reach through that hollow tone to the ache in her Sister. "I too found the sea a cruel task maker."

Sparrow turned to her, some of the bleakness receding from those honey-brown eyes of hers.

"The Qu'entar of the White Ilses took my heartbound, Selena. Her ship disappeared. We never did find out if it was a storm, rocks...whatever. A few planks of bow and stern appeared on one of the island beaches a season later. There was just enough of the writing to piece together the ship's name, but never anything else."

An understanding nod met her. Then haltingly, Sparrow turned to Brit. "I won't ever fall, *Soroi*. I won't leave you that way."

Brit mustered a grateful smile, but said truthfully, "I know you won't. And I know how much you need the stunts too—for reminding you of being strong, when things are going slow and wearing on your nerves."

"It's just...Khirla is such a long way's away. And this isn't some simple trading trip."

"I know," Brit's gentleness touched her smile, and then she put an arm about Sparrow's slim shoulders, hugging her near. "I know, Love."

Gwyn averted her eyes, an awkward tightness closing her throat. She prayed nothing ever mar their closeness.

* * *

Gwyn grinned as she came around the Healers' House, her saddle slung across her back. Brit was in the rear court with all six of their hosts at a long table that had been set up beneath the lantern lights of the kitchen's door. Between the overhead glow and that spilling out through the open doorway, there was a well-lit circle about them which was much needed, because the dried herbs and smudged parchments spread atop the table were under very close scrutiny by all of those women.

A faint chuckle drew her towards the cabin's back stoop, and Gwyn headed for the tinker-trades' wagon. Sparrow glanced up as Gwyn dropped the saddle and joined her on the steps, but nodded then at her partner and the others. "Every band of healers we meet, she spends half the night with—comparing remedies, challenging assumptions, trading medicines."

Thunder rumbled somewhere, and Gwyn appraised that gray-blue ceiling of clouds expectantly. The bright fullness of the early moon was strong enough to give the illusion of some twilight, but the storm front would soon quell even that and bring a thicker darkness. It wouldn't be long before Brit's little group was running inside.

"Look at them! I've never seen anyone as tireless and downright remorseless as a group of healers."

"Not even the Council of Ten?" Gwyn baited with mischief.

"Well...aside from the Council." At which Gwyn laughed and Sparrow screwed up her face in a funny grimace. That only made Gwyn laugh harder.

With a great sigh and contriving to look very much the martyr, Sparrow turned her attention to the saddle. Her fingernail pried between seams as she bent for a closer inspection, and the resinous glue crumbled off in a clumpish sort of way. She showed the moldy dust to Gwyn. "Definitely needs to come apart."

Gwyn accepted the pronouncement, wholly disgusted with the thing. "I should have known better than to break in new tack in this weather."

"Got it from the Marshal stocks in Gronday?"

"And as usual, something's not stitched or tied or glued too well."

"Hmmm, well at least it wasn't your own coin paying for it."

"Oh...no," Gwyn drawled sweetly, "only my service and my sweat are exchanged for it."

"*Ann* ," Sparrow commiserated. "Do you want to get into your extra gear tonight?"

Thunder grumbled again, and Gwyn decided, "I can wait for morning. Although—" a grin of irony suddenly appeared, "my extra saddle is an old stand-by. It's had so much oil rubbed into it that nothing would *dare* attempt the insult of soaking its stitching."

"Speaking of soaking?" Sparrow pointed above as yet another thunderous complaint rolled through. "Very shortly, we're going to be drenched. I know the summer storms down here don't last very long, and at least it'll ease this unbearable humidity. But are you sure you won't reconsider spending the night in the cabin with us? That little barn doesn't look like the winter's roofing damage has been properly repaired yet...our upper berth may prove much drier than the haymoss in that loft."

"Thank you, Sparrow, but no all the same. I'll be fine, and once my wayward pair of hunters return I'll have a warm enough bed."

Sparrow gave her a puzzled scowl. "How do you manage to get them into a loft? They're sandwolves, not winged-cats."

"The ladder's a wide slant step and pegged in place up top. It's close enough to stairs for them to manage. Don't look at me like that! I didn't do any coaxing of any kind. They were scrambling up before I'd had time to get my gear off Cinder."

With sandwolves, that was to be expected. Sparrow slid an impish glance at Gwyn. "Bet they make wonderful bedmates, so soaked to the skin. They're obviously not going to be back before this storm breaks."

On the heels of her words, thunder broke with a jagged streak of lightning to the north. The women at the table began to gather their things together.

Gwyn rose, groaning. Sparrow was all too obviously correct. "Wet woolly pack-mates—my favorite sort."

"May your dreams be smiling, *Niachero*." Her grin wickedly belied the honesty of that wish.

"And yours," Gwyn waved. She consoled herself with the fact that it could be worse; she could be outside in the corral with the horses. The barn was small, adequate for sheltering the two milkdeer and a goodly amount of hay-moss but not much else. As she crossed the front court, she glanced along the length of the passing road, hoping to see Ril and Ty appear. It was something she did mostly out of habit. But she froze in her stride from something else—the prickly sensation on the nape of her neck was back. Very definitely back.

The burgundy leaves were inky black now, only rustling shadows in the gloomy light. The breeze was growing stronger and smelling chilled, anticipating the imminent downpour. But there was stillness beyond the wind—no sounds of forest creatures scurrying for last bits of shelter, no stomp of horses from that distant corral—nothing.

Cautiously, the Amazon began to move across the front court again—towards that sword left with her gear in the loft. The barn seemed much further away than she wanted to think about. Suddenly she felt very naked with just her belt's dagger and those hidden knives in her sleeves...without her pack-mates lurking nearby. Belatedly, Gwyn realized how careless she'd become in traveling among Sisters; it felt deceptively secure within their company.

Jes should have told her one more time that "there is no safe place beyond the Gate House." It might have finally sunk in properly.

She slid to the side of the barn door. It was a sharp black rectangle in the thickening dimness, open as she had left it. She fingered the slots on the larger sliding doors that let animals and hay wagons pass; they were as they'd been, the heavy beams securely pegged in place.

She stepped in quick and left, crouching as soon as the darkness swallowed her. Hand on the water barrel beside her, she waited for her eyes to adjust. Still no sound greeted her.

Gwyn blinked. Silence? Where were the milkdeer?

She spun and leapt for the door as it slammed shut. Its thick wooden bar beyond bounced into place and sealed her in blackness. She screamed in furious protest as thunder erupted, covering her cry so it would never reach those in the back of the house. Her fist hit the wood in momentary frustration. Then she was sprinting for the corral doors at the other end.

They were already barred. She heard the horses whinny in confusion as another thunderbolt cracked. Rain pellets joined the raging winds' howl. Then suddenly Cinder's shriek called out in challenge. Gwyn yelled, pounding on that door—knowing mere storms would never bring that murderous shrill from any of her mounts. But the storm drowned her cries, and she forced herself still to listen again.

A harsh male voice shouted. Nia and Calypso loosed piercing whistles, joining Cinder's challenge. Gwyn took a quick breath and bit her lip, trying to think and knowing that some battle outside barred her mares from kicking in to reach her as surely as the storm kept her voice from reaching them.

Rough curses sputtered beneath the horses' screeches, and a chill shivered along Gwyn's spine. Then she smelled the smoke.

The wrist trigger sprung and she palmed a stiletto, plunging it into the crack between the two doors. With a wolfish growl she threw her shoulder into the door, trying to gain an angle for the blade. It was no good. The wood on the outer door overlapped the inner, and slanted, the blade wasn't long enough to reach that crossbar to lever it up.

But her sword was!

Mae n'Pour! With that sword she could go through the wall if she had to! If they'd not noticed, if it was yet in the loft...!

The knife snapped away as she dashed through the darkness. Her shin banged into an empty grain bucket and rolled as she kicked it aside. She reached forward, grabbing for the wooden steps' siding—finding it exactly where she'd expected it. She scrambled up, breathing shallow as the stench of something greasy and rancid seeped into the smoke.

Dear Goddess, they're going to cook me alive! Where's that damned blanket?

Her groping hands found it. She jerked the whole bedroll, sword, saddle packs on top—the whole lot—towards her and the loft's edge.

The roof crackled. She swept the bundle into her arms and jumped. Everything exploded above. The ceiling collapsed in one great flaming torrent as she rolled beneath the loft and found the only unexposed portion of floor.

The dry haymoss caught like the tinder it was, even with the sheets of rain pouring in. Gwyn lunged to her feet, freeing the sword, and awkwardly she cut at the wall with an overhand slice. Only a dull thud answered, and she was left coughing. In the loft, the wood cracked and popped. Smoke and flying cinder tried to blind her. She rubbed her face with her sleeve and grimly raised her weapon again. This time she concentrated—gathering, defying the panic. And within the hilt of her sword, the heat grew as the lifestone awoke.

Gwyn swung in an arch of blue light. Then a crash of brilliant orange and blue met the wall and split it. She choked on more smoke, snatching up the blanketed bundle and thrusting it shield-like before her as she hurled her body at that wooden wall. Sparks and splinters gave way to drenching rains. She hit mud and slipped, but kept rolling as the loft behind her fell in blazes.

Wet leathery noses pushed into her face. Teeth closed on jerkin and tunic to urge her—drag her—further away from the flames.

"Gwyn'l!"

Human hands added their help as another hacking spasm clutched at her. She couldn't get her footing. Rain drove hard against her shoulders. Her lungs felt hotter than the fire. Her packmates left off as her Sisters got her to a safe distance, and then finally they all let her succumb to that blistering cough.

The healers gathered around in a half-circle, torn between the need of an injured victim and the threat of the fire. Then Brit was waving them back to their buckets and shovels. But Gwyn was only aware of the rain raging down, drowning her, forcing her to roll into the mud as she fought for air.

And then she felt from deep within—she felt the fury of her packmates rise!

"Easy...easy now," Brit's broad hand wiped the dripping hair and sludge from Gwyn's face.

"R-Ril!" Her plea started another coughing bout, yet made Brit and Sparrow look around to find that both Ril and Ty were gone.

Suddenly the forest echoed with the cry of the sandwolf.

"No…!" Gwyn sputtered, trying to rise. "Ty!"

An answering howl cut through the storm.

"Stop…stop them!"

Brit's hands caught Gwyn, holding her as Sparrow shouldered her quiver of bolts into place, and bent low to face Gwyn. The *Niachero* blinked through the rain, desperately trying to focus. "Stop them….they'll kill…they won't think…don't let—!"

Another coughing fit took her, but Sparrow understood. She lashed her crossbow to her belt and rose, struggling against her own lust for vengeance. She stared at Brit grimly. Brit nodded once, and she went.

Gwyn gasped as the baying loosed from her packmates; their trail was assured. Gwyn's blood went icy. She knew her pack called only to panic its prey. They would grant no quarter; she had to get to them first.

"Honey, stop now." Brit's voice was firm, her arms unyielding as she pulled Gwyn closer. "Give it to Sparrow, *Kahmee*. Leave it be. You must leave it be."

Exhaustion, heartbreak at her helplessness, the sting of the rain in her face—all combined to defeat her. Despair rose from within. Gwyn nearly fell into Brit's embrace, and together they floundered down into the mud. Then like a child with a mother at her back, Gwyn found herself being rocked as the tears began. Her hands clutched at Brit's strong arms as she desperately clung to sheer safety.

"There were at least two of them," Brit murmured, oblivious to the healers rushing around them. The fire wasn't spreading to the main house, and the downpour had finally begun to dampen it. "One fellow got caught in the corral; we found the drays in the corner, protectively boxing in that pair of milkdeer." The healer shook her head in weary confusion. "Why would anyone loose the animals just to burn a person?"

"So I couldn't use them," Gwyn rasped. "So they couldn't kick a hole through for me."

Brit acknowledged that grim truth reluctantly, her face nodding against Gwyn's dirtied hair. "The fellow in the corral—Cinder, Nia, and Calypso apparently went after him when he started releasing those flaming arrows. Both Sparrow and I recognized him. He was one of those three roving hunters we met before Bratler's Hoe.

"There were also signs of a dampened fire torch on the front court here. Probably where the second fellow lit his arrows. There was a grease pot too…a couple oil bags emptied."

Gwyn nodded bleakly. Brit was saying not to blame the sandwolves for this killing. These men had chosen their paths and sided with the Fates for their own reasons; they had known the risks. But Gwyn didn't quite believe that rational. It took more than one to create conflict, didn't it?

* * *

The wind lashed down with dismembered branches and uprooted ground brush. Sparrow ducked and leapt, dodging through the debris in near darkness.

The baleful howls drove her on in her desperate sprint. She knew that sound from childhood...knew the savage kill of a pack threatened.

She followed by sound. Lightning flashed in eerie white sheets that blinded even as they illuminated everything. The crossbow bounced on her thigh, a hand automatically steadying it as she hurdled jagged rocks and hip-high roots.

The sounds ahead changed to bark and snarl. Then that ravaging muffled scream of human or horse came as the prey fell. Her legs pushed faster, her mind refusing to accept what must be happening.

She broke into a clearing and pulled up in mid-step. The hideous twisted shape of the dead mount partly straddled a jutting rise of rocks. The shadow of the rider was barely a lump beside it. On the rocky little pile stood the sandwolves, dark silhouettes of lowered heads and heaving flanks.

Lightning cracked. The scene lit in ghastly stark contrasts that burned into Sparrow's eye. She spun away as her stomach retched. But she couldn't stop seeing it. The sandwolves were plastered in blood and rain, their hairless muzzles and gleaming fangs streaming with garnet rivulets. The dark hide of the horse was gutted at its neck. The rider's head was nearly torn from his body. The vision printed itself irrevocably into Sparrow's mind.

It joined the ghosts of the frozen faces from the Exile's March to haunt her.

Chapter Seven

Despite the attack, they set out late that morning when the sandwolves finally reappeared. The healers had assured the Sisters that the local patrons would be quick to send the House help once the messengers went out, and everyone felt that their hosts might be more endangered by the travelers' continued presence. After all, only two of the three marauding hunters seemed accounted for. So Brit had concocted some strange brew for smoke inhalation and insisted Gwyn sit hunched over its steaming vapors, while she and Sparrow searched through the bodies and belongings of the hunters. And then the three women had left.

Sparrow's gruesome task had yielded a little information of immediate use. The two men had worn identical dark blue cloaks and each had carried a matching pair of sabers. The latter was a bit odd, not only because of the cost in steel they were boasting, but it was strange because long swords were much more common in the Ramains than sickle sabers. Then again, given the men's similarities in cloaks, beards, and weapons, perhaps it simply attested to the most likely of likelihoods—at some point, they had both been soldiers within one, very affluent company. Brit, however, couldn't remember any blue-caped, saber-wielding group among the Prince's troops....

Before mid-day, the road dipped and jagged to cross a rocky creek bed. The shallow rush of the stream was briny brown from the rains, yet posed little difficulty for the wagon's drays or for Gwyn's mares. From the high water marks and the recently torn brush, however, it was obvious that a flash flood had forced its way through during the night and that this creek was not always so benign.

On the far side of the stream bed, Ril summoned them. The women followed to find the third hunter of last night's party. The stiffened body lay battered and wedged between, half-beneath, a slide of cracked boulders. A wooden stirrup ripped from its tack was caught about his booted ankle. With a mutter of disgust, Brit turned Sparrow away, and they trudged back to the road; their scant sympathy for the hunters was long ago spent.

Ril and Ty lingered as Gwyn stood mutely, Cinder's reins slack in her hand. For an endless moment she simply stared. The sandwolves made no sound, their gazes sorrowfully resting on the man. Gwyn stirred with an unsteady breath. Clear eyes lifted to hers; they held neither remorse nor fire now, merely resignation. That same grim acceptance settled about Gwyn.

It was done. He was dead. She didn't want to ask if her packmates had caused the horse's panic and driven it into the flooding—if this was what they'd done after leaving Sparrow. It was possible—perhaps the rider had been brash and careless in deciding to try a crossing. It might even had been the sheer bad luck of the Fates washing down on him. It might have been...she sighed.

A little sunlight found a new angle through the treetops and slipped down to touch Gwyn. Her heart found no warmth in it, and she went to turn away—something flashed bright across the corner of her eye.

She blinked and looked back at the body.

The silver-white glint flickered out again. From the man's belt? A torn sheath and knife perhaps? She bent nearer and reached into the gurgling stream, brushing the loose rubble and rock aside—she froze. At his hip, a small, battered metal piece had partially torn free of it's leather pouch. It was a Clan's fire weapon.

She tugged and it came free easily. It's metal casing was crushed, rendering it beyond use. Vaguely she wondered if it had been damaged before the rider's fall, since last night the men had used arrows and oil pots to set the barn afire. Still—if a task could be done without a fire weapon's flame, it usually was. The Clan's reserves weren't unlimited, and Council rumors insisted that the Clan no longer had the skills to repair or refuel their weapons.

Well, this hand weapon was beyond mending, even by *dey Sorormin's* home world crafters.

"*Niachero...*, are you all right?"

Gwyn glanced up at Sparrow's call. She waved an arm in reassurance, then rose as her packmates watched pensively. She sighed and grimly agreed, "No, we're not all right. Come on—it's time to share the ill news."

* * *

"By the Mother's Hand—what are they doing?" Brit hissed, coming up behind her shadowmate.

Sparrow leaned back into that strong embrace, patting her lover's wrists reassuringly. "They'll be all right. They just need to be left alone."

They both looked to where Gwyn, Ril, and Ty sat around the camp's fire. The *Niachero's* feet were planted flat. Her long arms were loosely hanging over her knees. She stared unknowingly at some nebulous place between her boots. Near her were her two packmates. Ril and Ty sat as motionless as statues, their beige coats eerily stone-like in color with the firelight at their backs. They were on either side of Gwyn, yet more than an arm's length from her. Their unblinking eyes were fastened on their human.

"But what are they doing?" Brit whispered. She and Sparrow were still entwined, half-hidden by the cabin shadows beside the wagon. "They've been like that since eventide finished."

"They're healing."

The furrows deepened below that bristle brush line of hair, and Brit plainly admitted, "I don't understand."

A sigh underlined the difficulty. "It's hard to grasp, unless you've imprinted with pack-pups. Even harder, if you weren't at least raised around them."

"Are you telling me to mind my own business?"

The bluntness prompted a fond smile from Sparrow who glanced up to her lover. "*Soroi*, I know better than to do that with you."

A reluctant grin appeared. "All the same, I'd like to know. Sandwolves aren't as common as eitteh among the Marshals—or *dey Sorormin*—but they aren't particularly unusual either."

"I know." Sparrow paused again, her silence stretching. This time her shadowmate must have been more sensitive to the melancholy around the trio as she didn't press. And eventually, Sparrow stirred to continue. "It's sad tonight. Their killing last eve—it must have broken the pack bond in some way."

"A pack bond?" Brit murmured uncertainly. She couldn't place the term.

"It's a sort of pledge, yet more than that. A contract, almost a law, but one bound by emotional attachments and ethics, not merely expediency. All packs forge their own. It designates the role of each packmate. It establishes who is leader when. It outlines a code of conduct and responsibility, not only between members but between the pack and the rest of the world. It defines everything they are."

"Without words?" Brit marveled. The absolute quiet among the three, though, seemed to be a tangible sound in itself. Somehow, without physical gesture or verbal exchange, the solemn connections among the packmates were clearly visible.

"As an eitteh will understand the sense in your speech, a sandwolf will grasp the sense in your heart. Some say, once imprinted they speak to your very soul."

A tiny shiver skirted her spine, and Brit's arms tightened about Sparrow. "They say that too of Blue Sights."

"Aye, the perception is similar. Less complex, but similar. They very much *feel* what their packmates are feeling."

"But then how do they manage with something like last night? I knew Gwyn during the Wars. She left the fighting because she couldn't tolerate her pack being used as ambush specialists. She can't conceive of killing another unless it's in blatant self-defense."

"Most sandwolves have no such scruples. Perhaps that was why Jes gifted them to her?"

Brit nodded slowly. "Jes said as much to me once. Gwyn's sense of duty and responsibility to others in need is too strong to let her remain content in Valley Bay."

"She is *Niachero* in every sense," Sparrow acknowledged with respect.

"And yet she is poorly armed beyond the Gate House with such a conscience as hers."

"She is a Sister. Would you truly want her any other way?"

"Jaded as we've become? No, I wouldn't—unless it meant her death to be otherwise."

"The sandwolves will protect her."

"By killing?" Brit challenged softly. "Do they even understand what that does to her?"

"They grew up in her household, *ti Mae*. Their own sensitivities were shaped by Gwyn's convictions, and so they too mourn tonight the breaking of the bond. But their first instincts will always be to guard the pack."

"Always?"

"Unless they make a conscious decision not to. That too is part of their pack bond—when sacrifice should be given beyond any limit of personal safety. But still," Sparrow's thin shoulders rose in a shrug, "rage or fear can obliterate anyone's rational sense. Last night those men tried to burn Gwyn to death. They tried to kill her in a horrible way!"

"Probably hoped to make it look like an accident. Like she'd just knocked over a lantern in the haymoss."

"Aye, until the horses and sandwolves disrupted that."

"Doesn't change the fact of what they were doing, though."

"No, it doesn't."

Brit swallowed hard. "I wouldn't want to burn to death. I think I'd rather freeze on the Ice Plains than that."

"And I...I can't say I wouldn't have been the one hunting those men to their deaths, if it'd been you instead of Gwyn."

"Revenge...," Brit finally understood the damage among the packmates then. "To know you killed because of me...?"

"It would scar us both." Sparrow's eyes suddenly felt dry and scorched as she watched those silent friends in their struggle. How long would it have taken to make peace even with herself, if it had been Brit she'd killed for. She wondered.

Chapter Eight

Leaves whispered in the summer's night, the faint breeze lingering in defiance of the season's warmth. The odd-matched crescents of the Twin Moons peered at one another through trailing clouds. The wagon creaked as someone inside turned over in her sleep. At the sound, the tattered ear profile of a sandwolf's head rose from among the lumps beneath the low slung canopy of the neighboring tent. Motionless, she concentrated, identifying the sounds of the Sisters within the tinker-trades' wagon, the mares snoozing—the ever-so-distant sense of rightness that was her bondmate in the woods beyond; it was Ril's watch.

Contented finally that nothing was amiss, Ty permitted herself a quiet sigh and returned her chin to its warmed spot in the blankets. She tucked one massive paw underneath herself, edged against Gwyn's sleeping form, and went quite happily back to her own dreams.

Gwyn felt the stiff-backed push along her spine. She never wakened. She merely rolled a little more to her stomach, her hand checking her sword's placement from habit.

Her fingers stayed, tightening on that hilt. Her golden skin began to shade caramel and the silver of the unsheathed blade shimmered as the powers of that lifestone stirred. The bits of grass and soil seemed to sink, molding a cradle about the sword's length and framing Gwyn's hand as part of the grip, while within her dreams, fires arose.

A deep frown marred her sleeping expression. She'd had enough of those unsettling nightmares in the ten-day past…had thought them finally gone. She had no need for their return.

But the images persisted—her grip on the sword tightened. A subtle, unnamable difference from the usual memories registered, and curiosity began to curb her impatience. Gwyn found herself drawn into the commotion of fire and people—into a place too real in detail to be any mere dream.

Wind whipped ash into her face and she ducked, lifting an arm to protect herself as she coughed. Gwyn didn't recognize the clothing. There was no familiar stiffness to her leather jerkin, and as her hand fell to the sword at her hip, she thought the pommel felt too square to be her own.

The body that held her consciousness was upright again—shouting, pointing. A group of villagers with shovels ran to attack a new cache of flame. A girl stumbled by with an impossible load of empty pails—she was no older than Mak'inzi, Gwyn thought—and she nearly fell over her own feet. A hand reached out and caught her with surprising gentleness. Together they restacked the buckets, but as the child looked up her eyes went wide with disbelief. A muttered word of praise and a reassuring squeeze to the girl's shoulder sent her scrambling off again towards the water lines.

It wasn't going to be enough! Gwyn heard in this mind that wasn't hers…and she felt the rage of helpless frustration followed by a blast of icy cold determination.

That resolve disturbed and confused Gwyn. It was such a completely alien

72

essence—raw with passion but chilled by logic…no hint of the simpler furies that she knew from her bondmates. No, the sense of a greater whole surrounded her; Gwyn felt as if she'd walked into the middle of some long spun, intricate board game—as if she were some minute player suddenly elevated to the status of leader yet she had no concept of the strategy needed.

A shout brought her back to the chaos. She felt the weight of a heavy braid swing at her nape as she looked. Then she was running towards the blazing inn, the upper corner crumbling three stories above. Waving, warning—backing the folk away from the neighboring merchant's house which they'd all hoped to save. Then she was there dragging a fallen woman through the fiery cascade.

Others came to help as the two pulled clear of the worst. Gwyn felt the heaving of lungs, the smoke-sick feeling in the stomach, but there was no more than a single moment to recover. Orders flew—directions to regroup the water lines and to move the trench digging further back.

Yet all through the frantic hurry was the sinking despair that they couldn't do enough. The east end of the village was going to be lost. Their hope now lay in keeping the fire from the brushberries and the hoe farms…in not letting it jump the rushing stream at mid-town.

Their hopes had been in her to prevent just this! The savage thought flew—she was failing them in allowing the Clan's destruction to go so unchallenged!

Failing them? By the Mother's Hand there must be a way! There would be a way.

Gwyn felt the surge of fury reforge an inner strength of commitment. She stood back with that body then and with a few others of that burning village, watching the raging fires devour the hopes. A curt directive sent a companion off to check on the trench workers. Another moved the water brigades into a broader pattern. But most of what could be done was already in place now.

The night sky glittered with sparks and billowed with blackened smoke. The Twin Moons' crescents looked on gravely. Gwyn felt her own somberness rise as the grand heights of the inn finally collapsed completely, shards of breaking timbers caving inwards with one final roar. She felt her own sadness at the waste, and yet she sensed that same steady commitment still.

There would be no more of this. Somehow there would be an end—and it began here. Tonight.

The quiet confidence that accepted the challenge—the calm, compelling, absolute surety that Gwyn met—astounded her. She felt no arrogance, no vanity in that manner. She felt no sense of revenge or haunting of further helplessness. All she found was certainty—a sense of self and responsibility that simply transformed that pledge into fact.

It was a sense of self Gwyn's deepest soul knew could not be her own.

She awoke with that fright, dropping her sword as she bolted upright in her bedding. Ty lurched to her feet, crouching and alert with a faint warning growl. Gwyn blinked, disoriented to find everything about them slumbering so peacefully. She glanced overhead at the Twin Moons and breathed the Goddess a short prayer. Ty edged nearer, still tense, and Gwyn relaxed with her packmate's tangible presence.

"Forgive me, *Dumauz.*" She rumpled those great furry shoulders and buried her face in Ty's thick ruff. "I've been dreaming, nothing more."

There was a haunting sense of wrongness lingering after those words, and suddenly, uneasily, Gwyn wondered how true they were. An echo of that confident resolve brushed through her awareness again. It was less startling now in its muted tones, but no less compelling. She still couldn't imagine herself possessing that solemn acceptance at swearing to perform the impossible. She couldn't imagine trusting herself alone to have that kind of strength, that kind of ability. Perhaps with her packmates beside her...but alone? No, she had never met that sort of woman, not among any of the Marshals and not among all of *dey Sorormin*. It was her fantasy that such a woman could even exist.

Wasn't it...?

* * *

The signs in the morning were even more disturbing, Gwyn found.

"I can't say I've ever seen anything like it." Brit bent over some as she squinted at the place Gwyn's sword had lain the night before.

"Has it something to do with your strange alloy?" Sparrow suggested. She was on her knees, fingers probing the shallow depression in the soil where the length and shape of the long sword was imprinted. Even the curled fist of Gwyn's grasp at the hilt was still recognizable. There had not been a single blade of grass cut, however, and the crust of the topsoil itself had not been broken, merely sunken. Most trail readers would have sworn this indentation was at least a season old, and the obvious fact that it was not, only disturbed them all more.

"It's possible...," Brit mused obliquely.

"What is?"

"That Sparrow's right about our metal's alloy."

With deliberate patience, Gwyn drew a very slow breath and counted to cool her temper. She knew she was more upset by the print—and the dream—than she was at her old friend's muttering ways. Her patience won, and Brit went on without noticing her ire. "The Council of Ten has always maintained that the lifestones are the essence of life energies, in a manner of speaking. We've known since the earliest dealing of that first n'Athena with the Council that the combination of our alien alloys with a lifestone act in unison. They create a sort of energy collector for channeling amarin."

"*Ann...nehna?*" Gwyn shrugged, missing the point Brit was trying to make.

"Well, the stone in your hilt allows your concentration to guide the power of your sword blow. It enhances the strength of the alloy. It seems to do all that by gathering the life energies together into a directed purpose." Both Gwyn and Sparrow nodded, following now. "So, why should the channeling be limited to destructive purposes? If your amarin aren't bent on slashing something apart, wouldn't the channeled energy be more apt to do something less...less violent?"

Gwyn sat down with a bump. A fly-away strand of red hair was brushed aside from an eye as she frowned, but it was an idea she found intriguing...and a bit unsettling because of its novelty. "What you're suggesting, Brit...it's almost like saying a piece of Valley Bay steel welded to a lifestone creates a funnel for amarin. Like a Blue Sight projecting intentions to create an illusion or something?"

"Hmmf…doesn't sound quite so feasible when you say it like that, does it?"

"And wouldn't someone else have noticed before this?" Sparrow challenged. "I mean, the Council—"

"The Council," Brit interrupted somewhat sternly, "might in fact be responsible for no one knowing it, if we are right."

The corner of Gwyn's mouth lifted in irony. "They do have a way of secreting off certain knowledge, until it's less dangerous for the populace to have it."

"Which implies an even more disturbing idea," Sparrow whispered, and the others looked inquiringly at the thin woman. "Don't you see? When the Council considers knowledge dangerous, usually it's because people haven't yet got the common sense not to abuse the information. The only time it's allowed to surface is when there's no longer any danger of any abuse. Or…"

"Or there's an even greater danger that requires the drastic risk of loosening the knowledge prematurely," Brit finished in a dark tone.

"I like that even less than my dream."

"No…no," Brit shook her head quickly. "I don't accept it. The Council has its means and methods, certainly. But I don't believe in their omniscience. The Seers have their blind spots. The Council Masters have their prejudices. They do well enough as guides for Aggar, but they are not always right, nor are they always aware of what is important."

"Meaning?"

"I don't know, Gwyn'l. I don't think we've got all the pieces to our puzzle yet. It's certainly too soon to tell if your little experience was anything like a vision or if the sword's sensitivity to your amarin was responsible for this hollow. And I'm not ready to allow that the Council is consciously trying to communicate with us. Fates' Cellars, Women! They could just send one of their eitteh friends down with a message!"

"Certainly would be clearer," Sparrow allowed with a wry grin. "And they do seem to prefer brevity and clarity when dealing with Sisters."

"Right about that," Brit nodded. "We don't play men's games, and they know it. Better to deal openly with us and us with them."

"Basic respect," Gwyn murmured, only half following their words. A scowl creased the golden skin between her brows, and Gwyn proposed, "Could it be that this is related to Khirlan and the Clan? The Clan is richer in alloys than most, even despite the Council's quiet distribution of the scrapped metals. Could I be seeing something because my sword's lifestone is collecting energies from a wider source? Could the Clan's metals be acting like some sort of nebulous web?"

"The Council's Seers would have noticed that long ago," Brit countered. "To them, that sort of anomaly would have been like a flare going up during a single moon!"

"And I agree with Brit," Sparrow inserted. "The Council doesn't play games with *dey Sorormin*. They would have warned us when they sent Brit and me to you."

"Then what kind of amarin web would I be sensitive to?"

"Through your sword?" Brit pressed.

"Aye," Gwyn nodded slowly, still frowning. The pieces still refused to form any coherent pattern. "What *could* I sense that the Seers wouldn't?"

A scoffing snort from Brit answered her abruptly. "Damn little, Gwyn'l. Damn little."

* * *

They came upon the farmstead almost unexpectedly, the small house and larger barn blending well into the natural landscape of giant honeywoods. That the place was several generations old was evident not only in the varying coloration of its mud bricks, but in the way the neighboring trees twisted and bent their roots protectively about the buildings. This particular family had not only adapted their crops to hoe farming symbiosis, it appeared that they had also taken on the ideal as a way of life.

"Reminds me of our oldest Shea Holes," Brit muttered as she stiffly climbed down from the wagon's seat.

"Most homes in central and southern Khirlan are built like this," Sparrow commented in confusion, glancing between her two Sisters with surprise at their apparent unease. "I had thought it more civilized—like my Desert Peoples—to build in congruence with what is here."

"What? You live in sand dunes?" Brit groused.

Sparrow studied her shadowmate a moment, then returned calmly, "No, in burrows or in sand-bricked structures. But they often do look like sand dunes. The shape minimizes the destruction from the winds."

Brit drew a steadying breath and opened an arm to hug her lover. "Forgive me, *Soroi*. It merely touches ancient dreads."

At Brit's silence and Sparrow's continued puzzlement, Gwyn offered to explain. "There was an era, Sparrow, when the Clan hunted the Amazons—the last of us were seeking to leave the Terran encampments and join the Valley Bay settlement. A good many of those Sisters had been living secretly among the Clan members—had fought in the galactic wars among them. But they had never said anything about their affiliations with *dey Sorormin* nor about the expectation that the Terrans' Empire would abandon Aggar before the wars were done. The bitterness at being abandoned and at the Sisterhood's apparent part in it, led to some very bloody confrontations. So the crones n'Shea came south from Valley Bay and established the Shea Holes as aid stations for the fleeing Sisters. In those hidden places of the Great Forest, the n'Shea sheltered and healed a great number—but they buried many too."

"Too many," Brit murmured. "Reminders of that time…well…brings up ambivalent feelings to say the least."

Sparrow nodded solemnly and hugged Brit around the waist. "Now is now, *Soroi*."

"Aye." Brit drew another deep, long breath, then seemed steadier. "Let's announce ourselves, shall we?"

"*Sae!*" Gwyn forced a lighter tone. "I have no wish for an arrow to mistake me as some marauder!"

Taking up a pair of decorative sticks, Sparrow beat out a cheerful staccato on the high-pitched drum tube. She waited a moment, then repeated the pattern before dropping the sticks back into their small canister.

"Well?" Hands on hips, Brit turned and surveyed the forest's unyielding depths. "Do we wait politely or boldly make ourselves at home, I wonder?"

Gwyn chuckled, pointing at the water trough's enameled insignia and at the stone grills set on either side of the courtyard. "Everything's marked for public use. I don't think they'll have any trouble with us bedding down for the night."

"Courtyard's plenty big—just hope the privies are clean!" Brit marched off, and Sparrow exchanged a wry look with Gwyn before following.

Their hosts didn't show themselves until nearly darkfall, which was very late considering how lengthy the summer evenings were in Khirlan. However, the woman and her son were cordial enough for even Brit's tastes, and after they'd washed off the better part of their farm's dirt and enjoyed their own eventide, the two reappeared in the courtyard offering a sweet pie. Brit returned the hospitality with a small bottle of surprisingly tasty mead, and everyone settled down comfortably to the usual review of the Plateau's Treaty and northern news. When the youngster, Sek, asked Gwyn about her work as a Royal Marshal and was obviously enthralled with the thought of her horses, she excused herself and took him off to introduce him to her mares.

She left him in Nia's gentle care, trotting about the corral quite happily, and returned to the fireside to find less cheery topics under way.

"Kora was just telling us about the Steward's Swords that rode through here a couple of ten-day back," Brit explained as Gwyn accepted another small cup of mead. "Seems they were acting rather peculiar."

The *Niachero* tilted a questioning brow towards the stocky, gray-haired farmer. "Forgive me, Min, but I'm not familiar with all the titles in Khirla. What guild sponsors the Steward's Swords?"

"Why no guild at all, Marshal! That's why I was telling these tinks here, why it seemed so strange. They're from the Dracoon's court, from her Steward's own guards. Supposed to be the best of the District's corps, don't you see? Yet they come through here and, even with us all needing to pack an' leave for Khirla's big feasts, they don't give much mind to this old sowie we've got loose. Maybe it's just 'cause they're city corps, you know? Maybe they know about fightin' the Clan and all, but city breed don't always grasp the farming plights, if you see my meaning?"

"I do," Gwyn grinned. The woman's faltering tone underlined her sudden uncertainty at Gwyn's background, and the idea that she might have inadvertently insulted a Royal Marshal was somewhat daunting. "My sister, Kimarie, has a plains farm and a small herd."

"Ahh," Kora nodded hesitantly, then accepted the comment as reassurance. "We've got this buntsow roving about—wild, nasty sort. Had a newcomer settle here last fall, thought to raise a catch of little ones—tame them, you know? 'Course didn't work, never does. 'Bout once in a hand of tenmoons we get a bright youngster who thinks of a new way to try tamin' them, usually no harm in it. When things doesn't work out, we just slaughter the beasts young and go back to huntin' them for the regular meats. But this time, one got itself loose before the fella gave up."

"It's gone feral then?" Gwyn saw the problem immediately. Vicious and without its natural fear of humans, the buntsow would ravage the hoe farmers' crops, the milkdeer herds, and the domesticated fowls without a thought to the humans about. And given the chance, the thing would be as likely to take a child for its eventide as a lexion. "And these Steward's Swords did nothing?"

"Ahh...well...they tried, they said."

Gwyn was unimpressed. Kora was obviously not going to openly demean anyone of authority and so was still wary of Gwyn's alliance. It made the *Niachero* wonder what sort of soldiers were found among these Steward's Swords. "They went hunting it, though?"

"For a few days. Mostly after midday—back before eventide."

Brit gave a dismissive grunt; Sparrow nearly sputtered in her drink.

Unfortunately, Gwyn had to agree. "Seems they weren't aware of quite a few basics."

Brit sent Gwyn a sour look that suggested exactly how despicably stupid that particular comment was as an understatement. The *Niachero* ignored the Amazon.

"If I remember correctly, the habits of the buntsows are to scavenge the roots about the time of the midnight moon's rising." The farmer was nodding, her face brightening as Gwyn continued. "And if they're after fresh meat, they're out at twilight—morning or eve."

"The Swords left pretty quick." Kora resumed her tale, more confident now that Gwyn's sympathy—and intelligence—had been established. "Said they were doing the Dracoon's business—about the Clan most likely. Rumors have it that those raiders are coming easterly more and more. Think they were after a scoutin' party. Could forgive 'm for that, I guess. Get those monsters too close an' it won't matter what sowie's feral. There won't be nothing left to argue with the sowies over. Why just last ten-day there was this massacre over in Diblum. Whole east end of the village went burning from one of those fire weapons, I hear...."

"I'm afraid it did," Gwyn affirmed softly. So, her dreaming had been vision-stirred!

"Well, curs'd Fates it is. An' with this being the Feasts, near everybody's down in the city—none of us prepared for surprises. Even here, my boy's the only one for leagues. Usually my place acts like a little commons, you know? Draws all the old chatter folk, least once a ten-day. Certainly so, when strangers go plunking at the drum tube. Whole area knows there'll be news and such then, and it gets all of 'em running over after eventide. 'Til recent, that is. With this ole sowie loose now, it's getting too dangerous to go visiting at dusk."

Gwyn's head jerked up at the silent implication. Her copper eyes blazing hard. "And they still left you? These Steward's Swords left you with a feral buntsow that's actually *attacking* your folks?"

The stocky frame shifted uneasily on that bench, and Kora's dark gaze dropped to the remains of the cooking fire. "It's done more than attack."

Gwyn's breath went short, and she tore her eyes from the farmer. Carefully, she laid her ceramic mug on the ground. Her hands curled into white knuckled fists as her gold skin flushed to an angry brown. Quiet and cutting, she demanded, "How bad?"

Kora shrugged awkwardly. "Two maimed. One in the leg, another lost an arm altogether."

Again the unspoken hung over the fire. Gwyn felt her stomach clench hard with sheer fury. "And...?"

"And another's dead."

"When?"

"Firs...first day after the Swords arrived." The cup in the woman's hands shook faintly. "One of my own found the fella, already dead. Awful sight she said, head cut clean from the whole mess. Not much left of the rest, and—well, it was a cruel kind of Fates' Jest I think. The young fella Padder was the very one who'd tried tamin' the things. We should of known better, he being a city brat an' all. Just new arrived, up from Khirla last fall. But he seem'd to know his livestocks—was a livery apprentice in the city, you see. Still...maybe we should of told him again 'bout the troubles he was courtin'. Then...well, maybe we could've made it end different."

Gwyn sat immobile, anger turning her to granite-hard stone. From the far side of the courtyard, Ril and Ty came loping in from the shadows. Their sensitivity to their bondmate's anger was strong, their hackles already bristling.

Brit and Sparrow turned worried gazes to the silent, snarling expressions those beasts brought with them even as the farmer drew back with wide-eyed fright. Brit reached a comforting hand to the woman and offered a grim smile. Kora swallowed hard and muttered, "Jus' never seen one before."

"Gwyn? Kora's story...," Sparrow began very, very quietly. "It explains why there were no signs of the sowie when the Swords went hunting." She didn't wholly believe her words, but she recognized this dangerous tension in sandwolves from her earliest days. She could only try to bring Gwyn's reason forward and hope her Sister would control them. "The thing would have...the buntsow wouldn't have been hungry enough to be out scavenging or anything. At least, not for a while."

"It does not excuse these Swords," Gwyn growled. Her sharp eyes locked onto Brit. "Tomorrow you two go on without me."

Brit frowned soberly and began to shake her head, until with a quick slash of her hand, Gwyn silenced all objections. "There's only a ten-day left in the Khirla Feasts. You're business is there, mine is here first. My bondmates and I will handle it."

The farmer seemed to relax some at that hope, although her nervous attention kept darting back to the crouched beasts behind Gwyn. Sparrow stared hard at her hands, feeling the ire rise in her own shadowmate beside her. In the end, Brit only barely managed to hold her tongue. But it was a narrow-eyed, near hateful glare that she sent Gwyn across the width of the fire pit; the *Niachero* had quite adroitly tied their hands from helping, and she didn't like being manipulated—not even with the truth. And it was truth. Their business with the Dracoon would not be aided by drawing anyone's suspicions in Khirla. Yet there was nothing more suspicious than a tinker-trade arriving *after* a fair's end. All along they had planned to enter Khirla separately; this buntsow's ravaging was only presenting them with an obvious reason to part company. Gwyn's logic was indisputable. The need for the caution was undeniable.

But she didn't have to like it. She didn't have to like it one little bit.

* * *

Mae n'Pour! This obviously wasn't going to work.

79

Gwyn scowled grimly as Cinder stomped and chaffed on her bone bit. A guttural grunting from a thorny hedge taunted her. Beyond the far side of that brambly sanctuary, warily guarding against a rear escape, the two sandwolves sulked atop the arching roots of a mammoth honeywood. Their tree was considerably larger than the ones about Gwyn, though. The younger growth here had filled in what once had been a clearing and these non-mammoth trees were part of the problem. Cinder wasn't as mobile within this press of rough-barked trunks, and in the saddle, Gwyn would soon be fighting the lower tree limbs rather than that buntsow.

She eyed the stony outcrop to the left, the pocket-sized trampled flats before the thorn brush, the overhanging limbs of the smaller trees—and beyond that a single, massive honeywood with its sheltering roots. Roots that supported the nasty thorn bed. The snuffling grunts of her gloating adversary shuffled around inside the thicket. The tight twist and weave of the thorny brush hid all but the barest glimpses of the beast. With a bone-plated shell that swept back from its ears to protect the jugular and with a leathery, black-red hide to camouflage it, there was no accurate way to get an arrow through for a kill.

Disgruntled, the Amazon unstrung her short bow and slid it away behind her knee. For being less than a tenmoon old, this buntsow was remarkably adroit in choosing its ground. And for all practical purposes, the appearance of the sandwolves hadn't alarmed it in the least—had merely sent it into its favorite defensive maneuver. That was out of character for a wild sowie certainly, but not so much for one accustomed to human idiosyncrasies.

Gwyn reminded herself to be careful.

Then again, being cautious wasn't going to get rid of this particular little demon. The den was too well protected. She knew the scavenger was counting on her to dismount and come in on foot. She only hoped it didn't also count on meeting a *Niachero's* strength.

The thorn hedge shook with positively elated, panting sort of grunts as Gwyn drew out the silent, graceful length of her sword. The grunting got louder as she dismounted. Beyond on the arching root, Ril and Ty began a lumbering, back and forth shift of weight—keying their tension and alertness to a fine pitch.

Well, Gwyn mused, despite the wicked lair, the advantage might just be theirs. After all, the three of them had worked together for a very long time.

Her back to Cinder, Gwyn took a moment more to gauge her position afoot; the lifestone began its warm thrumming beneath her gloved grip. She spied a quick retreat of the ebony curled tusks and jagged teeth that marked the protruding undercut of the buntsow. Like its schefea cousins, the buntsow had a nasty talent for using those teeth to dismember joints; fortunately—unlike its cousins—the buntsow wasn't venomous.

Keen, little eyes peered through the tangle, and Gwyn swallowed hard, feeling that measuring gaze as the beast went utterly still. It was now or never. She pushed forward into the waist-high brambles towards that small clearing before the sowie's thicket. A piece of her absently applauded the foresight that had made her don her hard leather leg sheaths.

The buntsow snorted once, then went silent again.

The sword shifted to her right hand as she emerged into that trampled flat—she had every intention of dodging a charging run. She'd bait it until her packmates could close and help.

But the creature surprised her; it did nothing.

Z'ki Sak, Diana? The corners of her mouth tensed, disturbed. What had she missed? This near she couldn't risk a searching glance to answer that. Ril or Ty would have noticed if there'd been signs of a mate around, so that couldn't be it...*nehna?*

Warily she began to circle right, away from the dangers of getting cornered against the stone ridge. Concentrating with her peripheral vision, she sought any clue to this unexpected show of patience.

Maybe it was more uneasy of her packmates than she'd credited?

The tautness in her stance eased minutely at the thought—and the thing charged! She scrambled backwards.

It grunted its victory, thinking her trapped against a tree between the bracken. But Gwyn went straight up in a leap. Her left arm snaked out to clutch the burly overhanging limb and her feet tucked high quickly. The beast shrieked as it rammed into solid wood. It shook its ugly, tuft-haired head and bark bits went flying. Then suddenly the sandwolves were there, nipping at its heels. It spun, tusks slashing sideways. The pack pair retreated, feigned in and retreated again.

The buntsow rasped at the sandwolves, shaking its head and whole body in rage. Then it stilled in that instinctual half-breath before the attack—and Gwyn dropped from above. Her sword sizzled blue, descending with the weight of her body in a two-handed plunge. Her feet landed square as she straddled the beast and drove her blade deeper.

The thing's shrill whistle protested. It twisted and bucked, but its own neck shell kept it from reaching her—until it went down under the thrust, blood splattering. It gnashed and writhed. She sank the sword through and into the ground, pinning the sowie—holding on for dear life! Spasms finally took it, then lessened... then at last, eased it into death.

Gwyn straightened stiffly, taking her weight from her sword with an unsteady breath. She forced a stern calm over the quivering in her stomach and stepped away for a moment, not quite willing yet to totally trust that the thing was dead. Then the bloody mess of gloves and clothes registered—for the umpteenth time, she found herself appreciative of her Marshal's clothing. There'd be no permanent damage to most of it, save for her shirt. The thick, shiny leathers of her leg sheaths, jerkin and gloves were all well oiled and would come clean, if she tended them soon. And she had to soon—for her sanity's sake.

This had been anything but a clean kill, and she was not proud of the fact. Ril whined in sympathy as the bondmates nosed into Gwyn reassuringly. She consoled herself with their safety and with the reminder of the maiming and killing this sowie had managed.

With a steely resolve, Gwyn left it at that.

Chapter Nine

The split rail fence beneath Gwyn's elbows went 'whack', but Gwyn had been half-expecting it. She only grinned at the young boy scrambling frantically to catch his lost footing and clear the top. Then Ty bounded up and lightly nipped his collar before twisting away.

"Arghh!" the lad bellowed, near falling off the railing. "She got me!"

"That she did," Gwyn agreed and rubbed a hand through his raggedy mop of hair. Ty whined, panting hard with her flanks heaving, and Gwyn gave her a fond ruffle as well. "She always does, you know. I've never met anyone who can dodge her."

"But I almost out ran her!" Sek said, grinning rakishly, hair half-hiding his bright eyes.

Gwyn laughed and leaned back against the fence, shaking her head at his exuberance.

"Anyone ever do that? Out race her, I mean?"

"On foot? Never."

"Not even you?" His eyes widened in astonished disbelief.

"Not even me!"

"Eieh!" Sek looked at the tatter-eared sandwolf with renewed respect. Then, still dangling from the fence, the lad suddenly asked, "How long you had her?"

"Had her?" Gwyn's smile softened her rebuke. "I don't 'have' her, Sek. I don't own her any more than you do your mother. However, the three of us have been together for a little more than four tenmoons."

"But...I mean, you can't leave them anywhere without you. Can you? They're like those Council shadow-things—"

"Shadow-things?" Gwyn cocked a quizzical brow at him. "Do you mean shadowmates? The guardian-guide people?"

"Shadows are real people?" Again his young eyes grew saucer-wide.

"Of course they are. What did you think they were?" Gwyn felt amusement fade a little in the face of such ignorance. What era had these Khirlan folk gotten lost in?

"They're...aren't they suppose to be Council spirits? Like made by the Seers and...and they have to do all the stuff the Council orders...only they do it outside the Keep, in the places the Council doesn't live."

Ahh, then it's not necessarily Khirlan folk—perhaps just a little half-understood information the boy had overheard. Gwyn relaxed and settled more comfortably against the rails. Ty promptly lay down on a boot and rolled her weight into Gwyn's calf, that silly, slit-eyed grin of hers appearing.

"You ever met one?"

"A shadow? I have. A couple of them." Well, she was certain of Sparrow, and she had strong suspicions about a few of the other Marshals' apprentices, especially the ones who'd served in the Wars and were still apprentices. Not that it was *that* unusual to decline the full-status of a Marshal; some simply never felt prepared for the challenge of full responsibility.

"What're they like?"

Gwyn shrugged. "A lot like you or me."

"No—they can't be." He was genuinely crestfallen at that. "They're suppos'd to be special."

"They are," Gwyn assured him. "And so are you and I."

"I'm just a hoe farmer. Don't even get to herd the milkdeer from one moss batch to another yet."

"Well, that's how lots of shadows—and Marshals!—start out. But then they go to the Keep or to Churv to get trained. At the Keep, the shadows learn about Aggar's history. They study all sorts of things like agriculture, healing, weapons play, and sometimes even languages."

"Ugh," he made a face. "I know my numbers and 'nough to read the People's Book."

"Good to know the law," Gwyn inserted soberly.

"Ole Ma Tessie says the same. An' I need to write and read so I can keep the farm accounts when I get older. But I don't like books and study so much. I'm better with my hands—you know I can thatch a roof hole all by myself? An' I'm just coming on five seasons old now!"

"Very nice." Suitably impressed Gwyn gave a measure more of respect. "I also noticed how you handled Nia the other day. You've a fine touch with animals."

He beamed at her proudly. Then he abruptly switched thoughts to ask, "What did they teach you in Churv? You know, to be a Marshal?"

"Law—and some weapons play."

"Laws? That's all? The People's Book isn't that big!"

Gwyn stifled a laugh. "I didn't study just one book, Sek. I studied *all* the books. All the books for all the districts for the last hundred seasons or so. And all the books on why the laws were written the way they are and what the intentions of the monarchs were at the time they helped to make those laws. There are an awful lot of details involved, you see."

"Just so you could go fight Changlings?"

Lips pursed, Gwyn studied the boy for a long moment. Finally she asked, "What do you think being a Marshal is about, Tad'l?"

He considered that seriously, then he gave a gradual nod of understanding. "You're not just soldiers, are you? You do more figuring and studying then regular sword carriers."

"And why do you think we do that?"

"Because...," he puzzled this one through more quickly. "Because lots of times you have to think about a problem. Just fighting with whoever's to blame...well it doesn't always solve everything, does it?"

She encouraged him with a faint nod, and more sure of himself, Sek's shoulders squared off as he balanced one-footed on his rail perch and concentrated. "It's like when Padder's sowie got loose and started hurting people. Maybe it was his fault more'n other folks, for the trouble being there. But fighting him 'cause he was to blame wouldn't have stopped the trouble. Makin' him pay a fine—well it might keep other city folk from comin' out here and trying foolish scheming, but it wouldn't have solved the worst problem. The sowie would still be out hurting people.

"And them city Swords, they were all ready to fight the Clan's parties to keep us farmers from getting hurt, but they didn't want no part of this. Wasn't very fancy stuff to them. But what's the difference between Padder getting his head sliced off from the sowie's tusks or a Clan's sword?

"Seems to me…," he chewed on the thought a second or two more, before confidently concluding, "they didn't think about the problem enough. So what'd we get? Another fellow hurt so bad, he lost an arm."

"Now answer me this, Sek. Are these city Swords to blame for that crippling? Should I go after them?"

A frown creased deep between his brows, but only briefly 'til the boy asserted, "Yes, they are to blame some. Not all of it, though. It was a lot of things—Padder trying something that went wrong, them Swords choosing wrong, but mostly it was the buntsow itself. And what the Swords were doing out here is necessary too. If the Clan's raiding nearby, that needs to get stopped. You go arrest the city Swords, then the Clan only rides around free until someone else gets out here to chase after them. That would hurt more people, so maybe it's better to just wait until the city Swords are through with their work and then…I don't know. Maybe sit 'em down and explain how impor'ant feral stock is to farmers' safety, and…and maybe fine'm to make'm remember real good."

A small smile broke through at that last phrasing, but Gwyn was pleased. "Aye, it might be a good reminder at that. Adults have a way of remembering when it costs money, especially if they hadn't expected to spend it. And I agree with you, these Swords were only partly responsible."

"That why you're going on to the Khirla Feasts instead of after them?"

"Partly—and I have other business to attend in Khirla or more folks may be hurt later. See Sek, that's what Marshals try to do most often—help people settle problems without using our swords or arrows or fists. We try to make sure as few people get hurt as possible, and not just for today. We try to think about what might happen tomorrow or the day after—or ten seasons from now! Because sometimes what we do now, affects what your own children are going to be arguing about someday."

"So's you studied all those books about laws that used to be and about laws in other districts to learn how to do the best thing for everybody, eh?"

"That's why."

"An' that's why you decided goin' after the sowie was more important than goin' after the Swords or to the Khirla Feasts, and why you had to go huntin' for it every day instead of waiting for it to be seen attacking someone again? You didn't want to risk anybody else getting his neck sliced like Padder did."

"True enough." But that was the second time he'd said "sliced," Gwyn noticed uneasily. Something tumbled about in her mind and abruptly she remembered Kora had also described Padder's death in a similar way; she had said "cut." Now that was odd—not torn, not gashed or ripped, but cut and sliced? That implied a clean severing, not the usual messy style of a buntsow. "Sek, can you help me on something?"

"Maybe." He said it with considered attentiveness.

"Were you there when they found Padder?"

"Ah no." He was more disappointed at not being able to help her than he was at the idea of that grisly scene. "I was out in the west patches weeding the sweet beets an' knobby nips."

"Nips?" Gwyn was thoroughly confused at the strange term.

"Turnips," he enunciated promptly.

"Ah—can you tell me what you did see of Padder, if anything?"

"Not much. They'd moved him in and set up the pyre 'fore I was back. His pieces were all wrapped tight for burning by the time I saw him."

"Pieces?"

"Well...aye," Sek shrugged uncomfortably. "His head and his leg...they weren't part of him no more."

"Ahh...do you know where he was when it happened? Where your elder sib found him?"

"Oh that! It was west on the milkdeer path—between the afternoon watering creek and the road."

"Which road?"

"This one. South over there. The milkdeer path is used by near everyone. Less at night with the herds, of course. Even without Padder's sowie loose, there's always a few buntsows hunting somewhere, and we do best to keep the milkers in the barns. But people they leave be—'specially in groups—so we use it lots. It cuts short 'tween couple of farms, just less than a league from here. The path's maybe a stone's throw north of our district road marker."

"The fresh scrubbed one?" She'd seen it on her sowie hunts.

"Aye! The stone one!" He was suddenly looking very proud of himself again. "Could you read it fine?"

She understood then and gave him a smile. "I could indeed. Must be a very responsible family tending it this season."

"We do! It's us—I did the scouring myself just a ten-day past."

"You did an excellent job of it, Tad Sek. I am impressed."

"So you're goin' out there tomorrow? Instead of to Khirla? I could show you the way easy!"

Gently she declined his offer. "I'd best see it alone, Sek, but thank you. I need to be out early and then on for the city."

"Got'a be there for the races, uh? Thought so, with those mares. They're beauties. Cinder's got the spice for the winning too, hasn't she? Hasn't been a Marshal representin' the Royal Family since my Ole Ma's own grannie was a girl—or so Ole Ma says. But now the Wars are over, that'll be changing. Won't it? Now the King an' Crowned can be sending us help for against the Clan! It's like Ole Ma Tessie said—the districts had to be strong by themselves 'til the Changlings were dealt with, but we're a proper country and have a ruler King. Now there'll be money when there's flooding and less taxes when the crops fail. And the Clan folk won't be terrors for much longer. Now there'll be help for everybody needing it. Won't there?"

He said it with such certainty that there was really very little question in his voice, and as he hopped down from the corral, it was clear that he expected no answer from her. After all, she was here and that was an obvious enough answer for his young mind. But it was his very surety that raised bumps on Gwyn's skin. A boy not yet allowed to herd the milkdeer was worrying about the economics of floods and crop failures, and this in a area that appeared to be thriving? It was a sad testimony to Khirlan's state of affairs. It was even more unsettling, considering no one in Churv even knew the Clan's raids had worsened.

Unfortunately, she wasn't in the position of knowing a great deal more herself—at least, not yet.

* * *

The gray light of dawn found Gwyn and her packmates near the creek on the milkdeer path. The place of attack was evident despite the fact that it'd been through a pair of ten-day and a soaking rain. On the path, leaves had been torn and thoroughly mulched into the damp soil. Grit and stones laid aside, kicked out of their usual depressions, still patiently waiting for the next hundred hooves to plant them again. Some of the tree roots were speckled a more ruddy brown than normal—from blood stains. But Gwyn thought there was an eerie sense of wrongness to the whole scene. Her packmates were quick to agree. As torn up as the place seemed to be, there wasn't any sign here or below at the creek of the zig-zagging sort of tracks usually created by a buntsow pursuit.

Every fiber of her was certain. It had been staged. Oh, undoubtedly the sowie had been through here, and most likely it had been drawn by the scent of fresh blood. What the farmers had seen was indeed a body savaged by that feral beast, but the creature had not done the killing.

Ril gave a sharp yap, and Gwyn twisted about in the saddle to find her. The sandwolf was upstream, standing atop a pair of hulking roots, and eager to show her human something. Cinder carefully sloshed along through the water, until Gwyn reined in with surprise. Beyond the sheltering arms of the honeywood roots was a camp clearing, complete with a stone grill and split logs set face-down for benches.

That in itself wasn't startling. Sek had described this as a popular watering spot, so a great many mid-day meals and a few overnights were bound to be hosted here. And, of course, its location would make it a likely place for courting among the younger folk; wild sowies might bother stray milkdeer, but they'd adamantly avoid human gatherings.

No, the camp itself wasn't odd. However, the dark stains in the shadowy corner of one great root and its trunk were. There was also a chip in the bronze-red bark that was at an uncomfortably suspicious height. It was just about head high for a *Niachero*...or for a male of Aggar. It was higher than even the most ambitious lunge of the biggest buntsow, and it was cut too cleanly.

Then, glancing over those darkened stains again, Gwyn noticed the singed mark beneath the blood. It was a stake-straight hole the size of a fist, driven deep and scarred black. Few Marshals had ever seen that mark, but none would have mistaken it for anything other than what it was—the mark of a fire weapon. If the tree had been anything but the hard, hard wood of the aged honeywoods, it was have shattered and gone up in flames.

A quiet whine called Gwyn to turn about, and this time both Ty and Ril were waiting. By the look of the carved rings along the outer root's side, it seemed they'd found the picket line. Again the horses' signs were consistently worn enough to be a pair of ten-day old. Then Gwyn leaned forward at Ty's pawing gesture. She guided Cinder out into the stream a bit further to move their shadows, and the prints on the sloping bank grew clearer. Before Ty was the mark of a weighty, large horse. Beside it lay a partial print of a chipped hoof that belonged to a lighter mount. That chipped imprint was undeniably familiar; these tracks had been left by her arsonists' horses.

It seemed the Clan raiders had taken to impersonating the Dracoon's own sword carriers. Gwyn wondered—was their masquerade limited to the rural regions or had they managed it within the Dracoon's Court as well?

Ty growled low in distaste, and Ril seemed to sigh in a resigned manner. With a humorless grin, Gwyn agreed with her friends. "Aye, it's certainly not good news. But thank you—you did well to find these."

Ril lifted her leathery brows in an inquiring fashion.

"No, I'm not sure what it means," the Amazon admitted. "It suggests caution at the very least, but we knew that already. We'd do best to hurry onto Khirla, *Dumauzen*. Too much seems to be happening with too little explanation. It's clear someone was expecting us—or at least they were expecting some traveler representing the King and Crowned. And that someone's probably affiliated with both Khirla's Court and the Clan.

"So, can you two do without hunting until you see me to Khirla's gates? I know dried meats and porridge are not your favorite things. But...?"

Even Ty looked disgusted that she need ask.

"Then let's collect the other mares back on the path."

As they went, Gwyn realized how distinctly prejudiced she was becoming. For a fleeting moment she actually wished the attempts to negotiate a treaty between Clan and Dracoon were adamantly refused by the Clan—because she wanted to go after these fire weapons. She wanted the Clan's technology and all the fear it intimated banished—destroyed! It was difficult to remember that not every soul of the Clan folk could possible be as ambitious as these militia-raiders, very difficult. Unless...? Gwyn checked her rising anger, remembering the truth of every people: no one voice spoke for all. Which meant it was quite possible that some within the Clan were tired of their isolation and their militia's ways. For that matter, Gwyn saw, if the militia-raiders controlled most of the fire weapons, then they might very well be as intimidating to the Clan folk as they were to Khirlan's people. Ruling by threat and strength was no longer common among the Ramains' districts, but it certainly should be considered here.

"*Mae n'Pour!*" Gwyn prayed beneath her breath as a more immediate threat registered. "Oh—this is not going to be pleasant."

Gwyn suddenly hoped she wasn't riding into a trap.

Those three arsonists had killed Padder. They had wanted to kill a Royal Marshal too, namely Gwyn. That much was clear. And they had been able to pass themselves off as Steward's Swords to everyone in the area—to everyone expect Padder.

Why? Because Padder was from the city and had known these men weren't really what they claimed to be.

Aye, it was coming together. This was why the similarity in cloaks, weapons and beards suggested a military corp—the three were from a troop. But they weren't from one of the Prince's northern campaigns; they served as Steward's Swords in Khirla. That was why Brit hadn't recognized their costumes as one of the Prince's corp. Furthermore, it explained why the trio openly traveled together and yet lacked any sign of intimacy among them; the Clan was notorious for their phobias against same-sexed pairings.

It also accounted for the trio's inordinate interest in identifying Gwyn once they'd suspected she was a Marshal. Common sense would have warned the Clan's leaders that once the Wars were done the Prince's forces could easily be shifted against them, if need was shown. Prudence would have sent them scouting beyond Khirlan's borders to intercept or divert any Royal messenger, especially a Marshal. Now the Dracoon's and Khirlan's isolation was doubly important to maintain, because the Prince's troops were still mobile and at full strength. If the Clan could buy a season or two of ambiguous time, then the Prince's corps would be largely disbanded. Without that readied army, the King and the Crowned Rule would be less apt to strike against the Clan and more apt to negotiate new treaties.

But, even worse, what if Padder had not merely been killed because he'd known these men were impostors, but because he had known *them*. He had left the city only last fall, Kora had said. Fall was not the time to take up farming, not even the adventuresome sowie sorts. No, he'd fled because he'd discovered impostors within the Steward's Swords themselves—because he could identify them and they knew it. So, he had left the city and come here—until in this obscure, little corner of Forest, they'd stumbled across him again. This time, they hadn't let him escape.

Clan folk within Khirla's most elite corp? It would certainly explain Khirla's inability to counter the attacks of the Clan's raiders. It would also explain how messages were being exchanged between the traitors and the Clan without drawing anyone's attentions. After all, there were patrols riding out all the time; it wouldn't be hard to carry away a message and leave it at some pre-established point.

And it would suggest, Gwyn thought darkly, that accidents and disappearances within the city itself might be awaiting most any suspicious stranger.

She fervently hoped Brit and Sparrow didn't seem too suspicious.

* * *

The night was humid with no promise of rain for relief, and Gwyn had again left her tent open, hoping to catch the stray breezes. She slept easily after the day's long ride, barely waking as Ty rose to exchange watch with Ril. The sandwolves seldom disturbed her before dawn. Then she would rise to cook and break camp while they both caught a last nap before the day's trek. At the present, Ril was as content as usual to merely lie beside her favorite human and doze. It wasn't long before her soft sigh faded off with a little rumble.

Gwyn's hand slipped into that curly fur, welcoming Ril's presence. The sword edged beneath her left hip as she stirred. Half-consciously she moved it out from under her back and off the bedroll, but then her grasp stayed, her palm flat along its silvery length.

The ebb of rising amarin touched the lifestone within the sword's hilt as the grasses and leaves bent underneath the weapon. Her hand tensed, and once again Gwyn's dreams were invaded through that shimmering steel.

A steady pulse glowed within the rough-barked honeywood. It was a tree of middling age, huge but not so mammoth as to stand high on arching roots yet. Beneath her hand the flowing energies of its life seemed tangible, unselfishly strengthening her weary body's reserves. Yet the hand upon that tree was not Gwyn's own—there was no sign of the white stone ring of *dey Sorormin*. Still it was a graceful hand, Gwyn thought. The lines were slender and long, strong in its leanness. Much like her own right hand, it was slightly callused with the telling marks of a sword carrier. Although the marks suggested only a light use of the weapon. Or perhaps she's as left-handed as I tend to be, Gwyn mused.

In her sleep, Gwyn didn't think to question why this body had become a "she" or why the amarin of that honeywood felt so vividly alive to her touch. Instead, she found herself drinking in the sweet taste of the Goddess' living cycles. Fascinated, she watched the almost caressing stroke of that gentle hand along the ruddy bark. Her fingertips tingled in an exquisite sensation, making her toes want to curl in pleasure. Then, oddly, Gwyn noticed the very pale brown of the hand's skin was the golden tan of wind and sun, not the emotion laden, rich darkness of most on Aggar.

Shock registered.

The vision shifted abruptly, annoyance flooding strong as that body snapped away from the tree to rigidly await the approaching intruder. Gwyn couldn't tell if the anxiety and surprise sprang from herself at her sudden realization—this woman tanned!—or if the emotion was drawn from the woman's vexation at the interruption.

Gwyn felt another jolt then, this time undeniably all her own. The man who materialized from the trees was heavily bearded and caped in blue. He was greeted as a Steward's Sword—and he was addressing this woman as Dracoon!

Gwyn's attention was caught again by the blue-caped Sword. She disliked him as much as the woman who hosted her awareness did. He swaggered arrogantly with that bully confidence often supplied by weapons, and he was armed by two saber swords that hung from his hips. He reported with a curt, impersonal manner that the sentries had been posted, the forward scouts had returned, and that the cook was announcing eventide. Then he departed with an equally dispassionate, "By your leave, Min."

Gwyn couldn't quite decide, if he was being insubordinate or not in omitting the Dracoon's title now.

Irritation flared into a spurt of rage and a fist swung out into the tree. The honeywood calmly absorbed the passions. Her palm opened, fingers spreading wide again to drink in that sweet balm. The woman—no, Llinolae, Gwyn mentally corrected—it was Llinolae drawing this steadying breath. Reluctantly the Dracoon left the sanctuary of that deeper woods, carrying Gwyn with her towards the small group of the camp.

She—or should I think we? Gwyn wondered—paused beside the picket line to murmur a greeting to the big gray. The horse wuffled into her shoulder briefly, before burying its soft nose once more in the depths of the bushy haymoss piled at its feet.

A woman of perhaps ten or twelve seasons approached with a tentative greeting. Shyly, she offered a ceramic cup of spice tea. At the Dracoon's word of thanks, the young woman blushed a rich brown and fled back to the matronly cook's fire. Amusement tendered genuine fondness at the recognition of the younger's infatuation. For a wistful moment, a more personal notion was considered, then discarded—that inner sense of compassion and responsibility as always was too strong to court casual liaisons, but Gwyn was thoroughly unsettled at finding any of the attraction was mutual.

She tried to watch the young woman aiding the cook more closely then, wanting to understand Llinolae's interest. More slightly built than many, the woman wore neither sword nor cooking apron. She was sorely out-of-place among the stocky, burly caste of the blue-caped soldiers who gathered near the stew pot. Like most women of Aggar, she was at least a head shorter than the men, and since most of these males were tall even for soldiers, she seemed particularly petite next to them. The cook's square frame didn't detract from the perception much either.

It all combined to create an aura of innocence and vulnerability about her that, personally, Gwyn did not find appealing. Then Gwyn noticed the ink stains on those fingers as they dished out the stew. Behind the soldiers she saw a bedroll set apart with a scribe's bound sheaf and pens. Begrudgingly, Gwyn allowed there might be more to this person than first appeared. The thought only annoyed her more.

Abruptly, Gwyn realized that this perverse irritation had become outright jealousy!

Pain suddenly lanced through her left hand and woke her.

Gwyn froze, waiting for the momentary disorientation to pass. Ril gently nudged her with a wet nose, and her quiet demeanor reassured the *Niachero* that all was well around them. Cautiously, Gwyn looked at her hand. There was a small cut along her littlest finger where it had tightened about her sword's edge. It was such an ordinary sort of stupid thing to do to herself that Gwyn almost laughed, and the world returned to a more practical level of events.

The cut stung but wasn't very deep, and she sucked on it absently as she rose to fetch some ointment. Wryly she reminded herself that at least the source of her dreams had been identified. In truth, the dream had come from the combination of her lifestone and sword's alloy, but it had been conjured first by the touch of Llinolae's Blue Sight.

Gwyn knew such a sensitive awareness of amarin—that wondrous taste of strength—could be drawn from those trees only by a Blue Sight. Her sister, Kimarie, had first introduced her to those nurturing life energies when they were children. Later, Selena had shared those sweet amarin with her. And now—now the Blue Gift of this Llinolae was so deeply rooted in the fiber of the Great Forest that the lifestone in Gwyn's sword was once more exposing Gwyn to those forces.

She held no doubts now—this woman in her dreams must be the Dracoon Llinolae. Even without the soldier's confirmation, Gwyn would have known. There could not be two in this District who were so powerful with the Blue Sight. To casually manage such oneness with the flowing amarin of Aggar and yet retain any individual sense of self required a very, very strong Gift—and a great deal of personal resolve. That level of power fit with what Gwyn knew of Llinolae's Blue Gift. This Dracoon had the strength and skill to reach across both stars and time to *dey Sorormin's* home world; she was certainly capable of reaching Gwyn's sword through the Forest's shifting amarin—whether she'd intended to or not.

No, there couldn't have been two such talented women associated with the Steward's Swords of Khirla.

The more surprising thing to Gwyn, though, was Llinolae's skin tone. Aggar's natural genetics did not allow for sun tanning, only the addition of *dey Sorormin* and Clan blood had introduced that characteristic. However, it had not proven to be a very viable genetic trait in many respects. It was bred out by the second generation from the occasional mixed marriage of Clan and Ramains' folk. Even with Sisters, who relied upon the lifestone interventions for their reproduction (a bonding that precluded mutations), the skin's sensitivity to the sun was seen exclusively among the *Niachero*. It had certainly never been seen among the Blue Sights.

Until now, Gwyn granted.

For a moment, she wondered what this Llinolae actually looked like. She wished she'd questioned *M'Sormee* more closely. It wasn't surprising that Bryana hadn't mentioned the novelty of Llinolae's coloring, because like many gifted with the Sight her mother was often so preoccupied with inner amarin that the significance of mere physical details got lost. Still, for Gwyn the physical suddenly became quite intriguing—until she abruptly remembered Llinolae's speculative appraisal of the young scribe.

Even awake, Gwyn found she still resented that attraction.

Then a ghastly thought struck her. What if this scribe—the one who tempted the Dracoon to consider a more personal liaison—what if she was somehow in league with the court traitor? Llinolae had told Bryana that the Royal Family was ignoring her written pleas for help, yet Bryana had found the reports reaching Churv were giving no hint of trouble. And though there might be traitors in the Steward's Swords, odds were still good that there was at least one scribe in league with them; there were no easy ways to forge official signatures nor the varnished, resin-tight seals.

Yet the young woman in Llinolae's camp was too young to be a full Scribe, most likely she was still an apprentice. And she was decidedly too young to be crafty enough to deceive a Blue Sight's intuitive recognition of 'wrongness.' That feat was accomplished only by very tightly leashed emotions and a steel-clad, determined calm—it meant harnessing the intensity of a fanatic's passion without losing one's rational mind to that passion. But such intensity could blur the amarin and leave those with the Blue Sight uncertain of their companions' deeper motives. The young scribe might have been infatuated, but impassioned? No, the girl was definitely not the traitor.

Still, if there was a senior scribe with fewer scruples who supervised her...?

Mae n'Pour! How she hated schemers! Sometimes—just sometimes!—the sandwolves' toothier solutions to trouble might have some value, especially when it came to dealing with the satin-robed sowies of the royal courts.

Chapter Ten

At the scritch-scratching noise, Gwyn froze. Squatting above on the great bough of a honeywood with her short bow in hand, she waited. It came again; a quick tap and the dry leaves rustled. Carefully she moved to her right, straining to see through the midnight shimmer and shadow. Then she smiled. No, this wasn't some human scout. But it was eventide! As belated as that meal was, this bird was going to be sorely appreciated by both herself and her packmates. And it was big enough to serve them all—she disregarded the fact that its size meant it was fairly old and was probably going to be as tough as shrunken leather to chew.

The fowl continued to forage along the edge of a decaying log. Gwyn lifted her notched arrow, hoping her packmates held still just one moment more! Slowly she drew, painfully easing back past each click and whirl—the tiny gears and pulleys of her short bow preparing to hurl that arrow with far more force than an ordinary long bow.

The string loosed. Feathers flurried, then there was stillness. But the frantic flutter had been purely reflexive, and eventide was theirs. Ril appeared from nowhere to gingerly retrieve the catch. It took the sandwolf a moment to pry the arrow from the wood underneath, and Gwyn appreciated the care her friend took; the metal shaft arrows were a luxury not easily found outside of Valley Bay. As Ril moved back into the shadows, Gwyn returned her attention to the open brush land and to those city lights of Khirla. She pulled another arrow from the quiver at her back as she frowned at those stony walls.

It was said that some of the finer sweet wines had once come from this region—before the Wars. Given the broad expanse of brushberries spread about the city, Gwyn could readily believe the old rumors. The scruffy bushes were more commonly seen scattered through the Great Forests and usually marked areas of regrowth that began after fires had been through. But here the folk had deliberately cultivated the stuff to keep the great trees at bay and yet retain some usable quantity of topsoil. It had also been a brilliant defensive idea, Gwyn admitted. It allowed the City Guards better visibility of approaching raiders, and it would let them literally burn back enemy encroachers if they became too persistent. As it was, this season's current burn-backs had allowed space directly below the western gates for the livestock traders and nearer the northeastern road, for the Feasts' visiting merchant wagons.

Torches and cooking fires brightened the two camps. Music and laughter rose and stilled with the wind's dance, testimony to the continued festivities despite the night's descent. Along the upper galleries of the city's wall, Gwyn could see the guards walking. In the bluish caste of the Twin Moons' light, those fortress walls looked like bundled racks of stonemoss. But Gwyn knew the masonry was flame resistant enough to withstand even some of the Clan's fire weapons. Beyond the walls, the visible rooftops seemed to be equally fire retardant with their ceramic tiles and slated stones. Even the two palace towers that courted the stars were crowned only with narrow balconies of honeywood. Their slender lengths were fashioned of stone and peaked with caps of shining tiles.

Since the Clan had been abandoned by their starry empire, this place had known only struggle—a fierce conflict that had ultimately closed the once-prosperous trade routes between the northern and southern continents. Through it all, however, the Khirlan folk had held strong, never losing their patience nor their steady hope for eventual peace.

Well, everything about Khirlan suggested the people had earned a right to hope, Gwyn granted. Celebrating beneath the shadows overcast by those walls—beneath that ever-present reminder of dangers—was a show of indomitable character and strength in itself. She remembered the discouragement of so many in the northern ravaged territories. It had been a hard siege, but compared to this? Her respect for these hoe farmers nudged up a notch or two more. No wonder their Dracoon held such unshakable determination—to lead such folk, she must.

* * *

Gwyn circled west down to the entrance on the main trade road, preferring to imply she had traveled inland and south from the Royal Court of Churv. Given the obviously long absence of Marshals from the district, she expected her mid-day arrival to raise a certain amount of comment from both the gate guards and the general folk. But she hadn't in any way anticipated the total shock that greeted her as she rode through the outer encampment of merchants and visitors.

Roving vendors stopped in their tracks, barely shuffling aside with open-mouthed amazement and nearly tripping on the edges of their long robed coats. Children ran, calling to their parents who emerged from the dimness of tents to clutch their brood close and silently stare. Youngsters stopped their teasings, rakish charmers forgot their intendeds, and frowning elders folded their arms with squint-eyed consideration. Even the chattering, little prippers went bounding up their owners' shoulders, anxious and flustered at the sudden hush.

Cinder tossed her black mane with annoyance, and the two bays behind her snorted, equally unnerved. Gwyn once again felt vulnerably exposed without the sandwolves flanking her, but she breathed a prayer of relief that they'd agreed to stay in the woods. This sort of greeting would not have been to their liking—it certainly wasn't to hers. Studiously, she kept her hand from wandering to her sword hilt and her anxiety from reflecting in her expression. She only hoped that the dusty apricot of her tan would keep her unease from showing too clearly in her skin tones.

All but the oldest spectators cringed from the directness of her gaze, and Gwyn mentally reviewed her costume and gear in an effort to explain the strangeness these folks must be seeing. But the mares she led were only lightly packed with nebulous, canvassed bundles, and Cinder was behaving, her burly frame dressed in leathers as brightly polished as Gwyn's own. Gwyn had donned her leg sheaths again, and their honeywood sheen was a striking contrast against the darker red-brown of her trousers but clearly matched both the stiff leather jerkin that she wore and Cinder's tack. The undyed linen of her bloused shirt was the same shade of stonemoss that many favored here. The wide vambraces on her wrists seemed to be merely a variation of the styles worn by those around her. And behind her, across Cinder's saddle packs, the thick quilt of her Marshal's coat was prominently displayed—the ruddy bulk of its quilting, the bronze colored strings, and the glittering glass buttons were all unmistakable. Considering her coloring, her matched mares, and that coat, her identity as a Marshal surely could not be in question.

Gwyn noted one old matron with a bag of cider slung over a shoulder and a belt of ceramic mugs tied about her girth. The stubborn thrust of the squared jaw and the unwavering stare of her challenge bespoke of courage—just what Gwyn was looking for. She guided Cinder nearer the vendor and halted. Her copper gaze held the elder's grey eyes, noting the fear that sprang forward, but defiance blazed forth again quickly. Gwyn continued to look at her steadily, pulling a glass coin from her belt pouch and leaning forward slowly to extend it.

"A cup if you please, Min."

The woman's eyes narrowed shrewdly, weighing the respect of Gwyn's manner against the foreign accents of the Trade Tongue. Then in a bold gesture she stepped forward, accepted the coin and wiped a cup clean announcing, "It's spiced. My own recipe."

Gwyn smiled graciously and accepted the mug. She raised it in a faint toast of honor to the woman and sipped it. "It's quite good. You're to be commended."

A bright beaming smile and a proud glance or two were exchanged with those around them, and the tension broke. Murmurs rippled through the crowd, and Gwyn went to hide a grin in the mug…at which point she found herself hiding a grimace from the fuller mouthful. It really wasn't such bad stuff—for spiced wine. Usually though, she preferred hers to be watered down; she'd nearly forgotten the bite in an unadulterated brew. But the rising hum of curiosity was reward enough to endure a bit of soured syrups.

Pieces of the mumbled speculations reached her. But politely Gwyn pretended not to hear as she finished her drink, until suddenly, "Then how come her face is all brown?"

Startled, Gwyn glanced back as the child's shrill voice faded beneath a mother's frantic hushing. At Gwyn's attention, everyone abruptly stilled again.

"For…forgive the girl, Min." The old matron at Gwyn's knee took the emptied mug back, shifting uncertainly beneath the *Niachero's* concerned gaze. "She's not old enough to know what she's saying."

The ominous quiet hovered. Gwyn decided it wasn't the girl's age, but her honesty that was most telling. The skinny, little figure with pigtails was now firmly back in her mother's nervous grasp, and Gwyn produced a wry, but kind smile for her. She gave the girl a nod of encouragement and asked, "What did you want to know about me, Min'l?"

The child twisted about to look up at her mother for permission. But the woman had eyes only for Gwyn, mutely pleading for patience. Her skin color darkened with fright as she seemingly despaired of finding any tolerance in such a stranger as Gwyn.

Getting no voiced objection from her parent, however, the youngster stepped forward. Quite matter-of-factly, she demanded of Gwyn, "Are you from the Clan folk?"

"No," Gwyn answered, her polite smile softening with genuine amusement at that unexpected idea. "I'm a Royal Marshal. Why would you think I'm from the Clan?"

"'Cause...'cause your face is all brown like the Clan's folk get, and your hair is all fire red like some Clan folk, and...and you're a woman, but you're so tall!"

Gwyn chuckled softly. She was amazed at herself for overlooking such obvious details of mistrust in this district of all districts.

"Was one of your parents from the Clan maybe?"

"No." Gwyn shook her head and explained gently, "I'm an Amazon, Min'l."

"Amazon...the Valley north....!" The shock rushed through the crowd like flames in a wind.

"You see...," Gwyn went on, for the girl's sake, "I was born in Valley Bay. And yes, like the Clan's women an Amazon can have light hair, sun-browned skin, or be very tall. But I'm a little like you too. When I get excited, I flush dark. And when I get sick, I get bruises under my eyes just like you."

"You do?"

"I do."

Rumbles of relief and the awkward laughter of embarrassment began to tumble about, tempering the awe of her. Gwyn felt the tension in her own stomach release as well, thankful again that her sun's tan covered her skin's lighter shadings of emotion. The girl grinned at her. Gwyn nodded good-bye, leaving the youngster shining with pride that a Royal Marshal had actually answered her questions—and that her mother was hugging her happily rather than scolding.

The atmosphere was certainly easier after that. At least it was, until she came to the City Gates.

The Gates' gaping hole in the wall wasn't particularly meant to be imposing. Its bright tiles of rusty red, gold and sky blue tones glinted in the late morning sun, adding a beautiful relief to the somber beige stones of the walls. The long corridor through the wall itself was lively with torch light dancing from yet more tiles and from the festive bustle of the people moving along. But a somber-faced trio of guards in their bark-red capes dampened the welcoming auras quickly. Two of them were male with thick, short beards and bushy brows. Theirs was a scowling, unfriendly sort of demeanor. The woman beside them was no less imposing. Short and sturdy as most female sword carriers were, she still seemed to convey her deep suspicion as her arms crossed and her stance set wide. She was the only one of the three not playing with the hilt of her sword, Gwyn noted, and credited her with a slightly cooler head than the fellows she served with. The Amazon wasn't certain that made her any kind of an ally, however.

Cinder shied as the men approached. One of them reached out and roughly grabbed the reins under the mare's chin. She pulled back resentfully, until Gwyn calmed her with an unobtrusive pat on the withers. The mare settled only a little, the whites of her eyes still showing.

The other male laid an equally unwelcomed hand upon Gwyn's ankle and growled something at her in the local tongue.

Her copper hued eyes skirted between the three Guards. The young woman was stepping back, forcing the passersby to circle wider; she was opening room for her sword if need came. A very somber commitment to duty, Gwyn mused, and odd—considering the fact that this was supposed to be a festival.

The City Guard jangled her foot impatiently, repeating his question. A grim steeliness rose about Gwyn; there was no reason for his impudent use of the local dialect—the Trade Tongue had been bandied about freely in the encampment behind her, hadn't it?

"I am Royal Marshal to the King and Crowned Rule, First Family of all Ramains and Rightful Monarchs of the Districts. I deal only in the Trade Tongue of Travelers—as decreed by the People's Book, so that any who hear may understand and heed." Her words came clipped and were clearly enunciated. She was suddenly very glad of the glossy leg sheath that tempered the touch of his sweaty palm.

Cinder danced uneasily beneath her. The mount was as impatient as her rider was unhappy. Behind her, Calypso and Nia were growing edgy as well.

"Are you Marshal or Amazon then?" He spat off into the stones in contrived disinterest, but at least he was finally extending her the courtesy of using the Trade Tongue.

"Both."

His head shot around, imagining some insult to her tone, but Gwyn quite abruptly lost her patience with his game. Her lips peeled back in a silent, pack snarl as she met his accusing stare, giving him look for look.

The sword woman backed to the far side of the tunnel, nearly losing herself amidst the swirl of festival folk.

The Guard's dark gaze narrowed as he eyed Gwyn again, speculatively. A warier respect seemed to hover at the corners of his awareness, then for some reason was disregarded. He snapped his fingers, "Tags!"

She pulled the thong over her head and dangled the glass pieces low enough for him to read. She jerked them back as he went to snatch them, lowering them again only to allow him to read them. He made no attempt to claim them this time, although the hand on her ankle had become as stiff as a hardwood shackle. Gwyn wasn't about to risk losing those precious tags to anyone. From experience she knew that she could seldom afford to lose her proof of authority—and especially not here in this particular Court.

"What's your business in Khirla?" His belligerence continued as Gwyn strung the tags about her neck again—the sword woman had disappeared completely. "We haven't seen a Marshal in nearly two generations. Why send you here now?"

"I am a Marshal," Gwyn repeated evenly, ignoring his exaggeration; Churv's inattention had not been quite that extreme, she knew. "Tradition and Crowned give me leave to be where I will."

"And just what kind of business is that?" he sneered.

She wondered who had tutored this moron. Marshals went where they pleased, when they pleased; none but one in dire distress had any right to question a Marshal's priorities. Even the King acknowledged that they often rendered aid before he or the Crowned were alerted to many troubles.

The Guard turned to his fellow with a taunting guffaw, "You ever hear such a lame answer?"

"Not answer enough, certain to me!" Taunted the skinny soldier holding Cinder's bridle. The burly mare shook her head at his rude noise, and roughly he snatched at her ear, twisting to bring her nose down again. "Tell Herself that and you'll be laughed from the city."

And who was Herself? Gwyn wondered briefly.

"So give us another reason for your being here, Mar-shal?" Their drawling impudence rankled.

"Before the Wars, Marshals ran the races in Feast Days. Did they not?" She didn't give a damn about the racing, but she was certainly not about to say the Dracoon needed her.

"Bah!" The man to the front renewed his hold on Cinder's ear with a wicked pull. "These bulky wagon drays? What sorry tale can you spin next?"

Enough was enough!

Cinder agreed, and Gwyn let her go. With a wild shriek she reared high, taking the Guard up with her. The white teeth flashed as her ebony hooves pummeled, and the man fell from her bridle. A whistle shrilled as the mare rose again on her haunches. The street crowds fled as the downed Guard cringed in a wounded ball, waiting for the death blows to fall with the weight of the mare behind them.

Cinder screamed again. The bone bite shattered in her teeth. Shards of white and frothing lather flew, and she danced on her hind legs, pawing the air—still holding her two-hoofed arabesque.

"Tell him to move." Gwyn ordered icily.

The standing Guard stared at her without comprehension. He barely registered the steadiness of her seat and the quietness of her hands upon her knees. The only thing he grasped was that she no longer held the reins!

Behind Gwyn both Nia and Calypso snorted and stomped, pressing forward menacingly.

"Tell him to *move*!"

He scrambled, half-dragging the other to safety.

Cinder came down with a thud, snorting hotly and shaking her head. Her mistress stroked her neck, murmuring in quieter tones, and with a final stamp, the bay let herself be calmed.

"You arrogant, Clan-wedded witch!" And he left the shaken mass of his comrade huddled at the wall. "Fates' Cellars will see that horse before you ride out of here! Do you hear me?"

Cinder neighed shrilly again, tossing her head at his cry and threatened to rise once more. Gwyn's knees brought her down swiftly.

The City Guard reached for his sword. Gwyn's hand crossed for hers as the bays behind her reared, shrieking their own challenges.

"Hold!"

From the corner of her eye, Gwyn identified the newcomers. The sword woman had returned with a sergeant.

He was not tall for a man. His shoulders were broad and his neck thick. Age had salted his hair, and steel had marked his clean-shaven face with a scar that almost closed his left eye. But his gristly voice echoed a command that was not to be ignored, and the younger Guard's hand flew from his sword's hilt as if it had been burnt.

That dark gaze swung to the Amazon.

Gwyn hesitated, still suspicious as she took measure of this sergeant in his bark red cape and worn blue vest.

"You're a Royal Marshal," that rough timbre rang out again. He spoke in Trade Tongue. "You travel with the Crowned's immunity."

Slowly Gwyn straightened from her low crouch along Cinder's neck. Her hand withdrew from her sword a little less reluctantly. At least here was someone acquainted with the Law.

The sergeant turned, squaring his shoulders with a gruff air. He walked over to examine the quivering hulk that had once so arrogantly tried to bully Cinder. Sharp words chided the young Guard, and Gwyn suddenly realized how incredibly young all three of these City Guards were. A roughish hand helped drag the youth back to his feet, but Gwyn noticed it was more show than a damaging shove that sent him and his friend back to their posts. The sergeant waved the sword woman aside, pointing to the far corner of the tunnel where the festival crowd was staring, and the woman hurried to move everyone along again. His charges properly chastised and returned to task, the sergeant gave his attention to Gwyn. She said nothing as he stepped to Cinder's head; he made no move to touch the bridle.

"You trained your lady well. Didn't even crack his ribs." He took a moment to look over her small band of horses and baggage, feet firmly planted in the ground and arms crossed at his chest.

Gwyn liked his open scrutiny; he didn't need the reassurance of toying with his sword's hilt as the others had.

"May I ask what brings you to us, Marshal? Or rather, may I ask if you require immediate audience with the Steward?"

The Steward? Gwyn again wondered at the structure of this Dracoon's court. "A word with your Dracoon Llinolae would be appropriate."

His gaze dropped. He seemed to study his boots, weighing out his words carefully before saying, "This ain't Churv, Min. I've no intent to hinder you. But—" He shrugged and then straightened. "You'll have to judge the differences yourself. If you like, I can show you the way to the Palace. There's no Audience holding today, those are reserved for before 'nd after the Feasts. You can present yourself to the authorities, though. I can't say what they're apt to do for you. Again, I mean no disrespect to yourself or your position, Marshal."

"None taken," Gwyn assured him quietly. She nodded with decision, approving of his directness. "Lead on."

He stepped off without a backward glance, his cape flying.

The streets were narrow and made of cobblestones with a central slant towards the gutter track. Between the press of the festival visitors and the footing underneath, Gwyn quickly found herself dismounting and opting to lead her mares. The sergeant's stride slackened only slightly as the crowds thickened. Apparently, the colors of his blue surcoat and ruddy cape were enough to wordlessly clear their path.

"Generally, most walk within the City Gates," the sergeant explained after a moment. His low rumble of a voice calmly cut through the swelling laughter and chatter of the merriment around them. They turned a corner onto another small street which seemed even narrower with its shadows from all the three and four storied buildings. "Steward's Swords and Royal Messengers have exceptions made, of course. But the stones make poor footing for fast paced beasts, so there's less danger of accidents when we insist on the merchants having at least one handler at the head of each cart."

"Must make the Feast Races exciting," Gwyn remarked. She was not at all certain she wanted to risk Cinder's limbs on such a poor surface, regardless of how insulting she might seem to the traditions.

"Ho!" The man split a broad half-grin, the scar on his cheek twisting the left side of his face into something more sour. "There's no need to worry for your fine lady beasts, Marshal. The race is run 'round the outer sides of the city walls and only cuts in up the southern hill behind the Palace—that's along the track where the Dracoon's stables have entry. It's dirt packed, the whole circle. Lets folk see what's happening better too. Can't imagine trying to get a good glimpse of the runners in these alley ways. Can you?"

"No, not by much."

Gwyn took closer stock of the city as the street opened into a market square. The music of both public dances and troubadour performances mingled with the cries and smells of vendors. Bright banners hung from the upper windows of the local mercantile houses. There were streamers and ribbons fluttering from booth crosses, and the bottle-glass windows from a nearby inn gleamed from polishing. But underneath it all, Gwyn felt a pervading sense of struggle. The timber frames in the stone masonry were old. The plaster along the upper walls was frayed. The cobblestones underfoot were slicker than she had known in the northern cities, and she suddenly realized it was because of the rounded indentations of wear.

She followed her guide away from the market along another small lane, and then she began to understand what she was really seeing. The subtle disrepair of age surrounded her. Here in this street, she doubted the sun ever shone more than a single quarter of a quarterday, because the original houses and establishments around them had been built tall, and then built upon again. The lower levels were well-oiled where there was wood, sometimes the plaster was fresh with paint, but on the whole the tired, drooping structures looked as if they relied upon their mutual leanings for support. They seemed too weary to actually bother to crumble. Glass was scarce as well, even in the upper levels. Gwyn caught glimpses of open-tied shutters, but only the merchants seemed to have any sort of bottle glass, and even the clothiers' shops they passed had no broad panes of the stuff.

The clothing of the folk milling around her was a match to their city's depleting resources. Turned out as they were in their best, there was still a muteness of color and a limpness of cloth that came only from frequent wear. No, Gwyn corrected, it came from frequent patching and over wear. She noticed too that the clink of glass coins seemed rare within the cheerful barter about her, and looking more closely, Gwyn saw the trading of goods-for-goods was more often done than money exchanges.

They were as hard put in their survival here as any of the northern cities had become with the Changlings' Wars, she realized. And because of that northern chaos, the Royal Family had left this distant district go forgotten—as had her own corp of Marshals. Briefly, guilt pained her heart, and she allowed that the very thing the Crowned Rule had sought to prevent during the Wars—by posting Marshals as roving agents among the districts—had come to pass in Khirlan anyway; those in need far from the northern fighting had still gone neglected.

Yet it was not to be forgotten, the traitor within the ranks of this Dracoon's own court had been a great contributor to this negligence. As had the Clan in going from occasional raids to nearly the extreme of outright warfare.

It was not the Marshal's nor the Crowned Rule's fault that word had never reached Churv of the rising trouble. It was not the neglect of the Royal Family that had spawned the destruction. Had it been known Khirlan was in need of help, then the Marshals would have been sent.

Mae n'Pour! Gwyn prayed, let it not be too late now that I am here.

"The Palace is set to the south and west of the city," the sergeant began abruptly, almost too abruptly Gwyn thought. She wondered what he had read in her silence to suddenly prompt such a studied nonchalance. "It was built there before the Clan was ever even conceived of. Originally it sat on the hill, in order to keep watch on the overland route."

"A very long past," Gwyn observed dryly. She doubted that even the Council's archivists could easily produce those most ancient of ancient records anymore.

"Well, traditions linger. We fought Aggar's bullies in the beginning. Seems we fight them again now, perhaps to the demise of Khirla itself this time."

"So the Clan's giving trouble."

He looked at her hard and long, conscious of that placid acceptance of his assertion and the complete lack of surprise in her manner. He took another moment or two to think about her as they wove in and out of the crowds. Then forthrightly, he asked, "You here for more than the races?"

"I am," Gwyn answered evenly. She chose not to elaborate.

"Hmm...how much do they know outside the district?"

"Little." Gwyn smiled at the thought of Bryana and Jes, however. Together, her parents made a very formidable pair. "Enough to pursue it vigorously, if I should disappear though."

"Good," he nodded. With an abrupt decision, he extended his left hand forward, palm down in the formal greeting of the district. "I'm called Rutkins. And lowly sergeant that I've become, I welcome you to this place anyways." His lips twisted into that queer grin again. "You may want someone to watch your back. Keep me in mind."

Warily, Gwyn grasped his hand. She met his grin with a dry, sardonic one of her own. "Why trust you?"

"I'm not a Steward's Sword." He seemed to think that succinctly said it all. Then as his dark gaze fixed unwaveringly ahead of them, he added softly, "Before the Swords, I was Mha'del's Captain of Guard. Maybe that tells you a little more of something than other tales could."

Mha'del had been Llinolae's father, and a King's Dracoon as well. Gwyn remembered that easily enough from her studies in Churv. But it certainly did open interesting possibilities where Sergeant Rutkins was concerned—some of them alternately good and bad. Gwyn felt the empathic suspicion of her distant bondmates rise within herself, warning her against trusting anyone inside this fortress of a city. Ril and Ty were undeniably right, it was too soon for trust. Yet it was their past teachings that prompted her to consider him as a possible ally; the scent of his sweat was not the stench of fear or impatience. His faint uneasiness in being with her had begun only after she'd admitted to being here for more than the racing. And he still felt no need to toy with that sword at his hip. A level-headed soldier, smart enough to make captain and yet demoted—not jailed or exiled but *demoted*—at the advent of new rule. And there was more. Despite the risk of accompanying a stranger through this city—despite his obvious perception that it was, in truth, a risk to be with her—he was here.

He stopped, startling Gwyn and the mares. Calypso protested the halt with a snort as the man pointed ahead.

Gwyn looked across the bustling intersection and made out the Palace Square. The fountain at its gate sparkled gaily, water dancing down its sculpted tiers. Beyond that, she saw the upper galleries of golden honeywood that circled the Palace itself.

"I'll be better use to you, if I leave you here," Rutkins muttered. "Take the left and follow 'long to the back of the south wing. There'll be a host of blue cloaks to ask directions of—"

"Blue cloaks?"

"The Steward's Swords."

"Ahh—"

"Towards the far end of the livestock pavilions you'll see an open portal on the right. It'll be tiled like the City Gate was, but there'll be two banners hanging. One ruddy colored, like my cloak here—that's the Dracoon's. The other's dark'n blue. That's the Steward's own. Go on in with your horses and ask for the Regiment Clerical. He's one of the Steward's Swords, and if the Dracoon or Steward can be seen, he'll arrange it for you.

"But like I said, Marshal. I can't promise he'll hurry the news in, despite your wishes."

Gwyn nodded. "I understand."

"They'll probably try an' get you to board your mares outside the city walls in the visitor pens. The Palace stables have never been too big, so you can judge yourself if it'll be meant as insult or not. Again, I can't help with that, but if you want to get word to me, there's an honest handler by the name of Min Roan 'round the visitor pens. She runs a smaller tent. More expensive in some ways but better treatment for the beasts, so most think it's worth it. If you're outside the walls and looking for me, she'll let me know. Far as inside goes, try the Broken Chalice most nights. If I'm not in the commons, the bartender'll get me a message. Both places, just ask for me by name—not rank. They'll know the difference as important, even if you are speaking Trade Tongue."

"All right," Gwyn held his dark gaze for a moment, committing to nothing. Yet tacitly, she had to acknowledge the courage he could be showing in simply having this conversation.

He hesitated, then turned on his heel and was gone.

Chapter Eleven

Gwyn waited in the dark. The air around her smelled of familiar things like gingerbark tea, fabric lint, and bloomwater lotions—the last brought a smile as Gwyn remembered a night spent with Selena using that sweet body cream. There were too the scents of lamp oil mingling with sun-warmed, fresh bread, and beneath those both, she could catch a hint of a beastie wool blanket. The hot summer day had baked this small cabin to a pleasant well-doneness. Then the moons' touch had slowly cooled it, until now when Gwyn found herself surrounded with that exquisite essence of home. And in every sense of the word, Brit and Sparrow had made a home here in this troubadour's wagon. So despite the hour—or the usually appealing clamor of the festival outside—Gwyn was content to simply sit and wait in these shadows.

That sense of home, however, had not betrayed her into complacency. After the fiasco in the healers' barn, Gwyn wasn't about to feel completely safe anywhere outside of Valley Bay ever again—Sisters near or not. And so, though she sat in the silence of the wagon's cabin, relishing the feel of loving around her, she sat unstirring and without light, half listening to those outer folks as they passed just as a precaution.

When she had settled down to her wait, Gwyn had known it would be a long one. She had seen Sparrow's drays patiently dozing near the performance rings in the livestock camps during her earlier walk, and from the posted order of hand banners, it had been clear that her friend was scheduled for late in the evening. Gwyn had known Brit would seek out Sparrow rather than return here alone, should her healing services finish early. When Gwyn glimpsed Sparrow's saffron vest disappearing amidst the other performers, she'd assumed that Sparrow had seen her too. Confident then that her Sisters were faring well and that they now knew she was in town, Gwyn had moved on. She'd been wary of risking any kind of a more obvious contact, given the pair of Steward's Swords following her.

Because of those Steward's Swords, Gwyn hadn't returned for Sparrow's performance either. Instead she had wandered rather haphazardly, learning the general lay of the city, both within the walls and without, and pricing trinkets or savoring pasties just like any other festival visitor might. She had gone on in that manner until she was sure her two watchers were thoroughly bored, and then in a moment of distraction when a juggler and an errant pripper collided, she'd neatly vanished. She was certain the next disappearance would not be so easily managed, but the two who had been charged with keeping track of her whereabouts had been fairly inexperienced in city traffics; they had obviously assumed a woman as tall and uniquely red-haired as she, couldn't blend into any crowd quickly. They had underestimated the deceptions the simple don-ning of a cloak and a shift in posture could create. She doubted that whoever "was-in-charge" was going to send such innocents to trail her again. But then, she did have a few more eloquent tricks for future occasions.

A faint chuckle and a recognizable shuffle brought Gwyn alert. The gruffer voices of strangers came too. Her gloved hand curled over her sword's hilt. Its blade lay unsheathed along the bench, hidden behind her outstretched legs. The wagon rocked with the weight shift on the back step, and the door cracked open a bit. A bulky shadow blocked the torch light from reaching Gwyn and prevented the accompanying group from seeing into the cabin. Laughter rumbled softly around the small band as they all made their farewells. Then Brit's heavy frame squeezed through the door, and a balled up bit of rag went sailing through the air at Gwyn.

The *Niachero* grinned in the darkness and caught her kerchief neatly; she'd dropped it on the outer step to identify herself to her Sisters. Brit gave no other acknowledgment. Instead she puttered around the cabin, lighting a shielded lantern, closing the window slats on both sides of the wagon, and humming tunelessly to herself.

"Sparrow'll be in shortly."

If Gwyn hadn't been listening for it, she would have missed the words entirely. She nodded, holding her silence.

A soft rap beneath her back bone nearly peeled the skin from her neck as she shot off the bench. Just barely she managed to keep to the shadows and ended in a crouch near the door. Brit closed the last of the shutters with a rich chuckle.

Her Sister then leaned across the wide bench and pushed at the back padding. The entire panel of the center seat swung inward to allow a black clad Sparrow to roll in. Gwyn swallowed her heart back into place, shakily realizing there must be a false door beneath the driver's bench outside, and then admiringly she offered a lopsided, little grin. "You're good. I didn't hear you coming."

Sparrow tipped her head, pleased at the compliment. She helped Brit refasten the corner pegs of the bench, reporting, "No one's around watching that I can tell. Normal folk and festivities roaming. That was about it."

"Were you followed?" Brit asked Gwyn, turning the lantern light up a bit now that they were securely shuttered in.

"At first."

"Well, they still seem to be lost." Sparrow unfolded the two hinged bed halves away from the side benches, converting the back of the cabin into a wide bed. Then she promptly flopped herself down, toes prying the short shoes from her heels and hands folding neatly behind her head. She gave up a deep, satisfied sigh and wiggled her stockinged toes. "I assume, you're spending the night in our upper loft?"

"Cramped as it is, I thought I might," Gwyn drawled, sliding her sword back into its sheath. "If I'm not imposing too much?"

Brit snorted, dismissing the impish mischief of her shadowmate's expression. She was obviously quite weary from the day and simply sat on the bed's edge with a heavy creak.

"When did you get in?" Sparrow asked, abandoning pretenses and sitting up to massage Brit's neck. "We'd been hoping to see you a few days ago. Did you have more trouble along the way?"

"No, none." Gwyn spun a small keg clear of its niche and straddled it like a stool. "The sowie was rather craftier than I'd expected, that's all. Took a while to corner it properly. Then I camped outside the brushberry fields last night and presented myself late this morning."

"Did you get in to see the Dracoon?" Brit glanced up quickly, but she gave a nod of unsurprised resignation when Gwyn shook her head. "Been some odd things to notice 'round here, Gwyn'l."

Gwyn leaned forward, elbows on knees, and waited a moment. But Brit wasn't prepared to do much talking yet. Gwyn tugged the gloves from her hands and reviewed her own observations for them. Remembering only too well her welcome at the City Gates, she ended on a droll note, "This is not the most hospitable of places. And it's also the largest city I've ever been in that hasn't got an active Traders' Guild Inn."

Sparrow lifted a brow at that anomaly. She and Brit had merely assumed it was part of the Dracoon's grounds, a rather typical arrangement in outlying cities.

"So I'm staying in the Palace proper, courtesy of some Steward's orders. They put me back near the stables—" Gwyn lifted a brow tauntingly. "Lovely view of manure and stench."

"*Mae n'Pour!* And they expect you to tolerate that insult?" Sparrow looked genuinely appalled.

"Oh, they were quite profuse in their apologies for the quarters. But it is Khirla's Feasts, you know. There were no announcements anticipating my arrival. They are so sorry. Very, very sorry! But there are simply no other accommodations to be had." Gwyn grinned outright then. "I rather like it, actually. Any further in, and I'd have the Fates' Jesting with me every time I tried to sneak out on my own. As it is, they've given me a window. Oh—it's a good handspan above most soldier's jumping ability, but I manage to let myself in and out as I please."

Brit snorted rudely. "Fine thing to give you, a back door they can see from a league off."

"Why what other kind should I request, *Soroe?*"

"And your horses?" Sparrow broke in. "Are they getting any better treatment?"

"I lodged them myself with a handler outside the city walls. The Steward's Swords didn't seem to take any offense at the idea. In fact, they were rather pleased not to have me snooping around their precious tack and gear. Apparently, there's some sort of armory in one of the barn halls."

"Aye," Brit nodded. She wasn't really dozing at all beneath Sparrow's gentle rubbing. "The regular guard has no access to the place. Certainly sounded peculiar to me."

"Thought I'd take some time to scout around there come the single moon," Sparrow added.

"Good." Gwyn frowned. "What have you found out about this Steward of theirs? Short of declaring myself an emergency emissary from the Royal Court, I'm not going to be able to get in to see either the Steward or the Dracoon until after the festival's over. And even then, it appears I'll have to pass the Steward's scrutiny before I rate the Dracoon's Audience!"

"That woman has lots of power," Sparrow muttered darkly.

"So it appears. Is it a woman?"

"Oh yes, most definitely." Brit sighed and gathered herself together.

Patting Sparrow's hand in absent thanks, she finally addressed Gwyn with what she had. "She's a most disturbing personage as far as the folks of this city are concerned. If the Dracoon is well-liked, it seems mostly due to the Steward's unpopularity, and to the fact that the Dracoon is seldom seen by any within the city itself. Seems she spends most of her time with the patrols, try-ing to fend off the Clan's raids. Her absence is supported by the local folk, but the Steward's presence is—well, let's say she's tolerated because of a very per-sonal fear."

"That makes little sense, Brit. When has a mere steward ever earned the public's animosity?"

"With enough time and effort, anyone can do it," Sparrow interjected softly. The bitterness was quite clear in her voice.

"This one's apparently not the usual sort of detail organizer in most dra-coons' employ." Brit shook her head in a puzzled manner. "It's not entirely explicable. But at some point this Steward was awarded ruling powers, proba-bly because Llinolae was so young when she inherited the Dracoon's position."

"Well, the old Dracoon Mha'del died in a hunting accident when Llinolae was—what? Only five or six tenmoons? Appointing an adult to rule as regent while she matured, wouldn't have been a bad idea."

"But they've continued the arrangement beyond any age tradition or ritual could have demanded. Llinolae is as old as you are, Gwyn. She should have taken over the legislative duties seasons ago. Instead, she appears to endorse the Steward's absolute authority in all administrative and judicial matters—she's limited her own activities to Clan issues."

"That's somewhat like the Royal Family's delegation of duties, isn't it?" Gwyn shrugged hesitantly, failing to see why this was making her Sisters sus-picious. "It works that our Crowned Rule oversees the courts and law-making, while the Prince coordinates the military efforts. Given the Clan's been mak-ing life so miserable in these parts for so long, why shouldn't the Dracoon's pri-orities be focused on them?"

"Because this Steward's priorities support excessive taxation and administ-ration by tyranny!" Brit bit back her temper. "Gwyn, did you know that the merchant tolls for bringing goods into Khirla proper is nearly four times that of Churv's own Traders' Guild? And as you so rightly noticed yourself, *Soroe* , there's not even a Guild's Inn to support here!"

"Healers are taxed too," Sparrow inserted quietly. "For their services and for a license to practice."

Gwyn drew a tight breath at that one. By the People's Book, neither tax nor tariff was ever to be levied against a practicing healer. Life was too precious to demand an exchange of material goods for healing services. Every healer in the realm accepted only what was offered by their patients—no one bartered for payment! And the Royal Family respected and supported this tradition by exempting the healers from taxation. How dare this Court openly demand what the Crowned and King themselves would not even suggest?"

"There's a law book here that supposedly supplements the People's Book," Brit continued. "It's endorsed by the Steward and seems to specifically revolve around her own edicts."

"Her? The Steward—not the Dracoon?"

"Well...," Brit considered that dutifully, then admitted, "the book is written by the Steward's Scribe and enforced by the Steward's Swords. Tax collection, arrests, and judicial appeals all fall under the jurisdiction of the Steward's Hand. Hearsay is that the Dracoon doesn't actually have time to scrutinize this Steward's doings, and so the folk believe she doesn't know how liberally the Steward has been abusing the authority. But the Dracoon is known to support the Steward as a general rule. I admit, it might not be so clear where one should be blamed versus the other. I suppose that it's possible the Dracoon approves of the Steward's measures. Perhaps their need for provisioning against the Clan is worse than we've imagined. Still...?"

Brit's skepticism trailed off into ominous silence as Gwyn frowned. An entirely irrational, emotional bias leapt to life within her, and Gwyn found herself furious at the very suggestion that this Llinolae might be some sort of a tyrant. She calmed herself slightly with the more logical argument; it was simply implausible that Bryana wouldn't have sensed something amiss. "Brit, M'Sormee found Llinolae to be of admirable character. That doesn't fit with someone approving of the measures you're describing in the Steward's Book. I mean, this sort of law-making doesn't sound indicative of anything admirable, does it?" Gwyn rubbed her hands together, the itchy suspicious feeling that had plagued the nape of her neck before the barn fire was now making her palms tingle uncomfortably. "So, I have a Dracoon I can't see for another four-possibly five days, and I have a Steward of questionable ethics politely interfering in my attempts to push any meeting forward. I have Steward's Swords trailing my whereabouts whenever possible, despite my covert exits through bedroom windows, and the evidence of my buntsow chase leads me to believe some of the Steward's elite are actually Clan folk."

"That would fit with what we've seen here," Brit agreed, not in the least startled to hear the latter bit of information.

Sparrow was not so accepting, however. "What do you mean Clan folk within the Steward's Swords?"

"Think about it." Brit ticked off the points on her fingers. "First, we've got an elite militia all heavily armed with dual sabers. Metal is expensive, especially this far from the Maltar mines; the only other, readily available source of the stuff is from the Clan's ancient machine wrecks. And they don't let anyone near those old stockpiles—not alive, at any rate. So who can get in *and out* with the metal from those stores? Clan folk.

"Second, the Swords are all men and thirdly, all bearded. What other organized militia do you know of—on this entire planet!—that separates the sexes? But the Clan folk would have to, if they were to infiltrate the Khirlan militia. Their women are generally too tall—unless they're going to pose as Amazons."

"Not a chance," Sparrow muttered.

"Therefore, they have to use men, or the genetic differences will be too blatant to hide."

"And the beards?" Sparrow pressed.

"To hide the sun browning!" Gwyn saw at once.

"Or the lack of emotional skin tones," Brit amended. "You notice? The entire lot of them always wear gloves."

"But what you're saying...?" Gwyn felt a knot close in her throat. "Brit, are you suggesting the *entire* corp of the Steward's Swords are Clan folk?!"

"No—" But the thought did stop the elder woman for a moment of serious reconsideration. "No, I wasn't...perhaps I should be."

"That's not viable." Sparrow rejected the idea as flatly preposterous. "I'll grant that maybe some of them are. I agree, it would be the perfect place to hide a spy or two...or even a half dozen! But not all of them! Brit, someone would have noticed that many strangers! Khirla isn't that big a district. I mean, three dozen or four? Just how many mysterious appearances of skilled sword fighters can there be, before things get suspicious? Especially considering how lousy they've all been against these Clan raiders! That in itself must be raising a nasty question here and there!"

"Aye," Brit nodded. "But someone high enough up to discourage the recruitment of women sword carriers and to establish a ruffian dress code of bearded chins is probably someone high enough up to dismiss or misdirect most awkward questions."

"Or to order the disappearance of the questioners," Gwyn allowed grimly. "There's another consideration too, Sparrow. The Changlings' Wars up north have been training and discharging a lot of good sword carriers for over a generation now. It wouldn't seem so unusual to anyone if a batch or two of those mustered out decided to come and join the Steward's Swords. Few would think it suspicious for those veterans to have different customs and decent sword steel."

"Which means there's more of the Steward's Swords you can't trust, than you can," Sparrow saw at last. She sighed shakily, stunned at the audacity of such an idea. If true, the odds against them just got despairingly bad.

"Now the City Guards...," Brit smiled, a feral little glint glowing in her eyes. "There's a crew that wears their loyalties plain to see. A fair half of them are women, less than half of the rest espouse to beards."

"So whoever isn't imitating the infamous Steward's Swords may have dissenting opinions with them?" Sparrow nodded. "That sergeant we keep hearing about, the one I run into when I follow those Guards back to roost? He'd be suspicious of the Steward's blue cloaks."

"I'd wager, he would," Brit grinned.

"His name isn't Rutkins by any chance, is it?" Gwyn smiled at their startled looks. "I thought so. What do you know about him?"

"One of the old guard," Brit sketched a line across her left cheek and eye. "Got a wicked scar here and carries a long sword instead of a saber. Seems the City Guards are all armed with single blades, but his had the look of a master crafter."

"Saw him draw it only once," Sparrow supplied. "But it's got bright, clean edges with engravings along the length, just like the better crafters of the pre-war smithing."

"He seems to have a good rein on a number of the youngsters in the Guard," Brit went on. "Mostly among the young women—and that would fit. If the elite is becoming all male, there's probably a growing prejudice against promoting the women. But Rutkins has also got a contingent of older swords. They're made up of both men and women."

"Perhaps those of older loyalties?" Gwyn's brow lifted at that interesting prospect. "He said, he used to be old Mha'del's Captain of Guard."

"Very possible," Brit mused. "In any event, his people have an uncanny knack of disappearing into crowds with those plain ruddy colors of theirs—as opposed to those velvety blue things of the Steward's Swords. And he seems to use that talent of theirs pretty frequently."

At Brit's nod, Sparrow picked up the story. "Every time I've taken to trailing a pair of the Steward's Swords, I've found them returning directly to the Palace—or I've found at least one of these Rutkins' favored Guards following the Steward's Swords as well. I don't think they've spotted me yet." Sparrow grinned somewhat proudly. "Without my troubadour colors, I don't stand out much at all. Anyway, the Swords seem to bring trouble when there gets to be more than three or four of them in the same place—it's about then that Rutkins' people have a way of showing up. They rather auspiciously appear at just the right moment to prevent the local folk from getting hauled off or sliced up."

"There seems to be a very interesting, but uneasy truce between the two factions," Brit mused. "They draw tacit lines in fair tents or commons' rooms. Sometimes the blue cloaks will get all surly and belligerent. Then the City Guards back down."

"But somehow..." Sparrow drawled with a hint of malicious delight, "the Guards seem to get the last word. They're polite and duly subordinate to a fault, just not particularly believable."

"Leave agreeably, but make sure the bad taste lingers behind, ehh?" Gwyn couldn't help smiling herself. That tactic certainly seemed to fit the style of the man she'd met so briefly today. Then abruptly, Gwyn found herself shifting thoughts, "There's something else to remember."

Both Sparrow and Brit looked up expectantly.

"This is Khirlan. The Steward's Swords may purposely try to resemble the Clan members—it would make them more effective infiltrating the Clan's Plateau, wouldn't it? And yet by sheer looks, they wouldn't be well-liked by many of the local folk at all."

Brit pursed her lips sullenly, but she had to admit the plausibility of that idea. "Recruit the best fighters with the most suspicious backgrounds—the mixed parental heritage of Clan and Ramains' folk is usually hard to live with in these parts. Yet create a separate corp with an honor code of its own and you'd certainly have something to bind them together. You're right too—it would keep them aloof from the City Guards. And children with at least one parent from the Clan might have access to knowledge—verbal descriptions or...or some information about the Clan's Plateau. That could be an aid to the Dracoon."

"Their mixed blood might bind them not just to each other, but to the Dracoon as well," Sparrow murmured, glancing at each woman in turn. "She has that same mixed heritage, remember. Might explain why they'd follow her—even against the fire weapons."

"It would make them vulnerable to Clan spies both inside the city and out." Gwyn ground her teeth in muted frustration. The pieces were insistent. "But there's got to be someone close to the Dracoon—or to the Steward—someone working against Khirlan in aiding the Clan. Everything suggests

108

they're part of the Steward's own corp. I wonder—did you just say this Steward's Book was written by the Steward's Scribes?"

Sparrow and Brit nodded.

"Who wants to wager that at least one of those scribes also has access to what's written and sealed into the Dracoon's reports?"

"No wagering about it," Brit scoffed the nonsense aside. "It'd be more odd, if they didn't."

"I see...," Sparrow began slowly. "Hand-writing can be forged with enough practice. It's tampering with the seals they'd have trouble disguising from Churv's people. But these scribes would be the ones to dip the scrolls and date the shell varnish. They'd be able to alter the reports any way they'd like, *before* sealing them and sending them on to Churv."

"Obviously," Brit shifted tiredly on the bed's edge, "this Dracoon's Court is sorely broken in loyalties. Where precisely the lines of deceit are drawn though? Your guess is as good as mine."

"Only the Dracoon knows that!" Gwyn grieved, in exasperation.

"But if she knew, would we be here?" Sparrow asked pointedly.

"I meant she can say which of her militia are slow in obeying orders or which survived a Clan's ambush once too often and in suspiciously good health. At least," Gwyn sighed, "I hope she can—or this will never begin to unravel without hurting the innocent!"

"There's one thing more you should know." Brit met Gwyn's gaze steadily. "Llinolae's Palace was crafted not just from stone, but from bedrock."

"Mae n'Pour !"

"Most of the city walls and central buildings are made from it too."

"Suddenly the lack of interest the Council has shown in Llinolae becomes very reasonable," Gwyn saw. "Amarin barely stir through most rock and less still in stuff that's never even been marred by fossils! I doubt the Council Seers can ever decipher anything closeted away like that."

"I know they can't!" Brit spat.

"It would also explain why she's arranged the governing duties to frequently take her out of the city."

"Now *that*—I hadn't thought of," Brit granted, in grudging surprise. "Accepting you're right, Gwyn, what else could it tell us about her?"

"That she's been trained by someone extraordinary!" Sparrow exclaimed promptly. "Not only is her Blue Sight powerful enough to reach across the stars to the home world, but she obviously has an extra trick or two for dealing with stone!"

"I wonder...," Brit mused, "how much exposure to others' amarin is needed, before mere rock begins to—"

"More likely," Gwyn interrupted, suddenly realizing, "it wasn't Llinolae's mentor whose instructions were so extraordinary, but her own interpretation of those lessons *because* of the environment!"

"And so the bedrock suddenly became a friend for her, instead of foe!" Brit gasped. Sparrow looked at them both in confusion, not following their logic at all this time. "Don't you see? The rock would conceal her Gift from the courtiers—give her a safe place to experiment in. When she was her very youngest, it probably insulated others from the usual accidents and illusionary

109

tricks that flag the Blue Sight's presence. As she grew, it would have given her hiding places—practice spaces to try new skills, make mistakes without others discovering her abilities! And as for the Palace itself—well it is a palace! It's been home for generations of dracoons and friends. It's not like some claustrophobic tomb that could stifle her Sight and suffocate her breath! The accumulated amarin of all those ages, in the fixtures and furnitures—in the cloth and wood and the general clutter of sheer living! Those would always be present to reassure her through her Sight."

"Dear Mother!" Sparrow breathed in pure astonishment. "No Blue Sight has ever had freedom such as that. There's no telling what she's become capable of!"

"Aye, but more," Brit rejoined eagerly. "Those stone walls would still dampen the clamoring amarin of every one—of every living thing! The incessant distractions would be muted."

"Like the Seers' Baths at the Council's Keep?" Sparrow ventured. "A sort of retreat?"

"Precisely," Brit grinned.

"It also might give her the time and ability to develop other skills," Gwyn mused with a crooked grin. "Such as strategy and warfare, perhaps?"

"Or diplomacy?" The old healer nodded in satisfaction. "The public persona she's developed is amazing, Gwyn. She's got the district's people solidly behind her every effort. Despite the Steward's liberties, despite the Clan's terrorizing raids, despite their fire weapons—despite it all, the folk believe in her! In Llinolae, Heir of Mha'del and annointed Dracoon of Khirlan! They believe she will find their peace for them. Some how...some way, they believe she'll do it."

"From sheer charisma?" Sparrow was awed, barely comprehending just how impressive a Blue Sight projecting such personal confidence might seem.

"It may be more than that," Gwyn amended. "We don't know the extent of her powers or skills."

"Aye." A tantalizing shiver ran down Brit's spine. "Through their Seers, the Council has formed Firecaps, settled earthquakes, foreseen and forestalled disasters."

"She isn't a Seer," Sparrow murmured.

"No," Gwyn acknowledged. "But she has a strong Gift and an even stronger personal commitment to serve her people. We don't know what her limitations are—or aren't."

With a speculative squint, Brit added, "Might be that her enemies literally begin to quake at the mere sight of her."

"Or that they should?" Gwyn quipped. The glance she exchanged with Brit belied their humor, however. Gwyn sighed then, returning to priorities with a shake of her head. "I need to get in to see her. There has to be a way to weave through all the protocol and past that damned Steward to meet her! Too much can happen in four or five days. I've got to get to her sooner!"

"So ride in the races, day after tomorrow." Brit and Gwyn turned to Sparrow in puzzlement at her abrupt change of subject. "I'm serious. Take Cinder in and win the stupid race. The winner is awarded the City Crest for a tenmoon and the plaque is presented personally by—who? The Dracoon!"

Gwyn looked suspicious. Brit began to smile and tried to rub the thing from her face, but it stubbornly came back as a chuckle. Sparrow shrugged matter-of-factly, directing Gwyn back to her shadowmate. And the *Niachero* found a grin of her own.

"It couldn't be that simple…could it?"

Brit opened her palms with a hearty laugh.

"Marshals!" Sparrow scoffed, folding her arms and shaking her head at them as if they were barely two seasons old. "The lot of you are impossible! Too much imagination and…"

"Not enough common sense!" Brit finished, still laughing. "She has that right sometimes, you know?"

"Aye!" Gwyn assented whole-heartedly. "She certainly does."

Chapter Twelve

he next day Gwyn spent a quiet morning secluded in her Palace room, seemingly to recover from a night of carousing—which was normal enough for any Feast visitor. She made her brief, obligatory appearance at the mid-day meal of officers and honored guests; she noted nearly everyone there was blue-cloaked. The few merchants who weren't, however, avoided her like a plague carrier.

Finding that Brit's summation was true didn't make her feel much better; there weren't any women among the Swords. There were no women among the merchants either, at least none in attendance. Uneasily, Gwyn realized she'd never been in a room this crowded and yet peopled entirely by men.

Somehow she didn't think she was likely to forget the experience. It had not been pleasant.

The wary sense of tension from the dining hall continued to follow her as she left for the fairs. This time Gwyn exited by way of the usual corridors instead of her window; predictable patterns could get one hurt.

She didn't like her new phantom at all, however. She knew the tingling brush along the nape of her neck had nothing to do with the fly-away bits of her short braid, and it had everything to do with that peripheral shadow in her vision. Yet try as she might, Gwyn couldn't get a clear view of the man. She proceeded cautiously through the rest of the day. In some ways she was relieved to know her opponent was so obviously skilled. At least now she wouldn't underestimate him—or the perversity of the Fates! It had been her misfortune in the past to run headlong into bungling pursuers, simply because ignorance was so damned unpredictable.

Gwyn found she was taking an uneasy comfort from the knives in her vambraces. Still—when she found her instincts again and again prompting her to unsheath her sword, she abandoned all pretense of casual enjoyment of the Feasts. She folded her cloak back over her left shoulder to free her sword arm and openly began to avoid the narrower streets.

It seemed to her that this watcher who trailed her exuded a distaste that bordered upon hate. It was then she suddenly realized the rules had been altered in this game. Sometime during her absence last night, she had graduated from the lowly position of a suspicious visitor to the dangerous status of an outright threat. She didn't like that, but she'd be a fool to ignore her impressions, and she knew it.

The other unsettling fact, which finally registered as she worked her way through the crowds, was the people's lack of caution in dealing with her. With her sword near drawn and teeth near bared, the folk should have been much more anxious when she approached their booths. But the vendors' eagerness to serve her seemed no different from their attentions to others.

Gwyn felt her skin darken anxiously. No doubt, she could be abducted before a dozen witnesses here, and few would give it any notice.

But as she studied the townsfolk more closely, Gwyn began to see they weren't quite so unprepared for trouble as one might imagine. The city dwellers were the most heavily armed. There were stout poles, decorative pins that could double as stiletto knives, glass daggers and dirks on each belt—the list was endless. The ingenious arrangements spoke of long practice, and Gwyn cracked a wry grin; she doubted the knives on her own wrists went unnoticed.

The visiting crowd was less well-armed, but after some consideration Gwyn decided that they were better defended than her first glance had assessed. Again carving tools, shepherding poles, and belt knives were more common than not. And very few of the strangers wandered alone within these city walls. Pairs were infrequent as well. It appeared that small groups of four and five were judged to be safer.

Everything she saw, underlined all that Brit and Sparrow had said of the Steward's rule—these people lived with a constant fear. And it didn't come from the threats beyond their city walls.

Gwyn scowled and headed for the outer encampments. She suddenly wanted more of the evening air than the streets could offer.

On the way, she tried a few meandering tricks without much success at losing her watcher. She hadn't expected to really. She had rather hoped to seem as if she were merely following cautious habits. Her sense was that there was still only one fellow, and she didn't want him tempted by any grandiose illusions into trying something stupid in an alley.

Towards her goal of actually meeting with the Dracoon, Gwyn made a careful round of inspection in the livestock pens. She saw nothing which seemed remotely capable of defeating Cinder in a flat-out race. But as Gwyn went along to find her own mares, she was still uncertain of the race's outcome. The quality of her horses was blatantly evident to her—as it would be to others. That made it very likely the real challenge would come in the form of sabotage...especially if the Steward's Swords were wary of her meeting their Dracoon.

I'm getting in over my head, Gwyn realized begrudgingly.

She had nothing concrete to tell the Royal Family, yet she was already a marked target. Brit and Sparrow were not going to find answers as quickly as she needed them. That left her two immediate options—retreat to Churv with phantom stories or find help closer in.

"Evenin' to you, Marshal."

Gwyn paused in her tracks as a young man rose from his shadowy seat among the saddle bins. He palmed a short staff with a wicked hook and point at its end, stepping into the light respectfully so that she could identify him.

"Evening, Tad." Gwyn smiled encouragingly. It was only the livery boy standing his duty. After an extensive perusal of the animal pens, Gwyn had chosen this one for its stable hands' competency as well as for its security. From the regular posting of sentries to the rental of saddle bins for gear, Gwyn had been impressed. The posted watchers didn't drink, the bins were secured with combination puzzle locks, and the prices were high but not too high given their services. It was also, Gwyn had discovered, owned by none other than the Min Roan, Rutkins' friend. And right now, Gwyn thought, that might be something to gamble on. "Is the Min around?"

The youth nodded once, slow and solemn-like. He pointed to the open tent set beyond the far end of the corral pens. "The orange lantern's hung out, so she's still hearing business."

"My thanks to you." She half-turned to leave, but hesitated.

"Something more I can do, Marshal?"

"No," she smiled again and moved on, deciding not to risk his safety by involving him directly. He seemed just a little over-eager, the type who might be more apt to challenge a suspicious character by himself, instead of slipping off to report and get help. And it was too quiet out here on the brushberry edges—no one would hear if he simply called for help. She didn't want him hurt.

The stout woman who was bent over the ledgers looked up quick, frowning at the rustle of straw and step. As Gwyn moved into the lantern glow, the Min Roan relaxed and offered a grin with a wave to the vacant seat across the table from her.

"Thank you, but I won't take much of your time." Gwyn's voice was as neutral as her expression was bland. She leaned slightly against the tent pole, effectively screening out the rest of the world from their conversation.

"There were some Steward's Swords here earlier," Min Roan took the initiative before Gwyn could continue. "Showed a keen interest in your three bays. I told 'em you weren't in the sellin' market. Kept two of my hands grooming and mucking out close by. I'll take an oath that the blue cloaks didn't get any chance to tamper with either the feed or water. But I put extra eyes out watching tonight, just in case."

Satisfied, Gwyn could think of nothing more she'd have wanted. It was certainly more than she'd expected. "I'm grateful, Min. And...I have another favor to ask."

The woman nodded, her grey eyes narrowing attentively.

"Tell Rutkins, I'll be in the Broken Chalice after the midnight moon's rising."

"He'll hear."

"Thanks." Gwyn dug a few coins from her hip pouch and gently laid them on the table. At the gathering sternness in the matron's face, she explained, "For your stable hands on extra watch. Something special at tomorrow's midday perhaps?"

A wide grin slowly appeared. Min Roan decided that Rutkins had done well in supporting this one. "I'll see to it, Marshal. Count on it."

"Good." Gwyn went to visit her mares. That watcher was still out there, though. Despite the dry straw and animal musks, she swore she could smell him!

Calypso neighed a cheerful greeting, and Gwyn tucked her gloves away in her belt, before reaching out to stroke that silky, black muzzle. Nia and Cinder trotted near, determined not to be outdone or left out. They brought a soft laugh from Gwyn as she climbed through the split rails and found herself surrounded by those warm, massive bodies. For the first time in hours, she felt something akin to *safe* , and she let them nudge her over towards the watering trough.

"You selfish rascals!" Gwyn chided, seeing their ruse for a bit of fresher water. But she complied at the pump before sitting down on its broad wooden edge. The bays slurped greedily on either side of her, pausing now and again to push a nose into her chest or wuffle wetly through her hair.

"I'm going to be a slobbering mess by the time you're all done with me!" Her tone was more affectionate than protesting, however, and after a few moments her mares settled down, staying near yet dozing. All except for Cinder who grunted quite contentedly, head low as Gwyn scratched the black star on her forehead. Cinder butted Gwyn gently in the stomach, hoping for some attention to her ears, but a sudden 'bang' shied her back.

"It's only my sword, silly." Gwyn pulled it from the sheath and irreverently planted it blade down in the dirt between her feet. "You've seen it before—oh, what? Going to be a skitterish, little pripper anyway, ehh?" But Gwyn found her mood had lightened considerably. She sighed and folded her hands atop her sword's hilt, eyes smiling as she watched the big bay dance away another few steps.

She wondered suddenly at the warmth beneath her fingertips. Her throat tightened as she did a quick assessment of the murky calm around her. "Too calm," a voice inside her warned—yet in that instant she wasn't certain if she was overhearing Llinolae's mind or if it was her own instincts of cautions. Abruptly, it became urgent to know which.

"My friends!" The mares heads snapped up, ears flicking towards her at that low tone of command, "*cheroa'!*"

The three immediately crowded around her, alert and facing outwards in protective stances. Until Gwyn countermanded her order, the mares would stand ready to fight. Anyone or anything foolish enough to try approaching Gwyn would have to get past those hooves and teeth first.

Gwyn steadied herself with a breath. Then eyes closing, she slid her grasp down over the lifestone in that sword grip, and for the first time, she consciously sought Llinolae's awareness.

Shock reverberated through her whole body. Somewhere another woman screamed in frightened protest. Time seemed to slow as the knees beneath her began to buckle. Beyond the fire ring, silver flashed. The screaming stopped. A blue cloak moved away, and there in the firelight she suddenly saw the dead bodies of two women. The cook...why? And...*no!* She was so young—only an apprentice scribe!

Then the ground jarred as her knees hit. Blackness shrank her vision inward—and everything went black.

Gwyn came back to herself with a gasp and a violent start—that utter darkness had almost taken her; it groped for her still. She gulped in the humid air and blinked, forcing her eyes to see and her body to obey. Her hand jerked free from the lifestone, and she was left staring at the sword in astonishment.

The Dracoon's scouting party had been taken! What was she even doing so far away from the city with the Feast in progress?

Stupid questions, irrelevant tangents! *Niachero*—think for yourself! Llinolae had gone after the Clan raiders—she'd seen that in the last vision, remember? Aye, they'd gone somewhere east. And now there'd been at least one blue cloak in her patrol who had betrayed her...who had killed others in the camp. So presume the worst. No, no—not the worst. That had been some sort of blow to the head, not a sword severing. Llinolae was alive for some purpose—for a Clan purpose.

Then find out where in Fates' Cellars they were taking her—*and get her back!*

* * *

The midnight moon was quarter full and shining white as it lifted over the eastern walls into a starry sky of indigo. The early moon was well above the Palace towers, and the bright twilight of Aggar's night had only begun to dim because of the growing cloud cover. The elder farmers had taken wagers from the city folk against the odds of rains, and Gwyn tended to believe the hoe farmers. Humid as it was, there was no 'feel' of that gathering power which usually preceded the thunderstorms she'd known. The only gathering forces she was aware of were human—though the charged tensions swirling in this empty street behind the Palace were nearly tangible enough to spit lightning themselves.

She stepped into the darkness beneath the arches of the portico and disappeared. Without a sound, she drew her sword. The humidity muffled her steps as she hurried, changing directions and slipping in behind a stone column. The clouds passing above thickened the shadows. She welcomed the shroud provided by each and steadied her breathing. Then with sword readied, its silver pressed against her chest and hidden by the fold of her cloak, she waited—listening, scenting, *sensing* the world around her as her packmates had taught her.

The night rustled with the faint creak of a shutter, with the distant scratch of a scavenging pripper in some alley. Sluggish breezes stirred, bringing the dusky scent of horses and stables. And still she strained to listen, her palms growing damp within her leather gloves.

A foot scuffled.

Her head jerked right. The sound had come from deeper in the recesses of those shadows behind her, no longer from the open street. There was a ring of blade against scabbard, and a muffled grunt, before the dull thud of a heavy collapse reached her.

Gwyn's cloak shrugged aside without a sound. She licked her lips, flexing her fingers in her two-handed grip. *Mae n'Pour!* Patience now.

A cautious tread of boots approached.

She swung her blade. Fires of orange and blue sizzled along its length. Steel clattered as the other's sword halved and fell.

"Yielding!" Hands spread wide, palms open.

Her blade's point froze a breath from Rutkins' stubbly chin. Gwyn scowled and backed away some, sword still leveled and legs still braced in a fighting stance. "Explain yourself."

"Small favors from the Mother," he breathed in quiet thanks. The low tone of his voice barely seemed to stir the heavy air. But his eyes shifted respectfully between her gaze and her blade. "I received a message to meet you at the commons of the Broken Chalice. I was on my way 'cross city to do so, when a few of my—ahh, youngsters?" At her nod, he continued. "Brought me word that this fellow...," Rutkins pointed behind him, taking great care not to lower his hands any, "...was on the prowl. He's a specialist. Jefrez by name. I figured he was probably going to lead me to you shortly enough, seeing as the Swords only send him on special assignments."

116

"Such as?"

"He makes people disappear—permanently."

Gwyn had suspected as much. She relaxed and stepped down, sheathing her blade with an efficiency that wasn't lost on Rutkins. The sergeant flexed his hands a bit and took a deep breath in obvious relief. She watched him a moment, then toed the corner of the broken sword lying between them. "Next time, announce yourself better."

"Fates' Cellars, Marshal!" He bent to retrieve his sword pieces. "You didn't even seem to know you were being followed. How was I to assume you were planning your own ambush?" He frowned at his shattered blade pieces. The steel was riddled with fissures like a cracked eggshell. "Do you have any idea how many Steward's Swords have tried their fancy sabers against this ratty, ole piece? Yet one utterly insane Amazon...?" He clucked his tongue mournfully as he shook his head, slipping the useless pieces back into his scabbard. "I should have left you with those irate, young gate Guards. You'd have sliced them to ribbons but at least you'd have been denied city entrance. At this rate, you're going to be the death of me."

Gwyn stifled a sudden spurt of laughter and followed as he motioned them to move on. This was not a good place to linger.

"You're headin' to the stables?" He nodded at the dim outline of the stone barns as they rounded a corner. They ducked quickly into the alcove of a doorway as they caught sight of several grooms; the gambling party was settled comfortably beneath a barn lantern with stick-and-dice as well as a goodly supply of brushberry wine.

"It's still awfully quiet around here," Gwyn observed in concern. "Aside from you and that assassin, I haven't seen any folks tending stables or taking out the kitchen trash—no one's doing anything in the ordinary."

"It's Feast Days. Everyone's out having a good time. Everyone except us, that is." At Gwyn's silent rebuke, Rutkins grinned a twisted grin and challenged, "What'd you do, Marshal? To get into the Steward's good graces so quick, I mean."

"I'm not certain."

"Nothing is 'round here."

"But I think I just arrived at an awkward moment. Your Dracoon isn't in Khirla, you know."

He gave Gwyn an assessing once-over and apparently decided she hadn't lost her mind completely. "Well, I already said it, nothing's too certain around here. Any idea where she is?"

"She rode east about six days back. As of tonight, however, the Clan has her."

A gruff grunt answered that. "She's not dead? Just tied up and out of the way? Steward'll be in sweet distress over that one, I wager. All the power, all the authority, and no one to answer to 'til the Crowned starts getting suspicious. By that time, the tyrant'll be so entrenched here it'll take the Clan's own fire weapons to burn her out."

He leaned a shoulder against the stone with a frustrated bump. His arms folded to his bemused expression. "Or are you going to prevent all this by your lonely self?"

"It wouldn't be my first choice," Gwyn admitted.

"What? Changing the Steward's plans or doing it alone?"

"Doing it alone." She smiled at him, sweet with sarcasm as she folded her own arms in a mocking imitation. "Need I remind you that most of the Royal Marshals only organize and direct the local efforts? It's why we seldom need to travel in numbers. We're not soldiers in the usual sense."

"Aye." Amusement twisted his gristly features. "You just keep old reprobates in their places by cleaving our blades in two, hmm?"

She pursed her lips to hide a grin.

"So—all right," the sergeant relented. "Here I am. Your local garrison. Sorry we're a bit thin in the ranks at the moment, but then you weren't expecting much help anyway. Organize away."

Gwyn scowled at him without humor.

"I'm serious, Marshal. I may not be much to look at, but I may be of help yet. I do know this city like the knots in my boot laces. And I can raise a fair number of loyal sword carriers before dawn, if needs be."

An idea began to take shape for her. Gwyn glanced across at the gambling grooms. "Do you know where the Dracoon's tack is usually kept?"

"I do." He straightened from his lackadaisical pose. "Most of it probably went with her when she rode out, though."

"There aren't any ceremonial pieces or such?"

He shook his head. "She seldom used them. Most pro'ble they're sitting in the tailor's bower, waiting on some fancy new stitching."

Damn! She tried again. "Then the Palace?"

"Do I know it well? I was Mha'del's Captain for nearly ten seasons, Marshal. I know the private chambers of the old Dracoon himself! And I know the serving staff; I can get you in nearly anywhere for any time—and unseen."

"Do you know Llinolae's suite?"

"Aye." He looked puzzled and a thumb jabbed above them. "Top of this very tower, no less. Haven't been there in seasons. She's pretty reclusive by nature, even with the Swords."

Gwyn gazed upwards in confusion. A Blue Sight in such a narrow tower of stone? Uhh! She shuddered. Kimarie or Bryana would have fled; Selena had once asserted that being left in a stone room was the equivalent of being buried alive for a Blue Sight. But she needed to remember that Llinolae wasn't like any other Blue Sight she'd known.

Her fingers curled, the skin on her palm reminding her of the lifestone's heat in her sword's hilt. No—she had quite tangible proof that Llinolae was not like other Blue Sights.

* * *

Once above in Llinolae's chamber, however, her qualms still didn't slacken. And try as she might, Gwyn couldn't quite shake her unease. She couldn't tell if her anxiety was the lingering aftereffects of being followed all day or if it grew from some new threat's approach?

Or maybe—she thought with a wry bit of humor—*M'Sormee* had instilled her with a rock phobia!

Llinolae's room was round with thick, grey walls of stones. The bedroom roughly encompassed the whole of the tower's top, save for the platform and the stairs used to gain entrance. Even the encircling row of arched windows were only framed in honeywood, their shutters were made of thin slats of stone.

"Is there just the one way up?" Gwyn asked in a whisper.

"Aye." Rutkins hovered by the door, peering cautiously down into the dark stairwell.

The furniture and shelves seemed ancient and Gwyn approved; those well worn, but oiled woods always carried strong impressions of past owners and life energies. Gwyn knew those amarin would have been an immense comfort to any Blue Sight, even to one housed here.

She frowned faintly at the stiffness beneath her boots. With a toe she pushed the dilapidated edges of the overlapping carpets aside. Dear Goddess! Even the floor was stone. Llinolae was a different one.

"What're you searching for?" Rutkins pressed.

Gwyn pulled herself back to their task. "Something that would carry her scent well."

"You work with an eitteh or a sandwolf?"

"I do—a pair of sandwolves." Amused, Gwyn smiled. A certain degree of awe had crept into that gruff, old voice. "They've been combing the woods around Khirla since my arrival."

Rutkins responded with a disappointed sigh, regretting he wouldn't be meeting her packmates. Gwyn sympathized, it would have been a rare chance for him. Since she came to Khirlan, she'd neither seen nor heard of pairing between humans, sandwolves—or eitteh!

Rutkins suddenly flattened himself against the wall. Gwyn dropped to a crouch beside a chest.

The faint 'crack' in the stairwell below faded back to silence. They looked to one another, then the sergeant pulled a long knife from his belt. Its black glass gleamed wickedly even in this dim light; the blade must have been two handspans in length.

"I'll see to it."

She nodded, and he went to investigate.

Gwyn forced her attention back to the room. Clothing would be the best, she knew, but the linens and leathers hanging in the wardrobe were clean—too clean. Apparently, the Palace laundry took its duty very seriously. She pushed aside a ceremonial cape, but it caught something on the cabinet's floor. Gwyn noticed the shoe rack and bent. With a triumphant pounce, she snatched up a pair of indoor slippers that had been dropped to the side. Soft and pliant, thickly padded and worn to restitching in places; these favored pieces were used so often that stacking them neatly in the rack was a waste of time.

They were perfect!

A whisper of sound drew her around sharply. Then blackness and silence welled up from the depths of the open doorway. Her packmates' rule to mistrust all urged caution. Abruptly she darted across the room into the shadowy lines beside the entrance. Again, a hint of noise—a brush of cloth against cloth perhaps? Or a soft soled boot gently placed upon a stone step?

With the slippers tucked into her jerkin and with her sword drawn in measured quiet, Gwyn slipped out into the blackness. Of one thing she was certain, it was not Rutkins. The sergeant was clever enough not to risk her attack twice in one evening. But that knowledge only chilled her, because whoever hunted her now must have already dealt with him.

She descended slowly, eyes straining for shadows against shadows—ears clinging to wisps of nothing-sounds. Her breath grew shallow. Her step became so deliberate that the hard leather soles of her boots made no noise at all.

A movement without form surprised her—she swung. Metal clashed against metal. Her opponent faltered. Gwyn paused at a rattle, fearing something had been tossed on the stairs to threaten her footing. Again the strange sound came.

Then suddenly the air exploded in red fury. Her sword came up broadside, instinctively protecting her eyes as the fireball struck. Her blade resounded with the ear-deafening crack of a thunderbolt! But the lifestone in the hilt held the steel intact—the force reflected back to its source!

A scream pierced the bright smoke. Gwyn jumped forward, sword slashing through the fiery cloud as the man dropped his burning weapon. His gurgled half-cry went silent. Gwyn stumbled back to the far wall, her stomach churning at the bloodied, charred mess before her.

Not now!—she warned herself desperately. But her eyes stared, held by the disfigured, nearly inhuman remains. This was no time to be sick!

Mae n'Pour! She suddenly recognized that heap of molten steel which still sputtered and crackled with flame. It was another fire weapon! What was a Steward's Sword doing with a Clan's fire weapon in the Palace itself?

A groan from below pulled her up abruptly.

Rutkins! Blessings and small favors, was he still alive? She dashed down into the darkness to find out.

Chapter Thirteen

Brit!" The desperate whisper woke Sparrow instantly. She was armed with knives and pitching herself through the bench panel before her beloved was barely conscious.

She crawled from beneath the driver's seat over the foot boards and quickly rolled across the rough ground into the cloaking darkness of the neighboring wagon. She heard Brit's faint mumble of "coming," but the sleepy tone didn't deceive her. Sparrow knew her shadowmate was playing for time and when Brit did open the door, it would be with the flint-tipped whip near at hand.

She peered at the huddled shapes of their waiting visitors. There were two of them, both tall. One was nearly carrying the other and that other was seriously in need of a healer's attentions, if the slumped silhouette was anything to go by. A sliver of moons' light crept free from the overcast, and the breath caught in her throat as she glimpsed the white stone ring on the hand supporting the wounded one.

"*Niachero!*" Sparrow hissed, rushing forward and sheathing her knives as she went. Gwyn started at her sudden appearance, before offering a weary smile of reassurance. Sparrow pushed close to take some of the man's weight, and then Brit's hands came to guide them into the sanctuary of the wagon.

"*Sae!*" Gwyn bid them quiet even inside, sending an anxious glance to Sparrow.

She nodded and slipped back out to check for followers. When Sparrow returned in a few moments, she found Brit tending a nasty knife wound in the man's side. Pictures of past wounds crowded into her mind's eye with all the disturbing details her visual memory never failed to provide. She snatched a quick breath and thanked the Goddess that at least it wasn't Brit who was injured this time. She felt herself grow grim with calm resignation as she recognized the fellow's scarred face—this was the City Guard's sergeant. She noted the bruise on his forehead. It hosted an equally wicked looking cut, and she didn't wonder that he had needed help to reach them.

"*Nehna?*" Gwyn asked quietly, coming to stand at Sparrow's elbow.

"No one," Sparrow murmured. The man made a strangled noise of pain, and Sparrow felt her stomach clench a little. She shook the tension from her body with a quick, purposeful shudder and turned to the *Niachero*. "You trust him?"

Gwyn nodded, a stern set to her darkly browned features. Then abruptly she announced, "I need to leave Khirla—tonight. I 'saw' Llinolae again. The Clan's got her. Her patrol was betrayed by a Steward's Sword while one of them back here tried to assassinate me."

"I'm liking these blue cloaks less and less," Brit grunted, her hands still busy with the antiseptic and bandages.

"Another did this to him and made a second attempt for me."

Sparrow drew back half a step, startled by the silent snarl that suddenly curled across the *Niachero's* lips.

"He was carrying a fire weapon."

Brit only grunted again. Sparrow blinked, shaken.

"My wager is that the armory in the stable halls—the one so inaccessible to the regular guard?—is a stockpile of more."

This time, Brit didn't even bother to grunt. Nothing about this venture was going to surprise her shadowmate anymore, Sparrow realized. Somehow that made her own fears easier to deal with. She concentrated, then looked to Gwyn. "The single moon comes in five days. If I can get into the armory and if I do find there are more of the fire weapons, should I do something about it?"

"What if these folk are using those weapons against the Clan itself?" Brit prompted. "Ever think of that?"

"We haven't yet," Rutkins suddenly inserted. He swallowed a gasp as Brit turned her attentions to his head wound.

"Possession and use are forbidden by both Ramains' Law and Council Request," Gwyn rejoined flatly. "Even our Ring of *dey Sorormin* prohibits the use of such machines. There is no excuse for the Steward to differ. This district still answers to King and Crowned!"

Sparrow agreed with that completely. "So I'll see if I can't take something in to do a little damage."

"I've got a dry acid compound," Brit mused, almost in an absent-minded fashion as she clipped thread from the last stitch in Rutkins' head. "Could create a few fireworks with those maybe?"

"Do it." Gwyn turned and studied the sergeant for a very long moment as Sparrow watched in puzzlement. There was caution and indecision in that scrutiny, and then she understood as Gwyn asked gently, "Rutkins, can you keep your thinking clear for a bit yet?"

"Aye," he swallowed thickly, sitting up a little straighter with help from Brit.

Sparrow spun, drawing a mug of water from the pitcher for him. Brit sent her a brief smile of gratitude and drew a blanket around the sergeant's clammy shoulders. His hands shook as he tried a sip.

"Make it quick, Gwyn'l. He's close to shock. I don't know how long he'll stay coherent."

He probably wasn't now, Sparrow fretted. Despite Brit's ministrations, his skin was as black as stained mahogany and the bruises of exhaustion beneath his eyes were as purple as the bump around his stitches.

Gwyn apparently saw the same. She squatted down on the floor in front of him. "Can you tell me, has anyone taken notice of these two? Are they going to be endangered if I leave them in Khirla?"

"No." He swayed as his words slurred, but he managed to refocus his gaze on her. "The blue coats haven't shown any interest in any tinker-trades, an' I'll keep 'em safe. My youngsters'll watch out for 'em…personal favor to me."

If you stay around long enough to tell them, Sparrow thought anxiously.

"He'll be all right," Brit returned softly as Gwyn glanced at her with that same tacit question.

"Been worse," Rutkins found a twisted, half-grin to reassure them all. "Can prob'ly put it down to festival brawling. No one'll even notice."

Gwyn nodded slowly, then pressed, "Do you know anything more than I do, about why they were after me?"

"No...sorry."

"And Llinolae...?" Gwyn hesitated, clearly torn between revealing too much with her questioning and yet needing to ask. "Rutkins, can you tell me what she looks like? Is there anything—odd or striking about her?"

"Damn pretty for a mixed-blood." He winced at his attempt at humor. "Sorry, didn't mean that the way it sounded. She's a good sort, from what I know. Only thing really stands out 'bout her is those blue eyes from her mother. Rest is mostly what's usual in the half'n'halfs of hereabouts."

"She's got blue eyes?" Gwyn pressed urgently.

"Black hair'n'blue eyes. Pretty combination too. They tell me, it's not uncommon in the Clan folk—blue eyes I mean. An' her mother had 'em. Leastwise I never heard of Aggar-sort having eyes like that without the Sight. But she does."

Sparrow met Brit's solemn gaze over the top of Gwyn's head. Then the *Niachero* rose, and the three of them mutely agreed to hold the secret. Llinolae had reasons in hiding her talents for all these tenmoons, and it was certainly not their place to challenge that now. Given the intrigues of this night, it was probably one of the few advantages the Dracoon possessed in this struggle of Khirlan.

Gwyn reached a hand to the sergeant, squeezing his good shoulder in thanks. "Let them take care of you, all right?"

"'Til they kick me out," Rutkins agreed. He grimaced again and quickly aborted the nod as the pain in his head protested.

"Brit?" Gwyn glanced at her friend, remembering this man's injuries might not have been so bad if he'd been carrying his own sword. "Do you still carry those Black Falls blades below the floorboards?"

"Aye, " the Amazon nodded warily. The pieces in question were reserves she always carried for Amazon Marshals in need. They were priceless because they were forged by the best smith house in the Ramains and because they were made from the ancient alloys of *dey Sorormin's* home world as well as from Aggar's own metals. They were lighter, stronger and finer swords than any others crafted outside of Valley Bay.

"The sergeant has need of a new blade."

Brit weighed that for a moment, then she nodded. "He can have his choice. There's one in particular that should fit his reach well."

"Thank you, *Soroe*."

"Marshal—" Rutkins tried to protest through the hoarseness of his throat. But Gwyn silenced him with a gentle shake of her head. Their gaze met and held, then finally that scarred face winced in its half smile. Gwyn grinned right back at him.

"And where do you go now?" Brit reclaimed Gwyn's attention softly. "To Churv? Or to find this Llinolae?"

"They'll expect me to ride west for the capital, so I would prefer not to. And they can't know that I've realized she's not in Khirla or that she's been caught."

"You'll go east then, after her?" Sparrow guessed, knowing the answer before Gwyn spoke.

"I must. From what Rutkins tells me, this Steward will be ambivalent in paying any ransom. Llinolae won't last long in their hands, once they know there'll be no profit from it."

"East then," Brit agreed. Her grey eyes squinted as she considered the possibilities. "All right, we'll deal with the armory. Then as soon as it's safe, we'll follow you. There's a half-burned village sou'east of here—Diblum. It'd be a good venture for traders, and it lies on the route we'd take for the southern continent. We can disappear from there more easily than here."

"After that, how do we find you?" Sparrow pressed with sudden concern. "Gwyn, there's a lot of forest to get lost in, once we're off the road. And the Clan will be all over the place."

"She's right," Rutkins interrupted. "They control most of the Great Forests to the north and east now. They might risk one wagon of tinker-trades passing, especially if you'll do some fair tradin' with their scouts and seem to be open enough about everything. But the North Road up to the Suiri is a long, well-watched route. Sure as the Fates' Jest, they aren't goin' let a Marshal through there—or anybody with a Marshal."

Gwyn smiled very faintly as she tipped her head and looked to Brit. "Shall N'Shea again hide us from the hunters, *Soroe* ?"

"The Shea Holes, you mean?"

Puzzled, Sparrow glanced at Brit, then remembered the story Gwyn had told of the n'Athena Sisters whom the Clan had once hunted—trying to keep those Sisters from leaving the Clan's settlement and reaching Valley Bay. The healers n'Shea had come south to hide their Sisters in the Shea Holes. Well, Brit wasn't n'Shea, but she was a healer. "Still," Sparrow felt wary and asked, "That was a very long time ago. Is there anything left to use?"

Brit nodded. "A few places should be as sound as ever."

"Aye," Gwyn nodded. "Brit, the Virgin's Nest would be accessible to the wagon. You should even be able to reach it without using the North Trade Road."

"Fair choice. Then we'd meet in what? Two ten-day, at the most?" Sparrow watched as Brit found a smile, despite her obvious distaste for the use of the Shea Holes. "I admit it's an excellent thought, Gwyn'l. You're invoking that intrinsic wisdom of the *Niachero* , I see."

"Doubtless," Gwyn shook her head at the teasing and Sparrow grinned. As always, Brit could keep their sense of humor in tact.

Gwyn turned then and Brit drew her close in a strong hug. From behind her shadowmate, Sparrow extended a hand to Gwyn's, and the *Niachero* took it in a warm grasp. For a long moment they stood like that, until reluctantly Gwyn drew back, facing the fact that it was time for her to leave them.

Her gaze fell to Rutkins. She tried a smile. "Tend yourself well, my friend."

Rutkins offered a pained grin of his own in return. "Sound advice for both of us. Mother's Wind ride with you, Marshal."

"With us all," Gwyn amended.

But as the *Niachero* left them, Sparrow felt a coldness clutch at her heart. Memories flooded her briefly; so many hadn't come back. She moved closer to Brit, and her beloved wrapped a reassuring arm about her. Sparrow found it helped—a little.

Chapter Fourteen

Despite the clear scent Ril and Ty took from Llinolae's slippers, Gwyn had feared that setting out nearly seven days behind the Dracoon's patrol might prevent her bondmates from ever finding the route taken. But the sandwolves had not been idle in their roamings of the past few days. They had acquainted themselves with most of the human and horse scents of the easterly departures, attending most especially to those along the less traveled routes. And before the morning's fog had even lifted, they'd identified two of the most likely patrols. Gwyn kept moving east towards the Clan's Plateau as her packmates split to follow each one of the trails. Eventually—somewhere—the riders of those patrols would have to dismount and camp, and at those points the presence or absence of the Dracoon's individual scent would be discernible. Early that afternoon Ril's empathic sense of triumph summoned Ty in and together they circled back to lead Gwyn to the proper trail. At that point, their race truly began.

The next few days brought Gwyn memories of the summer they'd spent with Jes and Brit in the Changlings' Wars. Halts were brief, rest usually half of what was needed, and intuition played as large a role as skill in the hunt. The sandwolves persistently found the traces of riders and mounts, while Gwyn studied her maps to deduce directions and plots. Then with the guidance of her packmates, Gwyn made use of the animal trails to skirt the curves and bends of the roadways to save leagues and time. Her own ability to switch between her three bays, to alternately place each of the sandwolves up on the supply pillion and so allow them to rest as they continued to travel, and the sheer stamina of her Valley Bay mares all combined to let the group move at an almost impossible pace.

Days melted into the bluish-grey veils of the Twin Moons' nights unnoticed, their small band pressing on through the depths of the Great Forest and caring only for the distance devoured.

And then in the twilight of the fourth day, the vast spires and arches of the honeywoods sang with the eerie howl of a sandwolf's tragedy. The air split again as that stuttering yelp stretched into the long, wailing note of a lone mourner.

Gwyn dropped the tether line over the mossy remains of a giant root and kicked Cinder about as her sword whipped from its saddle sheath. And then they were racing through the woods. A half-hidden rock schism sent Cinder jumping without warning to Gwyn, but they hit the ground beyond in balanced unison, barely breaking stride. Ducking, dodging, dropping to the saddle side and righting again, Gwyn stuck like a burr as the mare continued to lunge and tear through the gaps of fallen boughs and hanging mosses. A blur joined them, and Ril matched stride to gallop as again that death keel rang.

The underbrush crackled and broke as Cinder skidded abruptly to a stiff-legged halt. Sunlight spilled into the clearing through a gaping hole in the forest's canopy. Charred lines streaked the trees' bark. The stream water had become a putrid, foaming gray from ashen clumps of burnt moss. Amidst the small craters of blasted earth and the churned pockmarks of horses' hooves, Ty sat with her mighty head pointed skyward, and her sandy eyes closed against the pain as yet another wail loosed.

Ril moved forward to her bondmate, tentatively nudging Ty's shoulder. The yelping broke into a small whine of choked sorrow, and Ty turned to bury her face in her packmate's thick ruff. In bleak silence, Gwyn returned her sword to its sheath and stepped down from the saddle. She took in the savaged campsite about her, and tears began to gather in the corners of her own copper eyes.

The tattered remains of two shaggy horses bloodied the far edge of the scarred space; the forest's scavengers had been busy with them. The glinting bits of sword steel were mixed in with the black of overturned soil and embedded in the wood of splintered roots—a daunting reminder of the power in the Clan's fire weapons.

At the edges of the devastation, Gwyn saw scraps of leather and a wisp of blue fabric. It leant sparse comfort to know that at least one of the Steward's Swords had resisted the betrayal enough to die.

Senses dulled and numb, she slowly turned until she saw the bodies of two women. Half-burned, half-buried, the cook and scribe lay in the center of what once had been a fire pit.

Images rose from that dreamspun vision and Gwyn remembered the young woman with Llinolae. There had been such innocence in her desire.

Somehow in the corral—between Llinolae's fading consciousness and Gwyn's own struggle to break their contact—the *Niachero* hadn't quite recognized whose deaths she had been witnessing in that lifestone's vision. But now, as she stood beside the fallen women, Gwyn began to feel the loss of those comrades—through Llinolae's eyes…through Llinolae's heart.

The Clan raiders hadn't even finished the cremation properly.

"You didn't deserve this," Gwyn whispered, the mourning chords of grief rising within her. "None of you deserved this."

Behind her, the two sandwolves lifted their heads in unison, and their wailing song began again. Tears came to wet her cheeks. Her voice joined in the chorus.

* * *

"I don't care that you don't like it!" Gwyn hissed in muted fury, and immediately Ty dropped flat in a pleading submission. The leather of cinch and strap went snap. The last of the supplies and excess equipment were now secured to Nia.

Ril's paw lifted tentatively as she leaned forward from where she sat. Gwyn's glance cut her short and she froze in mid-motion.

"Not a single protest! Not one more, do you hear me?" Gwyn rasped in a quiet, hushed voice. But the power of her unswerving refusal thrummed along the wordless line of their pack bond like a crack of thunder. "Strategy is my role and I say we split forces! It's my decision! Support me or leave!"

Worriedly, the two sandwolves looked to each other, but there was no indecision between them. Ty remained prone. Ril eased herself down in clear acceptance of the terms. They'd not desert her, especially not in this reckless mood of hurt and anger. The risks of this sort of impulsiveness, they understood well; it was simply seldom they'd ever seen it in their human packmate.

126

The last time Gwyn had been like this was after the men-cats' attack in the upper pasture lands and her sister, Kimarie, had gone missing—but even there Gwyn's plans had not failed them. No, taking risks because of emotional involvement was perfectly justifiable to them; it was not grounds for breaking a pack bond. They didn't quite understand why Gwyn was so intensely wound up in this venture now, but they didn't need to. They only needed to trust her and hope her plan—to send Ty in one direction and take Ril in another—was going to be successful, despite the risks.

"Thank you." The black tips of their ears perked out of their thick curl coats. Their expressive brows wrinkled hopefully at her softened tone. Gwyn turned to them then, a crooked smile chiding herself as she admitted, "I couldn't do this without you, you know."

Ty graced her with a tongue lolling, panting grin and grunt which uncannily mimicked a human's chuckle. Ril gave Ty a rebuking glare for that ill-mannered display, then heaved herself to her feet and offered Gwyn a gentler reassurance with a nudge of her nose.

"So—" Both sandwolves quickly grew attentive at Gwyn's familiar down-to-business manner. "We have to try tomorrow night. With the single moon setting early, more than half the night will be in darkness. If there's any chance of getting in and out in one piece, it'll be then. After that it's a matter of getting them to go in one direction, while we take another down to the Shea Hole. Which is what you and Nia will be doing, Ty. If you can get Nia far enough up the road towards Clantown to lay prints going north, there's a good chance we can get them to believe Llinolae stole a mount and fled for the Council's Keep instead of home."

Gwyn paused and took a deep breath. "At least, they should think so. It took her maybe seven days to get this far north with hard riding on a single mount? And it's nearly another day's northeasterly travel up the plateau to Clantown from where they caught her? Yes! They should follow you and Nia. With a good horse and staying to the old Trade Road, she'd out-race them. She'd reach the Keep within five days."

Ty cocked her to the side, weighing the idea.

"The gear Nia's carrying now is about the weight of a single rider—that should help. Stay to the Trade Road for about a day, before you let Nia circle back through the woods. That ought to give them enough of a trail to convince them. Though if Nia can't manage or if rain sweeps in, break off when you have to. Just stay cautious when you guide her back west! The sooner you both get down into the gorges, the better it'll be. All right?"

Her tattered ear flicked briefly, a habit of Ty's when she was considering something. Then her teeth snapped shut decisively, and her nose dipped quick in that sneeze-like nod.

"Good."

Ty's sandy eyed gaze shifted questioningly between Gwyn and Ril.

"Aye, I'll still let Ril guide," Gwyn promised grimly. "I won't set foot into town until she's scouted it thoroughly. You have my word."

"But, when I go in," Gwyn faced Ril and pressed, "I'll need a legitimate distraction—preferably one which scatters the horses and makes it more likely that Llinolae could have stolen one! And you're going to have to manage to do it with as few prints as possible.

"The last thing we want them thinking about is sandwolves and marshals!" Ril shifted to lean a little against Gwyn's leg reassuringly. She'd manage.

"All right then, let's get out of here." Gwyn bent swiftly to give them both a hug, then hesitated and went to one knee to face Ty. "You take care of yourself...and Nia."

Ty touched her face lightly.

"Aye, in four days."

* * *

Dawn came with a misty fog. It found Gwyn making camp in the shady cavern beneath the moss strewn roots of a particularly ancient honeywood. Cinder and Calypso only begrudgingly agreed to leave the moist over-hangings alone and accepted the grain rations instead. Gwyn endured a bland, cold meal herself; she was determined that neither torn moss nor fire smoke would betray them to any roving Clan sentries.

When she finally did settle to rest, her sleep wasn't much more comforting than the jumier jerky had been. Though the milkdeer had carved quite a nice trail up the Clan's Plateau, Gwyn was uneasy about the fact that she had made such good time along it, especially given the evidence of others' use. By the prints, more than the wild milkdeer and braygoats frequented the path, and Gwyn suspected Ril had led her in by way of the Clan's own 'back door.' Which meant scouts might be trekking past her hidden little campsite at any moment. It understandably boded ill for sound sleeping.

The risks of surprise only increased with Ril's absence. But it was imperative to know where Llinolae was being held, before Gwyn made that midnight sleuth into Clantown, and Ril was better equipped to track down the Dracoon's whereabouts than Gwyn was. So, the *Niachero* attempted to nap in the coolness of that damp, shady hollow and tried not to worry too much about Ril's absence nor her own vulnerability.

The morning's dampness gradually gave way to an afternoon of heated humidity. The mares snuffled about, hopeful of discovering a missed handful of feed. Yellow crickets peered in through the hanging haymoss, then hopped back to the upper boughs, cheerfully undisturbed. Nested birds chattered angrily at the wild prippers who scuttled too near, until slowly the Great Forest eased into the sluggish peace of its mid-summer day slumber.

A sudden 'thwack' broke Gwyn's doze. Her head reeled with a splitting pain and harsh voices crowded her senses. In her sleep—still safe beneath the arching canopy of the honeywood's roots—Gwyn's figure trembled and curled tight into a protective knot about her sword.

Boots tripped—kicked, striking fast. She folded over, falling from her knees as swift, hard leathers swept in again and again. More scouts joined the fray. Scrambling, snatching at clothes and even her braid to bind her as she still fought. She twisted, rolling, and nearly broke away! Suddenly a broad fist punched down. Laughter taunted as she crumpled, and all was lost then as images blurred with pain. Vomit and blood mixed, spewing out in choking gasps. The laughing ridicule of the Clan scouts turned cruel with the mess. Callused anger had them stripping her naked, and their flashing silver blades sawed the dirtied hair short. Injuries protested the lifting, then suddenly the icy water of the trough was nearly drowning her. She came up sputtering. The pain shrieked through her until....

Gwyn jerked awake, scrambling back on all fours.

Eyes wide she met Ril's challenging glare. She inched further away as the sandwolf growled menacingly. She saw then, half of the sword's crossbar was clutched in those shining jaws and the sandwolf's body was crouched low over the blade's length. The whites of Ril's eyes rolled, and the beast defied Gwyn to object.

Abruptly, understanding flooded into her awareness. It made Gwyn gasp. A hand went to her head as she felt the dizziness lingering. It had been an abrupt withdrawal from Llinolae, and the vividness—the strength of that forced mingling—had been more overwhelming than ever before.

Goddess, dear Llinolae, what are you doing?

"Running," came the immediate awareness.

The answer was so clear that Gwyn was startled again. For a moment, she almost thought the bond had somehow reforged itself. Yet there was no sense of losing her own consciousness this time, and after a moment Gwyn realized this knowledge had come with the original image. She—Llinolae—had been running away, trying to escape, and then had been caught. The blow to Llinolae's head had stunned Gwyn's own perceptions of the scene, but as the shock wore off the pieces were ushering themselves together as naturally as if Gwyn had been the one held captive.

Ril rumbled a little, in a tentative, questioning tone that called Gwyn out of her thoughts. She smiled at her bondmate gratefully and extended a hand in peace. The sandwolf dropped the sword and crawled across the last few feet with a plaintive whine; Gwyn had seldom tolerated anyone handling her steel weapons.

"No—no, you did well," Gwyn murmured and folded the furry beast close into her arms. "I hold no grudge...no grudge at all."

She took a long, deep breath, echoing Ril's own sigh as the last of the tremors left her body. Ril nuzzled her chin in concern, and Gwyn finally admitted, "It does frighten me, *Dumauz*. The intensity of this touching—I haven't felt anything of this kind since Selena and I...."

"Llinolae's Blue Sight is powerful. I understand that. Perhaps even more than *M'Sormee* , and I shouldn't expect her to temper that strength as our Valley-trained Sisters do. I know I shouldn't but, Ril, there is more. It's in her intensity. Maybe it's shock... I don't know! I do know that neither Kimarie nor *M'Sormee*—not even Selena!—ever engulfed my consciousness with a touch so...so commanding!"

She sighed, despairing of finding words that could make any sense out of the reality of this—this *experiencing*. "I think I'm scared by it, Ril—scared by her. I simply have no reference for this."

Sandy eyes looked on her with compassionate pity, and Gwyn slumped against her packmate, pressing her face into the curly warmth of Ril's coat. Gently the sandwolf's reassurance rose to embrace Gwyn, a subtle sense of wellness flowing along their pack bond to calm her. It brought a sad smile to Gwyn's lips, and she rubbed her cheek against Ril's coarse ruff. She couldn't tell if her bondmate was merely being sympathetic to this confusion—or if Ril's empathic sense was recognizing something Gwyn was missing.

"I don't want to know, if you are," Gwyn mumbled. Ril seemed to smile at her kindly, and it made Gwyn chuckle a bit. "Let me pretend there's wisdom in ignorance. Just for a night or two more?"

Ril challenged her with a playful snap of those gleaming jaws. Then abruptly she pushed Gwyn over onto her back. The *Niachero* began sputtering in protest, but her words dissolved into helpless laughter as Ril's lapping tongue found that ticklish place under Gwyn's chin, and the coaxing assault banished the doubts to a better day.

Chapter Fifteen

The thick bed of decaying leaves cushioned Gwyn's movements along the edge of the Clantown clearing. The forest behind her was dark, foreboding in its dense blackness. Ahead of her, the brush had been studiously cut back again and again by the Clans, in order to limit the encroachment of the woods and wild things. Now all that was left was hard-packed dirt, sparsely covered with scraggly weeds. But tonight, the openness was a Goddess-sent blessing to Gwyn and Ril. Tonight the lack of small bush and thorns left them an unhindered view of the village, and it would lend no noise of warning to the passing sentries when Gwyn chose to leave the sanctuary of the trees. She hoped to be neither seen nor heard.

She'd changed into a ruddy brown shirt to match her trousers and had donned not only her protective leg sheaths, but her upper arm leathers too. Her hair had been rebraided to stay tight, a head band securing the bits and pieces that usually flew about her face. She was armed not only with her sword, a steel hunting knife, and the vambraces from Jes, but with a few other shorter blades tucked into her boots and arm sheaths. Her preference was to get in and out with as little bloodshed as possible, especially on the way in. If she could create the illusion that Llinolae's escape had been accomplished solely with the Dracoon's skills, then the Court traitors might not assume a Marshal was involved—and the Clan pursuers might not anticipate the need to face a Marshal with sandwolves.

At least that was her hope. She knew the chances of accomplishing it were poor.

The sky above still reflected an expanse of bright, silverish light created by the early moon. Gwyn and Ril bided their time, watching the town. Darkness would come soon enough; the midnight moon faced away tonight. Ril rumbled deep in her throat with complaint, and Gwyn's skin began to take on the dark sheen of bitter tea. The tension seemed to prolong their waiting interminably.

Gwyn found the village she watched to be made of an odd style. A single, long lane ran through the middle of the clustered buildings. There was little variety in the structures, save for differences in heights. Even though she was accustomed to the white-washed stones of Valley Bay, the plaster and wood designs used for these places felt distinctly alien. She supposed that was good. Something more familiar might have invited carelessness. Still—in such a rainy climate, she couldn't help but wonder at the practicality of having flat-roofed structures.

Another pair of sentries wandered past. One of them cradled a fire weapon with seemingly negligent care, and Gwyn sank low into the safety of the shadows. Ril's contempt for these Clan folk came to Gwyn through their pack bond. She put out a quick, silencing hand, warning against distraction rather than sound. Besides, this was the Clan's home town; it would not do to underestimate the advantage it gave them. And if the idea of anyone even attempting to enter the Clantown seemed so audacious to the Clan folk that it lulled the peripheral guards into complacency, then that was something to use to their own advantage and not to scoff at.

Ril's ears flicked flat as the moon's light began to dim overhead. Gwyn nodded, and the sandwolf slunk off into the shadows.

In the west, the single moon slipped below a forested horizon, and the last of the silver glow whispered away. Total darkness fell swiftly, and even the forest noises behind Gwyn hushed. Only the music from the Clantown's tavern paid no heed and continued. The yellow haze on the town lane came from lanterns which hung along the porches, although only two buildings were still lit. One was the tavern where the music played. The other lay at the south end of town—this side of the road and catty-corner to the stables where Ril was stalking. It was the southern-most building where Ril had scented Llinolae.

Unfortunately, the sandwolf had found that nearly every scout in Clantown also frequented the place.

Gwyn watched as the sentries rounded the corner beyond that building, and after several minutes she made out their figures on the street beyond. They were pausing to exchange words with their change of watch, and neither pair seemed to be in a hurry to move on. She breathed a faint sigh of relief at the assurance; they were obviously not intent on starting some generator to counter the night's blackness. She'd been afraid that they might have a more sophisticated system of artificial lighting, when according to Brit the energy core from just one of their fire weapons could power an electrical generator for nearly a generation. Just because they didn't have the thermal power of the Firecaps available, shouldn't have meant they needed to rely on smoky oil lanterns.

It merely underlined how little she understood the Clan—another reminder that she shouldn't assume anything.

She sighed and rose. It was time.

Beneath the moonless sky, she moved almost invisibly across the open clearing. A hand on her sword kept it from swinging as she walked. It also prevented the straight length of the silhouette from suggesting she didn't carry a Clan's curving saber. It was important that anyone catching a glimpse of her from the tavern's rear windows should see nothing suspicious about her. With her unhurried pace and tall form, she hoped they'd mistake her for any of the intermittent scouts who seemed to be reporting in late. It could seem odd that she was choosing the route across the cleared lands, but then it was a shorter distance than the way around by the lighted street.

She reached the back corner of the building as the new pair of sentries began their rounds. Ducking between a log pile and water barrel, she disappeared neatly.

The pair walked by within arm's length of her, then halted abruptly with an exclamation of some sort. One twisted 'round fast and trotted back to the porch on the building's far side. The other spat a short curse but remained behind to wait.

Gwyn held her breath, a mere pebble's pitch from the sentry. The Clan woman began to pace in a bit of a circle, and Gwyn was suddenly very, very thankful she'd thought not to wear the Marshal's usual light toned tunic. It would been noticed.

The man returned just as suddenly as he'd sprinted off. With a quick laugh, he held out something to show his partner and they continued on their rounds.

Gwyn sent a silent prayer to the Goddess. Cautiously, she straightened and moved around the corner to the west side of the place, giving her attention again to that three-storied box of a building.

The windows nearest her were shuttered and dark, but a closer inspection showed the slanted wood slats were meant to be permanent. They acted more as shades than closures. The back room within was as dark as the northern rooms seemed, but further along towards the porch she heard mumbled voices and saw light.

She edged closer to the sill to get a good look in, then pulled back quickly as inside someone came near. But the figure kept walking and then there was a scrape of furniture. She crept near again and saw a male pulling his chair up to the center table, his back to her now.

It was a large, front room that extended the length of the structure. About a half-dozen scouts, female and male, were scattered around the place; they seemed to be passing out hot drinks from a pot on a tiled stove. Along the furthest wall, a rack shinning of metal caught Gwyn's eye—fire weapons. Just as a long sword was often more dangerous than a pairing knife, Gwyn knew the longer the style of a fire weapon, the more powerful; these slender pieces were frightening—easily an arm's length each. Another unsettling thing she noted was the sheer number of fire weapons hung on each rack—and there were a lot of racks. She couldn't decide if that meant there were scores of other scouts barracked in the building, or if this was some sort of central depot and stock pile. Fates' Jest, it was probably both.

The heavy clump of booted feet alerted her, and suddenly a pale design of lights descended from above. Gwyn froze as stripes of white hit the dirt a few feet further out from where she stood. The hollow stomp resumed, coming from within and yet above her. She drew away slightly as a bulky fellow in trousers and a nightshirt, his hair in sleepy disarray, passed by the window. Then she retreated to get a better glimpse at the new light above.

A shuttered window sat directly overhead. She made out the railing as it angled along the wall inside. As she watched, a figure wearily climbed the flight of stairs. She noticed another lit window above the first. The scout continued stomping upwards to the upper landing, and then the drifting timbre of disgruntled voices reached Gwyn. The window shadows exchanged something with a flash of silver and one began to descend again.

Assuming the silverish glint had come from a fire weapon, then someone upstairs was being watched very closely.

She glanced inside at the front room again. The guard from above arrived to fling a steel ring of keys onto the table. He proceeded to spout some belligerent complaint that touched off a heated discussion.

Gwyn slipped away quickly to hide herself between the barrel and logs once more, expecting the sentries to reappear shortly. They soon did, still in their leisurely stroll. She waited as they reached the street and reversed directions to begin their rounds again.

Though the voices in the front room had grown louder, Gwyn was quick to note the sentries remained unconcerned. They passed her and the building without pause.

Gwyn glanced above again. The top floor obviously housed someone of importance. She noticed the windows there were boarded shut tightly. None had the slanted shutters designed to let breezes in. Those rooms would get unbearably stuffy in any summer weather—which suggested it held prisoners rather than honored captains.

This was all nice as a piece of speculation, Gwyn wryly reminded herself. Still—if worse came to worst, she could probably persuade the Clan to exchange one of their leaders for Khirla's.

Now, she just needed to get up there.

After a cursory inspection of the water tube above the barrel, Gwyn dismissed it. The wood was near rotting and wouldn't have supported Sparrow's weight let alone her own. However, a closer examination of the plaster and stone itself gave her a better idea. The white-washed mud comprised only the thinnest of crusts; much of it was already cracked, breaking away from the rocks and mortar beneath it. And the stuff underneath could provide Gwyn with all the nooks and crannies she desired!

There wasn't a daughter raised in Valley Bay who hadn't scaled a few of the neighboring Firecaps' cliffs at one time or another. Add her *Niachero's* strength to that and she was more than a match for this old wall.

She eagerly untied the thigh lace of her sword sheath and adjusted the scabbard's belt so the thing wouldn't thunk about too awkwardly, then chose the corner of the building that lay behind the staircase for her assault. It was better than risk climbing past a room of light sleepers, and hopefully the sentry up top would mistake any outside scuffle for inside traffic near the lower landings.

A group of the Clan's folk began stumping their way up inside. Gwyn almost chuckled. This was going to work!

She started her climb and her humor turned a bit self-derisive. It had never been quite as easy as it looked on the Firecaps' cliffs either.

Her gloved fingers prodded and held. Her weight balanced on the edges of her boot soles, and she enviously remembered the supple, fish skin boots that rasped and gripped against most anything. But the rhythm of test-adjust-pull began to come back to her.

Gwyn felt the feral pleasure of a sandwolf's pride resonate strong along her pack bond; it urged her on, embracing the challenge. Fingers sought cracks in the hard plaster coating, digging into the mortar behind as she carved one finger's hold after another, to claw her way up the building's side. At the top, beams from the wooden frame jutted out sharply. She grabbed one, neatly pulled herself up, and then used it to step over the stone lip onto the roof.

An explosion suddenly shook the building beneath her, and Gwyn went reeling to her back. She rolled and wedged close into the low wall which ringed the deck. It barely registered that she was alone here—the attack was not against her!—when another blast blew a hole skyward through the far side of the roof.

She ducked her head as the debris fell. A fleeting image of white and red flame danced through her mind as she desperately sought to reach Ril through their pack bond—"*Stay!*" Then she sent reassurance and compelling stillness along that wordless line, urging the sandwolf not to loose bedlam among the stabled livestock—not to tip the lanterns in fiery diversion. Not yet!

The stench of smoke and tar surrounded her as she struggled to stifle a choking cough. Shouts and frenzied shrieks had replaced the music of the distant tavern. Gwyn scurried around the fragmented hole to see the main street, peering down to hear doors slam and see figures racing from the porch in commotion. Orders and bodies jumbled frantically, fighting for space at the pumps and troughs—stringing the bucket brigade from stable to fire.

A sudden flickering of blue in the gray around her—like the sword fire from a lifestone—caught her eye's edge and spun Gwyn around. There was a groan from the timbers and then a sharp 'crack' as more of the roofing caved in to open a gaping abyss. Smoke billowed and sparks leapt free.

Damned fire weapons! Unpredictable! Unreliable! Fates' Own Jest incarnate! Gwyn cursed, scrambling forward and tearing her kerchief from a pocket. Her eyes streamed with tears as she squinted and tied the cloth into a mask across her face, trying to make sense of the chaos below.

Shining fragments of one fire weapon lay clenched in the charred grasp of what may have been a corpse. A motionless male lay further to the side, his clothing smoldering and his body bent impossibly; if he wasn't already dead, he would be soon. Fire ringed the edges of the room. The door pounding from below her ended abruptly with an oath. A vague sense of recognition swept through Gwyn—a whispered hint of that familiar brushing touch, a Blue Sight's touch of amarin—then smoke swept it away.

"You...!"

Gwyn started. Below her amidst the smoking fumes and wreckage, a woman suddenly appeared.

"Can you get me out of here?" The imperious tone of command reflected no recognition of Gwyn. "Will you...?"

Gwyn answered with a curt nod, accepting that this was not the place for long introductions as she tore at the buckle of her sword's belt. "You're Llinolae, yes?"

An equally brief nod acknowledged it. Then a hacking cough caught the woman like a swift kick to her stomach and she bent in two, clutching at her ribs in pain.

"Royal Marshal," Gwyn offered along with the dangling end of her scabbard on its belt. The woman nodded disjointedly, reaching high despite her coughing to grab the sheathed sword. Then Gwyn had her up and through the ragged bits of roofing quickly.

Nearly choking, Llinolae let Gwyn move them to the southern corner before she sank down against the wall. Gwyn's copper gaze narrowed in concern at the dark-skinned, bruised-eyed evidence of exhaustion. There was more that bespoke of poor handling. Even without the dreaming vision, Gwyn would have guessed at the rough dealings the Clan folk had given this woman. The torn, sleeveless top was clearly an undergarment, the short-legged pants were close fitting in the style of the Clan women and looked distinctly odd without the high boots to sheathe the bared calves. Her hair had been haphazardly shorn, then left an unruly shortness of odd lengths which sweat and charred grime had further entangled. And beneath her skin's rich color, bruises from fists and fingers had begun to rise in a painful yellow-green hue.

"Can you travel?" Gwyn demanded anxiously as the woman gasped a steadier breath, the coughing fit finally done. They had no choice, she must be able to!

"Lead, Marshal—I'll crawl through Fates' Cellars if I have to. Just get me out of here."

Again that ruthless self-determination, Gwyn thought. She sent a grim glance over the wall's edge; below, the Clan folk had abandoned their bucket brigades and were racing to get armloads of fire weapons out of the burning building. She had the sense that this rooftop was much closer to Eternity than she'd like it to be. Determination flamed within her own stubborn self then. "Come on, Dracoon—over the side."

Gwyn lowered Llinolae most of the way to the porch roof, again with the help of scabbard and belt. Then dropped the belt to her companion's hands. Recklessly she scrambled over the edge herself—sliding, slipping dangerously faster than common sense and crumbling plaster warranted—until she hit that porch roof with a thud on her back.

She lay frozen, half-curled with her feet still in the air, listening.

The frenzy below them gave no sign of notice though. At Llinolae's nod, Gwyn got them moving again—this time towards the western end and the barren stretch near the forests. Behind and beneath somewhere a lantern shattered. Gwyn grabbed Llinolae by the elbow and jumped into the darkness as a rushing roar of flame seized the southeastern porch.

Llinolae stumbled in gaining her feet. Gwyn's arm hooked around her shoulders without losing a stride. Sheath in hand and Llinolae half under arm, she pushed their hobbling into a run for the forest. And silently through their pack bond, she sent out the urgency of *"Come!"* The image flashed through her mind of a lunge and leap past feed bins, and she knew Ril had heard—a shrill stallion's whistle split through the human voices. The small herd broke free as the stables began to flame and beyond the chaos the shadows of the Great Forest beckoned the women to safety.

The night *boomed* in violent thunder, shaking the ground with its sudden blast. Heat pushed them both forward in a crashing wave, and Gwyn twisted as they were lifted, putting herself between Llinolae's body and the smashing power of the root they hit. Her head rang and she shook back the blackness, barely keeping them upright as they were dropped. Bark scraped against her shoulders' leathers, her heels scrambled frantically for footing, and her body levered back hard against the tree root as she kept them upright.

A stifled sob turned into a rasping cough as Llinolae fought the renewed pain of ribs and bruises. Gwyn gathered the woman closer, holding her up as knees tried to buckle.

But behind them! Gwyn's copper eyes went wide with shock of her own. A raging inferno consumed what once had been a building. Even here across the clearing and behind the first line of arching tree roots, the heat was blazing. The roar of a great waterfall seemed to surround them, and only dimly could Gwyn reconcile that din came from the fire.

Sparks leapt towards the stars. Against the night's velvet they looked like the fireworks at Churv's festivals. Yet here, the winds whipped greedy flames about, reaching hungrily for the towering citadels of honeywood.

"They won't catch. It's not hot enough. Not to light them."

The low murmur finally registered through her amazement. Gwyn started and looked to find that Llinolae had moved away. She was standing alone now, her blue gaze caught too by the burning fury. "The resin in their leaves and red bark is fire retardant. Unless you cut the honeywoods down, strip them, they'll rarely burn in this Forest. It's so amazing. Sometimes I believe the old tales— that they truly are ancient guardians set here by the Mother's Hand."

Gwyn nodded slowly, turning back to the bonfire as she too remembered the age-old verse:

"...The great staves of honey'd wood came to Hand.
Twin'd Moons sail'd high. In watch, the Mother stands."

She glanced back at Llinolae where the faintest of smiles upon those slender lips wedded melancholy to regret. The flickering light of the distant fire touched her dark skin, the brown richness a startling contrast to those sapphire-hued eyes. Yet in her beauty, Gwyn saw a haunting grief that was undeniable.

Gwyn swallowed hard. With a weary sigh, she twisted the kerchief loose and freed her own face. She was too tired to wrestle with the knot and her gloves, so she left the thing tied about her neck and turned her attention to strapping her sword back on.

"You're a woman!"

Gwyn glanced up at that surprised murmur, managing a nod as she bent to tie the thigh lace. "Amazon."

"From Valley Bay?"

She grinned at that and straightened. "Certainly not from 'cross the stars."

That brought an amused smile and blue eyes shifted to meet Gwyn's fully. "Beg your patience. I've never met a woman as tall as myself. Least, none aside from these Clantown folk." Those last words dulled; they took the smile away again.

Gwyn frowned in puzzlement as that blue gaze went back to the fires. She'd felt none of the familiar mind-to-mind touching which usually came from locking eyes with a Blue Sight. She'd met a Seer at the Keep once who'd had the skill to pass unnoticed through her consciousness, but never anyone else. Not Selena, not even Bryana!

"Do we go? Marshal?" A gentle hand touched Gwyn's elbow.

"Yes!" Gwyn started. Annoyed, she pulled herself together. This wasn't like her! And they certainly couldn't afford her to get distracted here, tonight of all nights! "There are horses—this way."

But as they moved off into the darkness, Gwyn suddenly wondered if the chaotic feelings growing inside her weren't much, much worse than mere distraction.

Part II
Flames of Desire

Chapter One

Sparrow dropped from the low roof into the pitch blackness of the corner, briefly regretting the long drop as her stomach uncharacteristically protested her acrobatics again. She shook her head, slightly disgusted with herself—she had no more time for this queasiness now than she'd had the other morning.

Behind her the great stone wall of the city ascended. Beside her the rock and mortar of a winery protected piles of kegs. These vast quantities of brushberry spirits in their wooden barrels were much too flammable to be housed within the city proper, so most of the local wineries were nestled against the snaking contours of Khirla's outer walls. The location afforded the businesses some measure of safety against raiders—be they Clan folk or other—as well as allowing the businesses ready access to the brushberry fields they harvested. At the moment, the place also neatly concealed one small Shadow. It was a corner Sparrow was exceedingly grateful to have as she gave herself a moment to catch her breath.

A stone's throw from her black niche, however, the road that circled the city was lined with tall torches, all ablaze. She was midway between the livestock pens and the visitors' encampments, and despite the fact that the festival had been over for two days, there was still a busy scuffle of people along the lane.

"Doesn't anybody in this city ever sleep?" Sparrow muttered, disgruntled to find the traffic unaffected by the setting of the single moon. Not that anyone had probably noticed. With this incessant love for lanterns and torch light that kept even the less-used alleyways of Khirla well lit, it was a wonder they ever knew day from night.

She wrestled herself out of her knife straps and her wrap-around jacket reversing the lot to show a saffron suede lining. It was easier then shrugging back into the thing, hiding the knife harness and, unfortunately, putting the knives fairly out of reach...but she knew at this point that her best wager was in not getting caught at all. Then the black scarf unwound from her hair to become a tasseled sash at her waist, and the dark tops of her boots folded down into saffron trimmings, complete with fringe. Her fingerless gloves she tucked beneath her sash, and with a handful of dusty dirt, she rubbed away the more obvious traces of white resin on her fingers and breeches. When she'd finished, Sparrow looked like most anyone who'd been around the livestock pens or who'd been wandering through taverns—a bit disheveled about the edges, but generally presentable.

Just as long as she didn't look like a saboteur, Sparrow didn't care.

She inched her way closer to the road, crouching low to stay in the shadows as long as possible. A boisterous youngster staggered into his jesting friends, setting them and other passers-by off-balance a bit. Sparrow slipped forward, still bent, as everyone seemed to pull up or side-step to avoid the commotion. The fellow heartily apologized to whoever would listen, then began some song or other as his friends towed him off. Sparrow rose from adjusting her boot lace to move on with everyone else.

She spared a surreptitious glance behind as a pair of City Guards strolled by, but no one seemed to have taken much notice of her. With a faint smile, Sparrow continued on as she rubbed her aching wrist. It throbbed in grievance of her earlier mistreatment, and now in the better light, she could see it had taken on a nasty shade of purple that the deep brownness of her skin wouldn't hide. It was beginning to swell as well…unsurprisingly. She knew she hadn't broken anything, but she could foresee Brit's ire and the observation that she was blessed that it hadn't been worse. Sparrow had to agree; when the metal grate in the armory had fallen, it could easily have shattered a bone.

"Leave it to the Clan folk to waste metal on windows—" She could think of at least a half million more constructive uses for that precious commodity! Although to be fair, Sparrow admitted sourly, "This was probably done by that Steward."

A sudden scream split the night, and everyone on the road paused in startled fright. Again the terrified shriek came, followed by a child's wail. Then the baying "a-roo" of a chasing sandwolf echoed out.

Sandwolves? Gwyn's here? Confusion rooted Sparrow to the ground for a moment more. Then snorting, rasping barks broke the stilled air, and her stomach sickened, identifying the brutal beasts by their sounds—basker jackals!

"Baskers! Fates' Cellars are freed!" Someone yelled. "The Swords have loosed their baskers!"

The people around her panicked. A rushing onslaught flung itself down the hill slope towards her.

"Brit!" One thought seized Sparrow, and she broke into a wild run of her own, battling forward against the folks that were fleeing from the encampments above. She was pushed aside from the road, and with a leap she dodged into the stubbly root rows of the brushberries, hurdling herself over the low trellises and through the thinner crowds.

Parents clutched at their babies and dragged their children away in desperation. Lovers half-dressed, half-tangled in blankets—youngsters clinging to pet prippers, oldsters clinging to snatched bundles—all ran, chaos reigning, as Sparrow scrambled between them and forced her way forward as the gnash and bay of the baskers rang through the cries.

She topped the small ridge to see a wagon go up in a burst of flame. She ignored it. Clenching her eyes tight and standing her ground against the press of people, she concentrated—pulling in on herself. The lifestone in her wrist flared hot beneath its wristband, and then it pulled hard—to the left!

Eyes flew open and Sparrow was running again.

The yapping clamor of baskers came. The vicious yowling of those that cornered their prey spurred her on faster. Bouncing off people, darting toward the city gates, she kept running.

"Brit!"

Another tent went whoosh with flames, and Sparrow was jumping through a wall of debris as it too caught fire. And then there was Brit—struggling to get up from her knees with her skirt ends charred black.

"*Soroi!*" Sparrow got under her shoulder, lifting—sharing her weight.

"Red cloaks'll come!" Brit gasped and Sparrow understood. She pulled her lover about, forcing the stumbling steps and burly weight into a run. Angling, cutting through the fleeing crowd, they made for that tunnel where the flickering line of torches broke—for that place where Rutkins would lead his guards in!

Then the City Guards were there in force. Rutkins' broad arms swept out with orders, sending men and women through the panic in pairs. Their ruddy brown cloaks moved swiftly among the crumpled debris and the fires, helping trampled victims to safety, calming the trailing ends of the crowd, bringing blankets out to smother the fiery spots. Yet all the time, systematically, they were clearing the folk back from that central bonfire, sending them further down the hill slopes, until finally only the dozen or so figures were left—the Steward's Swords and the sleek, black silhouettes of their now harnessed baskers.

Sparrow squinted against the light of that one great bonfire, struggling to make out individual blue cloaks as they squared off to meet the wary approach of the Guards. Glittering edges of embroidery outlined the deep blue of the Swords' fine cloaks. Steel glistened, reflecting the dancing firelight along their curving lengths of sabers. Long-toothed fangs shimmered a wicked white against the sleek fur of the basker jackals; the slender animals snarled and strained against the leashes of their handlers. A short whip cracked, calling them to obedience, and the Sword Master turned slowly from the burning pavilion to face Rutkins and the encircling City Guard.

"What happened here?" Sparrow hissed, too afraid to watch and yet unable to look away as the Sergeant and Sword Master stepped menacingly closer to one another. Voices lashed out in bitterness, but their words wouldn't carry over the growling noise of the baskers and the roaring winds of the fire.

"The Swords came," Brit gasped. She leaned forward. Backside against the city's wall and hands on her knees, she tried to catch her breath again. And Sparrow suddenly realized the brownness of her love's face was marred with muddied blood. "No-no, I'm fine, *Soroi.*"

Sparrow ignored the feeble protests and tried to clean the worst from Brit's face with a kerchief.

"It's only a grazing, Love. Most of the bloody stuff's from the fellow who jumped me."

"Jumped you? Did you see who it was?" Sparrow felt the knots uncoil a little inside herself as she discovered Brit seemed to be right; most of the blood wasn't her beloved's own.

"Blue cloak."

"But why? What happened?"

"Don't know why. They came barging into the area seemin' half drunk and carryin' on about some cheatin' whore and a trickster of a healer. Next thing I knew, they're waving a raggedy cloth in front of those nasty monsters and settin' them free. The baskers tore through the camp, gnashing teeth—eyes red'n'burning. You'd have thought the Fates' just loosed them themselves. That's when folks went frantic—every which way! But when one of those hounds took for Tessie's throat—!"

"The old woman healer from Kora's place?"

"Aye."

"Why would anyone…?"

"You tell me!" Brit snapped, remembering that lunging devil rising out of nowhere. "I nipped the thing with my whip. Got Tessie time to get away. Then the next I'm knowing is some blue-cloaked bully is trying to use his fancy sword on my neck!" Sparrow's face set hard, but Brit was angrier at her own clumsiness as she growled, "Fool thing I did! Lost my whip 'round that basker's throat and left myself near bare-handed against the Sword! Had to roll the brigand through one of his own fires 'fore I could get to my knife and be done with him."

Sparrow cracked a short grin of approval.

"Should'a killed him though, now that I see the damage they brought. Goddess, just look at what they've done…." Her low voice trailed off despairingly, and together the two women surveyed the camp remains. Most of the fires were dampened or completely out. Wagons were overturned. Tent poles were collapsed. Shards of pottery, furniture bits, and trailing clothes lines were scattered in the dirt. Bits of ash floated on the air as the bonfire of the pavilion continued to roar. The near side of the encampment was totally devastated, although by the signs of it, the wagons and tents set further away had escaped some of the worst.

A few bodies were lying ominously still near the great fire, and it finally registered for Sparrow that the Tent of Healers was the one in flames. She felt her mouth open, but the words of disbelief wouldn't even form. In bewildered confusion, she pointed at the awful inferno.

"I know," Brit straightened and came nearer to wrap an arm about her partner. "The herb mixes and roots alone will take seasons to restock. But the books, the scrolls—I only pray we can convince the Council to let us retrieve some of it from the Keep's Archives. Even then, I'm not sure all the knowledge lost can be replaced. Nearly every Healer House in the district lost something in this tonight. We were just finishing the last of the Apprentice Lessons—"

"And these Steward's Swords gave no thought to any of that?" Sparrow could only stand there, shaking her head as she watched the Steward's burly sword carriers gather themselves and their blood-thirsty baskers together. A few of the City Guard trailed grimly behind the departing Swords, while the rest solemnly set about helping the families to sort through the chaos.

Rutkins appeared silently beside the City Gate, watching the last of the Swords and those restless baskers file through the tunnel. He turned to watch the camp and his Guards then, seemingly ignorant of the Amazons behind him.

"How's the head doing, Rutkins?" Brit asked in a low tone, making no attempt to move closer and face him.

"About as well as the ribs. But compare it to their sort of pain…," his head tipped towards the encampment, "…mine's less than nothing."

"Should still give yourself another couple days."

"Aye, and lose the livestock pens tomorrow? Should have thought ahead better, not gotten skewered so close to the single moon. Always seems to bring trouble from them…the Swords, I mean. Not the ghosts and demons."

"Same, aren't they?" Sparrow mumbled bitterly.

They stood in silence for a moment until Brit did move a little closer to Rutkins' back. Sparrow glanced about them nervously, still leery of leaving the shadows.

"I think it's the Feasts'n'all," Rutkins answered Brit's unspoken press for some sort of explanation. "The Steward's always demanding their best behaviors for the Feasts…limits them to pushing and shoving mostly, less sword play and bloody bullying. Probably she's meaning to keep rumors from spreading too far about Herself and the abuses."

"You mean she actually has a sense of civic duty, your Steward?" Sparrow quipped. She couldn't help it.

"Civic survival more likely," Brit interjected. "Rumors too close to the borders might get to the Council or King."

"Humpf," Rutkins grunted. "Hadn't thought of it that way. She's in a royal fuss with your Marshal disappearing so fast too. I can just see it—wrath of a striking snake. They got stung, her precious Swords—by herself no less. Bored and edgy already, the bristly little savages can't be happy at all in bearing the brunt of her displeasure!"

Brit's mouth twisted sourly. "So they find some insult for who-knows-what imagined reason and descend on the defenseless."

"Well…," Rutkins flashed his contorted, grotesque grin at them as he glanced back over his shoulder, "some of you seem less defenseless than others, I note."

"She almost got killed by those…!"

"Easy, Love," Brit interrupted Sparrow gently, taking the clenched fists into her own hands. "Black humor isn't to everyone's taste. But it comes from the same sorrows."

Sparrow forced the tension to ease in her shoulders. She accepted Rutkins' apologetic nod with one of her own.

"There's more you might need to know," Rutkins murmured. His gaze went back to the camp as his arms crossed. "The healer they were hunting? Seems she was from a homesteader's village along the route you came in on."

"So they were after Kora's kin!" Sparrow hissed, then bit her tongue as Brit's glance hushed her. There might be some things that were safer for Rutkins not to know.

"She went by the name of Tessie," Rutkins elaborated, deliberately ignoring Sparrow's outburst. "Seems she was inferring some rather insulting things 'bout some of our Steward's Swords."

"Such as?" Brit sidled a little nearer to let the sergeant's voice drop even lower.

"Mentions of mixed blood and that sort?" Rutkins shrugged uncomfortably. "My youngsters implied she might be referring to loyalties more than bloodlines—the fact of their mixed blood is usually taken as offense, but it's a rather commonplace complaint to toss about." They said nothing, and he continued, "Apparently though, there's this homesteader—by the name of Tadder or Batter or something—that the healer knew. Thought there was a bit a'truth in what he'd said 'bout some of these Swords' loyalties. Healer thought his suspicions explained what she'd been seein' and hearin' of the Clans these past few seasons."

"Suspicions others in Khirla share, perhaps?" Brit challenged.

Rutkins shrugged uncomfortably and settled his stance more solidly. "I wouldn't know."

"Then you might think on it," Brit returned quietly.

There was a pause and eventually a short nod. But it was admission enough that he would consider the notions. "Might I suggest something to you in turn—as a friend?"

"That it might be expedient to go tonight? With the others that are already packing for earlier-than-planned departures?"

"Might be wise, at that." Again he moved uneasily, his broad back still turned. "Especially with you being a healer, Amazon. I don't know, but if I was them I'd start thinking this old woman Tessie chattered to her associates a bit. Maybe she chattered a bit too much? Any rate, it's a risk to consider."

"In truth." Brit drew a tired breath and touched Sparrow's elbow lightly. "Let's go see the damage done to us, *Soroi.* "

"Mother's Wind ride with you." Rutkins added, glancing back one last time to catch Brit's eye. He nodded to Sparrow as well. "With the both of you."

"With *all* of us," Brit amended and pulled her shadowmate along with her, carefully skirting the edges of the firelight and torches.

They'd be better off than many, Sparrow guessed. They'd arrived late and had been parked fairly well towards the back fringes of the encampments. Yet, she still felt her mouth sour with the bile of memories. The wreckage tonight wasn't as thorough nor as bloody as many pillaged camps that she had seen during the Changlings' Wars—nor during the drunken conflicts between the acrobats' caravan and the swindled townfolks in her childhood days. But it was the same too—the violence and the bullies—a piece of it always seemed the same.

"I'm sorry—" Sparrow pulled back from her thoughts abruptly, belatedly realizing that Brit must have been speaking to her because the sound of Brit's gristly grumble seemed suddenly absent.

But Brit's smile was soft as it turned to her. Despite the dark shadows' dance in the wavering torch light and the grimy smudges across her face, the warm glow of Brit's gentle understanding reached in to touch Sparrow's aching soul with sweetness. The breath caught in Sparrow throat. Their tenderness dissolved the night's woe. And for just an instant Sparrow felt the peace of their heartbond utterly suspend time and tears. An answering chord gently curved a smile across her own lips.

The night noises began to intrude again, filtering in and bringing awareness back to the world at large.

Guiltily, Sparrow ducked under Brit's strong arm to offer what support she could. Her partner's stiffened gait bespoke of bruises yet to rise. Brit squeezed her lightly with a hug, at once both grateful for the help and reassuring in their love.

"What were you saying?" Sparrow prodded quietly.

They picked their way through the rubble and scattered folk for a moment or two before Brit answered. "I was wondering how your own endeavors had gone earlier?"

Brit's voice was kept low, it's tone as neutral as the words were vague. But Sparrow knew that was for the benefit of any who might be overhearing them, not from any lack of interest.

"I noticed," Brit continued softly, "that your right hand's a bit swollen."

"I'll wrap it before I go for the horses," Sparrow promised. Inside, she felt inexplicably wonderful, though. That lingering sense of their specialness was still warm within her. "Aside from my hand, I think it went well."

"Hmm," Brit picked up her skirts to shake a foot as the ankle of her trousers caught on a bit of broken timber. "Did you find anything interesting?"

"There were no surprises." The grimness crept back into her voice as Sparrow remembered that silver sheen caught by the moon's light she had reflected in her mirror. She would have preferred to prove Brit and Gwyn wrong, however; she had no fondness for the Clan's weapons regardless of who might wield them. She could not believe anyone would harbor those things for anything but evil interests.

"No surprises, huh? That's a pity." Brit sighed heavily, leaning more of her bulky, old weight into Sparrow's shoulder.

Sparrow's heart lifted at her lover's trust. She knew it had taken Brit a very long time to learn there was strength in this spindly, little shape of a shadow-mate-lover. And she knew that tonight was the kind of night her beloved need-ed tangible reminders of that strength. She sighed, feeling comforted in know-ing that this was one thing she could offer. And in this small way, she freed Brit—bolstered her with renewed confidence—to pursue and unravel the answers that ultimately might make things better for them all. Sparrow shifted her grasp to fit herself closer to Brit as the memories of past wreckage finally retreated from her mind's eye completely.

"Was there a way to deal with what you did find?"

Brit's question returned Sparrow to the issue of the armory's fire weapons. "I left the glass and palm mirrors in place as you suggested. The window vents were fairly high. I doubt anyone's going to get a glimpse enough to start suspi-cions, not even from the reflections. Least, not before late mid-day. And by then, it'll be too late."

Brit nodded. The sulfur compound she'd mixed was *very* sensitive.

Sparrow shrugged slightly, still beneath Brit's arm. "Some bird or pripper might change the angles."

"For one maybe. Unlikely that both would get shifted too far aside."

"We hope." They both knew it'd only take one focused little thread of bright light to set off that powder—and subsequently the chain reactions from the weapons' own explosive fuels.

"We could be a good ways away by mid-day," Brit observed absently. "We can probably skip off the roads earlier, forget the trading stop in the sou-east village altogether. With so many leaving, the tracks are going to be confused for leagues. It'll certainly save us time."

Sparrow glanced at her quickly, frowning.

"It would be foolish not to go."

"What?" Sparrow felt the anxiety stab beneath her breast as she suddenly realized what Brit *was* implying. "You can't be thinking of staying? Not now. Not after this…this rampage against healers! Brit, it's not safe!"

"No, it's not." Eyes narrowed shrewdly as if weighing some distant stakes in a gambling game. "There's more to this than we see though."

Sparrow considered that a moment. It was a thought that wouldn't have occurred to her. But then, bullies in arrogant, drunken attacks—that was a plausible rationale for most any violence in her opinion, given her personal history. But Brit thought in terms of power and plots, not merely in terms of loyalties and lusts. So through the seasons, Sparrow had come to realize that those using power often hid behind the facade of brainless lusts.

"All right," Sparrow allowed that Brit's experience might be better suited to interpreting tonight's events. "Should we stay or go?"

"We go." The older woman pursed her lips with an irritated frown. "It'd be too conspicuous not to. And we have a Sister needing our help."

But, you don't like it in the least, Sparrow read shrewdly. Her Love didn't like to be manipulated into doing anything. And the more Sparrow thought about it, the more she had to agree. In one form or another, it seemed that they were indeed being run out of the city.... She knew Brit would have preferred knowing just a little bit more about why.

Chapter Two

Llinolae?" Gwyn crouched low just outside of the cave-like den of the tree roots, holding a cloth bundle and cake of soap. The early afternoon air was humid and heavy with the promise of rain shortly, and she wasn't about to waste the opportunities a storm could present right now. Softly, she called again, "Llinolae?"

There was a sudden rustle. Then stillness was followed with a tentative, "Yes?"

"The rains will start soon."

"Yes." A shadowy figure resolved into Llinolae's disheveled self. She crawled out into the light with a blanket in hand. "Thank you for the rest. It has helped."

"Would a quick scrub and a fresh shirt help more?" Gwyn gestured at her armload with a lopsided grin. "Wish I could offer more, but most of my gear trotted off with Nia and Ty. And we won't meet up with them for another day or two."

Llinolae's blue eyes flickered between the soap and the game trail behind them. The tip of her tongue brushed her lower lip almost hungrily, and her hoarse voice carried a note of yearning, "Dare we?"

"Aye! Come on!" Gwyn tugged her gently by the wrist, and Llinolae discarded the blanket in eager compliance. The creek babbled and called from below the short slope, and in little time the two of them had scurried down to meet the bubbling waters. Lithe, Gwyn hopped across the stones to a flat rock in mid-stream that sat beneath a drooping, young honeywood. She tossed the towel and tunic over a limb as if it were a clothes rack and found the soap a rocky niche next to her feet. Laces fumbled loose, she went to strip that smoke-tainted vest and tunic from her body, glancing up quickly to Llinolae on the shore. Abruptly their gazes caught and they both froze, each stayed with fists full of fabric and arms cris-crossed in preparation of shedding their shirts. Then just as suddenly they were grinning like fools and sharing in silent laughter as they peeled out of the grimy clothes.

As Llinolae left the short trousers on the shore and waded into the ankle deep stream, Gwyn felt herself go still again. She didn't even move when the soap was snatched from its rocky shelf. She stood, half in shock from the swatch of bruises beneath Llinolae's left breast and half in stunned amazement at the sheer beauty of the lean body before her. Even smudged with soot and mud, her skin pale except for those purpled abuses of limbs and ribs, even with that hacked mess of a hair cut, this woman was beautiful. Tall as Gwyn was herself, small breasted with darkened nipples that grew taut in the splashing rinse of the creek's waters, sleek with strength and decisiveness in those quick movements—all converged to tie Gwyn's tongue in a way that hadn't been done since her adolescence. Speechless, she barely managed to draw a breath, and she felt a sudden rush of warmth as her skin flushed into that burnished gold of the richest apricot which so easily gave her emotions away—as if a Blue Sight would need obvious demonstrations!

Llinolae looked to her then, offering a puzzled but friendly sort of smile, and Gwyn started, realizing her arms were still bound in front by those half-removed garments. Yet as she discarded those things, all she could grasp was how much more attractive that smile and those eyes were with the dirty smudges washed away from them.

Gwyn squatted low to wet her own face and grinned a little self-derisively at just how fast her heart was beating. It was undoubtedly prudent to refrain from washing more than her top and hair today. She had no need to make a more foolish spectacle out of herself than she was already managing. Standing stark naked before a good friend was one thing, doing it in front of a graceful, lean and handsome woman who just happened to have the Blue Sight, then tell her why you'd suddenly become a stuttering youngster, was more than even a *Niachero's* ego could stand.

They scrubbed in silence for a time, but as Gwyn straightened and offered Llinolae the first use of the single towel, the other waved it aside. "You need it more. You're chilled already." Then as she bent to have another try at her hair, Llinolae asked, "Are all Amazons so susceptible to cold water?"

Gwyn accepted the polite evasion with a faint shake of her head, appreciative of the graceful excuse for her darkened skin tones. "Only some of us. Most of Valley Bay's Sisters have been much better bred than us throwbacks."

"Does that explain the hair also?"

Gwyn crooked an eyebrow high, pausing briefly in running the towel through her shoulder length tangles.

"I've never seen anything like..." The woman hesitated, shrugging slightly. "The color—I don't know what to call it."

"Red." Gwyn grinned a bit wickedly and sent the bunched towel flying at a startled Llinolae.

"Red?" A baffled amazement backed the denial. "No, it's fair. Almost like some of the Clan folk, I'll admit, but I'd not call it *red.*"

"Well, we do. And it comes in shades as dark as a bay mare's hide, as bright as a copper tile or as light as this feathery stuff."

That brought a hint of mischief alive in those blue eyes, and Llinolae challenged, "Feathery? Or straggly?"

"It's wet. What else would you expect?" But it was a happy retort, and a suspiciously pleased sort of titillating tingle stayed with her as Gwyn tugged the clean tunic from the tree limb and passed it to the woman. She sighed then, resignedly retrieving her own smoke-scented vest and shirt. With a flap or two, she separated the garments and tried to air the tunic better, but she knew that wasn't going to make much difference. Oh well, think of poor Nia trudging around with that gear for four days without respite.

"Marshal?" the whisper held warning.

Gwyn spun about, in one motion tugging her shirt into place and her belt's dagger from its sheath. Llinolae's cautious nod directed her towards the slope's crest, and she heaved a sigh of immense relief at Ril's bright-eyed pant.

"*Dumauz!* Scare us a bit more and you'll be dodging steel blades! What were you thinking?"

Ril whined a faint apology, then her dark ears perked up through her ruff as her body went taut in alertness. Gwyn silently made her way across the rocks, listening with all the concentration her bondpack had ever taught her. A faint rumble of thunder descended. The hushed scurry of small animals and the cooler touch of the stream's waters carried on the breezes. She glanced back at Ril, "But no Clan scouts?"

A sneeze-like dip answered her emphatically, and Gwyn was satisfied.

"Good. We'll be away from here soon." Llinolae's stillness registered then, and Gwyn touched the woman's arm lightly in reassurance. "This is Ril, one of my bondpack. Ril, this is Llinolae—Khirlan's wayward Dracoon, no less."

Ril flicked her ears forward in brief greeting. Then quite oddly she vanished, leaving Gwyn with a frown of confusion.

"One of your bondmates?" Llinolae pressed, sliding back into the short trousers hurriedly. "You've more than one sandwolf with you?"

"There're three of us," Gwyn muttered absently, still worriedly gazing after Ril. But as the thunder rolled again, they were both reminded to move for camp. As they topped the crest, Gwyn shook her unease aside and continued more sociably. "There's Ril, Ty and myself. At the moment, Ty's leading my third mount, Nia, on a meandering chase north that will lead the Clan scouts astray—I hope. It may take them a while to notice you didn't burn in that building, but I'd wager most anything that they will notice."

"Aye, they will." The Dracoon too was grimly certain of that.

"With this storm though, Ty will turn Nia back. Like us, she'll take advantage of the rain to cover their tracks. If we all keep off the worn game trails and the Trader's Road, this leaf mulch and rain will leave precious little trace of us."

"Oh yes." Llinolae seemed to pull her wits together with an impatient, internal little shake. "That's why risk the bathing...."

"This storm has the earmarks of a heavy one." Gwyn eyed her companion with concern. "The rains will wipe out any signs of us in the camp and down at the stream."

"Which I should have realized myself," Llinolae admitted ruefully. "Seems my head's not quite functioning yet."

"That was a nasty blow they gave you yesterday."

At Gwyn's gentled tone, a sarcastic curl twisted the slender line of Llinolae's lips. "Small blessings are favors too. I'm still alive, aren't I?"

* * *

Disgruntled, Gwyn glanced above at the darkening skies beyond the forest canopy. Those patches of ghostly glows were becoming duller by the moment. She couldn't tell if the cloud cover was thickening or if the early moon was preparing to set. She thought it was too soon for the latter, but given her nerves tonight that internal clock might well be wrong.

And they were still a good league from the gorge—*Mae n'Pour!*

Cinder shied as Ril emerged from the wooded shadows, and impatiently Gwyn kneed her mare back into obedience, but not before the sharp 'clack' betrayed a hoof striking against some rock or other. Gwyn admitted defeat with that hollow ring. They weren't going to make the valley floor before sunrise. At this rate they weren't even going to make the gorge edge without leaving a trail akin to a wounded buntsow's! The horses were stumbling around in the dark, the wind was chilled and picking up, and nothing but more rain and darker hours were to come. Certainly the sliver of the midnight moon tonight wouldn't cut through this overcast by itself, and if that early Twin was on the verge of setting, then they really did need to find shelter soon. And if the early moon wasn't setting, then the second half of this storm was going to be worse than Gwyn wanted to think about!

"Either is a good reason to hole up for the rest of the night," Gwyn muttered. Ril nudged her booted ankle with relieved agreement. It was enough to make Gwyn smile again. "All right, old friend. I stand rebuked. Now tell me—have you some place in mind already?"

Ril trotted off the game trail with an eagerness that made Gwyn chuckle, and they all followed. She should have known.

From behind Cinder, Calypso grunted with a weary satisfaction. The mare knew from long experience how the abrupt change in manner from a sandwolf meant the day's trek was nearly done. Gwyn couldn't blame either of her mares, nor the weary slump of the cloaked figure astride Calypso—she'd been pushing them hard. The more distance they claimed between rains, the fewer clues would be left for the Clan scouts. But even her own aching muscles attested to the fact that none of them were invincible. It was time to rest.

The cavernous honeywood Ril had chosen was split by a shelf of rock at its base. A twisted growth of an entrance provided a wide enough space to comfortably ride the horses in through—a gray mortar-like wall on one side, ruddy-barked wood on the other. With the smattering of light still available, Gwyn made out the curving bend that led deeper into the hollow and then the rough stone plateau above from which Ril gazed down at them.

"Perfect," Gwyn breathed, pride and pleasure coursing through that silent bond between her and her packmate. They'd be able to leave the horses below and to risk a fire up top. And Ril was right about their need for a fire—despite the evidence it would leave. With the chilled, wet weather, the lack of proper gear and general exhaustion from the past ten-day, they all needed warm, dry beds and full stomachs tonight.

She hoped Ty's natural exuberance didn't outweigh common sense this evening. Poor Nia was going to be in bad enough shape after three days of full pack, without Ty demanding a shivering martyrdom from her as well.

Ril caught Gwyn's eye with a reassuring grin. Ty did have more sense than that, even she knew it.

Gwyn chuckled, swinging down from her saddle with an absent pat to Cinder as she peered overhead into those mossy tree crevices again. It smelled fresh enough, not in the least dank, and that told her there had to be additional ventilation somewhere above. A little sulfur powder rolled into that haymoss, and the stuff should burn just fine…perhaps a bit slowly, but quite fine.

A muffled cry from Llinolae caught both Gwyn and Ril's attention. But it was Calypso's stock-still rigidity that sent Gwyn moving forward in alarm. Very carefully she reached to ease Llinolae down in that last, long step from stirrup to ground. Even then, beneath the oil slicked cloak and the tunic, Gwyn could feel the flinch of bruised muscles at the pressure of her touch. Guilt stung sharply, reminding Gwyn that worse things than hard travel had been plaguing Llinolae in the past few days.

"Thank you." The words were a mere hush. Llinolae barely moved, shifting only enough to bury her face in Calypso's silky, black mane. Her arms circled the mare's strong neck for support, and Gwyn hovered with growing concerns. A thread of laughter found its way into the rasping voice as Llinolae managed, "Saddle sore at my tender age—who'd believe me?"

With great gentleness, Gwyn laid a hand to the Dracoon's back. "Let me get you settled up with Ril, before I deal with the horses."

A weary shake of the head answered her. Llinolae straightened slightly. "It'll do me better to move some—stretch these knots out. I can brush them both down."

Gwyn frowned, hesitating.

"I'm all right, Marshal." Llinolae smiled a tired, touchingly sweet smile as she turned to catch Gwyn's hand. "Really I am. Go on now, get things organized to your liking."

Gwyn squeezed the other's grasp encouragingly and accepted the reassurance. "Say if you change your mind."

"I will."

It took a while, but not nearly as long as most would have expected, for Gwyn to convert that dingy space into a livable camp. She started with a few makeshift torches before climbing into the mossy heights and hacking away at the shaggy tendrils. A family of prippers darted deeper into the tree's upper crevices, chattering in rebellion. A single bed of glowing crickets emptied with a flurry that had Gwyn batting awkwardly with her sword hilt and clinging rather precariously to the webbed vines as she tried to keep the things out of her hair. But there was nothing more exciting to encounter, and she'd soon cut enough haymoss to supplement the mares' grain, feed a good fire for the night, and lend a springy cushion beneath their blankets as well. By the time she'd rolled several moss logs together and started the fire blazing, Llinolae was nearly done brushing Cinder.

Gwyn shared a smile with the woman, glad to see some of her stiffness had indeed worn off. "I left a pan of tea to brew—Ril's going to show me the fresh water she's found. I may be gone for a bit."

"Anything I should start cooking?"

"Not without more water," Gwyn admitted, shouldering their pair of empty water bags. Judging by Llinolae's rich skin tones and bruised eye shadows, Gwyn knew why neither of them were suggesting she accompany Gwyn; a long trek with heavy waterskins was obviously not in the woman's best interests just yet. "I'll send Ril back ahead of me, once I know where I'm going."

Llinolae nodded, faintly amused. "I suspect I'll be here."

With a crooked grin, Gwyn admitted that that was most likely what she'd expected too. But she couldn't quite think of anything else to say, and with an awkward shrug she left. Feeling tongue-tied was not a condition she was accustomed to, Gwyn found. Though oddly enough, she was almost enjoying it.

* * *

Thunder was beginning to grumble again when Gwyn returned. Her mares greeted her with soft wuffles, eager for the water she'd brought. She murmured fondly to them as she patiently filled and refilled the small canvas hollow she'd fixed in a rocky niche for their trough. Their thirst sated at last, she gave each of those velvety muzzles a hug and climbed around to the warmer heights of the fire.

She came over the edge of their small plateau and paused in surprise. The blankets had been neatly spread across the wide bed of haymoss. The damp horse blankets and oiled cloaks had been draped across the rocky edges to the right side of the fire. The tea was ready. And beyond the crackling flames, curled against a rock with her head pillowed in Ril's thick ruff, slept Llinolae.

The pleading eyes of her packmate begged stealth, and Gwyn didn't have the heart to refuse.

"Know that I am grateful, *Dumauz*. Your approval of her is important to me. Though, right now, I can see nothing any would disapprove of in her."

The bruised hollows around Llinolae's eyes had begun to recede. The slumber had taken some of the weariness too, and the pale brown of her skin was from the kiss of wind and sun. She'd scrounged out a rust-brown kerchief and donned it as a band to keep the odd lengths of hair from her eyes.

"She sleeps with such peace, Ril. Even after what she's been through she trusts and sleeps." Yet her strength of resolve and confidence had not been completely shed by slumber.

Gwyn felt her heart strings tug just a little more. Life for Khirlan's Dracoon would never be simple or peaceful enough to erase all mark of her responsibilities.

"And if I let myself come to care for you...," Gwyn shook her head faintly and sighed. "Caring for you would never be simple either, would it? But it would never be taken for granted either."

Last night and today, Gwyn had seen that Llinolae's determined passions were in no way cold. Instead Llinolae had shown her openness and self-assurance.

"I never would have expected you to turn and thank another for help in dismounting, but now I can barely imagine you losing your patience and withdrawing from honestly needed aid."

Would—could—Gwyn herself have been so trusting of a stranger? Even if that stranger held the title of a Royal Marshal, even if the Blue Sight suggested trust could be given?

Gwyn drew herself back with a slight shake. There were things needing attention. At least for the moment, she should try to remember that she was in charge of getting them done, because eventide certainly wasn't going to cook itself!

* * *

"That was good." Llinolae sighed, savoring the flavor of that last, warm spoonful of porridge.

Ril whined in a confused protest, and Gwyn glanced up with a faintly indulgent expression of her own. "It must be the fresh mumut."

"Hmmm...," the other woman ignored the sarcasm. Leaning back against the rock with a blanket wrapped around her and her eyes blissfully half-shut, Llinolae looked as contented as if she'd finished a ten course meal instead of a second bowl of sweetened mush. "I didn't know it grew so far north."

"What?"

"Mumut." Llinolae stirred enough to pass her empty bowl into Gwyn's waiting hand. "Does it grow in Valley Bay itself?"

"Ah—no. We've got something similar, though." Gwyn rinsed the last of their dishes, a crooked grin growing. "We call it *cinnamon.* "

"Cinnamon?" A puzzled frown folded a crease between those slender brows.

"It's not—"

"It's from your home world, isn't it?"

It was Gwyn's turn to be surprised.

"Yes, I remember now." A brief smile nearly stunned Gwyn before it vanished again. "You save the spice as those little stick things, then grind the ends down for a cooking powder or use the stick itself to stir flavor into a hot drink. Do I have the right spice?"

"Yes, you do."

"And it tastes a bit like mumut?"

For lack of anything more coherent to say, Gwyn simply nodded.

"I'd never guessed." Llinolae seemed pleased with that small discovery and drifted off into her thoughts, leaving Gwyn staring. Ril gave her new friend a gentle butt with her nose, and Llinolae remembered her presence, apologizing with a fond smile. The sandwolf's eyes glazed and nearly closed as Llinolae obligingly set to scratching behind a pointed, black ear.

"Do you enjoy cooking?" Gwyn found her sensibilities somewhere and settled herself away from the fire, tea in hand. "That you know about rare spices like cinnamon, I mean."

"No," Llinolae was amused by the very idea. "I just have an insatiable curiosity. With the everyday sorts of things, I tend to be the habitual observer."

What Blue Sight wasn't, Gwyn admitted to herself. She swirled the reddish tea in her cup, watching the small twigs and leaf bits collect in the middle. The feelings inside of her seemed to calm as the tea leaves danced in their age-old patterns. She fleetingly wondered if this warming peace might be Llinolae's doing with her Sight, but she couldn't deny that she'd welcome it, even if it was Llinolae's projections. They all could certainly use the respite. Although on further thought, Gwyn decided the feeling was probably just from the welcomed fire warding off that cold, thrumming rainstorm.

A strangled, little yowl drew a chuckle from Gwyn as she saw Ril nearly roll into Llinolae's lap, stretching to get her tummy rubbed. "Mind your manners, *Dumauz.* That woman's a lot sorer than you are, I'll wager."

Guiltily, Ril withdrew—but only to Llinolae's side. A reassuring rub along her stomach line returned the panting pleasure quickly, and in a very un-Ril-like, tongue-lolling manner, the sandwolf gazed up into Llinolae's blue eyes with sheer adoration.

Dear Goddess, not the both of us! Gwyn wryly recalled that archaic term of 'puppy love.'

"I want to thank the two of you." Gwyn started at the sound of Llinolae's voice. "I feel safe. Regardless of how premature that feeling may be...well, it seems a very long time since I could last say that. Thank you."

With a silent toast of her tea, Gwyn acknowledged the gratitude. But it was the quiet richness in Llinolae's tone that brought Gwyn's smile out. "You're sounding less hoarse, looking less bruised. The rest and fire has done you good already."

A rueful brow arched high as those icy blue eyes lifted from the sandwolf. "Can I withhold judgment on the bruises until morning?"

"That bad?"

"Yes and no." Llinolae shifted a bit against the hard rock behind her. The thin blanket wasn't much of a cushion for her back or tail bone. "I'm just getting stiff again."

"Still certain nothing's broken?"

"Not that I've noticed," Llinolae answered with a little amused reassurance.

"Would a back rub help?"

Ril's head came up, ears perked forward—as surprised as her Amazon was by that abrupt offer. And judging by the Dracoon's sudden stillness, it seemed that the usual implications were not lost on Llinolae either. But it had undeniably been Gwyn's voice that had done the asking; she supposed she should at least try to act like it was a rational idea. Though, it didn't feel like one. She saw her hand was fairly steady in holding the tea mug and noticed gratefully that her embarrassment hadn't flushed her skin much darker than its usual golden tan. The silence stretched, and she chanced a glance at the Dracoon, trying to remember that this *was* the Dracoon of Khirlan and that she *was* the Royal Marshal here on official errand—which didn't seem terribly relevant at the moment. With a faint strain, she cleared the dryness in her throat and elaborated, "It might help. Th-there's some creamed mint in my saddlebag. I admit I usually use it as a salve for the horses when they pull a tendon or such, but it's pretty useful on people as well."

"Ah-ha!" Llinolae's soft smile reappeared. "There's the drawback. Just how bad does this stuff smell, Marshal?"

Gwyn caught the teasing sparkle in the other's eye, and a grin started to tug on the corners of her own mouth. "Not bad at all. Do you want to try it?"

"If you're still offering—please!" And at Gwyn's nod, Llinolae began slowly—stiffly—to unwrap herself from both sandwolf and blanket.

As Gwyn rummaged through her pack for the salve, however, she thought she heard the woman mutter something to Ril about 'having accepted less eloquent propositions', and her sense of humor rose. Given how sore her companion was, anything but a massage was truly a deranged fantasy. The tension in Gwyn's stomach unknotted with her faint chuckle, and she returned to the fireside waving a tiny jar triumphantly.

It appeared that Llinolae too had shed her own trepidations—much more easily than her shirt, given her stiffness. With an almost naive eagerness, she prompted, "Where do you want me?"

"Face down on the bedding would probably be best." Gwyn fed another pair of rolled logs to the fire. "Are you going to be warm enough?"

Llinolae paused in bundling the tunic into a pillow, frowning faintly at the damp chill in the air. Her skin had already darkened enough to obscure the tan lines at her throat and wrists. Despite the fire's heat, there was a persistent updraft atop this rocky plateau.

"Here! Try this while I...," Gwyn tossed the discarded blanket at Llinolae as she was hurrying back to her packs.

A broad grin split her face as Gwyn spun about with a pair of woolly, leather-soled stockings held high in hand.

"My slippers?" Llinolae exclaimed in astonishment. "Why would you…no, of course. Your sandwolves needed my scent from something."

"Hope you don't mind much? I had to paw through your things a bit to get them."

"No," Llinolae laughed, delighted. "I don't mind at all!"

It was better when the short trousers, her bare shins and bare feet were finally covered. The fire seemed toasty and nearer as well. Together everything allowed a bruised, tired body to lie down and be about as comfortable as possible on a haymoss mattress. Gwyn settled gingerly on her knees, straddling Llinolae's hips yet worried about those sorer muscles. "Tell me if I get too heavy for you."

"You're fine," Llinolae asserted, although the words came out muffled against the tunic linen and were almost swallowed again by a sudden yawn.

Laughing gently, Gwyn opened the creamed mint. "You're not allowed to fall asleep yet—I haven't even started."

Llinolae made some inconsequential little sound of reply which promptly dissolved into a long moan of sheer relief as Gwyn's hands began.

"So now you can tell me," Gwyn murmured, "how's the cream smell?"

A purring, wordless assurance answered her, and pleased, Gwyn started to relax as her own body fell into the slow rhythm of stretch and pull. Her hands tingled cool and then grew warm as the salve was absorbed. Llinolae purred again, the cream's cool-hot touch beginning to ease even the worst of her stiffness.

And Gwyn continued. Her palms slid, slick and strong along the length of Llinolae's back. Her long fingered knuckles patiently ground through the tension, only to open again as her touch gentled and soothed the cool cream into the purpled bruises. She concentrated, the smoothness and softness of the woman beneath her luring Gwyn's focus into the single-minded purpose of healing. She found the tenseness of an ache beneath the soft, satiny skin. Her fingers pressed and played, coaxing tightness into unfolding like the slender kiss of the sun's ray opening a flower. Then she moved on to find the next tangled knot, then the next.

Slowly, the shining cream and caramel of skin blended beneath Gwyn's hands. Llinolae's skin tones grew deeper, richer…darker like a stained wood grows to shimmer when caressed with oil.

A sigh escaped her companion and Gwyn smiled fondly. Her hands went on in their steady, patient dance.

"You truly will put me to sleep soon," Llinolae mumbled, her words nearly slurred by her body's trance.

Gwyn leaned low, her hand kneading upwards to a little kink between Llinolae's shoulder and neck. She paused to brush a dark cluster of curls away from Llinolae's check, then kept working. Her own smile grew at the peacefulness she saw in Llinolae's face. Quietly she challenged, "Would that be bad?"

"Hmm, Gwyn…would what be bad?"

A single hand kept playing its rhythms while the other sought the ground to brace Gwyn as she bent even nearer. Tenderness crept into her tone as she asked again. "Is it so bad for you to fall asleep?"

A smile tried to curl in answer, but the lethargic, caring magic had taken its toll. In truth, Llinolae was already sleeping.

Gwyn brushed a feather-light kiss across Llinolae's cheek and carefully moved away. She drew the blanket up to cover the bared skin and found herself lingering a moment or two. Feeling foolish all of a sudden, she remembered her packmate and glanced at Ril who was stretched out by the fire. The sandwolf arched her head back questioningly at Gwyn's sudden attention to her.

With an unembarrassed shrug, Gwyn admitted she didn't quite know how to explain that impulsive action. But then she was suddenly smiling, because she did know, and Ril's warm compassion was there, thrumming softly along their packbond. "Just because she called me Gwyn for the first time…for the very first time."

And it had sounded so sweet.

Chapter Three

hat's wrong with it?" Llinolae asked, perplexed as Gwyn once again abandoned a quite adequate-looking trail which descended over the gorge edge. Ril hadn't even bothered to scout down the path. In fact, the sandwolf hadn't been doing much scouting of any kind in this slow, morning trek of theirs. But the Marshal was concentrating with a distracted scowl, searching the ground with its jutting rocks and straggly tree roots and didn't seem to hear any of the Dracoon's questions. So, Llinolae sighed and resigned herself to the presence of some mysterious trail markings and nudged Calypso onwards.

The gorge edge was actually more akin to a cliff face, and from a topographical standpoint, it would have been more apt to call this Great Forest a forest of steps. The floor of the gorge below them was very nearly at sea level, and in fact, it extended with a few gentle rolls east all the way to the Ramains' Plains which did border the western seas. The forested cliffs here began a jagged ascent which was intermittently leveled by plateaus until the very broad wastelands of the Clans' lands were reached. West beyond that were only rough, mountainous peaks which eventually plunged into the depths of the southern Qu'entar, forming a very formidable and uninhabitable eastern sea-coast.

Gwyn stiffened suddenly. Llinolae reined in Calypso, watching mutely as Ril went racing forward. A wild pripper clamored upwards, chattering and scolding in a fluster of panic at Ril's quick pounce over a slender tree root. The sandwolf buried her nose in a patch of fern and froze.

Llinolae glanced curiously at Gwyn, acutely aware of some soundless communication that these two used. But the Amazon was as unmoving as her packmate. Abruptly, Ril bounded off along the gorge edge ahead, and Gwyn broke into a cheerful grin.

"Ty's been here."

As if that answers everything, Llinolae thought with amusement. But as she obediently sent Calypso trotting after Cinder she remembered the third member of Gwyn's bondpack was Ty.

"There it is!" Gwyn pointed ahead.

Llinolae peered, still puzzled, and finally had to ask, "There what is?"

"The tree that marks descent to the Shea Hole."

The information didn't clarify much. Although the honeywoods here weren't anywhere as massive as the ones set further back from the cliff edges, the pillars of red bark and haymoss were still sturdy sizes. Sturdy and anonymous sentries. They offered Llinolae some vague sense of stoic strength, but there was scarcely anything more identifying about each as individuals.

"See...where Ril stands? The two limbs were knotted and then grew upwards again."

Not such a surprising thing, given the spring winds these honeywoods were subjected to so close to the gorge edge. But as Gwyn pointed again, Llinolae did make out the gnarled signature. The limbs in question were thigh width, each of them…meaning they'd either been very convenient trail markers or this place of refuge the Amazon was taking her to had been in existence for more than a hundred tenmoons!

"Whenever you see this sort of knotted limb in the Great Forest, my Sisters have left a trail to safety," Gwyn explained quietly. She halted Cinder beside Ril, dismounting and giving the sandwolf an absent pat as she studied the ground of unearthed stone that made up the gorge edge. She circled back and around to the far side of the honeywood, calling finally, "Aye, here it is. We'd best take it by foot."

Llinolae swung off Calypso, relishing the cool feel of leaves and dirt beneath her bare toes. Gwyn had offered her an extra pair of socks, but until the rain stopped threatening, Llinolae wasn't willing to risk drenched, woolen footwear; bare feet were infinitely preferable to that. Especially for her, since it left her unimpeded contact with the soil and so kept her bound within that encouraging strength of the life cycles surrounding her.

"Ril, you go first—horses second. We'll bring up the tail."

An odd arrangement, Llinolae thought fleetingly. But Gwyn was no longer distracted with trail markings and noticed her misgivings immediately.

"The footing may be a little washed out by the rains below. The mares need all they can get. You and me…well," Gwyn grinned with a shrug, "we can scramble across much less if we have to. And Ril will make sure there's at least enough for Cinder and Calypso without wearing much of it away herself."

Llinolae smiled wryly. "You're the guide. And I did promise to follow—even through Fates' Cellars."

Gwyn laughed. "You just never thought I'd lead off a cliff."

"Well…," Llinolae took a closer look at that dubiously narrow, steep path as it lay half-hidden by the tree beside them. "I suppose I should be more careful of my promises in the future."

"Don't fret. It's only the first dozen steps that are the worst."

"Which if I don't make, I won't have to worry about the rest. Right?"

"My point precisely."

Llinolae glanced at Gwyn, catching the dance of mischief in those copper-bright eyes. An absolutely contagious mischief, she found, and she couldn't help the lift to her own lips. "Lead on, Marshal."

It took Gwyn only a couple of minutes to redistribute the small packs more evenly between Calypso and Cinder, making certain the bulk of the gear's weight was secured forward over the mares' withers. The stirrups were removed and strapped flat as well, to keep them from snagging on rocks or roots. Then Ril was padding off quickly, followed quite unquestioningly by the burly mares.

Llinolae watched the bulk and lurch of ruddy horseflesh disappear with an impossible twist. The illusion was very strong—that the animals had simply stepped over the cumbersome tree roots and off the cliff edge without so much as a whinny of protest. As she followed Gwyn, however, she saw the quick cutback into a rocky niche that literally widened to a wagon width beneath the overhang of the gorge edge.

"Who'd have ever thought this was here?" Llinolae marveled, running a hand over the smoothed bedrock beside them. The stone was damp from the recent rains, but above it was solidly dry, and she had no doubt that this passage could indeed have been in existence for more than a hundred seasons. She shivered, shaking herself abruptly in annoyance at that slight protest from her Sight—having spent most of her life in the stone fortress of Khirla, she had no patience for the Sight's silly sensitivity to rock.

"It'll be better in a few more steps." Gwyn offered a gentle smile, then was busy concentrating on her own footing again. "Most of this path is as overgrown as any other in the Forest, but this top portion was hand-wedged from the rock."

Llinolae nodded, seeing the ancient lines of chip and chisel now that she knew to look for them. As Gwyn spared her another brief, encouraging smile Llinolae's stomach clenched tight, and she forgot the stonework completely. The disquieting feeling of…of wrongness was pressing again.

She scowled gloomily, the slender arches of her dark brows straightening, folding a crease between. It was an awkwardness—not truly a mistrustful sort of feeling. But still, some gnawing sense of…exposure…was lingering.

Whatever it was, Llinolae didn't like it.

As they broke into the damp moss and dirt of a more open track, Llinolae found her brooding stare had focused onto the back of that ruddy red vest. The easy swing of the sword at Gwyn's hip, the confident square of those shoulders, the quiet assurance of a Marshal's authority all should have countered this nagging doubt.

Should have, yet didn't—like the amarin's intricate shadows of duplicity and secrets in the Palace! Llinolae fumed.

And then suddenly Llinolae could put her finger on it. "I've spent most of my lifetime hoarding secrets!"

"What did you say?" Gwyn called back quickly.

"Nothing of any consequence," Llinolae grinned ruefully. "I'm just muttering to myself like a surly old infantry veteran."

Gwyn's laughter rippled back and left Llinolae only more mindful of the difference this Marshal was introducing to her. Save for the rare visits her harmon made to *dey Sorormin's* home world, she'd never had the luxury of a Sister's freedom.

Until now. And Llinolae found, it was unsettling. Gwyn acted as if they were equals—as if they were simply Marshal and Dracoon…as if Gwyn herself was privy to all Llinolae's secrets and completely non-judgmental about what such knowledge entailed.

The seeming arrogance of such unconditional acceptance was beyond Llinolae's sensibilities. Life with court baskers and military schemers had taught her much more caution. Need for that caution tugged at her, challenged her appraisal of Gwyn—devalued the woman's character. That in itself fired an equally unwieldy conflict within Llinolae because she found she wanted to respect this woman. She wanted to like Gwyn! And that equally puzzling prejudice only made Llinolae frown all the more as they trudged along.

* * *

"Mind the footing, Ril!" Gwyn called ahead as they neared the gorge floor. Yet she too felt that insistent pull of excitement. She could almost hear the low throated whine of Ty's impatience below.

The track returned to firmer stuff, and this time Gwyn did not call out to slow Ril. Ty was so near—so very near! The packbond between the three of them fairly thrummed with their anticipation. If Gwyn had stopped to think about it, she would have been proud of her bondmate's patience in waiting below on the gorge floor, because this trail certainly offered no safe place for a rambunctious reunion. But after two-and-a-half days of separation, she was as caught in the excitement of re-unifying the pack just as completely as Ril and Ty were.

Almost from habit, or perhaps from wanting to share such uncontainable joy, Gwyn glanced over her shoulder to Llinolae. Copper and blue gazes met, and the Dracoon gasped, startled into an abrupt halt as her hand instinctively reached to the earthen wall beside her for support. Gwyn paused expectantly but unconcerned. Her skin flushed the deep, deep brown of rich topaz; her eyes brightened, sparkling with flecks of gold like sunlight.

"It's our packmate, Ty! Just *feel* how close she is!" Gwyn reached back to Llinolae, vaguely thinking the long downward trek had begun to exhaust the other. But her hand was waved aside before they'd even touched; Llinolae's own skin tones darkened from a weary caramel to a sultry cocoa in a swift rush.

The lightest of frowns began to mar the beauty of Gwyn's flushed face. She took a hesitant step towards Llinolae only to have a hand wave her assistance aside before they touched again.

"I'm fine. I just need a short rest." The Dracoon pointed down the trail. "Go ahead. Go greet your friend."

Hesitation held Gwyn motionless until Llinolae nodded her on with a brighter smile and firm, "Go!"

The Amazon turned, almost darting off with the released excitement. As she disappeared around the bend of the trail, Llinolae sagged into the rough dirt wall of the trail's side. Her knees felt like honey butter. Her heart was racing as madly as if she'd run the horse course 'round Khirla on foot.

Nothing—nothing!—had prepared her for the utter, incredible beauty in that woman's sheer joy. Gwyn's smile alone had taken the breath from Llinolae's throat, the voice from her tongue...frozen her very wits. In that single shared glance, the ground beneath her feet had hummed with the vibrancy of spring and her entire being had been fused—suspended, cradled—in perfect harmony between the wondrous rapture of one joyous woman and the answering choir of rejoicing life cycles.

"Mother!" With a jolt, Llinolae realized, "I'm in love!"

There was nothing else that could explain that sense of...of sweet, utter wholeness joining her to both Gwyn and Aggar. Nothing save her blue sighted sensitivity could have called that beauty of spring from the surrounding forest's amarin in an answering chord to Gwyn's unguarded rapture.

She shook her head a little bit to clear it, a hand absently reaching to that banded kerchief about her brow. Her fingers jerked back as if burnt, and she stared at that hand with widening eyes of disbelief.

Unlike the clean tunic Gwyn had loaned her, this kerchief had been worn recently—in fact, it was the same the Amazon had used to mask her face against the smoke during the rescue the other night. It still carried a very strong imprint of the Amazon's personal amarin, and it had been that lingering essence of the Amazon that had been drawing Llinolae's touch.

"Amazon?" Llinolae muttered, amazement numbing her again. Had she ever even called this woman by her true name? Her ice blue eyes looked blankly down the trail. "Amazon...Marshal...Gwyn...." She paused and looked at that hand before her again. Slowly, the ancient-learned words of her Blue Sight Mistress and her n'Athena mentor rose in a frightened whisper, "*Soroe n'ti Mau...Soroi...Soroi n'Athena. Ti mae n'Gwyn n'Athena?*"

And then something clenched hard in her stomach, and Llinolae finally registered the words Gwyn had used in turning to her with that wondrous smile. The icy, frozen feeling descended again, and both hands grasped the gorge's rocky soil as she sank to the trail. Stunned, she heard those words again and again—there was nothing but a single, clear, unhidden meaning of amarin carried within them.

"...*our packmate—Ty! Just* feel *how near she is!*"

Gwyn knew of her Blue Sight.

Llinolae felt winter sweep in with her deepest fears.

Gwyn knew. She wasn't merely making some assumption because of the color of Llinolae's eyes. All the old feigns that it was simply an anomaly of her mixed blood, all the care she had practiced to keep her Sight unnoticed all these tenmoons by the Court, the guards, even the Steward!—all she had done to avoid discovery by the Council of Ten. Only two days with her, and she knew? But no, Gwyn had never been fooled! The restless, uneasy feeling that had plagued Llinolae—that she felt somehow exposed before this woman—was because her secret was, in truth, exposed.

And Gwyn was a Royal Marshal, duty bound to report this. Then in Churv the Crowned Heir, too, would be required to inform the Council of Ten—who would claim her for their Keep. It wouldn't matter after that. They might train her for someone's Shadow, give her the choice of becoming some mindless Seer or perhaps, if the Mother's Hand held her very, very near she would only need to become a Seer's Apprentice. But her life would not be her own anymore—not ever again.

"Yet Dearest Mother, I love her." Eyes closed in a sigh of weary resignation and dejection as her head leant back against the gorge wall. "By Your Hand, Mother, I do."

* * *

A cool-nosed, leathery-skinned muzzle nudged Llinolae's hands where they dangled over her knees. For a long moment, there was no movement from the woman. Her legs were drawn up, head bowed against her knees, but Ril was patient and did not hurry that slow return from the amarin of Aggar. She had known the Dracoon was long aware of her approach just as the woman had known of the sandwolf's vigilant guard since mid-afternoon, even though Ril had kept a respectful distance down trail until now. If there had been a danger threatening during any of that silent time, Ril also knew the Blue Gift would have sensed it equally as clearly, and Llinolae would have brought herself out of this weary trance-like state quite abruptly.

A hand moved a bit.

Ril's ears perked forward attentively, her head cocked a little to one side. The sandwolf's empathic understanding of strangers did have its limits. In some ways she was more sensitive to this woman's character because of their shared awareness of amarin and sentient emotions. But Ril had been raised among the Blue Sights of Valley Bay and had been trained among the Council's Seers. She knew no Blue Sights such as this woman.

Not only had Ril met few with the Sight whose innate talents were more powerful than Ring Binder Bryana's, but Ril had never remembered anyone quite like this woman in style; Llinolae was very different in her use of the Blue Gift. It felt to Ril something like Gwyn once felt when they'd suddenly come face-to-face with a traveler who hadn't spoken any language Gwyn knew—it was bemusing and sometimes frustrating. Ril had the disconcerted feeling, however, that Llinolae was rapidly learning to understand this sandwolf more quickly than Ril was learning of Llinolae.

A slow, deep breath was drawn. Eyes still closed, the woman lifted her head in a stretching arch until she rested straight-backed against the gorge wall.

That was another thing of difference Ril had noticed. This Blue Sight Llinolae reached into her harmon-self center, before extending downward into the outer amarin beneath her. Then Llinolae literally took her harmon—the part of her amarin that made her life essence uniquely *hers* —and she literally flung her harmon outward into Aggar's life cycles to meet and weave herself through the threads of amarin.

As Ril understood things, this was impressively different from the Council's Seers. Those Blue Sighted Seers drowned in the sweet amarin of Aggar to lose all sense of themselves, and eventually they were eclipsed, their personal sense of identity forgotten or lost amid the intertwining patterns and weaves. This allowed the Seers to read and describe the patterns of the amarin when the Council Masters questioned them, or to reweave the physical patterns around them when prompted. The result of the Council and Seers' work was admirable enough—they'd nearly done away with things such as earthquakes and droughts.

She was different in respect to Seeing as well. Ril knew Blue Sighted Shadows or Valley Bay Sisters kept somewhat anchored to their self-identity. Some of them were quite powerful; through skill and out-of-time Seeing, some could reach the Amazons' home world or reach back into the history of Aggar. Then there were those with an affinity for understanding animals as if they were bloodkin, or for deciphering human loyalties—their talents depended on their training and individual strengths. But Llinolae did not 'look' at the tree or star or neighboring companion when she used her Sight. The Blue Sights of Ril's acquaintance had always 'looked' outward. They literally needed to see the amarin—eyes open. Ril knew they couldn't do anything, when blind-folded. In some way, they visually had to 'See.'

The sandwolf's head tipped aside once more, peering closely at the woman. But Llinolae's eyes were closed. This was certainly not what the Sisters of Valley Bay managed.

Apparently Llinolae's harmon truly did co-exist with the amarin of Aggar's life cycles. Through air or soil, emotion or sound, sight or smell, she could fling her harmon into the amarin through all of them.

What fascinated the sandwolf even more was that when Llinolae did this, it was a meeting of amarin—a meeting of life cycles and self—a meeting of essence to essence with an equality that Ril had never seen any other of the

Sight display. It meant that Llinolae's awareness of her personal amarin was exchanged with a Primal Awareness of Life's Quintessence. That was a daunting concept—an individual calmly meeting some vast, omniscient consciousness and returning with her sanity still in place.

It was a difficult for Ril to grasp what that might do to a human's harmon. How could any individual simply bond to something as all-encompassing, as completely different in thought, mood and perspective, as the naked energies of Life?

Then again, the sandwolf pondered, perhaps it was a matter of simplicity and acceptance not prideful recognition. Packmates could be combinations of sandwolf, human and eitteh. All three were sentient beings, yet all very different. Communication was sometimes difficult because of those differences, but that was why the bonding was undertaken as a lifetime commitment to the chosen pack—it was why packbonds honored affectionate respect and trust above all else.

For the pack to thrive, the packmates had to value an intimate understanding of one another. Without the entire pack's commitment to mutual understanding, communication disintegrated because of individual differences. And so the bonding had evolved within the sandwolves to an instinctive imprinting at an early age, to provide an even finer sense of communion and projection of meanings to the 'others' within the pack.

The inherent respect for differences, the patience to learn new communication skills without rushing trusts—Ril's own empathetic senses told her that Llinolae cherished these things dearly. That was the basis for many strong relationships, and sandwolves accepted it without question—which raised another interesting observation: Llinolae's attraction to Gwyn.

The woman stirred again.

Returning abruptly to practicalities, Ril eyed the damp trail somewhat disgustedly. The Terran fabric of those short trousers was tightly woven, but it wasn't waterproof. Llinolae was going to feel very cold soon.

The Dracoon's legs unfolded stiffly. Her hands dropped to press flat against the ground.

The touch of Llinolae's amarin withdrew from Ril's empathic senses and Ril's attention shifted again. Perplexed, the sandwolf's brow wrinkled. She stared harder at the ground, but found no lingering traces of Llinolae's amarin within the Great Forest's own.

"I am still here, Ril."

The sandwolf glanced up at the face of the woman, finding a soft smile of greeting. She returned it with a toothy one of her own. It shouldn't have surprised her that Llinolae would still be sensitive to her, when Ril was so close. After all, Llinolae had reached across stars to the home world of *dey Sorormin* and across leagues to Gwyn's own sword and lifestone. An arm's length wouldn't have thwarted her in the least.

"Thank you for returning."

Ril tipped her head, moving forward to accept the offered ruffle of the curly fur behind her crown. Then the woman did something only a very few of Gwyn's kin had ever even dared—she gently touched the smooth, leathery hide of Ril's forehead.

At the sandwolf's startled but pleased acceptance, Llinolae did more. She took Ril's face between her hands and lifted that sandy-clear gaze to meet her own. "And thank you for watching over me so patiently. I know I've been a very, very long while away."

Ril pushed closer, lightly butting Llinolae's pale cheek in reassurance. She had been uneasy with this woman in the beginning, because of how deeply the sword's images had affected Gwyn. And she had known through the depths of the packbond what Gwyn had been hiding from—that Gwyn would inevitably fall for this Blue Sight once they met.

Being a sandwolf, Ril did not presume to understand the heartbonds of human-to-human attachments, but she could grasp the feelings and the weight of their importance easily enough. She found it good to discover Llinolae's growing affections were matching Gwyn's own, and she credited Llinolae's pledge with the honesty it deserved.

"I'm honored by your trust." Llinolae's smile softened, not expecting and yet touched by this last note. "Your approval means much. I promise you—I've no wish to hurt her. In truth, I'll do my best not to."

Unfortunately, Ril knew how there was often much said that couldn't be done. She could only hope, for both Gwyn's and Llinolae's sakes, that the hindrances of the Fates and hearts wouldn't clash too often—nor wound too deeply.

She rose with Llinolae to turn down the trail.

From a distance, thunder rolled in through the dimness of the late afternoon clouds. Ril sighed as she trotted after Llinolae—to her, that deep rumble sounded ominously like the Fates' jesting.

Chapter Four

A gust of wind swept the dampness in with Gwyn's entry, and hastily she rounded to tie the tent flaps shut again. Llinolae glanced up from brushing Ril, slightly startled at the heightened excitement and anxiety in Gwyn's amarin. The sandwolf nosed Llinolae's hand reassuringly, and the woman tried hard not to sigh in agreement; her Sight was not always very helpful in what it allowed her to See. Most often she only caught hints of uncomfortable emotions or plotting intentions. Unfortunately, this afternoon her Gift had made it alarmingly clear that Ty's reason for abruptly withdrawing from the camp had been her dislike of Llinolae.

"...admit I'm surprised this old healer's tent is holding together so well."

Llinolae smiled weakly as Gwyn's voice registered. But the Amazon was busy shedding her drenched cloak and boots, and her back was still to the pair on the floor. Llinolae returned to Ril's grooming, absently noticing their surroundings again.

The tent was nearly as broad as it was tall. The heavy canvas walls were supported by a circular, wooden frame, with four center poles fitting snugly around a ceramic brazier. There was a sort of chimney flap, also fastened to the center poles, raised above the rest of the cloth roofing and outer canvas. And although the brazier contained only embers at the moment, it was large enough to hold a cooking fire when desired.

The rest of the tent was equally well designed. Wall braces served double-duty as pegged racks for clothing. The planks of the storage crates had been transformed into a platform, raising the canvas and thick woven rugs of the flooring well above the damp ground. Wide bed pallets doubled as low couches when folded back against the wall braces. A collapsible table and set of camp chairs had also been unpacked from the Shea Hole's supplies, as well as saddle racks and a set of short shelves. Glass lanterns hung from the rafters, sitting in little roped nests well above head height. All this, while still the structure seemed airy and reasonably uncrowded. But then it had been intended to house wounded and to allow the healers to work standing.

A Shea Hole, Llinolae had discovered, was not a shelter in itself. Rather, it was a hidden cache of necessary camp goods. Nestled in a small boxed canyon at the foot of the gorge, the ceramic lockers had been fashioned to resemble, in both color and shape, the tree roots and cliff rocks of its niche. With inner seals waxed tight to protect against wet and decay, the non-perishable supplies had been hiding, innocuously, longer than her lifetime.

"The horses' tent is just as dry." Gwyn reclaimed the Dracoon's wandering attentions, sighing deeply as she sat herself down on one of the couches. "I didn't bother with the picket lines tonight. If anything happens, I'd rather the mares be loose."

"Afraid of lightning in a gorge?" Llinolae murmured absently.

Gwyn shrugged. "Perhaps more of a flash flood."

"There were no high water marks." Llinolae's gaze didn't leave Ril nor did her hands falter with those long, rhythmic brush strokes.

Mutely Gwyn watched them, but in her mind she saw the flooded stream bed of another rain storm and the broken body of the man that had tried to burn her with the barn. She felt a gentle tug along her packbond and found Ril's soft, sandy eyes on her. A melancholy smile accepted the sandwolf's assurances, but Ril's compassion suddenly felt very minuscule within the tent's empty, growing unease.

The sandwolf's glance left her, and with that withdrawal Gwyn realized how hurt and confused she was by Ty's absence. It was not at all like their packmate to volunteer for sentry patrols and refuse their company when neither Gwyn nor Ril thought there was any need yet for sentry posts—especially not after their three days of separation. It made Gwyn wonder if her bondmate had run into some kind of trouble with the Clans earlier, but Ril would have known of that. And she'd have gone out circling on Ty's heels if there were wild baskers or buntsows to worry about.

It didn't make sense. Gwyn had a distinctly disquieting impression that she should have understood Ty's evasiveness. Actually, she had the impression that she ought to understand someone else's moodiness as well.

Her copper gaze drifted to Llinolae and the Dracoon's hand paused in mid-air at the attention. At least my presence isn't being completely ignored, Gwyn thought.

"I beg your patience," Llinolae sighed. The hand with Ril's brush dropped abruptly as did her facade of nonchalance. Weariness suddenly shadowed every line of her body, from the faintly bruised hollows beneath her eyes to the slump of her shoulders. Even Llinolae's skin tone had notably darkened a shade more than her normal light tan.

The transformation was subtle, as if Llinolae had looked this tired all evening and Gwyn had merely not been aware of it before now. But Gwyn's experience with Selena and Kimarie—and especially with Bryana—had taught her differently. She was not in the least fooled by that shift of amarin; Llinolae had intentionally been projecting an illusion earlier—to hide her fatigue. After the closeness they had shared last night, it hurt Gwyn to know Llinolae felt any need to hide from her.

Two rejections in the same evening? What was she doing to be so unpopular? Gwyn tried to muster together some kind of smile saying, "Have you decided my barbering skills were even worse than my cooking? That you should trust me so little, so suddenly?"

Tenderness touched the melancholy in Llinolae. She looked up at Gwyn finally, amending, "No, I like my new haircut quite well. Thank you. I know you would have preferred for someone else to have done it, but I am grateful."

"I suppose…," Gwyn's shrug was awkward. "It turned out well."

"It did."

Gwyn smiled at that richening tone of sincerity. And she had to admit that at least she'd gotten one thing right since eventide.

Llinolae's hair was now short-clipped at both the sides and back, barely a finger-width long, and the black curls that wrestled on top were just long enough for one or two to fall forward over her forehead.

Guiltily Gwyn jerked her gaze aside, realizing she'd been on the verge of staring. The ice-clear blue of Llinolae's eyes and the inky black sheen of her hair made a vibrant contrast—beautiful even in this weary state. Why didn't it make her look younger, more innocent, Gwyn wondered. Instead, the high curve of her cheekbones and the slender arches of her eyebrows only seemed more prominent, more expressive. Llinolae's subtle amarin of determination and intelligence were now underscored by her pondering expressiveness. Without the obstructions of either tangled hair or smoky soot, Llinolae was simply more compelling in her strength.

She should have been an Amazon, Gwyn mourned. Then the truth dawned; she was, in truth, more of an Amazon than any Gwyn had known from Valley Bay. Because Llinolae had been born of Terran descent—just as the Founding Mothers of *dey Sorormin's* home world had been. Because she was a woman-loving-woman who cherished others' lives so much that she risked everything as their guardian—just as the n'Athena had in bringing their ships and families across the stars to guard Aggar in that Imperial decline. Aye, she was an Amazon—by blood, by heart, by ethics of soul—she undeniably was.

So why is it so strange that I've lost my heart to her? Gwyn rebuked herself, and the audacity of that idea suddenly shook her.

"Don't chide yourself so," Llinolae's soft voice came.

Gwyn caught her breath. Heart racing and skin flushing from deep gold to burnished brown in a single beat, she kept her eyes downcast to the whitened knuckles of her fists.

"The ill will between your sandwolf, Ty, and myself is from a misperception. We'll sort it out. I promise you." At the confusion of Gwyn's amarin, Llinolae added, "Ril was leery of me too in the beginning. Remember?"

With an effort, Gwyn managed a shaky nod. She concentrated on breathing and relaxing, until bit-by-bit her fingers began to uncurl. Perhaps she was going to be politely left alone in this foolishness. Or more likely, the intensity of her inner turmoil wasn't allowing Llinolae's Sight to accurately decipher details quite yet. That wouldn't matter much in the long run, Gwyn knew. Sooner or later her amarin would be clearly discernible for what it was.

A brief memory of the young scribe in camp with Llinolae returned to Gwyn, and she felt the knotted muscles in her shoulders gradually release more of their tension. There had been compassion, not ridicule, in Llinolae's deciphering that evening. Gwyn had nearly forgotten who she was dealing with—this woman who so valued others. There was nothing Gwyn need fear in what Llinolae would learn with her Sight. And it wasn't as if Gwyn expected her companion to return the interest!

"There is something else...."

"Well...," a derisive little smile lifted the corner of Gwyn's mouth at that tactful comment. "None of us is perfect. Are we?"

Llinolae glanced across to her then, and their eyes met, glowing softly as humor rose to gentle both of their nerves. They shared a chuckle that grew. Then suddenly they were both laughing, skin tones flushing even darker while Ril's ears pricked forward; she seemed puzzled, but their laughter was warm and chased the anxiety from the tent. Llinolae noticed the poor sandwolf's confusion, and she laid a reassuring hand to her ruff, trying to catch her breath before explaining, "It's all right, my friend. We're simply being silly."

At which point, Ril heaved something of an exasperated sigh and returned her head to her paws for slumbering.

"A most proper response for sandwolves to take when humans are being hopelessly human," Gwyn quipped, half to Llinolae and half to her packmate.

Ril opened a single eye in disdain, then shut it with a snorting "humpf."

Feeling better, Llinolae stroked that furry back sympathetically. In a moment she shifted her attention back to Gwyn. But she too was aware of the camaraderie that had returned. A lump tightened in Llinolae's throat. She knew that what she was about to bring up might strain this new friendship beyond repair.

Gwyn waited, watching her expectantly. Llinolae exchanged her hesitation for directness. "I need to ask you something you may not like."

Gwyn's head tilted inquiringly, a feathery strand of red slipping into her eyes. She tucked it absently behind her ear again, noticing Llinolae's distraction at the movement. But she only said, "I'm listening."

"I need you to tell me why you came to Khirlan in the first place—to Clantown in particular. And why you're so certain my blue eyes mark me with the Sight."

"I came because Bryana told me of your need."

"My need...*me?*" Llinolae pointed at herself, brow wrinkled and only partially comprehending.

Gwyn nodded. "Bryana reasoned your dilemma was King's business and asked me to come."

"Bryana...?" She tongued the sound as she groped for a face to match that name, and then she had it. "The Ring Binder of Valley Bay? *That* Bryana?"

"Aye," Gwyn sent her a rueful grin. "Actually, she's my mother."

"Your—?" Llinolae blinked, remembering the slightly built woman in the garden apron.

"You did ask her not to involve the Council in anything."

"I remember."

"But she felt your complaints about the neglect of King and Crowned legitimate enough to warrant some investigation. So, she spoke with me."

"How is it you're the Binder's daughter *and* a Royal Marshal?"

Gwyn shrugged. "I don't know. I've always wanted to be more like Jes than Bryana. I'm built a lot like Jes, taller and stronger than most of Valley Bay. She's a Marshal herself, and I'm not Sighted. My sibling Kimarie now—she's a head smaller than myself and has *M'Sormee's* Blue Gift as well. Although, I admit she's never aspired to be arbitrator nor adventurer, so she had no intention of vying for a seat on the Ring of Decisions either. And she certainly has no patience for out-of-time Seeing, so she could never connect the Ring of Valley Bay to n'Sappho of our home world for conferences. She much prefers wandering the meadowlands of the upper Valley and herding the beasites about."

"I see...," Llinolae said, assimilating that thoughtfully.

"Actually, when I set out I expected to be riding south with Jes. But there was an accident and...well...."

It was Gwyn hesitating now, Llinolae noticed. Then abruptly she realized, "So the Council's been involved after all."

Gwyn nearly winced at that flat accusation. "Not precisely."

"What's that mean?" She wasn't any less suspicious.

"The Council sent two of my Sisterhood to aid me instead, Brit and Sparrowhawk. They pose as tinker-trades. Brit's also a healer as well as a Royal Marshal herself. They've worked with the Council on-and-off through the Changlings' Wars, but they aren't here to do the Council's bidding. They came because I needed help, because aiding you was not something I could expect to do alone, and Jes couldn't come."

"What you're saying is...those two are your Sisters first and Council pawns second?"

Gwyn scowled at the choice of words, yet reluctantly yielded a nod. "Basically, yes...that's true."

Llinolae weighed that carefully, lips pursed in a growing frown of concentration. Then she pressed, "And your own oaths to the Crowned Rule? Do you hold your mother's vow to me above the Marshal's Oath of Fealty?"

At that, Gwyn grew as grim as the Dracoon sounded. She leaned forward, folding a leg under her and half kneeling on the couch as she challenged back, "*You* are a Dracoon. Do *you* hold personal pledge above duty?"

Llinolae blinked at the suddenness of the cold attack. Then a solemn calm settled over her features, and she answered quietly but firmly, "They are one and the same to me."

"Exactly!" Gwyn pounced. "My loyalty is sworn to the Crowned and her cause. My love is freely given to both my parents and my Sisterhood. But my judgments are my own. I stand by my decisions and accept the responsibilities for my actions. I am a Marshal, Dracoon. Not someone's pawn—not a soldier blindly following anyone's orders!"

"Patience!" Llinolae raised a palm, silencing the protest.

Gwyn's tone grew gentler as she relented. "I beg forgiveness—please."

"Gwyn, I'm sorry. I...." She broke off in frustration and paused for a long breath. Trying again, she explained, "When you say you are a Marshal, I worry that you're saying you're honor-bound to tell the King and Crowned Rule that I have the Blue Sight. If you do that, then they in turn must surely tell the Council. I simply do not wish the Council involved in my personal life." She paused again, then admitted, "Frankly, I've enough to deal with as it is. I don't need superstitious, meddling oligarchies interfering now! When I spoke so freely with Bryana, it was only because I felt she'd not betray me to the Council."

"She hasn't. I haven't. Neither Brit nor Sparrowhawk has. Nor will they, any more than I intend to. Your reasons for keeping the Gift to yourself, Llinolae, are only King's business if this isolation from the Council is compounding the problems you're having with the Clans."

Llinolae nodded faintly, absorbing the limits and rational of that statement to find it fair. "And if it does appear to be interfering with my duties here...?"

Gwyn's copper eyes met Llinolae's blue, and the Dracoon gave a snort as she glanced aside abruptly. "You're right, of course. I'd tell them myself."

"Aye," Gwyn agreed softly. "It's that overly developed sense of selflessness—we both have it."

"Ethical responsibility?" Llinolae muttered. "Stubbornness might be a better

171

description, don't you think?"

"Integrity is often stubborn, but only with need."

Gwyn's smile almost stole Llinolae's breath; the amarin of beauty and sensitivity were so clear.

This is why I love her, Llinolae grasped. This total acceptance, this nearly instinctual understanding of what I value. She doesn't simply hear my words, she knows the depths of commitment they reflect for me. And she doesn't find it daunting or impressive—or foolish. Of all the women Llinolae had loved—though there hadn't been such a great number—none of them had ever completely understood her sense of need and action. Duty had meant only work to them; it was equated with power or perhaps with some degree of honor, but never had they felt the bone-deep obligation to others—to attempt the near-impossible simply because there was no one else capable of the attempt. It mattered less if she failed, than if she never tried—

No, Llinolae mused bleakly, those were her father's words, talking to his child in her first seasons of learning. Now, in Khirlan, it did matter *terribly* if she failed. There had to be a way to make peace between Clan and District folk. There had to be a way to ban or destroy their Fire weapons. There had to be, even if it meant her own happiness—her own life!—was to be forfeited. Otherwise the price, in lives and blood, was going to be too high.

Perhaps that was why the Mother had guided this other pair of *dey Sorormin* to aid Gwyn. Perhaps it was meant that her life be exchanged for truce—only not by dying, as she'd once assumed such an exchange could demand. She'd forgotten how many alternatives could be created instead. It was a cold thought—that forfeiting her life to the Fates might mean becoming a Council's tool. It was also suddenly a very tangible possibility.

"No...," Llinolae murmured absently, "I can't quite believe that is to be...not yet."

"What?"

She glanced back to find Gwyn still watching her closely. The Marshal had planted one stockinged foot flat on the pallet and settled an elbow on the upraised knee, her hand supporting the side of her head. Her long fingers were curled in the disarray of her red-blond hair, loosening that short braid and adding more to the general unruliness. The apricot glow of Gwyn's fair, tanned skin had returned. The clarity and patience of her purpose reflected in those copper-bright eyes; the strength of her body was visible in her bared forearms.

Llinolae shut her eyes against the bittersweet intrusion of shirtless images from yesterday's bathing.

"What can't you quite believe yet?" Gwyn prodded softly.

Her chin lowered. With a sigh, Llinolae took a moment to gather her wits again. It was an effort to return to business. "I'm not convinced the Council's aid will provide the solution between the Clans and my folk. Least, I'm not quite ready to turn the District over to them completely."

Gwyn shrugged. "They'd probably prefer you—or the Crowned—to settle a truce without their direct influence anyway. Aggar gains nothing through fighting. Doesn't matter if the conflicts are between the District and Clan or if they're between human and Changling it only brings blood and devastation—neither is the Council's goal."

"No, they aren't, are they?" Llinolae scoffed. An acidic-tasting chuckle echoed her unvoiced thoughts—that the Council preferred more insidiously passive methods, even when direct confrontation would be more prudent.

"May I ask why you were out with the scouting party?"

Again Gwyn's candor was startling in contrast to the Court intrigues Llinolae was accustomed to. A smile cracked as she shook her head. "Forgive me. I've not dealt with many Marshals...and none in the last several seasons."

An answering grin met hers. Gwyn wasn't in the least slighted. "I'd expected to find you in the city, given the Feast Days. When you weren't there...well," she shrugged, "it didn't take me long to come looking elsewhere."

"How did you know where to come?" Llinolae asked abruptly. "I thought there were only two in the City who knew my errand."

"Which errand?" Gwyn asked pointedly.

Blue eyes widened in surprise. The question almost shocked Llinolae in its forthright challenge; it went against a lifetime of protocol and deference to the title she held. Belatedly, she remembered what Gwyn was and a touch of humor chided her bruised pride. "Are all Marshals so dogged?"

"Like a basker jackal on scent," Gwyn returned flippantly, her grin broadening.

"A very fair-haired basker," Llinolae noted.

Gwyn shrugged, then lifted a brow. "Are you not going to tell me?"

"Of my errand? No, certainly I will." Llinolae's tone was somber again. "During the Feast Days I traditionally do stay city-bound. I'd hoped that the first ten-day of the Feasts would distract most of the Court from noticing my absence—my Father's tradition was to suspend official functions and simply mingle with the festival folk, and I've carried on the practice. But I didn't want any interference in this. I wanted to speak with the Clan Leads secretly."

"About establishing some sort of truce?"

"Aye, and that's still my intention." Llinolae paused, frowning deliberately. "There must be a common ground for us—somewhere. The District and Plateau are big enough for—for something to be settled!"

"Any ideas of what?"

A frustrated little shrug underlined her scowl. "Nothing specific. I'm assuming land or a more civilized access to the Traders' Guild might be useful for them. But I assume those would be important, because historically those sorts of resources are often viable bartering pieces at a negotiating table. The Clan may have completely different ambitions, however. I simply don't know. And I won't know, until I can manage to talk with them."

"You met with no success at all in Clantown?"

"None. But I would never expect their militia to aspire to peaceful ambitions, especially not with their supply of fire weapons to play with!"

"I see your point," Gwyn allowed.

"My only real hope to reach the Clan Leads is to convince someone with less stake in the militia's warfare..."

"So you were going further east into the Plateau to the farmsteads and crafters."

"A Lead in their farming community, or even a Lead Scout—the scouts seem to represent a balance of farmers and military."

Gwyn considered that venture reluctantly. It wasn't precisely an easy task to manage. Still, the Dracoon was correct in assuming the farmers might have more stake in trade and resources than the Clan militia. And the farmers and crafters provided the foundation for the Clan's social structure. They were the ones that designated the Clan Leads, and the Leads in turn appointed the militia commanders. So, it was also quite possible that a Lead Scout might listen— might just be the ones who know the most about all different factions of the Clan. It was quite possible they'd hear the Dracoon's offer. Possible...but not probable, Gwyn knew. She looked to Llinolae again. "Did you learn anything useful during your days among them?"

"A bit. Seems their stockpile of fire weapons lies in the northeast nearer the original off-worlder settlements."

"Impressive tidbit. How did you uncover that one?"

Llinolae's mouth curled in a less than amused smile. "They'd been sorting through a small shipment just fetched, when the scouts brought me back from my aborted escape. I saw neither the weapons nor their maps, but I Saw a fair lot of the poor pack horse they dropped me next to at the watering trough while someone went to fetch me a few clothes. The amarin of the travels still clung to the beast and weren't so hard to decipher. Besides, it gave me something to concentrate on aside from pain."

"Not pleasant."

"Not in the least." Llinolae stretched the stiffened muscles in her side carefully. It seemed to hurt more, merely thinking about it. She shook the notion aside, continuing with, "There was something more. There was an amarin of anxiety about these Clan folk, Gwyn—especially for the militia. I Saw an overwhelming sense of fear among them. I felt the commitment of purpose that unites them was actually grounded in desperation."

"That sort of incentive leads to extreme measures pretty rapidly," Gwyn noted with legitimate concern.

"Apparently, it already has in some cases."

"Aye—like that village fire." At Llinolae's puzzlement Gwyn elaborated, "Burning the whole east end of Diblum was fairly extreme, wouldn't you say?"

"Unfortunately, yes. More and more of that sort of thing has been happening—" She stopped in mid-sentence, blue eyes narrowing as they returned abruptly to Gwyn. "You seem to know an amazing portion of my recent doings, Marshal. I'd thought you'd only just arrived Khirlan."

"I have. And no, I haven't been snooping around your Court for very long either." Gwyn pointed at the rack. Her sheathed sword hung next to their cloaks. "The lifestone in my hilt seems to be sensitive to your Sight."

"A lifestone?" She knew only vague rumors of those, but then she'd not thought they were used by many aside from the Council. "So between your sword's stone and Aunt Taysa's directions...?"

"I didn't speak with your aunt."

Llinolae sighed at the implications in that. Unfortunately, she could probably imagine why Taysa would avoid a Royal Marshal. Dutifully, she pressed, "Why wouldn't she see you?"

"The Steward is your aunt, isn't she?" Gwyn fleetingly hoped there had been a mistake somewhere, somehow, but Llinolae nodded as Gwyn had expected her to. "She didn't give me a reason—or at least not one any of her Swords passed on to me. They told me she would be available after the Feasts, but not before. Then they stuck me in a Palace room back by the stables—"

"What!"

"Then after one fairly uneventful day, the next found two of her Swords trying to kill me."

"Who?" Suddenly that tone was flat and steely.

"The first fellow I think was a Jefriz?"

"And the other? Were they working together?"

"No, they weren't together. As for the second attempt, I beg your patience…," Gwyn drawled slightly, a wry twist to her grimace. "But there isn't always time to get a name."

Biting back a curse, Llinolae shut her eyes and sank her frustration down through the wools, canvas, and wood—down into the damp soil of Aggar itself.

"It gets worse," Gwyn's quiet tone had shed any hint of sarcasm.

"Tell me."

"The nameless one used a fire weapon."

Just as the traitors within her camp had, Llinolae added to herself. Her palms went flat against the rugs and she drew a deep, weary breath. Then the sweet strength and patience of the Great Forest's life cycles came at her beckoning, and Llinolae felt the inner balance of her harmon return. With a slow release, her breath loosed and her eyes flickered open again. Sorrow and apology, practicality and common sense, all colored the compassion she finally extended to Gwyn. "I am sorry, Gwyn'l. Truly sorry. You've not seen Khirlan at its best. But then, sadly, it's been a very long time since there was much better to be seen."

Llinolae sighed, shaking her head again. "My aunt…the irony is that she was twisting my own orders against you. I'd sworn her to silence, along with Samcin, her Master of Arms. I was trying to guard my patrol against the risk that some of the less…reasonable?…of the Clans' scouts might intercede before I could reach one of their more tolerant Leads, or one of the farming folk even. I didn't want my task to be discovered. Not that most of the Clan wouldn't be generally delighted to hang my head as a triumph, or blackmail Churv for some ransom."

"You and your patrol were still ambushed," Gwyn noted quietly.

"Aye, and they took only me."

The pain of those deaths brushed them both in silence.

Gwyn closed her eyes and rubbed a tired hand across her face. There was nothing to be done for those lost now.

"I can't just go back to Khirlan!" Llinolae reiterated her earlier words with a sudden vehemence. "My companions' deaths…the loss of so many folk in Khirlan will be for nothing, should I simply leave. I wish there was another way to reach one of the Leads. If I can't talk with someone, there is only one choice."

"Destroying their weapons arsenal, you mean?"

"Aye. Did your mother speak of that as well or…?"

"Some," Gwyn admitted honestly. "I'm not quite opposed nor in favor of the idea yet. You shared the ambition with me as well—again when your Sight reached me through my sword's lifestone on that night of the town fire."

Llinolae frowned thoughtfully. Maybe she should have paid more attention to those troubadour rhymes of lifestones as a child. But then, she had never really had all that much time for any of the usual childhood pastimes. She sighed and shook the musings away. "What do you think of the idea?"

"Ambitious. Sometimes I nearly convince myself it would be the best of all plans. It would balance the power."

Llinolae waited for her to say more.

Gwyn half-shrugged and admitted her discomfort, "But it would deprive the Clans of their only true resource. Is it...," she hesitated, choosing her words and struggling to define her own thoughts even as she spoke, "is it necessary to deprive them of their strength so completely? They have so poorly integrated with Aggar's peoples and have always clung so tenaciously to their off-worlder heritage. If we deprive them of the symbol this technology must offer them as well as the very real strength and wealth that the weapons represent, aren't we threatening to isolate them even more? Threatening to drive them to even greater lengths of desperation?"

A faint scowl conceded the point even as Llinolae saw, "You're not saying I shouldn't attempt it."

"No, I'm not saying you shouldn't attempt it. I agree with you it would be best to try to talk to a Lead. But no, that doesn't look very realistic." Gwyn looked at her then. She felt the force of that silent determination flow up from the life cycles around her as Llinolae met her gaze steadily. But there was no sharp blade slicing through her mind's eye, imposing that decree upon her. This was different from others of the Blue Sight, Gwyn realized distractedly. But the intensity of Llinolae's commitment pressed more urgently. Gwyn accepted the awareness with a nod, abandoning attempts to grasp the subtleties of Blue Sighted differences for a time.

Gwyn sighed, nodding once more. "We've a while to stay. Brit and Sparrow won't be arriving for another few days. Even then, the scouts searching for you will still make traveling too dangerous. I'd suggest a good ten-day-and-a-half should pass before we try to leave the Shea Hole."

Llinolae smiled, "I'll still be set on moving east into their farmsteads."

"And nearer their weapons' stockpile."

With a shrug, the Dracoon admitted, "I have only a vague notion of its location. If it comes to that...."

"If?" Gwyn interrupted, disbelief echoing in her voice. "Or when?"

Llinolae's gaze dropped to Ril as she went to resume brushing the sand-wolf. Neither of the women were fooled. Her silence was answer enough.

* * *

Gwyn trudged up along the small creek towards the bend at the top of their canyon, relishing the anticipation of cool water and a good scrub. All morning she and Llinolae had been busy cleaning tack, washing clothes, and tending the mares, especially poor Nia's chaffed sores from carrying all that wet gear for so long. Gwyn had been heartily glad that the separation had been brief and that Jes had always taught her the proper care for tack and mares; with equipment that was less well-padded, the skin damage would have been outright cruel from the chaffing, wet leathers. As it was, Nia's ruddy hide had been left tender but unbroken; a ten-day of rest and attention should more than see the mare ready for work again.

The Amazon had been as proud of Ty's judgment as of Nia's endurance. Her bondmate had obviously done her best to find the mare dry niches in cliff and tree for the worst of the storms. Although now that the last of their immediate traveling was done, the cloud bursts seemed finished as well.

Fates' Jest was all, she conceded wryly. The warm sun was welcome, reaching into the forests with its dusty light. In their tiny valley the heat had dried the ground early. By the afternoon, the cooler shadows from those great trees above on the gorge's rim lent some aid, and Gwyn had sent Llinolae off to tend herself. Although the woman had protested, Llinolae had clearly been relieved in the end—her body was still more bruised than not.

Gwyn felt her heart skip a beat at the memory of that smile, and she laughed at herself. That absurd grin of Gwyn's had lingered even after the Dracoon had left—lingered through all of the haymoss gathering and through most of the hoof painting—until Cinder had snorted in protest when Gwyn inadvertently stiffened the hide on a foreleg with the liquid enamel. Chagrined, the Amazon had admitted that the enamel shells were better protections against hoof chips and cracks than skin rashes. But Cinder had been patient enough, obviously enjoying the extra attention the clean-up and salve provided.

With a sigh Gwyn escaped a sunny patch of heat as she rounded the canyon bend and ducked in through the draped haymoss. The vines and ruffled leaf bits dangled and spanned the short neck in the rock's fissure, creating a tunnel-like coolness. She breathed the sweetened air deeply then, emerging, she found herself squinting against the abrupt return of the sun's glare. The ground felt softer beneath her boots, and for a moment she paused, lifting a hand to shade her eyes. A plush lichen carpet of deep forest green, so dense a color that it was almost black, covered the ground entirely. There were mists from the tumbling little waterfall that cooled the small place, despite the break in the honeywoods' canopy so far above. The water fell from a much closer ledge, however, since it had carved something of a tiered stairway back into the gorge heights over the generations of its flow.

Splays of rainbows and the chatter from a squabbling bird's nest filled the air. The crevice walls were beige and bleached brown, rising in rocky tiers and sheer walls with only a smattering of the springy lichen above a knee's height.

A paleness stirred atop a sunlit slab of stone. Gwyn glanced to it, watching the shimmering arch of a rainbow's bend touch the woman lying there. A breeze rifled through the mists again, and the colors disappeared. But Gwyn's gaze stayed—fixed and captured by the naked ivory of Llinolae's length.

The woman stirred, her Blue Sight telling her of another's rapt attention. She sat and turned, staring mutely at Gwyn for an endless moment.

Panic frissoned within Gwyn's stomach. Embarrassment warred with consuming desire until her feet stumbled to flee in sheer blindness.

"Gwyn wait!"

She froze.

Llinolae appeared quickly beside her, sliding into a tunic for Gwyn's benefit. The shirt hem settled across her thighs, but still Gwyn didn't move. Hand clenched to the towel at her shoulder, eyes fastened on the moss vines before her—skin deepening more and more into that cocoa richness of sweet longings with each breath—she didn't dare to move.

"Gwyn…," Llinolae's voice was soft with a gentleness that made the Amazon's eyes slide closed in cherished agony. "It's all right.

"*Soroe?*" Llinolae spoke the word tentatively. Her hand ventured to risk a touch to Gwyn's arm. "*Soroe*, please, know that it's all right."

"No." Gwyn swallowed hard, shaking her head. She found her heart's courage with a whisper, "Not *Soroe. Soroi?*"

"I know," Llinolae murmured. Tenderly then she brought Gwyn around to face her, waiting with endless patience until Gwyn finally managed to open those copper-bright eyes. Uncertainty and confusion danced behind the threatening tears, but Llinolae merely laid a warm hand to Gwyn's cheek and smiled ever so faintly.

With a steadying breath drawn in slowly, Gwyn felt the panic loosen its vice in her chest. She tried in some way to return that gentle smile and then, at last, her own voice came again. "I beg your patience…I seem to have lost my heart amongst your things."

The words sweetly stole the breath from Llinolae with their honesty. She stepped nearer and took Gwyn's face in her hands, her blue gaze seeming to stare into Gwyn's very soul. "My own heart's a bit lost around you too, my dear Amazon."

Gwyn's surprise registered in shock, bringing Llinolae's gentle laughter then. But still, she was not released.

"If I were not Dracoon of Khirlan, I would beg sanctuary within your arms—within your Valley Bay of *dey Sorormin*. But my time and my duties are sworn to Khirlan's people, at least, until the Clan's troubles are settled. I can't promise you more than the hour of today—perhaps, a few of tomorrow. But vows and bonds…," Llinolae sighed. "I have no life of my own to offer. And everything I sense about you warns me of the pain that any fleeting encounter between us could bring you."

"I…I know," Gwyn managed hoarsely. "It's…selfish of—"

"No!" Llinolae pressed a thumb lightly against Gwyn's soft lips. "No, don't say it. Neither of us are wrong in wanting the possibility of more. It's merely…it's something I don't have to offer."

"Duty." Gwyn nodded. She understood only too well.

"If…," Llinolae paused to wet her lips, her own skin beginning to flush with a caramel that was so much richer than her tan. "If you could risk lesser…? If today or…or tomorrow alone could be chanced as enough…?"

Gwyn stood unmoving, bittersweet pain crowding her heart at that simple invitation.

"Well…," Llinolae's voice grew lower in its own sadness and acceptance, "it's something to think about."

Then she was gone. The breeze stirred in the leafy vines behind her, and Gwyn found she was left standing alone on that edge of chill and brilliant sunlight. The choice now was hers.

Chapter Five

Sparrow jerked upright, half-spinning on her rocky perch at the startled squeak of a pripper pair. The little bush-tailed felines dove from a high branch and disappeared beneath a tree's root just as a red hawk swooped past. The bird crashed back up through the forest's canopy, its faint shriek of frustration echoing behind. Then things grew quiet, gradually returning to the calming rustle of leaves and tumble of creek waters.

The serenity was lost on Sparrow. Skin dark as burnt caramel, eyes bruised and swollen from weeping—the young woman settled once more on her stone seat to watch the swirling ripples in the pool below her. It was less than a pool, actually—more a still niche created by the boulder she sat upon. But the reflection the water cast back at her was barely distorted, and Sparrow had thought it might bring her some comfort in this self-imposed isolation of hers.

Isolation—it wasn't what she wanted now. But realizing she was pregnant was all the turmoil she could manage. Telling Brit...she couldn't even imagine telling Brit.

Brit was worried about Sparrow's wrist, and in her fussing Brit hadn't given Sparrow much chance to think since they'd fled the city, though it was the unspoken confusions over her shadowmate's subdued manner that was Brit's true concern. Sparrow could only withdraw more and more in the face of Brit's growing anxieties, but she couldn't help it—especially since there was a genuine need for Brit to take concern.

Need? Sparrow shuddered. She didn't know what she needed. At first, desperately, she'd only sought to find peace enough to think. But thinking wasn't going to solve anything. And her healing wrist-sprain was the least of her worries; Sparrow was frightened for Brit—for herself—when her Love did learn of the truth.

But oh sweet Mother, what was that truth?

Sparrow only knew, she *couldn't* explain what had happened. And Brit was going to want an explanation! Of that, Sparrow had no doubt. Her shadowmate's temper was going to demand much more than a mere explanation! Yet Sparrow couldn't provide even that much.

She sniffled and tried to wipe the tears from her damp cheeks with a hand. It didn't seem to make the water's image any more presentable. She pulled out a kerchief and did a little better, dipping it into the icy waters to cool her flushed skin.

"I shouldn't tell her until we've met up with Gwyn. Brit will need a *Niachero's* strength then—Gwyn can give her that. At least I should do that much for her." Sparrow barely realized she'd spoken aloud. But the assertion sounded confident, and any sort of plan helped her right now. Then again, she didn't really have much choice. As much as Brit loved her, Sparrow knew this was going to be heart-wrenchingly painful to her shadowmate.

Brit—a wonderfully strong Amazon who'd had such trouble trusting any other to care for her. She was a proud Sister who'd balked at the Council's suggestion of a Shadow and who'd fought her own biases against both Sparrow's age and the lifestone's bond before accepting Sparrow's love. Her Brit, the healer, who would risk setting aside her sacred oaths to stand between Sparrow and a Changling's wrath—the woman who'd both laughed and cried in Sparrowhawk's arms at the end of that horrid, horrid Exile's Trek. Brit—who'd only this winter confessed her hope that they might leave their wanderings to start a family of their own in Valley Bay and so unknowingly echoed Sparrow's own deepest wish. How could Sparrow expect her lover's heart not to break when she told Brit that their family was already on the way? Knowing the child had not been conceived beneath the hands of n'Shea with their lifestones. With Sparrow not knowing, not remembering who had....

With Sparrow not remembering anything at all!

She shuddered and shut her eyes tight against that pain. She *needed* Gwyn to be near—for Brit's own sake, she dared not say anything sooner. Though how she would ever dare to say anything, even later, was beyond her too....

And Brit would suspect the worst. Sparrow couldn't deny that she did herself. The bruises on her ribs and body were faint. But they were there. She'd never paid much attention to how her acrobatic, mid-night escapades could scratch and bump her about. She'd initially assumed the markings were from the trip into Khirla's armory and from the riotous crowd's shoving when the baskers had been loosed.

Now she wasn't so certain.

Now, she no longer knew what to think. What had happened when? She couldn't remember anything being out of sorts. Surely, if she had...with her peculiar memory gifts, if she had been attacked, she would have remembered *something!* At least wouldn't she have noticed a *lack* of time she could account for?

She knew from her monarcs spent with the traveling acrobats that her picture-perfect memory did not shy from vivid portraits of abuse. She knew, from her own thrashings and witnessing others endure worse, that fear didn't dull any of her mind's recollections. Although from her training and travels since, Sparrow had come to recognize how common memory lapses were for many trauma survivors. Some she thought were blessed—they would never remember clearly. Others she'd held through the terrorizing nightmares and kept them safe through sudden bursts of panic when memories resurfaced. Yet Sparrow herself had never expected to experience anything but the absolutely unalterable imprint of reality that her memory always provided to her. Or so she'd been told by healers. As much as she had prayed to be free from some of those bloody scenes, she had never seriously expected it to happen.

If what she had witnessed as a child and as a Shadow hadn't driven her memories into blackness then...? Sparrow was terrified of the idea that it had happened now. If all she'd seen had never caused her to lose her memory's pictures, then how much more horrific must this incident have been?

How had she even survived it?

* * *

The dream whirled with a thick darkness, a black fog that circled and snaked in a winding spiral until slowly it spun outward. In the nest of murky images, a room emerged—and then a bed, canopied with fine satins and a fringe of silver lace. A bed of foreboding, as dim figures moved, shifted and became clear. A woman, thin and long of stature lay with fever, tossing in frenzied nightmares with a dream of seeking escape—of seeking safe haven. Another figure—a man with sword-callused hands whose fingers curled like talons, nervously closing and opening in tension. On silent feet, the intruder crept to the bed—yet even then face and body were veiled—identity unknown in those tendrils of swirling blackness. A vial of amethyst powder tipped. Dust glittered and danced upon the fresh water of the bedside basin. A finger dipped, stirring the waters until the last of the sparkle dissolved, and then a cup fetched cool liquid. One of those hands came near again—on a finger, a ring of carved wood—then with a touch, the feverish sleep of the woman was broken. The water was accepted and sipped thankfully. Exhaustion engulfed her again, slowing her life's flow as death's descent was summoned.

"No!"

"Shush...shush...it's all right. Llinolae, it's all right. You're safe."

Blue eyes blinked, awakening to the glow of the single lantern and the brazier's embers. The wind rippled across the outer layer of the watershed canvas. At the foot of her pallet Ril sat alertly, her eyes peaked in worry. Kneeling beside Llinolae, so careful in not touching her, was Gwyn.

Her red hair was loose, falling across the shoulders of her sleeping shirt. The color was a warm bronze in the reflected light of the lantern. Desire leapt to replace the nightmare's terror and with a mewed cry, Llinolae reached for Gwyn.

"You're safe now," Gwyn wrapped her near, sliding onto the bedside quickly. With one hand she cradled Llinolae's head to her shoulder as the other moved soothingly along the woman's back.

Llinolae pulled away slightly. Her eyes searched Gwyn's pleadingly. This...this platonic sort of comforting was not what she needed.

"It was a nightmare," Gwyn whispered. She made no move to release Llinolae.

"I know. I've...I've had it often. Ever since I was a child." And she wanted to run from it—then and now. Wouldn't Gwyn...couldn't Gwyn now?

"Do you know what it's from?" Gwyn struggled, forced the words out through the strain, her breath growing so shallow.

Llinolae's hands trembled, clenching fists of Gwyn's tunic—fire rising in such desperate desire. And she could barely shake her head—all so very slowly—her voice aching, nearly pleading, "It never comes on the trail! It only ever comes after...after the Court hearings...after arguing with Taysa over money to rebuild the villages or Samcin's...!"

"But it's all right now, you're safe here...with me." Please be with me, her mind echoed helplessly. Gwyn's throat closed in pain, the wanting was so strong. Her gaze fell to Llinolae's lips.

Suddenly Llinolae pulled back to arm's length, ducking her head and closing her eyes with a shuddering breath.

Gwyn felt the immediate recoil of her body as that blue-sighted influence fled. She went cold. Her flesh chilled with goose bumps. Her backbone stiffened. Even as she realized what had been happening, Gwyn grew angry at herself for almost succumbing to it. Llinolae's reaction had been a natural one—a human's need to physically connect with a protector as intimately as possible after being threatened. She did not blame her companion for that need, but she did chastise herself for not recognizing it sooner. She had lived among enough Blue Sights to have had the experience before—it wasn't appropriate to take advantage of Llinolae's vulnerability!

Gwyn took a deep, steadying breath of her own and brushed her fingertips across Llinolae's browned cheek. She leaned near again, gently urging, "Llinolae...?"

That ice blue gaze flew back to her face.

"I understand." Gwyn smiled in tender reassurance, quite suddenly feeling very strong and very protective of this dear woman. "It's all right now."

"Is it?"

"In truth, it is."

A broken gasp caught in her throat as Llinolae collapsed back into the safety of Gwyn's arms. Strength embraced her, steadfast in its comforting, and Llinolae shuddered with a ragged breath of trust and relief. "Thank you, *Soroe*. Thank you."

Chapter Six

Good morning!" Gwyn called, ducking into the horses' tent to find Llinolae nearly done with Cinder's grooming. "Have you eaten yet? Llinolae shook her head, bringing her own fetlock of black curls down over an eye. "I had some trail bread—I'm not much for eating first thing in the morning. My stomach doesn't usually wake up until mid-day."

Gwyn understood that habit well enough. Given a choice, it was her preference as well.

Finished, Llinolae stepped back and sharply clacked the brushes together a few times to clean the dander and hair from them. Calypso snorted with a short toss of her head, and Nia seconded her. They were eager to leave this yellow bright stuffiness inside their tent. The sun was far from being overhead, but the day's humidity and heat had already begun to collect within the canvas walls.

Cinder pulled slightly at her tether, nuzzling towards Gwyn, and contentedly ignored both her herd sisters for her favorite human. When her Amazon grinned and came to her, the mare gave a wuffle of pleasure in a soft, throaty tone and rubbed her broad head into Gwyn's chest. Gwyn laughed and hugged her in return, a hand lovingly sliding up along that muscular, broad bend of Cinder's neck. She found the bay's coat as satiny to the touch as it was shiny to the eye. Apparently the Dracoon was a well-practiced groom despite the availability of help in the Palace Stables.

"I didn't know if I should let them out. Do you usually set them on a picket line, hobble them—or what?"

"There's no need for any bindings here," Gwyn murmured, untying the tether from Cinder's halter. With a swat to that heavy horse rump, she sent the mare off through the opened tent flap. Then as Llinolae went to loosen Calypso, Gwyn turned to Nia explaining, "This canyon is enough like our natural pasture pens in Valley Bay that they'll all stay near. They'll treat this as a home territory to be protected from braygoats and sowies, not a place to be left. And if something does happen that's dire enough to spook them into running, Ty would round them up and bring them back."

"How awful does 'dire' have to get to spook them like that?"

Face set grim, Gwyn remembered the barn burning and the mares' shrill attack outside in the corral. "I know fire isn't enough...." She shrugged abruptly and forced a lighter note. "I've never encountered anything that disastrous, actually."

"Let's hope you never do."

The curry combs and brushes were returned to the short tack shelf, and together they set to work tying open the back canvas flaps. The breezes swept in quickly, cheerfully rippling across the clean haymoss Llinolae had bedded down the tent's ground with.

"We'll have to watch for prippers and grubbers moving in," Gwyn chuckled, glancing about at that bright sheltered space. "It looks much too inviting for critters. Although, I suppose we could always send Ril in to give them a good fright."

"Prippers are too curious. Even Ril wouldn't keep them frightened for long," Llinolae quipped. Then rather suddenly she sobered, remembering Gwyn's other bondmate. Tentatively, she ventured, "Is Ty still out by herself?"

"Aye…" and that deep sigh was weary enough. Gwyn picked up the horses' water bags and moved off towards the creek. She shouldn't be quite so worried about Ty, she knew. Both Ril and Llinolae had assured her that it was only some kind of misperception, and Gwyn knew how stubborn her packmate could be. Almost as stubborn as one particular *Niachero,* in fact.

"Do you think it would help, if I talked to her?"

Gwyn looked up from the creek side, surprised to find Llinolae had followed her.

"Ril didn't seem to think it was a good time quite yet."

The hesitation in Llinolae's voice was unmistakable, and Gwyn realized her companion was much more comfortable in being direct, even with difficult confrontations. That made a wry grin appear as Gwyn returned to her task—waiting was not a thing this *Niachero* did well either.

Silently, Llinolae filled the other water bag as Gwyn's thoughts turned again to Ty. But when it came to gauging feelings, Gwyn could only admit, "Ril's judgment is usually pretty sound…especially in regards to either Ty or myself. But I don't really understand what's going on."

Llinolae bent her head guiltily. She couldn't ignore the Amazon's quiet prompting. She sighed, half shaking her head; Gwyn did deserve an explanation. "It's us…or rather what I feel for you. Ty's jealous of me, and somewhat mistrustful. She's afraid I'll do you more harm than good, emotionally."

"No," Gwyn asserted with a surprising clarity and calm. "You won't."

Llinolae glanced at her to find the Amazon's amarin shimmering with a richness of honesty and certainty. The depth and beauty of Gwyn's trust that her amarin reflected was as unexpected a discovery for Llinolae as it was a precious one.

Gwyn looked up then, and for a heartbeat, their gazes met. She halted. Llinolae did the same, but it was Gwyn's deepening skin tones that stole Llinolae's attention—that sweet, apricot gold rising to glowing put to shame any tan. Llinolae's mouth went dry as her own skin flushed deeper. She felt her lips part as her breathing became excruciatingly, exquisitely impossible. But she would not—could not—think to look away.

"I know you won't…hurt me that way, I mean."

"How do you know?" Llinolae whispered.

Gwyn's eyes gentled, a tender smile tilting her head as a careful finger reached out to brush those unruly black curls back from Llinolae's forehead. "I do know. Whatever happens between us, I know it will be better than never having met you. I know that was true for Selena—when she died, it was hard for me. But I never regretted knowing her while I could. She gave me much, much more than mere loss. Now…meeting you…," Gwyn shrugged, suddenly feeling almost embarrassed. "You're already a part of me. You've already given me more than you could ever take."

Llinolae studied Gwyn for a long, long time. Then a faint sigh of exasperation replaced her pensiveness. Llinolae finally grasped how hopeless rational musings were in this moment—a fact that Gwyn had obviously already noted. A fond but crooked grin appeared and Llinolae dryly observed, "You are a hopeless romantic, Gwyn'l n'Athena."

"I'm *Niachero*," Gwyn replied softly—enigmatically. "I have to be."

* * *

"What's that you're doing?"

Gwyn glanced up from her whittling with surprise. A ready smile curved her lips and warmed her eyes as Llinolae joined her on the log seat beside the creek. Gwyn had nearly forgotten how effectively most Blue Sights blended into the amarin around them, not disturbing the life cycles and moving nearly unseen or unheard through pastures or woods. Within towns or houses, any place where Aggar's amarin had been reshaped by human hands, such stealth became a matter of innate talent and conscious skill. But out here amidst the ancient honeywoods...no, out here Llinolae's tread seldom disturbed even the cricket beds.

"Is it a flute of some kind?"

With a blink, Gwyn realized she'd been staring again, but, oh—staring at such beauty!

"I beg patience...," Llinolae murmured, sensing the amarin shift and intending to distract them both with a hint of gentle humor. But that purpose left her quite completely as her blue eyes lifted to Gwyn's face. Then her own soft smile grew and she began to study Gwyn in kind; like a touch her gaze skimmed across the cheekbones—across the straight, slender nose—watched the play of the forest's breeze in those red wisps of fly-away hair. She felt her lips part in tender temptation as her glance fell to Gwyn's lips, finding them trembling ever so faintly, feeling their breath growing so shallow in unison. Nearly feeling—tasting—the kiss that could be....

Then those trembling lips hinted at some approaching smile. Llinolae blinked, caught by disbelief. Gwyn's amarin distilled into intent—into anticipation. Her approach enticingly slow, Gwyn leaned forward to create that kiss.

Llinolae gasped at the first light touch of their lips, and Gwyn paused, a whisper away from her mouth—neither withdrawing nor pressing, merely waiting. Until Llinolae chose too, pressing forward—melting in sigh and sweet, sweet desire against her beloved. And their warm press lingered, overwhelming in its simplicity...'til gradually each began to move. At first barely a brush of satin to satin, then deepening warmth—rippling fullness as their mouths learned of shape, of form, of subtle fitting to one another. Caress giving pause, a nibble discovering the curve and bow of an upper lip...yielding again to the flickering tongue's touch at the delicate corner contour. Swift and sudden air swept in as both moved in single desire and tongue met tongue, tasting—drowning.

Alarm—disturbance rippled through the amarin. Llinolae's brow furrowed, agony of sense torn in two moods—and her kiss grew more commanding. Her fingers slid into Gwyn's hair...Gwyn's flushed cheek in her palm as the Amazon matched need with more need.

But instinct for survival won, and quite helplessly, Llinolae found herself pulling back. Her ragged breath protested the parting. Her hand shook where it lay against Gwyn's face, held tightly there with Gwyn's own grasp now. And Gwyn watched her with rising concern as Llinolae tried to focus on that internal sense of urgency—of wrongness. She twisted her head away, concentrating—reaching down into herself and then down into the flowing lines of the Great Forest's amarin. She blinked, then squeezed her eyes shut, straining beyond Gwyn's distracting presence—and found it was the Forest's sense of intrusion.

She snapped to alertness, half-spinning away from Gwyn. Then she looked east, down the creek bed towards the canyon's open end.

"What is it?" Gwyn demanded, already reaching behind herself to make certain the sword and scabbard at her hip were free from entanglements.

"I...don't quite know...."

"But there's something," Gwyn finished grimly.

Even the afternoon birds and prippers had become unusually quiet.

Then Gwyn noticed Ril's absence as well. She frowned, searching her packbond for other clues. And suddenly she was laughing.

Llinolae spun back about in her seat, readily Seeing Gwyn's relief yet she couldn't grasp the understanding.

"Ty's bringing Sparrow and Brit in along the creek. Ril's gone out to meet them too!"

Llinolae felt that thin thread of empathy among Gwyn's bondpack then. Undeniably, there was excitement and reassurance present. Still...that wasn't all to be Seen. Quietly, she asserted, "There's more. The forest says there's more...."

Words, images, hovered on the edge of her consciousness. But the concepts refused to take coherent form.

"They drive a tinker-trade's wagon," Gwyn offered tentatively. "That novelty of color and noise—the dray horses alone could unnerve the forest's creatures...?"

It was a legitimate possibility. Llinolae considered it seriously. Mutely, she stood, her eyes closing to focus inward and out.

"Or..." Gwyn warily amended, "their wagon's attracted the Clan scouts?"

"No," Llinolae muttered, barely hearing Gwyn's voice—more sensing her questions through the fluid swirls of amarin about them. "No, the intrusion is theirs alone...your Sisters."

The Amazon's audible sigh of relief brought Llinolae back to Gwyn's side with a rueful grin. "I should just trust your bondmates and not worry so much, hmm?"

A slightly embarrassed shrug allowed that Llinolae had quite succinctly summarized Gwyn's general attitude.

"Then I think...," Llinolae's tone grew lower, "I shall...." She moved to face Gwyn more fully. The intensity of her sheer stillness sent Gwyn's heart racing as the awareness of what had been interrupted resurfaced.

"Did you mind...?" Gwyn whispered, wanting so much to hear the words, although she did not in the least doubt the answer itself.

But Llinolae answered her first without the words. Her lips touching Gwyn's again, gently pulling in a coaxing kiss...a kiss that wandered aside to the burnished brown blush and line of Gwyn's cheek, then further on to warm

Gwyn's ear with her breath. A murmur, rich and vibrant, countered all fears with, "No, my Amazon, I don't mind. How could I ever mind any touch you might give me…?"

Llinolae smiled with her then, and Gwyn drew a less than steady breath almost wishing her Sisters' arrival was less imminent. Almost wishing it, but not quite.

With a brief touch of reassurance, Llinolae's fingertips brushed Gwyn's cheek. "Whatever you give…whatever you *want* to give me, Gwyn'l…it will be enough."

"In truth?" It hurt Gwyn, pierced her heart with the very thought, that her uncertainties could wound this woman all too easily. She had no wish to dance some flirting game; she cared too deeply for Llinolae to inadvertently taunt with false hopes, when what Gwyn understood of her own feelings was yet only confusion.

"I will make it enough, Gwyn. Please trust me. I am old enough to be responsible for myself."

"I didn't mean to imply you weren't."

"I know. You didn't."

A startled fowl somewhere sent out a shriek and flapped noisily off into the air. The rattle and clack of a tinker trade's wagon rolled in on that echo. Both women looked at each other in resignation. The Sisters, it seemed, were arriving.

Chapter Seven

Llinolae found some wild brushberries—"

"Bitter yet," Brit gruffly cut Gwyn short. The box lid slammed down with a bounce that literally shook the caravan sideboards where it was attached; apparently all the flour and seasonings needed were already secured in the broad bowl beneath Brit's arm. "Would think at least she'd know that...too early in the season.... You! You I'd expect that ignorance from, but it's her own damn'd district. Not impressed, *Niachero*. Not impressed at all."

Gwyn stood there a moment, hands on her hips, caught somewhere between perplexed surprise and outright disapproval. Head cocked sideways a little, she watched Brit's stout figure retreat around the corner of the wagon towards the camp's fire ring. Then her eyes narrowed dangerously. Mouth set in a grim line, Gwyn set out after the woman—enough was enough!

"Brit n'Minona! Stand your ground—*now.* "

The elder Sister stopped in her tracks. Back stiffening she spun with rage, glaring. "Do *not* bark orders at me, girl! I'm no mother who owes you patience. I'm not here to nurse you through heartaches—nor to pick you up off your sore little rump 'cause you've gone bump!

"And I am certainly *not* here to dilly-dally around with your lovesick, nepotistic...Blind Fool Puppet of a Dracoon!!"

"*Blind?*" Gwyn rasped, voice low and harsh in a fury so tightly harnessed— copper eyes blazing embers against the burnt topaz of her skin. "*Lovesick?! Goddess give us a mirror for your own soul, Soroe!* "

"I'm *not* the one—"

"Yes! *You* are. As Daughter of Mothers, I swear...*you are.*"

Pain washed through Brit in a single, engulfing revelation. Stricken— trembling, held in fear and anger—her expression went blank. The gray of her eyes dulled. The tea-black of her skin lost its sheen.

"Yes," Gwyn repeated more gently, but no less forcefully. "This comes from *you* , Soroe. Since you drove the drays in yesterday, you...*you* have found no kind word, given no chance of warm welcome...*allowed* no peace to settle within this camp.

"The Dracoon and I...yes, you see rightly that we do care for one anoth- er. Care deeply. But you have not spoken more than a dozen words to her—or to me!—which have been reasonable. You arrive, announce the Steward is the grand fault of the District, then balk at the simplest of explanations! Have you even noticed Llinolae is asking only of what and whereof you speak and is not denying any of your accusations? This so-called tyrannical Steward is her aunt, n'Minona! Yet she is choosing to accept *our word* and discard her family loyal- ty! Despite that, it hurts her, and you can see that it does hurt her! At some time or other she trusted her aunt, but do you recognize the heartache that might cause? No! Tell me—could you or I have done as well with any strangers' accusations against our own kin—no matter how much evidence we had? No matter how much truth we knew they spoke. Wouldn't I be screaming with protest inside if you proved Jes a traitor?

"Yet you don't respect Llinolae's efforts to deal with this chaos! You refuse to address any course of action other than a return to Khirla to confront Taysa—despite the immense stupidity of thinking a handful of Amazons and Rutkins' City Guards could stand any kind of chance against the Steward's fire weapons!"

"We destroyed those!" Brit roared. "Or have you forgotten already?"

"You destroyed the stuff in the armory of the Steward's stables," Gwyn corrected with fierce, clipped emphasis to each word. "And you *know* that place wasn't housing all the fire weapons in Khirla. Any one or all of the Steward's precious Swords would have a personal cache of the things tucked under a mattress or at the bottom of a chest.

"No, Brit. No," Gwyn shook her head slowly, the temper easing from her finally. "The discord in this camp was brought in with you and Sparrowhawk. It must be resolved between you and her.

"The brushberries are not too tart, this time of summer. The traitors in Khirla's Court are not of sole importance in this struggle between Clan and District. And Llinolae's caution—as well as my own!—against jumping at any sort of plan to unseat her aunt just yet is *not* due to infatuated foolishness.

"The confusions—the ill-tempers, *Soroe!*—they're between you and Sparrow." Gwyn gave a short sigh, compassion and concern furrowing her brow as she examined her friend. She hesitated, waiting, but Brit made no move even to meet her gaze. In the end, the utter shocked stillness of her Sister urged her forward a step. And she reached a hand for Brit urging softly, "Tell me, *please*...nothing can be so bad that silence betters...."

"I have to see to this bread baking," Brit announced abruptly and turned, shunning all touch or care offered.

Sadly, Gwyn let her go; her Sister's voice had seemed so very hollow. Perhaps she could sit with Ty later this evening...of the three packmates, the younger sandwolf had been closest to Brit in the season they'd all worked amongst the Changlings Wars. Perhaps her packmate would understand something more of this?

Gwyn smiled without much humor then, suddenly—ironically—realizing how alike Ty and Brit were. Both were so prone to those rash bursts of temper and suspicious judgments. Aye, too many judgments, too much silence.

Mae n'Pour—just too much hurt.

* * *

"So you come to See me now, because the news these two Sisters bring from Khirla confirms even more of your suspicions regarding your Aunt Taysa. But you must remember, Daughter," the Mistress n'Shea noted quietly, "this Brit and her Sparrow entered your city with fresh eyes. They were not there for all the times your aunt lent you her help. You've seen her genuine outrage—heard how vehemently she pleads. The Sisters haven't spent nearly all of their lives beside Taysa, listening and being coached to rely on her insights."

"In that respect—yes! The advantage was theirs!" Llinolae hissed. She wheeled about vehemently, loosening a fiery dust from her harmon's heel, and continued to pace. "And yes! They know Ramains' Law and the People's Book well, so naturally they'd notice any discrepancy between Churv and Khirlan's

189

barter codes.

"None of that excuses *me!* I may not be able to read the accursed books, but I know Churv's law inside out! I should have taken the time to learn Taysa's too. No! I should have *made the time* to learn the rhetoric in that Steward's Book! I'd had suspicions and yet I didn't—"

"Which is my point...you were already suspicious." The Blue Sight of the Mistress imbued those softly spoken words with a daunting power that gave Llinolae pause to heed. "Despite a lifetime of being told by courtiers and tradition to trust Taysa, you'd begun to suspect your aunt's motives. Even if these Sisters hadn't told you of the abused tariffs and altered reports, you would have soon discovered her treachery for yourself."

The quiet reasoning of her Mistress curbed Llinolae's ire. About them, the garden's twilight began to warm as the globes along the adobe walls lit up. The smell of blooming roses mingled with the sun-baked scent of a lazy prairie breeze, and somewhere not too far off a bird cried. The faint edges of Llinolae's harmon shimmered a translucent blue as the wind fluttered through her figure, inviting peace.

With a long sigh, Llinolae accepted the invitation and let all the self-pitying recriminations slip away.

The Mistress n̩'Shea smiled gently, her Sight reaching out now with encouraging reassurance.

"The truth can be difficult to accept," the young woman breathed, aching and melancholy.

"It is always painful to See a traitor among trusted kin."

"But that's the trouble. I can't See her! I can't...!" Llinolae broke off in frustration. Her fist grasped at air as intangibly as her comprehension grasped at reason. "I can't See *why* she does this!"

The older woman gave Llinolae's impatience no mind. Glancing about for the hemp rope to anchor herself a bit, she sank down onto the long bench of the garden swing. The length of her salt'n'pepper braid swung easily over a shoulder, and she settled comfortably—patting the seat beside her for Llinolae.

The young woman joined her, once again sighing in an attempt to rein in her emotions. She knew the glint and spark along the edges of her harmon reflected her passions too easily, too often. But then her Mistress had learned long ago that even the most vibrant, emotional displays seldom hindered Llinolae's control of the Sight.

"I know you well enough, Daughter." The Mistress n'Shea smiled, and Llinolae felt less alone, despite Taysa's betrayal. "You didn't come here simply to rave about your delusions of incompetence."

That brought a slow smile to Llinolae's face and her mentor laughed softly. Their blue gazes met then, and all the gentleness and confidence of their long association warmed their Sights' touch.

"Now, you said you couldn't See why your aunt had turned from you?"

"To be truthful, I'm no longer certain if she's ever been loyal." Llinolae looked back to the garden with a somber resignation. "When I think back, so many things seem...the circumstances seemed too contrived and her explanations too conveniently offered. She has this knack for stepping in with some tidbit of new information or for proffering some tidy reason, just as suspicions might start suggesting a traitor within the patrol led to its ambush or a Clan's party had altered its attack plans because they learned we were waiting."

"Those sorts of coincidences are suspicious," the Mistress agreed.

"Aye, but—*Mae n'Pour!*" Llinolae bit off with a savage shake of her head. "I wish n'Athena were nearer today!"

"It would help." The Mistress n'Shea merely nodded, not in the least offended by the younger woman's desires. "Di'nay is much shrewder at such intrigues than I. She will be back before dawn rises, if...?"

"It's longer than I should wait. And no, Mistress, it's not a grasp of schemes I need." Llinolae sighed and shook her head at her own inabilities. "It's just, even with my Sight's talents, I can't seem to...! I need skills I don't have. I need to decipher the individual amarin to unthread the bias of emotions from thought—from truth! And I can't do it !" Her hand went up in helpless frustration.

"You decipher both better than any Blue Sight I've ever known," her teacher corrected her, causing Llinolae only more confusion. The Mistress smiled in that patient way she had, and nodded. "Only Blue Sights trained as the Council's Seers—and even then, I think, only the eldest of them—might be able discern more details than you, yet they can merely describe what the Council Masters prompt them to report. So very much of what they perceive is left unspoken, because they no longer experience themselves as individuals and can't judge the importance of what should be shared. As for the other Blue Sights I've known...we may retain our sense of individuality, but we have a very hard time ushering all the pieces of life's puzzles together. We sense the amarin of others by suspending our perception of self for a brief moment or two. It lends us information, but it also overwhelms us with a barrage of impressions. Often there is simply too much information to organize those impressions into a coherent, recognizable pattern, because we didn't..." Now it was the elder who grasped for words.

Llinolae waved the struggle aside. "Patience Mistress, I do understand. It's a matter of too much or too little. The Seers immerse themselves in the amarin too long and completely lose their sense of self. The Blue Sights immerse themselves long enough to grasp some details. But you don't recognize the source or sense of it all, because you return too quickly to your own sense of self. Considering how adamantly I've always been in being *me*, I shouldn't be surprised at how few details I do perceive. It seems the skills I wouldn't learn as a child, I may come to rue as an adult."

"You have an intensity in you that has always been mirrored in your amarin, Llinolae. I would never say you See less than other Blue Sights." The Mistress seemed amused. "You merely See differently."

"Not surprising, all things considered," pointed out the young woman with matching humor. As a child, she had refused to learn the usual way of doing things with her Sight, and so she had spent much of her mentor's time exploring ideas for alternative approaches before returning her harmon to Khirla where she could experiment within the safety of stone. Such a trial-and-error method had often left much to be desired. Her visits to *dey Sorormin* had never seemed frequent enough. Her stolen practice time had always seemed too short. But as the Dracoon's heir, she'd had other duties to tend and a score of people to notice if she was late.

"You had an odd tutelage, I'd never deny that," the Mistress agreed, drawing Llinolae's attention back from those memories. "Di'nay was the first to recognize it, though. You had the tenacity to learn what you needed, despite the improbability of balancing time and patience and resources."

"In other words, I was stubborn," Llinolae surmised dryly.

"And ingenuous. You may use your Blue Gift differently, Daughter, but you use it impressively well."

Surprise widened her blue eyes as Llinolae suddenly realized, "You're serious."

"I am. When you first began to work with me, I was afraid of the limitations I might inadvertently be imposing upon you. Because I've no talent myself for out-of-time Seeing, I'd no way to know how the skills of the Blue Sight had been refined during the generations that lay between us. As a result, I tried very hard to let you decide what was appropriate for you to learn—though I was a bit uncomfortable letting a child make some of those decisions. But Di'nay was right...you were undaunted by any of it. Whether it concerned your love and loyalty to family, your responsibilities to Khirlan's folk, or your own development, you approached each challenge with passionate determination. And you succeed. Llinolae—you can do things I'd thought only Seers might attempt and yet you do them without a Seer's loss of self!

"So yes, you did learn ways to use your Blue Sight that are completely different from anyone I've imagined—I wouldn't even pretend that I actually understand how you manage some of what you do. But clearly you've taught yourself the control and precision as well."

"Then why have I been so blind to Taysa, Mistress?"

"My best guess would be, its because the intensity of her amarin is a passionate match for your own. It's the most common reason why a Blue Sight or Seer has trouble deciphering someone's amarin."

"But I don't do things that way." Llinolae felt the frustration begin to rise within her again. "I don't read emotions by locking gazes. I don't anticipate a sword's swing by sharing an opponent's own plans. I can't do it! I *won't* do it. I'd follow the barest trail of the most ancient fossils' amarin through a league of rock before I'd learn to impose my consciousness on another's soul!"

"The simple fact that you have often followed such fossil trails, should impress you with the strength of the powers and skills you do have."

"Exchanging pleasantries with a tree has little to do with deciphering the truth of a court's intrigue!"

"Llinolae, you absorb the Sense of truth and lies through the flux in Aggar's flowing cycles. You *always* See a happening as it actually occurred, not as an individual's biased perception. You *always* perceive the complexities of greater patterns. You are never limited to a single person's awareness, save when you choose your own. And it is your very own awareness which then allows you step back from the details and fit the facts together." The Sight wrapped about Llinolae in a cloak of compelling truth as the Mistress n'Shea leaned forward in eagerness. "Yes, your skills are best when away from the stone courts and chambers. Like all Blue Sights, you're more attuned to what is true or what is elusive, when you're physically closer to the natural webs of living amarin. But you've spent most of your life riding in and out of Aggar's Great Forest, Llinolae, and you've interacted with the awareness of those great Ancients well...with patience and respect, despite your tenacious refusal to be swallowed by their flowing Life Cycles. As a result, you're becoming more and more skilled at drawing upon the power they offer. Soon even your time in the cities will barely interfere with that bond. You've already begun to notice more subtleties in your Court—like the growing suspicions you've had for Taysa. Nothing in her interactions with you particularly changed, yet your perceptions shifted."

Sadness curved Llinolae's lips. As if she were not overwhelmed with court baskers and schemers already!

The Mistress n'Shea chuckled, Llinolae's Sight freely sharing that impression with her.

"Whether it's fortunate or not, I'm afraid I'm beginning to See what you mean, but it lends me the very discouraging impression that I'll find things in Khirla are every bit as bad as Brit's insinuated." The sigh Llinolae slowly released, was a weary one. Their swing swayed a little as she leaned forward to set her elbows on her knees, linking her hands together loosely. "Given I read people so differently, how do I assess what I See?"

"Separate what the Forest prompts you to know from what your personal feelings assume."

Llinolae's scowl returned.

"You find you still dislike what these Sisters imply."

"I do."

"What has the Forest shown you?"

"That they speak the truth. But there is more from what I know for myself." Llinolae remembered the devastation of the fire weapons sweeping through her small camp—and the two blue cloaked executioners among her Steward's Swords. "The morning we rode east for the Clan's Plateau, a pair of the sword carriers I'd chosen to accompany me were taken ill. I didn't think much of it. With Khirla's Feasts in celebration, it's not so unusual for a good number of folks to get sick from some new food or spice. Samcin quietly arranged for two replacements—walked them down himself to explain the others' absence."

"Samcin is your aunt's consort, isn't he?"

"He's also in charge of the Steward's Swords—very convenient for Taysa, I'm realizing. The replacements he arranged seemed anxious, but no more so than the rest of us. The others were anxious about being caught as we worked our way far enough into the Clan's lands to find a settlement other than Clantown. I'd hoped to persuade someone less involved with the militia's ambitions to approach the Clan Leads with my petition for peace negotiations.

"Samcin's two sword carriers weren't worried about the Clan scouts and the possibility of being ambushed, however." Llinolae stared grimly down at her hands. "Turned out they were waiting to do the ambushing. I Saw the tension and jitters in them that evening—they spread to most everyone pretty quick. Still I didn't think it was odd; we'd found signs of Clan scouts in the area and nerves were naturally taut." Llinolae fell silent, feeling the stunned shock of the Forest and her companions at those first bursts of death. She wondered again if that moment of immobility had been an eternity or an eye blink.

"What were they armed with?" the Mistress n'Shea prompted gently.

"Fire weapons—the small sort that belt on under a tunic. And a dozen or more descending Clan scouts as reinforcements."

The Mistress sighed.

"Obviously someone is very serious about keeping me away from the Clan Leads with my proposition. And Taysa made sure they'd succeed by planting a few sympathizers inside my own camp."

"You sound certain it was your aunt giving the orders and not Samcin's own doing."

"I am. Samcin may be a good soldier, but he's a mediocre commander. He doesn't eat or sleep without her instructions—it took me an unfortunate amount of time to notice just how doggedly loyal to her he is. But given the illegal taxes and tariffs Brit and Sparrow described, I suspect Taysa rather enjoys having him intimidate the merchants and crafters into mute acquiescence." The picture she was beginning to form of her aunt was growing less and less pretty as they went, Llinolae thought.

"What are you going to do about her?"

"Nothing for the moment."

The promptness of Llinolae's response surprised the Mistress n'Shea, despite the sensitivity of the Sight stretched between them.

"Look—I can't trust her. I can trust Gwyn."

"The Royal Marshal you spoke of?"

Llinolae affirmed it with a nod. "And as much as this Brit n'Minona dislikes me for my past stupidities regarding Taysa and Samcin, she and her companion are equally willing to help me end my District's struggles! No matter what Taysa's greed has engineered over the past seasons, two things remain clear—the fighting between Clan and Khirlan must stop, and the fire weapons must go.

"The Clan's fire weapons are the fundamental base for their militia's power. The weapons are being used more and more often to do more and more damage—the fact that the two Swords Taysa sent out with me had also been supplied with the nightmarish things only attests to the broadening problem. If she's bartering with someone for fire weapons in return for betrayal—then you can wager others are too."

A considering nod accepted that logic. The Mistress n'Shea smiled humorously. "As you speak, I can almost hear Di'nay saying something along the same lines."

"She taught me much of strategy and schemes," Llinolae acknowledged. "I could not propose to do what I am, if it had not been for her teachings."

"Both she and I would wish it otherwise for you, Daughter."

"I know."

The Mistress rubbed the bridge of her nose in a weary gesture that made Llinolae smile faintly. The gesture was an unconscious mime of the Mistress n'Athena that reminded the young woman of how many of the tenmoon seasons her two mentors had seen together. Llinolae wondered if she and Gwyn might ever decide to risk enough commitment to acquire a few reflective habits as well.

"Then you're still intent on trying to reach a Clan settlement, before you return to Khirla and deal with your aunt?"

"Aye, and arrange some contact with the Clan Leads."

"And the fire weapons?"

"If the Clan Leads will not negotiate for some reasonable limits...," Llinolae grew stony. "I'll find a way to negotiate their precious weapons completely out of existence."

The Mistress n'Shea met Llinolae's blue eyes without comment. The young woman needed to resort to the Sight to communicate the fiery determination of her vow. The Mistress remembered the unswerving tenacity in the student she'd once trained. She saw now how the child had grown as the challenges had, and with a brushing pain of grief, she knew the Dracoon would die rather than fail Khirlan's people.

Chapter Eight

Llinolae lifted the tent flap, pausing before moving outside to join the others around the dying camp fire. Even in the warm softness of the summer's evening the amarin were wearying with the mistrusts and despairs of the small band. The forest's sense of discord that she had Seen before the caravan's arrival yesterday still lingered strongly. At least Ty had finally deigned to join them for eventide. But even Ril had grown more tired of dealing with her packmate's intolerances than Llinolae had; Ril had withdrawn into the stabling tent quite a while back. Too bad Llinolae couldn't follow the example as easily. But then, she'd spent too many seasons dealing with Court to believe anything could be settled by avoiding either Ty or Brit.

At the moment, the threesome looked innocently content. Ty was spread out full-length on her side, beyond the fire's stone ring. Across from Ty, Gwyn was quietly whittling away on her flute, sitting on her usual rock. She wasn't too far from Brit's side. But the silences between the Amazons only seemed to stretch longer and longer as the evening wore on. Ty had made no move to curl nearer to her human packmate either.

As far as Llinolae could tell, the Amazons' tea mugs hadn't even gotten refilled since the dishes had been done. So much for brewing the fresh pot.

Mae n'Pour! Of all the tales she'd ever heard sung of Amazons, not one had mentioned the discord of sullen tempers and stubborn musings. Llinolae sighed. Well, short of being openly rude and giving yet more fuel to Brit n'Minona's ire, she couldn't very well avoid the Sisters for much longer. Reluctantly, she left the tent's comforting seclusion.

Further down the canyon then, she noticed something. The amarin in the evening's growing twilight shimmered—something not quite right moved beyond the caravan, drawing slowly nearer. Oh—Sparrowhawk, Llinolae recognized her absently. Then a frown touched her brow as Llinolae began to watch the approach of the smaller Amazon more intently.

Of the two new arrivals, Sparrow was the one Llinolae had found the least approachable. Yet she had felt the most affinity for her. The woman had been polite and gently clear in all of her dealings with Llinolae. Unlike Brit, Sparrowhawk was neither resentful nor judgmental of Llinolae's overtures. In truth, she seemed merely exhausted from her condition and eager to be left alone whenever possible. And that was certainly a desire Llinolae could respect.

Tonight though…tonight was overwhelming. The woman was pushing herself punishingly hard.

Llinolae halted a few feet behind Brit and Gwyn. Ty's head came up expectantly, sandy eyes challenging the Dracoon's approach. But Llinolae's attention was fixed on Sparrowhawk as the Amazon drew nearer.

And then with a sudden chill, Llinolae realized what the strain of that fatigue was on the verge of causing! She rushed forward in alarm, crying, "Sparrowhawk!"

Both Brit and Gwyn looked about, startled.

"You can't do this!" Llinolae snatched the heavy water skin from the small woman. "To be so exhausted! Yet carry so much!"

Grim-faced and still, Sparrow refused to answer. But her burnished, darkened skin was more than telling, and Llinolae took no notice of the silent rebuke. Abruptly Sparrow found herself relieved of her arm's load of firewood as well.

Gwyn glanced at Brit, puzzled. Her friend was tight-lipped and stern, almost as deeply browned as her shadowmate.

"At least sit down?" Llinolae pleaded gently, her hand hesitant in reaching out. Even with the water and wood set aside, her concern was unwavering. But the woman seemed on the verge of refusing even that simple act of self-care, and Llinolae grew desperate to break through that dangerous wall of dulled apathy. "What? *Why?* Do you *want* to miscarry?"

Sparrow's head snapped up—sandy eyes widening in horror as her hand rose protectively to press against her stomach. A sudden stillness stunned the camp and told that—*for all of them!*—this was a secret bared without proper warning.

Llinolae felt the others' jolt of near incomprehension, belatedly realizing none of them had even suspected this Sister was pregnant. But how could that be? Hadn't Gwyn said Brit was Sparrowhawk's mate?

Her blue eyes flew to Gwyn for guidance. But the whittling knife was poised motionless above the flute wood, that copper-bright gaze was fixed on Sparrow, and Gwyn's sun-kissed tan was slowly turning from its apricot hue to the deep, deep burnished brown of shock. Then Gwyn's own gaze started—jumped to Brit, then back to Sparrow as the younger woman began to step away, almost stumbling. And suddenly Sparrow was spinning about blindly to run.

"*Soroi!*" Brit's bark halted Sparrow in her tracks, but Brit's tenor grew caring and low in her next words. "*Ti Maez....*"

Llinolae felt her throat tighten at the sheer gentleness in Brit's tone...such gentleness could only have spoken of love and commitment—of unjudging reassurance.

"*Sae Soroi—tizmar?*"

Sparrow glanced back. Feet frozen in their place, she could only stare searchingly at the woman who sat so quietly on the camp chair, holding that tea mug with such a steady hand. Her breath caught with a shudder and she twisted away again. Both her arms came 'round her waist to hug herself as she slumped forward. Her sobs rose as the tears finally flowed. Only then did Brit put down the tea and rise, going to her beloved and gathering her tenderly into a strong embrace.

Brit's lips brushed across Sparrow's temple, and then she simply stood there, holding her treasured love. The moment thinned, drawing on through the dimming twilight, but no one dared to move for fear of interrupting the two. Even Ty merely watched, eyes peaked in muted concern and understanding.

The warm palm of Brit's hand came to lie against a wet cheek, and she brought Sparrow's gaze upwards to meet her own. "Come...."

Fear flickered through those still tearing eyes, and Brit's lips softly touched Sparrow's own.

"Now come," the older woman repeated as she wrapped an arm about her lover's shoulders, turning them towards the home of their caravan. "It's time to talk."

Her shadowmate nodded, swallowing painfully, but the unwavering, unconditional support of Brit's strength did not abandon her. Her trust in that steady strength began to rekindle despite the past days of mounting fears, and silently she let Brit lead them away from the camp's fire.

"I...I didn't know...," Llinolae murmured, heart aching as she watched the two go—the blur of their amarin blending. She brought a near helpless gaze back to Gwyn. "I wouldn't have said anything if...I didn't know!"

"It's all right." Gwyn smiled gently and stretched a hand out to Llinolae. "It will be all right."

The Amazon drew Llinolae down to sit beside her then. With a faint squeeze, she shook Llinolae's hand a little in emphasis of her words. "I promise you, it will be better between them. They've been grappling with the silence of this secret since their arrival—and longer. And for them, such silence could only have become more painful—and destructive—the longer it lasted."

Ty's ears flicked back at that. Her nose dropped thoughtfully to touch a curled-under forepaw. Then her sandy gaze rose to focus intently upon Llinolae.

The Dracoon turned abruptly at that unexpected touch from the sand-wolf's empathy. For the first time since they'd met, there was no bitterness nor challenge in Ty's demeanor. Her blue eyes narrowed in concentration, and slowly, Llinolae recognized Ty's reassurance for what it was. The sandwolf was not only agreeing with her human packmate, she had—for whatever reasons—decided to extend a tentative truce; something in Llinolae's manner tonight had won Ty's respect. And in return, Ty extended an honest assurance that she believed Llinolae had done nothing wrong here, and that—just maybe—Ty could trust her to genuinely care as much for what happened to Gwyn's heart.

Tears pricked the backs of her eyes, and Llinolae blinked them away as Gwyn's arm encircled her gently. Shaking—warily, she dared to accept the physical offer of reassurance and leaned into Gwyn's shoulder. Ty's amarin didn't waver; she still offered only approval.

With a grateful smile, Llinolae sent a silent 'thank you' to the sandwolf. She had nearly given up on ever earning any degree of acceptance from Ty. Yet ultimately, she had known how important Ty's acceptance was to the pack, especially to Gwyn. The faint trust Ty now gave was all the more sweet for the waiting. She pledged to both the sandwolf and herself that she would do her utmost to hold this new faith unbroken.

* * *

Llinolae stirred restlessly on her bed pallet, well aware that the mid-night moon had risen and that its early Twin was nearly gone. Dawn was yet a ways off, but she was reluctantly beginning to believe that she'd still be awake to greet it.

That dream—that damned, haunting dream of poisons and death just wouldn't let her go. In truth, the nightmare itself had not come again. But since Brit and Sparrow had arrived, the images seemed to be lingering, almost lurking, at the shadowy edges of her awareness. They were always waiting for her concentration to lapse just a little, before surging forward with all their vile horrors again.

She rolled onto her back, stifling a sigh. From the corner of her eye, she saw Ty's head lift in query. This wasn't fair to either of them. And if she wasn't careful she'd be waking Gwyn completely too.

At that, she did give up and pushed the coverlet aside. She pulled on the ruddy leather breeches and didn't think to bother with stockings nor boots. The night was more than mild enough for the light tunic and the breeches to suffice.

Ty's nose returned to the pillow of her curled paw as Llinolae slipped out of the tent. Then her eyes peaked in wrinkled little triangles of worry and the mismatched points of her ears flicked towards her human packmate.

Only half-asleep, Gwyn slowly turned over. She stared at the sluggish ripple of the canvas flaps as they settled. Outside the night seemed quiet in the way a forest's night is, yet isn't. The breezes moved leaf bits. The creek gurgled nearby. Yellow crickets, night birds, the odd snuffle or snort from the mares all mingled.

Gwyn could hear no footsteps. She could not follow Llinolae by any sound. She hadn't expected to be able to. She was sorry for that, though. She regretted she couldn't even offer that small bit of solace in dispelling the woman's aloneness. And sometimes, she knew, the gifts of Blue Sight could seem so very isolating.

Ty nuzzled the back of Gwyn's hand, and the Amazon smiled faintly. "*Dumauz*, thank you. It does help, knowing you've grown to judge her less harshly."

Gwyn sighed and rearranged herself on the pallet, Ty rising in answer to the tacit invitation of hers. The sandwolf stretched out atop the blanket, crowding close to her bondmate. Without shedding a tear, Gwyn buried her face in the warmth and comfort of Ty's ruff. It wasn't the kind of melancholy in her that stirred tears, really. It was just a hollow, helpless feeling. She didn't know what to do or say.

Ty nosed Gwyn's chin in gentle reproach.

"That's true," the Amazon smiled weakly. "I don't know what I can give yet, let alone if it'd be what she needs."

"Llinolae...?"

The hesitant voice was soft, uncertain in identifying the Dracoon's presence; and Llinolae looked ahead with a welcoming warmth. She had forgotten how sensitive Sparrow's lifestone made the woman to the amarin around her, even if that sensitivity was not on a wholly conscious level.

"Aye—it *is* you."

Llinolae nodded, climbing up to join Sparrow as the woman slid a little further along the stony seat to make room.

The night sparkled around them with the spray of the waterfall, the moons' light turning the mistiness to silver. The air smelled clean. The crescent of the midnight moon peered into the gorge. While around them all the dark honeywoods rose height upon height, setting the trees' crowns far above the rocks and waterfall.

"The Great Forest has settled with peace tonight," the small Amazon murmured.

"It has."

"I...," Sparrowhawk paused, rethought her words, then laughed with an awkward shake of her head. "Thank you doesn't seem quite the right thing to say."

Llinolae touched the back of the other's hand lightly, understanding well enough. "I know. Part of me wants to beg your patience while another is happy for you—for both of you. What you share with your healer, Brit, is very precious. And I've Seen how much better things have been between you two since...well, since my less-than-tactful announcement the other day."

"Yes, everything is much better. Thank you. It was...I simply didn't know how...to...tell her."

Blue eyes only turned to Sparrow with compassion; there was no pressing to continue. Sparrow drew a deep breath and let her tensions go with a sigh. "I was so frightened, simply because I am pregnant. Yet I was so afraid, too, of hurting Brit in telling her. I'd waited...hoped that Gwyn could help her through the pain it would bring. But I don't know...." Candidly, Sparrow looked to Llinolae, "I *am* grateful to you. I know now that I couldn't have done it myself."

Sparrow's grasp folded about hers, and thoughtfully Llinolae turned their hands over. Fingers entwining, she held on tightly as she searched for words and clearer images amongst the woman's amarin—searched for what Sparrow appeared to be so desperate to share with her. But Llinolae was not as good at deciphering the complexities of an individual's amarin as these Amazons seemed to expect her to be. Only Sparrowhawk's sincerity was clear to her; the sources of those earlier fears remained elusive.

In the end, Llinolae settled for something of a shrug and a smile, covering their clasped hands with her free one. "I understand probably too little of what you've been struggling with. But if I've helped, then I'm glad to have given you that. In truth, I am."

A ready grin and a great wash of relief swept over the smaller woman, and Llinolae found her own smile growing in return. Apparently, there were some things Sparrow was quite relieved in not pursuing further. Then the Amazon invited questions of an even rarer sort, "I know that *dey Sorormin's* ways can often seem strange to an outsider. I remember having a daunting amount of questions, when I first met Brit."

Disbelief, then gratitude at the open trust Sparrowhawk was offering held Llinolae silent for a long moment, until the subtler humor of it all registered. What hung unsaid was Sparrow's rather impish acknowledgment of Llinolae's attraction to Gwyn—and the rather obvious expectation that Llinolae's curiosities about the Sisters' customs were plaguing some of the sweeter dreams Llinolae had concerning Gwyn.

Llinolae couldn't help herself then, and her laughter rang bright, sparkling with the joy of the silver water mists. With an amused shake of her head, she thought Sparrow's suspicions couldn't be further from the truth of what kept her awake tonight. "Ah—I do thank you. But...Gwyn'l is not the problem I've been pondering."

"Oh." Sparrow blushed faintly in the dimness. "Seems Brit's rubbing off on me. She's always been accused of being an old gossip."

"No, you're not starting rumors," Llinolae amended more softly. "The affection is there between us. Where it will lead…it's too soon to say."

"Fairly noted. Gwyn would want it that way, I can see. Something with evoking the honor of the *Niachero* , no doubt." Sparrow tipped her head to the side a bit. "May I ask then, what has kept you up so late?"

The question spawned a more sober response, and Llinolae's gaze dropped to the pooling waters below them. "A dream…or maybe the ghosts of a dream would be a better way of explaining it."

"A nightmare?" Sparrow ventured tentatively.

"Yes…no." Llinolae shook herself slightly. "I remember it as a dream, but it has the vivid qualities of a real memory." She shrugged again, "It's not one of my own."

Sparrow understood memories well enough, even blue-sighted ones. She squeezed Llinolae's grasp, giving what reassurance she could. "At the Keep, the Council's shadow trainees—the Blue Sights I mean now, not those such as I— they often spoke of dreamspun visions. Sometimes they would describe things that had not yet happened, sometimes things that had already happened. But usually, it was a thing they'd not witnessed personally. Although the dreaming *was* always about a thing which would eventually affect them very, very deeply."

Llinolae considered that, nodding. "It certainly does…deeply."

Sparrow pursed her lips a moment, feet swinging absently where they dangled over the waters. But before she had decided to speak again, Llinolae closed a hand over hers. And at Sparrow's gaze, the other's smile grew only more sad. "I know what I must do. I need counsel less than courage. But thank you—for the offer of knowledge from your understanding of the Council's friends."

"All right," Sparrow lent her a gentle smile in return. "I'm of a mind to brew some midnight spice teas."

"The sort with the llinolae moss blossoms in it?"

"Aye, it is a rare skill for a northerner or a desert nomad to have, seeing the stuff grows only in Khirlan. But when we arrived and I noticed the moss blanket beyond the pool there, I couldn't resist a few little harvest-and-brew experiments with the dustiest of my old recipe notes." Sparrow chuckled at the disbelieving look the Dracoon gave her. "The Council taught Brit and me much more than simple healer or troubadour skills. When Brit let's me, I'm even a fair cook myself!"

"Then perhaps I'll join you fireside in a bit." Llinolae held Sparrow hand tightly for a longer moment, before seeking her eye with a humble admission. "I once shied from the Council's associates completely. Now I find that may have been a rather biased view to take."

"You've seen nothing but the worst of Brit and myself. You may yet—"

"No, I'm serious. Distracted and irascible as n'Minona was, she was never the monster so many believe the Council folk to be."

"It's a fear found only in Khirlan and the Clan's areas," Sparrow corrected without anger. "The isolation has begun to create bigotries again…just as the isolation of different beasts and people split Aggar's unity in the beginnings."

"Bears thinking about," Llinolae noted.

"Llinolae, if you ever have need...," Sparrow hesitated, but with a squeeze of a hand was encouraged to continue. She shared a fluttering bit of a grin and shrugged. "I am bound to Brit by the stone as your Blue Sight has shown you."

"Aye."

"Well...we—Brit and I—would lend you the aid of Sisterhood, healer or troubadour."

"I know."

"If ever we could offer more...Brit and I spoke of it earlier and not many know this, but should you *wish* the Council's help someday, Brit is empowered to speak for them. She'll not carry them tales without your knowledge, and never without need, but if you should ask for their support or advice?" Sparrow glanced at her again, still wary. "She was an Archivist for a time among them and has their trust. I thought...."

"You thought right." The quiet tone held no malice or pain, and Llinolae moved nearer to offer a light hug. "The Council's aid may eventually be of some help with this escapade, I don't know. But thank you."

"The offer will stand, even after this venture is sorted out, Llinolae."

It was a pleasing honor, Llinolae acknowledged with a nod. Then a sudden thought occurred, "Does Gwyn know? Or should I take care not to...?"

"No...she knows now." Abruptly Sparrow shifted, a hand going to her midriff. "My stomach is needing that tea, I think. I'd best go."

"Do you want help?"

Sparrow rose, cheerfully denying it. "I enjoy mixing bits of moss and herb and spice to taste."

"You are sounding proficient!"

"There'll be enough, if you want it later."

Llinolae watched the woman lithely scramble off, and she was reassured that her help was decidedly not missed. Then she turned back to the peace of the tumbling falls. Sighing, she drew herself up and focused her concentration. It was time to follow this dreamspun vision to it's inception.

She knew her answers might not be reached tonight as her experience in untangling the amarin of people and places from the past was less practiced. It was not a journey she anticipated enjoying either.

Yet the answers would not come by themselves, she rebuked herself gruffly. Whether it took a handspan of nights or a monarc of attempts, the doing would not be done any faster by avoiding it.

She sighed and folded her legs beneath her, shaking the remnants of tension from her shoulders and neck. Deeply she drew in the air, settling among the rhythms and flows of the life cycles about her. Her eyes slipped shut. Her head tipped back, face bared to the night sky and the waterfall's mist. A breeze drifted by, brushing her lips as lightly as a kiss. And then in her mind's Sense, she gazed outward along those shimmering tendrils of Life's amarin, gathering finely coiled cords of it, moving upwards beyond the honeywood ancients, and then reaching—flinging—those silver-blue lines out to uncoil. Further back through the tenmoon seasons...further back to that bedroom and time of death.

Chapter Nine

till no sign of them?"

Llinolae shook her head, amused at Brit's fussing, and put the wooden bread bowl she'd filled with brushberries on the camp table. Since the two Sisters had arrived, the amenities of the 'civilized life' that the wagon stocked hadn't ceased to impress the Dracoon. From the folding tables and chairs to tunics already tailored to fit *Niachero*-tall Amazons, the tinker-trades' goods had easily supplied all of their needs—and even a few of their whims! But it was Brit's own cooking and the available seasonings she had to work with that Llinolae most appreciated. Having spent more of her life out on patrols or housed at inns across the Clan-ravaged west-district than she'd spent in the Palace, Llinolae had come to measure 'good' in terms of quantity, not quality. Brit's penchant for mixing and brewing extended far beyond a healer's recipes, however, and now that she knew of Sparrow's pregnancy, she had taken on the task of "feeding them proper" with a true zeal. For this talent alone, Llinolae could see why Sparrow might have pledged the unending allegiance of a lifebond to the Amazon.

"You're movin' pretty limber today," Brit noted, adding another handful of flour to the cheesecloth before punching down the dough again. "How're the ribs feeling?"

"Good."

"Good. 'Fraid you'd broken something there, when Gwyn first told me. They gave you quite a beating...barely tell anymore. Scarcely a bruise left it seems."

"I've always been a fast mender."

"Most Blue Sights are. It's all that nurturing you tap into with the Life Cycles' amarin."

Llinolae grinned outright. "I don't think I'm ever going to get used to hearing you three say that...."

"Say what?" Brit caught her eye. "Oh—" The healer chuckled and reached for another handful of nuts-and-dried-berries. "Never mind me, I just rattle on. Safe enough 'round strangers, though. Don't have to worry about your secret breakin' loose...no one else's business anyway."

A grateful pride warmed inside her; Llinolae was glad to discover that she was no longer considered a stranger.

"Strangers...," the healer tisked with a shake of her head. "Wish I knew if Sparrow's worryin' about nothing or not."

The complete lack of anger in Brit surprised Llinolae almost as much as the confidence being shared with her; Sparrow had seemed so completely convinced that there would be a terrifying blaze of anger and rejection. She leaned back against the wagon wall, folding her arms she propped a foot up on a wheel spoke. "You're merely curious?"

Brit blinked, startled that she shouldn't be. "'Course I'm curious. Wouldn't you be?"

Llinolae frowned with a puzzled admission, "You're worried about her still. I can See that, but...but you're not angry. At least, not the sort I can recognize through your amarin."

"Why should I be angry? She can't help it, if some sadist took her." A touch of bitterness crept in then, but Brit shrugged it off in favor of practicalities. "If she gets to remembering that was the way of it, then we'll deal with it. 'Til then, we'll wait and see;. Couple of *months* we'll know anyway, won't we?"

"*Months*? " The odd reference distracted Llinolae for a moment. Then she recalled that Valley Bay still kept records in *years* as well as tenmoon seasons, for the sake of their communications with *dey Sorormin's* home world. But Brit's assumptions were still confusing her, and she gestured down the creek towards the trail Sparrow and Gwyn would presumably return by. "She's worried because she can't remember—? Remember *what* about some sadist?"

"My same point."

"Your same...?" Llinolae stared at Brit and suddenly—finally—understood. "Sparrow's scared she was raped?"

Brit looked at Llinolae with the uncanny assessment of a true Crone and, abruptly quit her kneading. "What's your Sight telling you is different?"

"She's not pregnant because she was raped, Brit."

"Goddess' blest!" The elder woman squeezed her eyes shut with the whisper. "You can See that...you know it for truth?"

"In truth," Llinolae readily answered that faint waiver of doubt. "Brit, I may not be able to decipher much about the subtleties of an individual, but the baby she's carrying is several ten-days along. I can See the child well enough to know she's yours and Sparrow's, no other's."

A sigh, then a faint, satisfied smile suddenly burst into a broad beaming grin of shining joy. And Brit blinked, the tears dancing in her gray eyes. "Thank you, *Dumauz*, thank you."

Llinolae touched that strong wrist reassuringly.

"It's just so rare...." With a sniff and a slight shift in her weight, Brit found her balance again and assessed the dough lump before shaking a few more nuts into the kneading. "You know...for the women on Aggar? In *dey Sorormin*, yes. Well, between the lifestones and our long herstory of gene selections before we ever, even dreamed of settling Valley Bay...you could say it's half-expected. Among us it's always considered a possibility. But....uhn...now that's an arrogant prejudice against Aggar's women, isn't it! Since when has rare meant never?"

A gleeful laugh shook Llinolae's tall frame, but Brit just grinned all the more, totally unabashed. Feigning some bare measure of politeness, Llinolae managed to cover her mouth with a half-curled hand before gulping out, "What *are* you talking about now, n'Minona?"

"Parthenogenesis," Brit rejoined just as cheerfully.

"Which to us poor, uneducated folk outside of Valley Bay is...?"

"When a woman's egg doesn't divide completely in developing—it can fertilize itself. Spontaneous reproduction...a type of identical twin, only as a daughter. Oh, arguably the risks for Aggar's women to miscarry may be higher in those cases, but Sparrowhawk...," Brit grinned and shook her head in an amused tolerance for her dear lover. "Sparrow could no more sit still for a single day than a hawk could resist flying for its whole life!"

"You're still wrong."

Concern flashed across the other's face, but Llinolae raised a quieting hand, "No, not about Sparrow being all right. She'll do just fine, I'm certain." An impish sort of smiled sprouted from Llinolae then as Brit relaxed, and she added, "Actually, the night after you two arrived—it seemed the exception to the usual."

"The entire ten-day was!" Brit sputtered in exasperation.

"But you're wrong in thinking this is Sparrow's daughter alone. It's yours too."

"Mine?"

"Quite clearly," Llinolae nodded. "Your amarin and Sparrow's both run through this baby."

"That's...that's just because we're so close, lifebonded and all."

"No." Llinolae moved her head silently, lips pursued in absolute denial.

"You mean...?" Brit's dough went forgotten again.

"She's yours—as much as she's Sparrowhawk's. Genetically, *yours.*"

"But...how?"

A smile cracked at that as Llinolae shrugged in guileless innocence. "*You're* the healer, Brit. You're the one who knows the customs of Valley Bay, Council—and even my own District better than I do! I'm just some lost Dracoon. How would I know *how?*"

"But that's just it. We didn't...," Brit stopped mid-sentence, the answer ringing through her mind even as she knew it was impossible. Yet, ultimately, there was no other explanation to be had.

"What is it, *Dumauz*? What's gone wrong?" Llinolae straightened, pushing away from the wagon's side.

"The lifestone—it must be the lifestone." Brit turned a perplexed but amazed sort of gaze on her. "We've used the things for generations now, to create our daughters. It—it was safer than the ways before. We learned it was possible from the first lifebond of the Sisterhood, but only because she was a Blue Sight like yourself. Yet the *only* cases of spontaneous conception between lifebonded partners has come about because the Blue Gift and the lifestones meshed the amarin—which then altered the egg's development to create the child! For that matter, conceptions guided with the lifestones still require a blue-sighted healer to intervene...."

"Until now?"

"Apparently so."

"Until now." Abruptly the flowing amarin around her nudged Llinolae into an awareness of much more that had happened here, and a softer smile gentled her humor. She slipped an arm around Brit's shoulders and bent to press a kiss against the older woman's temple. "Welcome into the Life Cycles of Aggar, *Soroe.*"

"As Daughter of Mothers, child! Valley Bay isn't...," Brit's laugh caught, and she took a moment or two more to turn the idea around in her mind. Then she smiled, almost surprised by what she found. "Aye—though Valley Bay is *dey Sorormin*...even the Council once suggested that eventually...." She glanced to Llinolae, still bemused, "We have become such partners of traders and scouts...of healers and protectors among both the Northern and Southern

Continents since our Foundings. So much a part...so much caring, have we barely noticed how deeply we do care?"

"You were a part of Aggar even before then. *Dey Sorormin* took Aggar's hand the day the Blue Sight was carried to your home world."

"It is possible." Eyes narrowed and slowly the herstorian n'Minona within Brit surfaced, and she glimpsed something more of the patterns. Then that childhood training shifted her perspective again, and she bit her lower lip in a sarcastic, little chuckle. "Strange tapestry in these weavings, *Soroe*, to have the amarin first engaging the Amazon strangers. Would have done Aggar more good to embrace the Changlings for a few seasons. At least, the Life Cycles might have given it a try! *Z'ki Zak!* Half the northern folks' problems come directly from poor communications."

"Or rather the total lack of any," Llinolae muttered. With little humor, she thought of the troubles with the Clan.

"Now, the winged-cats have the *sense* of understanding, if not always the responses we humans can grasp. And the sandwolves have the *feel* of understanding, even if they often seem so odd to some people. But how the Changlings will ever have a chance...? At our best, Sparrow 'nd I could barely manage a basic exchange of food or cloth with them. Always the concrete, never any of the abstract concepts at all."

"I could only hope the Clan turns out to be so concrete about their needs." Llinolae scowled briefly as Brit shook her head. "What then, n'Minona?"

"Your hopes for the Clan? I don't see anything but hopes and air there, Llinolae."

"And did the Changlings seem so poor a prospect to you too?"

Brit chuckled, unperturbed. "Changlings are different."

"So are the Clan folk," Llinolae persisted. "Respect and patience—"

"You have! As well as honor. I don't mean to mock you. Don't take it that way. But we're a long way from the Council, and we're even a longer way from merely talking to work our differences out with the Clan folk."

"I have to try."

"I wouldn't want it any other way," Brit admitted with sincerity. "I just wouldn't be too ready to count on doing things the easier way."

Unfortunately, Llinolae mused, she couldn't either.

* * *

The amarin stirred without a breeze of warning, and Llinolae paused in the clothes washing. Concern concentrated her Blue Gift as she looked downstream, until suddenly the tension broke. Her soft lips quivered with amusement.

Quickly, she turned to rinse the soap from the last of the garments and wrapped the lot loosely in the canvas carrier. Then heedless of how damp her camisole knit would get, she scurried off with the load to find Brit and tell her of the others' return.

"Humpf—'bout time," the stocky woman grumbled and fished a few more of her mumut dumplings out of the pot to roll through the crystallized honeyspice. "Can you See if they're bringing anything edible with them?"

"You sent them out hunting," Llinolae muttered good-naturedly. "You think they'd dare come back without meat?"

The wooden spoon went 'whack' against the ceramic pot's edge, and Llinolae jumped more than the boiling water but her grin only broadened. Brit scowled, then went back to her cooking and mumblings. Llinolae laughed as the woman feigned another annoyed grimace. She took herself off behind the main tent then to hang the laundry to dry. As she secured the extra lines for the bedding, the friendly noises of horse and Amazon drifted in to her, and she wasn't surprised to find Ril come 'round shortly to greet her.

"It's good to see you too." Llinolae knelt and hugged the great beast, laughing when Ril's calm suddenly gave way to excitement—her coarse curls and silky ears arched backwards up against Llinolae's neck as a lapping tongue wetly found her ear.

"Ril!"

The sandwolf started guiltily at Gwyn's outcry.

"Oh she's fine!" Llinolae assured them both, rubbing the furry tummy emphatically. "Aren't you, my friend?"

Ril wiggled from her shoulders to her hips in eager agreement, nuzzling Llinolae's chin happily as the Dracoon hugged her again. Gwyn's chuckle had them expectantly pausing to glance at her, but only briefly. Then amusement faded into something more intense as the Amazon drew nearer, and neither Ril's nor Llinolae's empathic sensitivities could ignore the silent soul ache.

Llinolae stared mutely at the booted feet planted on Ril's other side. Her throat tightened. She swallowed and dared to look up at Gwyn whose color deepened to a golden flush, and Llinolae's gaze shifted quickly back to those shiny boot tops as her own desires swept through her in a caramel blush.

Sandy eyes met her squarely, and Llinolae's heart dropped at the frankness Ril shared with her. The sandwolf flipped over neatly and rose to her feet to trot off, leaving Llinolae squatting there...feeling rather stupid at being so overwhelmed.

Gwyn's hand reached down to take hers. Somehow, she found herself on her feet staring into those questioning copper-bright—lovingly bright eyes. Eyes that turned gentle, banishing the nervousness, eyes that invited, coaxed—and Llinolae went willingly. Arms closed about her as sweetly as Gwyn's lips took hers, and for one heart-stopping moment she felt she was the most preciously treasured, respectfully cherished, most beautifully amazing woman Gwyn had ever held.... Then her blue eyes slipped shut, and her heart started pounding, because the feeling only grew—Gwyn was all those things and more to her in return.

Her senses melted, only to discover the wonderful strength beneath her hands as palms pressed—fingers kneaded—into Gwyn's back beneath that suede jerkin. Dust and horse and humid heat clung to skin, yet beneath—beyond?—that was the woman's own scent, an intoxicating, warm hint of.... Llinolae gasped without breaking their kiss and found surrender was given as freely as hers had been taken, and so in turn she took command. It was Gwyn's strength that seemed fainter, and grasp tightening, she drew Gwyn against her in reassurance.

Hands slid across Llinolae's shoulders to her neck and up into her hair. Fingers spread wide to slide through those tantalizing short bristles. And helpless to the nibbling lips against her neck, Llinolae tipped her head back. Gwyn gave a throaty growl of pleasure, and Llinolae found herself answering it, losing herself to the tongue tracing along the skin line of her camisole. They stopped then. Arms folding them each near, crushing nearly in their withdrawal. Skins flushed dark in cocoa-black sheens...faces buried in desperation against quaking shoulders.

"I...?"

"It's all right," Llinolae murmured quickly, tightening her hug in reassurance. She pressed a kiss against Gwyn's neck, and repeated, "Whatever you can manage is enough. Always."

They drew away so that they could almost see one another, their foreheads together...their breathing still erratic.

"It is enough...it is," Llinolae murmured again and again, finding the blurred amarin from her sweet love so frightened and yet wanting. There was more there to be Seen too, but Llinolae could not make sense of it—and for the first time in her entire life, she regretted having chosen a different training. There was so much...so much openness in wanting—needing!—to share with her. "Oh Gwyn, I wish I could, my Love...." She pulled Gwyn close again, this time in comfort.

"I know." The hoarse whisper was muffled against Llinolae's neck, then Gwyn forced a laugh and straightened—her hands gently framing Llinolae's face. She looked at her for a long moment, a thumb stroking away threatening tears. Gwyn smiled. Her heart filled with the wonder of simply holding—of knowing Llinolae at all. They laughed together a little, both realizing how silly it seemed to be so happy while in the same moment so indecisive.

Gwyn brushed the stray curl off of Llinolae's forehead; it only fell again. A smile danced tentatively across her face once more. Until finally, she met Llinolae's gaze properly. "I don't know much about you—in some ways."

"Like my use of the Sight," Llinolae murmured.

"Like that...or your favorite color?"

"Used to be blue...that satin blue of the Dracoon's formal colors."

"Used to be?" Gwyn tipped her head quizzically, and Llinolae laughed. "What?"

"When you do that...," Llinolae put a finger to Gwyn's chin, adjusting her head to the side again, "...when you turn your head like this, it reminds me of your sandwolves."

"Especially that irascible, inquisitive look Ty gets?"

"Yes—especially.... Do you mind?"

"That you noticed? No. It's nice that you do notice."

Llinolae's smiled fondly.

"Do you mind?" Gwyn pressed.

"What?"

"That I want to know more about you?"

"Like my favorite color now? It's a copperish...light...red." Her fingertips touched Gwyn's tousled bangs and traced the line beneath an eye. "I may have to change the Khirlan official colors. Do you think the King or Crowned Rule might forgive me?"

"Perhaps." Gwyn's eyes sparkled, pleased.

Llinolae looked at her in gathering silence. Gwyn waited.

"Do you think I should have told them of my Blue Sight?"

"No."

Llinolae assessed her carefully, but found no hint of reservations in Gwyn's amarin. "You trust me that much?"

"I do."

Llinolae took Gwyn's hands in her own, glancing nervously at their entwining fingers before asking, "Would you truly like to know more...about me and my Sight?"

Gwyn nodded, amending gently, "Only if you want to tell me."

"I do." Llinolae sighed. She turned. But she kept one hand in Gwyn's, inviting her love to walk beside her.

They followed the waters upstream until the creek disappeared through the rocky curtains of haymoss. Then Llinolae took them 'round towards the entrance to the waterfall, explaining, "I'd rather not be interrupted."

"I understand."

Beyond the dangling haymoss, Llinolae hesitated. The flat-rocked perch across from the falls didn't seem quite the best place for this. She nodded instead to the broad bed of green-black moss that swept across the stony flats to the right of the pool's leafy foliage. Gwyn's own glance lingered wistfully on the white churning waters that spilled into the shiny, black calm of the wider pool.

"Go ahead," Llinolae laughed, suddenly feeling much less pensive in the face of Gwyn's innocent shift of priorities.

Gwyn tossed her a look of sheer gratitude and began to tear off her weapons. "You're sure, you don't mind?"

"Hm-uhm." Llinolae nodded, still charmed and amused by her Amazon's eagerness.

"It's been so sticky and hot all day." The jerkin and tunic went quickly.

"Yes, I know, you've been in the saddle or skinning braygoat. It's all right, Gwyn—*go!*"

A hand to each boot, the laces loosened down her shins. Then with Llinolae watching in amazement, breeches, briefs, boots and socks all peeled off in a single layer. Must be a chore to untangle that mess, she caught herself thinking, and suddenly was laughing again as Gwyn took barely two steps and launched a long dive that carried her over as much land as black water, ending perfectly by sliding into that ebony coolness.

The laughter was gone—Llinolae's hand to her throat—stilled so quickly by that fleeting image of Gwyn—brown, lean, stretching—reflected in that mirror-clear blackness. A trick of light—no, of amarin perhaps?—but for the briefest of instants, to Llinolae it seemed the world was suspended above with the starry voids below—and Gwyn's beauty hung within both, binding both together at that point where they touched. Her hands slicing into the water, *Niachero* ascended to Grandmother's Stars.

Her Mistress n'Athena had once told her a *dey Sorormin* legend—

"...When it came time that the *divine woman* had finished Her work among the people, she returned to the great mountain where she stepped back into Grandmother Lybia's embrace. And ever after was *Niachero* known as—a Daughter of the Stars...."

Llinolae gulped for air, and Gwyn came up with a splash. She waved with a grin, bobbed under again, and Llinolae staggered beneath the amarin weight of normalcy.

"*Mae n'Pour!*" she breathed and managed to sit herself down on the mossy blanket with a bump, even though the moss cushioned her tail bone better than the horsehair pallets they were using in camp. She took another deep breath or two, still readjusting to the world as she knew it.

"What's wrong?"

Llinolae blinked, then smiled uneasily, realized she hadn't actually been alarmed enough to heed the amarin announcing Gwyn's approach. Was she trusting this woman more than she'd even noticed?

"Llinolae?" Gwyn dropped to her knees in concern, shrugging into her tunic hurriedly.

"I'm all right."

Gwyn shifted over to sit beside her with a blunt, "You don't look it."

She noticed her hand then. Her darker tones of color had returned. She shook her head, amused at her usual lack of subtlety. "There are occasions I do seem rather infatuated, don't I?"

Gwyn sent her companion a commiserating glance as she lay back, and propped herself up by the elbows. She studied Llinolae, not missing the weariness in those hunched shoulders as the woman sat with her feet planted flat and her hands dangling over her knees.

"The amarin still play tricks on me every so often...show me succinct little glimpses of a more powerful whole." Like they did just now, she admittedly silently.

Gwyn said nothing, content to let Llinolae choose her own words and time.

"I See...." A hand waved, at a loss for words. "What do I See? Usually, I Sense more than I See, at least in regard to people. I don't 'decipher' intentions or 'read' emotions all that well—for individuals I mean. I can't. I *chose* not to learn how to impose my perceptions on another or how to steal them from someone else's awareness. I couldn't—I still can't!—justify such intrusions on an un-Sighted companion."

"You don't consider it simply some form of communication?"

"No!" Llinolae swiveled half about, adamant in her denial at first, then she turned away again, repeating more calmly, "No. I don't. Communication is as much a choice as a tool, I think. An individual's choice in what to share and when to share it—as well as what *not* to share—is to be respected. I can't offer that respect if I manipulate their choosing by my Sight."

"What's different in using your Sight versus say—interpreting someone's sincerity or deception by their posture and inflections?"

"What's the difference in using a sword versus a fire weapon?" Llinolae glanced at her quickly, then shrugged. "I can't justify using the fire weapons we've confiscated over the seasons, either."

"Not even against the Clan itself?"

"Especially not then. It has to stop somewhere or nothing will ever get better."

Gwyn tipped her head, thinking the Steward's Swords obviously weren't supporting that particular judgment very well but decided discussions best waited for another day. She could certainly see the point Llinolae had that there was a 'choice' in not sharing some things.

"It's an imperfect analogy, I know. The other piece of it is less a matter of ethics and more a matter of selfishness."

Gwyn said nothing, and Llinolae smiled off at the beige stone heights, grateful yet amazed at this Amazon's patience. With a faint shake of her head, Llinolae admitted, "Coming from Valley Bay and with Bryana as a mother, I suspect this will strike you as somewhat ludicrous, but I've always had to fight very hard to earn my rights as an individual—turning around to lose that identity again to the amarin was just not acceptable."

"That doesn't strike me as ludicrous in the least."

She smiled again. "Thank you." Llinolae moved hesitantly to face Gwyn. Her fingers reached out to toy with a knobby little curl of moss. Then almost shyly, she lay down on her side, an arm curled beneath her head as she played with another bit of mossy growth.

Gwyn turned onto her side to face Llinolae, propping her elbow in the moss and her head on her hand. Then she waited until, gradually, Llinolae grew more at ease.

"I've never told anyone any of this—or about my mentors." She sighed and abandoned the moss bud, tucking her hand beneath her cheek. "My mother was a Clan refugee. She'd been found injured in the west district forests, fleeing her kinfolk. She'd been attacked by a pair of wild baskers, it seemed. My father was already in West Bough, arbitrating some town dispute, when they brought her in. He must have fallen in love at the first sight of her—she seemed so very strong and beautiful that day, he'd say—despite her being half-starved and exhausted from the blood loss and running. When she died of fever, her forearm and thigh were still carrying those scars—that was three tenmoons later. I remember Mother once saying, she'd only survived the baskers' attack because the beasts had been young, not fully grown.

"She was like that, noticing even the littlest of details...never seemed to panic at anything. Except once, when I was born and Father saw my blue eyes." A mirthless bit of a laugh made her pause. Her gaze shifted to Gwyn as she explained, "Mother had heard of the Blue Sights and of how the Council of Ten would take them for training. She didn't want to lose me so soon."

Llinolae's eyes grew shadowed at the next thought then, a blank stare turning back to the mossy cushion. "She lost me anyway, didn't she...in dying so young? I was only a season-and-a-half old...."

"I remember running about and once in a while even falling over my own feet—much too bright and energetic for any nursemaid—much too strong in my Sight even then. Mother had blue eyes herself, you see, so when she told Father mine were because of her Clan blood, he thought it odd but not refutable." Llinolae paused and gave a short sigh. "I think it was the only thing she ever lied to him about. He was dubious, kept watching for some sign of the Gift in me, but he was in Court a lot during the days—occasionally away overnight visiting the district townships for duties. So, she was always the first to notice my talent's eccentricities. She taught me to hide it—to keep it a secret.

"It was a game of ours from the beginning. Literally a hide-and-go-seek game. 'Be invisible!' she'd say, and somehow...? Well, now I know it was because of the Blue Sight, but I always understood it was terribly, terribly important that I be good at the game. So I was."

"Important to your mother," Gwyn interjected.

"Yes—or we would be separated 'too soon'...for however long that was, I don't know now."

Gwyn nodded, "The Clans keep their children young for a great many seasons more than most of us do."

"Yet I was young then...barely knee high...that made it important to me as well. But I could *imagine* being without her so clearly, because again the Sight itself was beginning to show me out-of-time glimpses of when she'd be gone."

"So you learned to hide well."

"Very, very well. Soon servants, grooms—whomever!—could walk right past and never see me."

"You were bending the amarin around you and you weren't even three seasons old?"

"Before I was two, actually."

Gwyn was amazed. Kimarie had been nearly three times that age before she'd been able to touch that kind of power.

"Consciously, no. Unconsciously though? From the assumption everyone did it, yes. I didn't control much consciously for another tenmoon-or-so. When Mother died, Father stopped worrying about whether or not I had the Sight—I think he suddenly couldn't bear the thought of losing me too. In his grief after her pyre burning, he begged me to always stay beside him. I promised I would." Llinolae looked at Gwyn solemnly. "It was the first promise I'd ever made."

From anyone else, Gwyn might have challenged that sort of comment. But given the strength of Llinolae's Blue Gift, she now understood just how the woman would know; every detail of her life would be as accessible as an etched carving to Llinolae. Her out-of-time Seeing ability would only allow her to draw sharper focus on the images. But the drawback would be in that clarity itself—those memories would not be the memories of a child necessarily, rather they'd be complex pictures of what had actually happened. All it would take— all it would ever take—was a determined enough, fierce concentration to sift through those images until the proper set were uncovered. Given the grief of her father's loss—of her own loss!—the child would never have been allowed to forget the importance of that promise to the widowed husband.

"At first, he held me as the most cherished reminder of her. He took me nearly everywhere with him. I'd sit in Court at his knee, ride through the District—first held before him in the saddle then soon beside him on my own shaggy bit-pony." Affection softened her tone and brought a smile to her lips. "He soon came to love me for myself and not merely for her sake."

"Except that he never knew of you as Sighted."

"Except for that—though sometimes he almost let himself suspect it again. Like when we were traveling and needing fresh meat, I'd always be the first to notice the sign of braygoat—or I'd be the first to give warning of a roaming pack of wild baskers. He convinced himself I was merely growing to be more like my mother, I think."

"Aware of the smallest details?"

"Aye. No one ever challenged his assessment, and there hadn't been a Blue Sight born near the city in nearly a generation. Most never returned from the Council once they'd left the outlying regions as children, so no one knew what the Sight could or couldn't be influencing in my talents."

"The emissaries from Churv never had a Seer or an unbonded Shadow trainee among them?"

"Only once, during one of the last few official visits. Before father died, the Changlings Wars had worsened. The delegations from Churv had already been stopped. When Taysa and I seemed able enough to cope without direct supervision after Father's death, the Royal Family only seemed grateful and relieved."

"Leaving you overwhelmed," Gwyn grimaced. Then she asked, "You said there was a Blue Sight visitor to Khirla's Court before your Father's death?"

"Yes, when I was three-or-so seasons. It was the day I...," she smiled with little humor. "You could say I ran away from home that day. Or from Aggar, more aptly. It was the journey that introduced me to my Mistress n'Shea and her n'Athena Amazon.

"It was around the time Taysa joined us. I remember she had just married my uncle—Father's younger brother. Father had gotten uneasy with the Blue Sight emissary during the afternoon, and he'd sent Taysa up to me before eventide to tell me a little about each of the Court visitors...he'd told her it would help me remember who they were during dinner. He'd never do that unless he was leery of someone, though—"

"Wait. You said he was always keeping you near. Why hadn't you been there when they arrived in Court?"

A rueful mischief lit Llinolae's blue eyes and nudged her to tease, "I wasn't such a big girl then, Gwyn'l. I was...what? About three-and-a-half tenmoons? We'd been traipsing around the brushberry farms all morning and my little legs had covered more leagues of soggy ditches than my little mind could count! When we got back to the Palace, Father promptly ordered me off to bed for a nap." She actually giggled, and Gwyn started smiling. "Did you think he was trying to make me into some clingy, fruit vine? I assure you—he had quite a lot of sense for a single parent with no nieces or nephews to learn from.

"Still—that day was different. He was frightened by the Blue Sight visitor...." The laughter died, and Llinolae remembered that eventide news again. She rolled onto her back, her Sight blurring as she recalled the fresh flush of fear that had rushed through her. It had made her physically ill at Taysa's announcement—she'd thrown up on her aunt's best satins. Then with calm complacency, she'd been bundled back into bed and cooed assurances that her tummy would be all right come morning.

Until finally she'd been left alone in the stony haven of her tower room. It was a hide-away-safe stone place which had once been her mother's sewing room and her playroom. She'd taken it as her bedroom after her mother's death, because Mother had assured her once that 'not even the Council's best Seers could find' her in there. But her mother had been talking about the Seers in the Council's Keep; this Sighted One was in the Palace itself, and she hadn't trusted the room with its door of honeywood and its drafty edges. So she had dressed and clutching her warm riding cloak around herself, she had disappeared into the black depths of the gaping fireplace.

Crawling...squirming she'd gotten in behind the mammoth stone crest plate with it's sooty engravings. Back into that thin space between stones where the air channeled up from other fire hearths below, then slanted above her own to finally drift into the open skies beyond....

Though the spring was wet, it was warm, and none of the fires in the tower were lit. The updrafts swept through the stone mazes making them chilly. The child shivered, trying to tuck the cloak around her better, as she looked up into the evening's twilight. Her only thought was to hide—to disappear to some place safe. Night fell darker. The early moon stayed hidden from the chimney vent, and the little girl watched as stars appeared. All her focus narrowed, guided by that stone chimney chute. Her eyes shut, clenching tight against shivers and distractions. And she 'reached' high to hide in the black velvet of the starry skies.

Bushes—she suddenly felt bushes around her. They were fragrant and sweet smelling things. In surprise, the child looked around at this strange new place of the night.

Voices and laughter were coming from nearby. The girl rose cautiously to her knees, all the while 'hiding' her best amidst this strange leafed brush.

A campfire blazed brightly with a circle of gray stones. A small cabin with a thatched roof and a single window stood off to the side of the clearing. A huge set of bay horses lazed in the corral beside the building. But as the laughter broke again, it was to the pair beyond the fire that the child turned.

Two women lay against a long seat, playing with a slender stick and an ashen bulb stuck to it. The younger woman laughed again, tossing a dark braid back over a shoulder as she pointed hurriedly at the bulb. Her companion tried to catch the thing as it began to disintegrate into gooey strands, dripping from the stick. Fingers danced back, then forward, juggling the branch and the thing's heat, until laughingly she abandoned all reason and shoved the sticky thing into her mouth.

"Oh *Soroi*, no!"

"Too late!" she panted, trying to suck the air in to cool the food and her burnt tongue. She almost choked on her laughter. And she gulped it down with a swallow, frantically fanning her open mouth again.

"Di'nay!"

"Hot!"

"But sweet." Fingers reached high to rearrange those short brown strands of hair back into a semblance of order.

The taller woman grew still with the touch, her dark gaze turning tender. She caught the fussing hand and pressed a kiss against the tooled leather band on the wrist. "Not nearly as sweet as you, Love."

The younger woman moved her hand to intercept the next kiss before it reached her lips. "I have something to tell you first."

At the quiet tone, the woman took the other's hand in her own. And her assurance was a loving one as she smiled, "I knew you brought me out camping for some time to talk with me alone."

Still the younger hesitated.

"*Ti' Mae*—tell me."

"I'm carrying your daughter."

The air seemed hushed, holding time suspended for a breath. "Your wh...? My—?" Shock made her blink, then sit straighter with a start. Her gaze locked to the brown flushed face of her lover. "You're carrying *my* daughter?"

"It's the lifestone...." The murmur was a faint one, uncertainty rising. "I know you wanted children, but—please believe me!—if I'd known this could happen I would have warned..."

"Warned me? No, no...." She cradled her lover's face with both hands, burying the fears beneath gentle kisses. Murmuring again, "No, my darling. There's nothing to warn me about, *ti'Mau...Soroi*, know you never have need of warning me."

"The stone's taken your life patterns and woven them into mine."

"That's what it's always done, hasn't it?" Her gentle eyes told only of marvel and joy at this miracle.

"I think...."

The indecision caused concern in that dark gaze finally. She asked quietly, "What are you afraid of, Elana?"

"My Sight," came the faint answer. She shrugged awkwardly. "I'm so sensitive to your amarin through it...it caused the lifestone to intervene again."

"Again?" A puzzled crease marred her forehead.

"As strongly as when we first bonded."

"Ahh...." Her frown cleared, and reassurance glowed again in a smile. "This daughter is ours because our hearts have wanted her so much. Are you trying to tell me it may happen again sometime, without warning? Or are you trying to tell me that since the Blue Sight helped create her, she will be as Sighted as her birth mother?"

"Both."

A deep throaty chuckle almost melted the last of the insecurities as a strong hug rocked them close. "Goddess blest, I love you! And I will love this Blue Gifted little shea as dearly as any child I could imagine—as dearly as any children you could ever give us!"

"And n'Sappho? This was not what they had in mind when they granted me a visa with Special Provisions, was it?"

"Ah! The heart's true fear at last! And no, I'm sure they hadn't had this in mind. But *dey Sorormin*—oh Love, they will welcome our daughters! Because they *are* our Daughters—as truly as Helen the First Born of this world once was. Ours will simply be the first born of the Sight."

The child in the bushes balked at the concept of such complete acceptance;

her balance slipped. Leaves rustled as amarin shimmered, and the young women beyond the fire sat forward in alarm!

Gwyn started.

The world dropped back into place around her. The crashing fall of the waters, the misty humidity of the air, the windy shuffle of the haymoss tendrils—all reappeared.

Llinolae stood, shivering a few paces away. Her hands briskly rubbed against the chill of her dark-skinned arms. She heard Gwyn shift to sit up and paused, almost turning. Then she decided against it. She shrugged, rubbing her arms again. "Forgive me."

Forgive her—for what precisely? Gwyn closed her eyes and privately took inventory of herself; she felt perfectly fine. She was confused, certainly. But she had known she was in this little canyon all along. Although, the place *beside* her had been...elsewhere?

Gwyn blinked and realized it'd felt similar to the sword's visions when the lifestone and Llinolae's Blue Sight had touched her earlier. This time, however, there had been no sense of 'being' someone else. Her awareness had been hers alone. It was almost as if she'd been remembering something—skimming through a memory rather than reliving it. Which was actually what had happened, she grasped suddenly. She looked at Llinolae pensively standing there with her back turned. She asked gently, "Do you remember my mother, Bryana?"

Llinolae hesitated, then nodded faintly. She made no move to face Gwyn yet.

"She projects images like yours, when she works with the Blue Sight of our home world."

"When she brings the Rings of Valley Bay and home together?"

"Yes."

Llinolae accepted that quietly; it seemed neither to excuse nor rebuke her carelessness. She cracked a brittle smile—to think she'd just been telling her Mistress how much better she could control her concentration these days! She sighed. "Forgive me, Gwyn. I've not subjected anyone to that sort of thing, since my tutors tried to teach me to read."

"Tried to?"

Her head tipped in measured agreement. Those old regrets were no longer as strong as they'd once been until, bleakly, Llinolae remembered the young scribe who'd ridden out from Khirla with her. If she'd been more literate, the girl wouldn't have had to come—the Dracoon would have had no need of another's help to tend the journals and messengers. She folded her arms and dropped the tension from her shoulders with an effort, explaining, "It's difficult to learn, if one has to filter out the Sight constantly from the very ink and paper. When I followed Father about, he'd tell me stories and teach me of strategies, plots...the laws as we did other things. 'Always listen with one ear,' he'd say. 'Keep the other open for surprises and inspiration.' I found learning that way and learning by doing—especially for horse or sword skills—worked well for me. But to sit quietly and try to work sense into letters...sounds into words with meanings? I quit trying the day I set the school room on fire."

Gwyn's mouth twitched a moment. Then she rose to her feet as she asked quietly, "How did you explain that one away?"

"I didn't." Amusement made Llinolae glance back to Gwyn. Then a mischievous grin crept free as she Saw Gwyn shared her humor. She turned about slowly, elaborating, "My tutor's back was to me when the book caught on fire. So I dumped the candlestick onto the parchments quickly and ran!"

She had promised herself she wouldn't, but Gwyn couldn't help it—the laughter snuck out anyway. Llinolae chuckled, then suddenly they were both laughing together again—feeling better. And when Gwyn took Llinolae into her arms, there was only a sense of welcome relief between them.

"Suddenly the mysterious but fiery accidents the night of your escape aren't so mysterious. Were you intending to be quite so dramatic?"

Llinolae sighed, shaking her head. "Things did get a little out of hand, didn't they?"

Gwyn nodded then wrapped her close, hugging her protectively as their humor faded. Wearily, Llinolae sagged into her.

"It's so hard sometimes...."

"I know."

"To have fires start merely because I learned the spelling for *flame*—do you know how frightening that is for a child?"

"Some of it I know," Gwyn murmured, soothing the tension from Llinolae's back and shoulders with warm, stroking hands. "Some of it I can imagine, but I'll never be completely overwhelmed by any of it. I promise you."

In a mixture of surprise and disbelief, Llinolae broke away to stare at her. Gwyn simply smiled and shrugged. "Not only is *M'Sormee* Sighted, but my younger sib, Kimarie, is too. I grew up beside her, going through some of those fears with her. I do have an idea of what I'm in for around you, my Love."

Then suddenly what they'd actually been Seeing registered, and Gwyn demanded, "Those two women? They became your mentors n'Athena and n'Shea?"

Llinolae nodded hesitantly, not quite grasping what struck Gwyn as so amazing.

"Did I understand them to say, their daughter was going to be the first Blue Sight born among *dey Sorormin?*"

"That's right. She was." Llinolae grinned at her then, realizing Gwyn was actually awe-struck at the notion. She gave Gwyn a slight nudge with her hip. "The child was also the first of the Sisterhood to be conceived solely through the spontaneous interaction of lifestone and Blue Sight. There was no planning, nor involvement by the Crones n'Shea."

"And you know them...these two...personally?"

Laughing, Llinolae could only begin to shake her head.

"But do you know *how much* those two simple incidents have..."

"...Influenced the development of *dey Sorormin* since? *Ann, ti Mau*—I do. How you bear children, the randomness restored to your genetic selections, the ecological balances the Sighted help you maintain the ties that bind Valley Bay and your home world—and more."

"The trusts that developed between Aggar and *dey Sorormin* alone were...!" Gwyn waved a hand, thoroughly overwhelmed, and her voice dropped to a murmur again. "Valley Bay wouldn't even exist if—"

"But n'Shea and n'Athena are just women—like you and me, Gwyn. They love. They fight. They cry—just like us. They tried to live their lives, doing their best to handle whatever was sent to them by Fates or Mother."

"But—"

"No," Llinolae halted her protests softly with a kiss. Gwyn grew calmer, and this time as Llinolae smiled, it was returned. "Soroi, few of us ever know how important or insignificant a life will be. Do you think Brit and Sparrow constantly worry how this daughter of theirs might again be changing so many things for Aggar and the Sisterhood?"

"Because their shadowmate lifestone has let Sparrow conceive?"

"Yes! Because it acted on the sheer strength of their mutual desires. Because it may eventually eliminate all need for any healer's intervention for Sisters to conceive. But to Brit and Sparrow those possibilities are secondary, Soroi, and they probably always will stay secondary! They're concerned for their baby. Their concerns are to bring her healthy and safely into this world, and their hopes are for her to grow strongly and be happy."

"Aye, and she will be—happy, I mean." Gwyn's eyes softened, thinking of Brit around youngsters. "As irate as Brit is with so many adults, she's accepting with children. Whether she's living with them for a season or visiting for a day, she is so very patient."

"Sparrow is equally as caring, I've Seen." Llinolae sighed and let Gwyn draw her close again. "They'll both make good parents."

"I don't know…," Gwyn sighed.

But there was no alarm in her wistful amarin, and Llinolae prodded softly, "Know what, Soroi?"

Those coppery eyes gleamed. "Is Aggar ready for such a child? With Brit's insatiable passion for crusades and Sparrow's boundless energy, there's no telling what may become of dey Sorormin or Aggar!"

Chapter Ten

Mists swirled. The dreamspun vision wavered behind that growing fog and then dissolved into fragments of nothing.

Llinolae shook her head abruptly. Breaking the trance-like stillness that held her body, she uncrossed her legs and got up off her pallet with impatience. Her booted feet fell into a steadying rhythm of tap-clack as steps turned to pacing, and the scowl deepened displeasure as she chewed her lower lip. Unlike past attempts to decipher more from her Sight's dreams, this particular meditation had been alarmingly clear.

The woman ill in her dream, she discovered, had been her own mother. And the assassin who poisoned the water had been none other than her uncle—her father's younger brother.

Still the murder made no sense to her. The amarin about his skinny frame had been clearly focused on gaining title and rule. Yet if her uncle had been so ambitious for power, then why had he targeted her mother? An outsider to court, her mother had been well enough liked, but she'd been kept apart from many of the Dracoons' more official dealings *because* of her Clan blood. It had been an arrangement made with her father before their marriage, and her mother had never felt particularly inclined to change it. She much preferred addressing the healers' concerns or the farmers' complaints than juggling trade taxes and district disputes. The result was the people of Khirlan had come to trust her. But her death had not affected the economic or political structure of the district in any serious way.

Perhaps her uncle had expected it to undermine her father's emotional strength? She paused in her circular walking, remembering how Mha'del had turned to her as a child. He had clung to her existence as proof of his wife's presence—as tangible proof of their love, Llinolae now realized. Had that somehow kept her father alive?

No—she discarded the idea completely. Her uncle had never lost her father's trust. That meant Mha'del had never suspected him of treachery, let alone of murder. There had been no hint of his ambitions for the Dracoon's seat during the two seasons following her mother's death. And she couldn't believe his age and uncertain health in those last monarcs would have completely swayed the sort of power-craven lust she'd Seen in him as he killed her mother. He must have been working on a much grander scale, and he had always valued patience before a strike—whether in board games, Clan raids or street riots. Her uncle had always been a shrewd man. If the flu pox hadn't struck him down that winter, she had to believe he would have moved against Mha'del eventually.

She sighed. It was possible he had anyway, through his own scribes and contacts. Only he had died before the fruition of his plans.

Lips pursed, Llinolae wondered about that suddenly. The Clan raids had begun to escalate just slightly that season, focusing more heavily on healers' supplies and food stocks. Still limited largely to trading caravans, they had extended their attacks further west than before. It had seemed obvious, at the time, that they too must be struggling with the outbreak of flu pox. No one had seen the raiding as odd.

But the shipment of medicines used to treat her uncle had...yes! It had been scattered and only half of the medicine recovered from a Clan raid on that caravan.

The chill she felt had nothing to do with the damp, cool air outside. It was the coldness of unpleasant truth as affirmed by Aggar's own Life Cycles. It was the realization of Clan involvement in her uncle's seemingly natural death. The medicine had been tampered with, somehow. And for some reason or another, the Clan had decided that her uncle was much more of a threat than Mha'del.

She dismissed the suspicion that they'd hoped to kill Mha'del as well. Her father had survived a lighter bout of the flu pox earlier that season. For that matter, so had she and Taysa. It had been common enough knowledge throughout the district. The assassins would have known it too.

Which brought her back to *why* her uncle?

"No...it brings me back to Taysa!" Llinolae muttered with a sudden fierce conviction that commanded the Sight to restore the time and folk of the deception's beginning.

The laughing images rose as Taysa's seductive flirting came through her Sight to spin quickly out before her. Taysa teasing both husband and brother—distracting Mha'del as an intruder slipped away...Taysa murmuring with her husband as Mha'del left to greet another...Taysa in wedding gown and...?

Wisps and whirls gave way to a dark alcove and hands moved, an exchange of money for poisons. Her uncle nodded, Taysa prompting him all the while with quiet, insidious rumors!

Llinolae jerked back from the shock of that truth. Her breath came hard as she blinked and shuddered. Taysa had been part of her uncle's plans from the very beginning of her liaison with him.

It began to fit. Her uncle's own ambitions would have left him a target for bribery. Undermining Mha'del's reputation with the royal family had been an effective stepping stone to power and easily done through placement of his own scribes, until he'd become expendable—because he knew of Taysa's affiliation with the Clan and knew which of the scribes were involved. His greed had won him death—by Taysa's own orders, Llinolae would wager. Thwart her, and Taysa would have retaliated without hesitation.

So now it was Taysa's scribes, aligned with the Clan, that still altered the reports to King and Crowned!

Half-sister to her mother, mixed blood as Llinolae herself, wife of the ambitious...? That marriage...Llinolae remembered her father's grief again. Her uncle had won her father's admiration and public support for that marriage to Taysa. So soon after her mother's death, she Saw how her father had sought to embrace anything that affirmed his wife's presence. And Taysa with her district kin had aided her mother's initial escape from the Clans, giving her refuge, then food, and sending her on deeper into the Khirlan district when the Clans pursued. Mha'del had known the tale well and had welcomed Taysa when her village home had been burnt out that late autumn. Her uncle had merely seen the marriage as another way to gain credibility in Mha'del's eyes—to distract Mha'del from whatever suspicions might have been stirring. And young Taysa had found both brothers foolishly naive as they played into her schemes for the Clan.

Llinolae Saw now how Taysa's passion for power had brought her position early among the Clan Lead's. She had already held the full support and backing of a sizable number in the militia; she had heralded a new ambition for the Clan with her scheming. No, Llinolae's uncle had been used even as he'd tried to use Taysa.

Llinolae rose and moved to the tent's entrance, drinking in the cleaner air of the small canyon's afternoon. It tasted sweet in the wake of the dust blown by such ill amarin.

Her uncle, her aunt—they had deserved one another. If he had lived long enough, Llinolae acknowledged grimly, she would have come to hate him. She could find no other word for Taysa either—scorn was too placid, rage was too irrational. No, what she felt was cold, hard, bitter hate.

Her uncle had left her a legacy of deceit to deal with—Taysa? Her aunt claimed not only the Clan's leadership, but much of Khirlan's own.

The irony in that was not in the least to Llinolae's liking.

* * *

"We have a problem."

The other three women in camp went silent at Gwyn's assertion. The twilight held everything in dim grayness, and the *Niachero* was so still her form and colors would have been lost in a denser place of honeywood and stonemoss. Ty stirred and sat up beside her, attention fixed outward with hers.

"Is it Ril?" Sparrow glanced across the table and wash-water to Llinolae. The Dracoon nodded faintly, the dish in hand poised to be rinsed as she tried to follow that packbond's sensitivity.

Brit shifted and the wood of her folding seat creaked once as she put aside her tea.

The *Niachero*'s chin dropped. Mutely, she met the sandwolf's sandy gaze. Her whittling was discarded, and she ruffled both Ty's ears with a brusque fondness. Ty nosed Gwyn's knee in encouragement and agreement, then bounded off to join their packmate.

"What's Ril found?" Llinolae pressed quietly. The grim amarin of determination about Gwyn seemed unerringly familiar—an almost mirrored reflection of her own.

"A Clan scout is tracking the braygoat herd that Sparrow and I raided yesterday. Ril expects him to find the remains of our kill soon—if not tonight, morning at the latest."

Llinolae frowned slightly. "Hasn't some basker pack or sowie pair probably rooted through and scattered the discards by now?"

"It's Fates' Jest, but he's crossed our outward trail and noticed the horse signs. Ril seems to think he's lost and trying to rejoin a scouting party."

"So he thinks your tracks are from them—that they've gone hunting to resupply or something, hoping he'd catch up with them himself." Brit shook her head with a resigned snort. "Even if he loses your trail, he'll think to backtrack once he's seen any sign of a kill. Usually these Clan groups stake out a base camp before they go hunting, then work the area for a few days. He'd just be expectin' them to circle in from wherever they'd come from."

"Either set of tracks—outgoing or incoming—will lead him here," Sparrow saw.

"Unless he's a very *poor* tracker?" Brit suggested almost hopefully.

"Poor enough to get lost," Llinolae observe dourly, "doesn't mean poor enough to stay lost. If Ril's concerned about him, then I am too."

"I agree. Ril's not the alarmist," Gwyn amended. "That's Ty's great art." The Amazon and Dracoon shared an amused grimace at that.

"They're getting a lot closer these days," Brit observed matter-of-factly, turning the mug of tea slowly as the leaves brewed.

With a sigh of resignation, Llinolae dumped out the wash-water. She reached for the hand towel and just barely managed not to moan. It was not a good thing to wish for another stack of stew bowls!

Sparrow finished the drying and tossed the damp rag to the camp table. Then with a pointed looked to Gwyn and Llinolae, "So what are we going to do? Corner this scout, scare him off or simply hope he'll keep wandering the wrong way?"

"I would prefer *not* to rely on the last," Gwyn suggested dryly. "I don't particularly feel like tempting the Fates quite that much, thank you."

"My vote'd be to scare him off and get ourselves out of here completely." Brit glanced at Llinolae with a lopsided shrug. But then, she was only being honest.

They waited as the Dracoon sat down, shifting pieces on some mental game board, until finally Brit prompted, "What do you propose?"

"This…is there a chance we could take him?"

"Why?" Sparrow hugged her legs to her chest and propped her chin on her knees as she puzzled, "The militia didn't care about talking while you were held in their jail cell. What would make them want to listen now?"

"No—it might work," Brit countered suddenly, seeing the potential of the idea as she considered it again. "You had no chance to get them to listen when they held you, because they were smug and complacent. And they were being good little soldiers under Taysa's instructions. But isolate one of *them*, and you might succeed in getting some attention."

"And he's young," Gwyn noted, heeding the finer details of the image in her packbond's awareness, now that the immediate shock of the scout's appearance had eased. "Corner and catch him, and it'll probably bruise his inexperienced little ego."

"Aye—at the very least that'd loosen his tongue about the searching patrols around here." Sparrow liked the practicality in that fact almost as much as she liked the chance, finally, to *do something!*

Gwyn grinned broadly, turning to Llinolae as she declared, "Shall we try a bit of your favored old sport? Hide-and-go-seek might work well here."

"If he's armed," Brit reminded them with pragmatic caution, "that'll be a dangerous game."

"Ril did see a small fire weapon strapped to his saddle," Gwyn agreed. "But it's a safer choice than ignoring him until he rides into camp!"

"Between my Sight and the sandwolves, we'd—"

"Your Sight should stay in camp!" Brit snapped. "I say it as a healer because you're well mended, but not whole yet. As a Marshal, I say it because you're the Dracoon and right now this District can't afford to have something happen to you! And as an old campaigner...," Brit shifted with a disgruntled sniff and admitted, "As an old campaigner, I know its best to guard my back."

"Meaning—" Gwyn had worked just long enough with the woman during the Wars to know what Brit was suggesting, "one of us should stay in camp, one of us should go hunting the scouting party he got separated from before *they* stumble onto us, and someone who doesn't look the least like a Royal Marshal—or an escaped Dracoon!—should keep the boy distracted in case the hide-and-go-seek allows him to get a glimpse of his opponents."

"I'd love to keep him off balance," Sparrow offered.

"Well, Love...," Brit leaned nearly off the side of her sturdy, old camp chair and wrapped an arm about her shadowmate's shoulder, "we're goin' to get the chance real soon!"

Gwyn shook the stillness from her body. The pack bond had snatched at the focus of her attention again, but the impressions had held images strong enough to dim other senses for the moment.

"More news?" Llinolae pressed.

A grin reassured them all quickly as she shared, "Only good news—he's bedded down for the night."

"Then we should go out 'bout first light?" Brit suggested, and sought Sparrow's opinion with a glance. Her shadowmate only agreed with an eager nod.

"Both Ril and Ty are staying out to watch him," Gwyn added.

"Shouldn't we send someone up to the northern ridge as well?" Sparrow ventured.

"I don't think we need to," Gwyn considered, then shrugged. "Even if the scouting party got close enough to the gorge edge to see us, Llinolae's Sight should warn her before they managed to trace a way in...."

"I'd know before they actually saw our camp from above," Llinolae confirmed.

"Still—we could leave the horses loose," Brit speculated. "For caution's sake, we might even put out the drays."

"Wonderful!" Sparrow quipped. "We'll let the big lugs slobber all over the invading Clan folk."

Gwyn and Llinolae chuckled.

"The point is, they'll seem *hugely* intimidating after Gwyn's smaller mares have gnashed a few teeth and kicked a few hooves."

"My mares are not that much smaller, Brit!" Gwyn protested.

"And they're nearly as husky." Llinolae's grin broadened.

"All right!" Brit tossed her hands into the air. "Don't leave the ole nags loose—do whatever you want! I don't care!"

"Oh yes, you do!" Sparrow smirked back. "It's what makes you so adorable."

Brit glared at her.

She smiled sweetly and batted her eyelids with innocence.

"Humpf!"

It couldn't be helped; both the Dracoon and *Niachero* dissolved into laughter.

Chapter Eleven

The night air was neither particularly hot nor cold as the drop in temperature and the increased humidity neatly formed a balance. Moist scents of greenery, mulch and soil permeated the forest. Yellow crickets chittered, and a pair of night toads croaked along in their summer mating songs. Beneath them all, the rhythms of the waterfall ran.

Gwyn sighed contentedly and stood to walk out of the pool, disturbing the glossy stillness of those quieter edge-waters. She reached for her towel, gazing around the small, cradled cove. She enjoyed being here, especially during these silverish hours of the Twin Moons. Even with the approach of the Clan scout, she found only a soothing calm here, and it became easier for her to trust her packmates' assurances that all was well for the night. Gwyn could see this place had been well chosen for a healing Shea's Hole.

She settled beside her clothes on the mossy bank, dried her hands a bit more, and reached up to pull the slender reed from her hair buckle. It felt good to shake her tousled mat free. She ran her fingers through the feathery tangles as the ends brushed across her shoulders, reminding her to ask Brit for a trim.

At that, Gwyn smiled to herself. She wrapped her arms about her legs and propped her chin on her knees at a most pleasant thought—Llinolae playing with these longer strands. Jes had once teased that she'd catch anyone's eye with 'that fly-away silk' if she'd only grow it long enough to give a woman a proper length to dally with. Gwyn had to admit, she liked the idea of that woman being Llinolae.

Her smile faded as Gwyn accepted she did want that woman to be Llinolae. It might mean wintering outside of Valley Bay, but it meant being with Llinolae. And that was what Gwyn wanted—needed. At the very least, Gwyn understood she *needed* to try—to risk—the turmoil to see if this heartbond could be welded strong. In the end, it was very simple; she wanted them to be together.

"Can I take it…," a quiet voice drifted through the silvers and shadows of the night, "that since your shift in amarin seems to include me, you wouldn't mind my company for a bit?"

Gwyn glanced to the wide, sloping blanket of thick moss and barely discerned a figure rising. She broke into a welcoming grin as Llinolae stepped into the moons' light. "How long have you been here?"

"Since before you came in, I'm afraid. Forgive me for holding silent?"

"Certainly. Or was I disturbing you?"

"No, you weren't," Llinolae murmured. She made no move to sit, and Gwyn had to lean back a little to look at her. "I'd been…trying something with my Sight. It wasn't working, and I caught myself dozing off. Then you were wading in and I found myself…well…." She shrugged a shoulder as amused at herself as she was embarrassed. "I enjoyed watching you swim. You have a way of moving—not just in your swimming, but with everything. You add grace to your beauty."

"Thank you," Gwyn was charmed by the confession. "That's two compliments you pay me."

"Two?"

"No, three. You trust me enough that my arrival doesn't disturb your Sight nor your sleep. You like the grace I do things with, and I think...you just said, I was beautiful—?"

Llinolae felt her skin flush slightly. "I did."

"Thank you."

"I was tempted—to say something sooner."

"Were you?"

Llinolae nodded and waved a hand a bit towards the water. "Going in seemed like a nice idea."

"Then why don't you?"

"You—you wouldn't mind?" Llinolae blinked, a little nonplussed.

"I wouldn't mind. Would you rather I leave you to it and meet you back at the tent?"

"No! I was...I mean you...I don't want to make you uncomfortable, Soroe."

"And what if...*Soroi?*" Gwyn's voice dropped low and her words grew rich with bold honesty. "What if I want you...to make my heart race a little faster...and my skin flush a little darker? What if I want to love you...am ready to love you—to touch you—in return, my sweet, sweet Llinolae? Would you still want me to be here...when you finish swimming?"

The loving warmth in both Gwyn's voice and amarin reached to surround her, and Llinolae's slight start of surprise yielded to pleasure. A slow smile grew on her lips as she breathed, "*Sae, Soroi...ti Soroi....*"

Gwyn's gaze held hers steadily and neither smile nor assurance faded. She slipped from her clothes, noticing a deeper richness begin to glow in Gwyn's paleness—the silverish light of the night nearly masking that subtle darkening of skin colors. Gwyn tipped her head to lay her cheek upon a knee and continued to smile at her.

Gwyn saw the question—the last faint brush of insecurity rising again. She smiled even more gently. "I will be here waiting...for whatever you want."

Llinolae waded into the pool, glancing back slowing, then spinning 'round entirely. Eyes on Gwyn, she could barely breath as she moved backwards through the waters—into something much deeper than sheer water, her heart realized.

Gwyn folded her arms over her knees and once again put her chin down, taking her own sweet turn at watching...anticipating. Then suddenly Llinolae was smiling and arching back into a joyous, twisting dive. Heels kicked up and toes flipped out, and she was gone in a splash that left Gwyn laughing in wet delight. And inside, Gwyn felt as silver as that spraying waters' dance with the moons' light.

* * *

Through her Sight, Llinolae felt Gwyn's sleep stir, and she took her eyes from that silver dusted chasm so far above to smile as she found again an even more beautiful thing to behold. The midnight moon still bathed their canyon cove, and Gwyn's naked figure, with milky light and the mossy bank, seemed almost as black as the moon's own sky. But now there was the scattered wink and white sparkle of fine-pointed blossoms as well, which mirrored the stars themselves. Those delicate moss petals of llinolae blooms had opened to gasp the cool, misty air and drink their fill only after the midnight moon had chased the final dregs of day's heat away. The wonder of her name-sake never ceased to amaze Llinolae, but tonight—tonight the enchantment was spellbinding, and she saw again that fleeting glimpse of Gwyn's dive into the stars. Only now, there was nothing fleeting in this sweet vision of her beloved *Niachero*.

Pale-skinned in the moon's light, one arm stretched in graceful curve above her head and the other resting beside her long length, Gwyn moved again in her waning sleep. A leg lifted slightly as a foot set flat. Her face turned towards Llinolae, cheek nuzzling against the downy soft petals that had uncurled there. Then she settled into her dreams once more.

Llinolae smiled, remembering how soft Gwyn's skin had felt against her own, even softer than those tiny flowers could feel. She rose and left her rocky perch at the edge of the moss and returned to her place beside her Amazon. Careful not to touch nor disturb her yet, Llinolae lay down very near. For a long moment more, she could do nothing—needed to do nothing—but marvel at the tousle of fine silken hair, at the slender line of limb and proud peak of breast...at Gwyn asleep. Then a slow smile began, and Llinolae tipped her head, affection and desire mingling as she felt the coursing flow of amarin around them. Anticipation of Gwyn's awakening prompted her to end their waiting.

She leaned forward with the gentlest kiss that softened, nibbled and again pressed full to warm Gwyn's lips. A sigh of drowsy pleasure rose as she drew back to wait once more.

A deep, full breath parted Gwyn's lips. The slow rise and fall of her breasts began a languid stretch of purring contentment. Her muscles went lazily limp again, hands still above her head, and eyes still closed in peace.

"I love you," Llinolae whispered in welcome.

"And I—" The pause grew so long, Gwyn lying so quiet that if Llinolae had not held the Sight, she might have thought Gwyn slept again. But the sweet amarin around them told Llinolae she held her lover close with dreams and memories. And then Gwyn's quiet voice came again, "Discover...."

Llinolae watched her curiously.

Gwyn breathed in the warm scent of their loving once more. Then with eyes unopening she began in a murmur...

> "Across the breezes of the night
> the scent—the brush...solely new...
> comes velvet touch to linger.
> Spoiling dreams of fantasy
> in sultry tease of waking..."

Copper-hued eyes opened to Llinolae...

> "To eyes of star-reflected light
> to fond curved bow of welcome—
> to kiss and pledge abandon...
> Then leap! In fire—stunned. Eclipsed!

Gwyn's gaze locked to Llinolae's own—

> Intoxicating blue descends,
> claims and fully takes me whole.
> Yet heed—! More than all I've won."

The words drifted into the night. The thrashing waterfall claiming them first, then the Forest's great amarin absorbing each, until again Llinolae felt their pulse of richness beat against her harmon. Amazement made her blink, shaking her head a little.

Gwyn smiled up at her, simply loving her with that gaze.

"You...are a poet?" Llinolae's words seemed inane to even herself as she spoke. But she could not help the surprise...nor the growing delight.

"Sometimes poems, sometimes lyrics—when I am not carving my flutes. Or did you fear..." a sword-callused hand lifted half curled, stroking Llinolae's cheek with the softer skin of a finger's back, "that I only wrestle with ruffians and outwit schemers?"

"No," Llinolae caught Gwyn's hand and placed a kiss to her wrist. "I harbor no fear of who you might be, merely pleasure at discovering...." Her sentence went unfinished as pain crowded close, unbidden. "I fear there is so much of you I may never uncover as our duties tug to separate us."

Fingers pressed her words silent. Gwyn shook her head, lips pursed in a reassuring hush. "There are paths around such dilemma, my Love. I know you've worried. As Dracoon you're bound to District and service, and I know it will have to be my own life that adapts, if we are to be together."

Llinolae's brow knit. "I can't bind you here, Gwyn. I...I couldn't ask that of you—to trade Valley Bay for Khirlan. I could never ask that of you."

"Then let me ask something else," Gwyn amended, both hands rising to take Llinolae's face. "I love you, Min Llinolae, Dracoon of Khirlan. With heart filled and past seasons discarded, I freely offer to join you in your Ramains' District. Will you...do you...welcome me?"

The gasp caught in Llinolae's throat not once, but twice. She felt herself begin to tremble and could barely comprehend it. Gwyn's gaze grew tender as her own blurred in tears. Then the sob broke, and she collapsed into the strength of those waiting arms.

"Love...*Soroi*," Gwyn held her, soothing her, protecting her...loving her undaunted. "*Ti Mau coraen Kau* ...."

A weak laugh took Gwyn as she felt the tears wet her breast and the shudders run through her lover. She only gathered Llinolae nearer, teasing gently, "My dearest Blue Sight—how could you not expect this of me? I love you. You can See that, can't you?"

Something of a nod answered the pause, and Gwyn drew back far enough to raise Llinolae's gaze to meet hers. She searched her lover's stricken expression for some way to reassure her. "I know what I'm doing. I know what I'm offering."

The tears stopped. Llinolae felt her heart ache within her ribs. But she couldn't deny, "I know you do."

Gwyn stared at her hard, for a long, silent time. Llinolae almost flinched from what she knew Gwyn must see. She was ashamed of her own lack of courage in this, yet needing to share even that…she did not turn away.

"You're afraid," Gwyn voiced finally, her tone soft and unaccusing though it hinted of her surprise. "Of what we share—of what we could share? Much as you want it, you are afraid of this."

"Yes."

"And you're thinking I'm not."

Llinolae blinked, distracted by the very thought. Her blue eyes squeezed shut and her lips pressed tight as she struggled with common sense. Then she looked at Gwyn again and tried a smile, "Forgive me…you overwhelm me with…I've never imagined…or rather, barely imagined…anyone…like you…."

"I know." Tenderness and understanding were shared as Gwyn nodded, "You are the same—for me."

Llinolae felt that truth. She smiled again. "We'd be fools not to be afraid, wouldn't we?"

"We'd be greater fools to deny our heartbond."

"Aye. So yes, *sae*. Be welcomed in Khirla, my Love."

"I come with a family."

"I've always known that." Llinolae gently took her turn in reassuring now. "With both Ril and Ty—I'd welcome all of you. If you're certain this is what you want."

"I'm certain."

"And Valley Bay?"

A crooked smile granted much would be missed. "I'll go for a visit now and again."

"Your Oath of Duty?"

"I'll wander when called. But the Wars are done. They'll be looking to post Marshals on a more permanent basis. There's no reason I can't request assignment to Khirla's Court. And the Royal Family has no policies against emotional liaisons."

"You've thought this through."

"Would you want me to offer, if I hadn't?"

"No."

"Well then—"

"Heartbound?"

"*Sae*?" Gwyn's breath caught as joy sparked warm trust in the blue, blue depths of her lover's eyes.

"Heartbound," Llinolae accepted. Her lips turned up at the corners then as she watched the paleness of Gwyn's skin begin to brown. Her pulse raced a little faster, desire rising to match her Amazon's own. Eyes fused by their sheer wanting. The tension between them grew exquisite in the waiting, and Llinolae felt fire singe the remains of doubts to ash, leaving her bolder. "Heartbound, *Soroi* … have you a special rite to seal the contract?"

Llinolae's tongue drew a line across her own lips, and Gwyn's gaze flickered to her mouth—caught in fascination.

"Have you, *Soroi*?"

"Several," Gwyn breathed, feeling her insides melt. Llinolae's fingertips came to lie so lightly atop Gwyn's heart—Gwyn's body spasmed then froze, the very breath in her stopping. Slowly those long fingers stretched outward as palm pressed flat, softness warming hot.

"Something like this, perhaps?" Llinolae hovered so very close that their lips brushed with each syllable. Her touch drifted, cupping, yet not quite claiming the fullness of Gwyn's breast.

Gwyn nearly laughed as patience snapped, and she arched into Llinolae's palm, covering Llinolae's hand with her own—laughter transcended into moan.

"*Sae.*" Llinolae approved. Her kiss found the delicious line of Gwyn's collar bone. Her thigh slipped between Gwyn's, and arms drew her nearer.

Chapter Twelve

Abruptly a prickly shiver ran up along Llinolae's back. She spun on her heel to thrust the canvas flap aside. The Great Forest cried—the amarin were today's.

She searched for a clear sense of the alarm. Overhead, the thick static air of the imminent storm was still blowing east, though more sluggishly than last night. The winds rippled through the honeywoods above the canyon walls. The stream tumbled by. But of creatures—pripper or bird—there were no sounds.

Her Sight prodded again. A whisper of alarm, then the touch of a friend, seemed to dance along the amarin.

"Ty?" Confusion creased a line between Llinolae's brows, and she stepped cautiously from the shelter of the tent.

Undeniably, it was Ty she Saw coming, from somewhere downstream and moving quickly, with urgency.

Why?

An image—the harmon of a wolf imposed upon a woman of height—leapt across her mind. Llinolae gasped, the strength of the picture striking hard. The imprint hit again. And in truth, it was a wolf she Saw. It was an animal like no sandwolf of her world, with a finely furred face and markings of amber-edged black upon white-gray. Yet within the ghost of that harmon was a tall woman of fiery bronze hair, though her features were obscured almost to vagueness by the power of the wolf image. The features of animal vied with those of human. Stature, structure—contradictions of four-footed in two seemed irrelevant, suddenly seeming to hold no contradictions at all!

Gwyn?

Llinolae choked, coughing and fighting for air with a hand to her stomach as she wrenched herself free from that emotional intensity. Then stumbling, she turned to re-enter the tent, seeking short bow and bolts along with the medicine purse. Because she finally understood. She was Seeing Gwyn as her bondmates could. And Gwyn needed Ty to bring help!

Waterskins, a long knife, and a pouch of trail rations hung from her belt as well as the medicine purse when Ty arrived. The sandwolf loped in amidst the waters of the stream, moving too fast to hide her tracks otherwise. But she barely paused at the camp's edge as Llinolae donned a cloak over the bolt quiver and grabbed the bow, already running.

Ty rounded and was off. Boots splashed undaunted to follow her close.

* * *

Llinolae crouched behind the thicket of stone-moss, sandwiched between a rocky little crevice and an overshadowing tree root. Ahead in the twilight she Saw the disturbance of Clan scouts. Two on horseback, at least. They were apart and circling in different directions, though both had been near within the late afternoon. Somewhere about the male one, she felt the more familiar amarin of Ril and Cinder as the sandwolf led the mare in diverting tracks. But Llinolae could tell neither from track signs nor amarin if the scouts were working together, or if the male was the apprentice and the other some more experienced patrol member searching for him. Of Brit and Sparrow she felt no presence at all. So if this was the apprentice, he had certainly proved more wily than any of them had anticipated. And if it was not him, then the two were somehow working in tandem and might expect the rest of the patrol to rendezvous soon.

When it came right down to it, Llinolae simply didn't like the fact that they were Clan folk. Anything else at the moment she considered trivial.

Twilight had come. The early moon was already up and bright despite the cloaking canopy of clouds and trees. Darkfall was not going to get much darker today.

She glanced at Ty who lay down beside her, still panting in exhaustion. The sandwolf cocked her head, tongue lolling, then snapped her mouth shut and managed one of those sneeze-like nods briefly. She panted again, and Llinolae sank her fingers deep into the curly ruff with a squeeze of reassurance. Ty was right, the rest was left to her.

Bow in hand, she crept out of their nest while bending the amarin around her in that uncomfortably familiar guise of 'hide.' She glanced about cautiously and ventured to stand. She wished she had a better sense of exactly where those scouts were. Knowing they were too far to See easily yet near enough to continue to disturb the amarin was *not* her idea of safe distance. They could be a single tree beyond her clear Sight or a half-league. If only a single tree beyond, then they could—with skill—target her on the scopes of those fire weapons with barely a notice from her Sight. The prospect of tree climbing right now did not make her happy; dividing her attention between 'hiding' and anything else was always a risky venture.

But tree climbing? Hah! She eyed the burly giant across the way. It was going to be more like cliff scaling from the look of that Ancient honeywood. By the Mother's hand, how had Gwyn ever managed to scale that thing?

Llinolae approached the aged honeywood, feeling the steady ebb and flow of its amarin. It had a richness and depth to it that few others of this behemoth's kind could equal. Age…seasons…she placed a palm gently against the smooth ridges of the ruddy bark. So, so old—the cork-flake texture of its bark had completely been lost. With time and weather, with fires, and, yes, even winters—this one had been little more than a sprout when it had first seen snow. Llinolae stroked the stone-armor, respect slipping to awe. She had never known that snow could fall below the altitude of the Clan's Plateau. To her knowledge, Khirlan proper had never boasted a true winter—at least not since the Council's Seers had shifted the amarin to create a place for the Clan to house their starcraft.

The amarin of the Ancient shimmered in affirmation; its seasons numbered much greater than even that.

A shiver ran through her. Fingers curled about deep ridges that were palm-wide and more. The satin feel of polished stone was somehow cool to the touch, yet it seemed so very warm with life. She gazed up along the rising lines that marked the scars and eons of survival, walking slowly along the base. She needed to go only a few steps before stopping. The shape and slope of its trunk became clearer to her Sight as she focused inward, and she found its roots were sunk deep. The tree grew virtually straight out from the ground with a diameter that could easily eclipse the width of Khirlan greatest city gates. It's smooth, hardened wood, nearly petrified by elements and time, offered little for the inexperienced hand and foot to use in climbing. Limbs as wide as silver-pine tree trunks stretched broad overhead. They were far, far overhead but of no aid to her here below. Yet the currents of this great one cradled Gwyn's own amarin. Llinolae stepped away, squinting upwards in concentration. The glimmering filaments of the Ancient's harmon grew more distinct to her—like starlight emerging from the twilight—and gradually Llinolae was drawn to a pattern of pinpricks. She drew back a bit more and Saw the zigzagging pattern of ascent up the trunk to a crevice that sidled around the corner of the lowest tree bough.

Lightning had once struck and split there, Llinolae realized. Though the growth had eventually mended, the rift further above and the haymoss played shadowy tricks that hid the place from normal sight, it was an excellent hideaway. No doubt Gwyn's initial thoughts had been to take refuge on the tree limb itself, high enough above the forest floor to be out of casual view on a branch that seemed inaccessible yet was wide enough to mask her from searching eyes. The Mother had been guiding her choice however, and the shelter within the tree's great trunk had become obvious when Gwyn had gotten above.

Yet how Gwyn had managed it? Baffled, Llinolae shook her head until suddenly she Saw that the zigging amarin trail was some sort of tree wounding. But they were small, insignificant insect nips to this Ancient and wouldn't have struck its amarin with such tell-tale signs, unless the tree was intending her to note them. So, not wounds. She tried to measure perspective by a more personal standard and grasped that they were narrow yet deep, thin as a finger... maybe twice a hand's depth? Made by a stiletto-styled, steel blade! And not merely one knife, but two!

Gwyn's vambraces! Those leathers on her forearms sheathed just such knives!

"Mae n'Pour!" Llinolae breathed and eyed the height of that long climb again. She knew the Amazons of old were strong, but to pull one's self up, hand over hand by knife strikes? "In truth you are Niachero, ti Soroi."

The tenor of the amarin shifted within the Ancient, and Llinolae felt a pulse of urgency reach to her. The bright print of Gwyn's knife-trail glittered like set gems while the rest dulled. She extended a soul-deep thanks to the Ancient. She thanked the Amazons as well for their practice of using metal arrows, because it was the only way she was going to reach those upper heights Unlike her beloved Niachero, Llinolae did not have the sheer and powerful upper body strength necessary to pull herself up this Great Tree using only knives! Which was a moot point anyway, since she didn't wear vambraces with hidden stilettos! She shrugged her cape aside, reaching into her quiver which she had filled from Gwyn's stock.

Blue eyes narrowed. She pulled and Sighted. Harmons pulsed and steadied, amarin shaping daughter, tree, and arrow to one purpose. Fingers opened—released!

With soundless harmony the strong, metal shafted arrow took flight and the first rung of Llinolae's ladder was planted in the lowest of the stiletto marks. She set the next arrow, and the next, sliding into an efficient rhythm of set-pull-release that needed no pause even as she stepped away to gain proper angles for her higher arches.

A nudge of praise brushed her as Llinolae finished, and she smiled over her shoulder in Ty's direction. It had been a task well done, she admitted. She slung her bow over her shoulder and secured it, then took to climbing. She had taken care to sink the arrows deep enough to hold, yet leave her room to step without damaging the fletching. Though she still had a half dozen in the quiver, she would rather not sacrifice the fourteen unless she absolutely had to, and she intended to retrieve as many of these as she possible could. Those Clan scouts were still too close.

Arms and once bruised muscles were beginning to shake towards the end, but she made it to that broad based limb soon enough. She sat a moment to catch her breath and wiped the sleeve across her flushed brow, feet dangling. A sense from Ty flickered across her mind's eye, and she learned Ril had begun to circle Cinder wide, to take her back to camp.

That was good, Llinolae nodded unconsciously. It meant that by the mid-night moon's rise, Ril would be standing sentry along with Ty. She glanced around herself to get her bearings in the gathering shadows. The wind was chillier, yet it carried more of the Forest's voices up here—yes, quite a ways up. She glanced between her feet again, judging the climb must have been six or seven times her own height. Shaking her head again at Gwyn's sheer strength, she got to her feet. She touched the haymoss, glancing upwards. The crevice started slightly below the limb here, but there was still a head's height or two to go before the rift opened properly. She turned to check for the scouts first and walked out for a better view.

It was a comfortable walk, with a bit of haymoss clumped here and there. This lower limb was too old to branch leaves and too far from the forest canopy to get proper sunlight anymore. She gave Gwyn credit for a gamble well made. They could have trotted a horse along this limb, and it certainly offered a wide view of the forest floor.

And it was, in truth, the lost Clan scout out there. Llinolae crouched low, more from habit then from risk of discovery. His amarin was unmistakable from this angle which might mean another scout was near who might be searching for this fellow's trail?

She spun a little on her boot soles, gaze narrowing as she searched off to the left beyond the tree's great trunk. The second scout was barely discernable, riding into the distance...riding away at an easy canter.

There was too much satisfaction and purpose in that direct line of depar-ture, however, and Llinolae didn't particularly like it.... It could mean a search pattern finished with an anticipation of eventide—or it could mean signs of the lost scout had been discovered. The latter meant the whole patrol could be descending later.

She frowned and made her way to the trunk's shelter. The arrow steps were not going to be easily missed unless she intervened with her Sight.

Still hidden below, Ty prodded Llinolae encouragingly with a light brush through her awareness. To Ty's senses, all was well at least for the moment.

It would have to do, Llinolae accepted. If the scouts returned, hopefully the sandwolf could alert her soon enough for her Blue tricks to conjure something useful. Right now, Gwyn was waiting.

She scampered up the last few feet, but as soon as she parted the haymoss, Llinolae realized the sluggish rhythms to Gwyn's body were not from sleep but from a concussion! The jumbling of amarin was a chaotic mesh, blending Gwyn's life signs with those of the Ancient tree. Like blood from a poorly stanched wound that flows into an icy creek with washing, Gwyn's uniqueness of self was quite literally bleeding away in the wash of the greater tide.

"Thank you for giving her shelter, but neither you nor Aggar can have her yet!" Llinolae announced, and the flare of her own Sight burst bright. In a whirlwind of blue light, her amarin raced about the perimeter from either side of her until at the far end of the craggy chamber the sides met and sealed. Sparks and jagged bits of indigo protested for a brief moment, but the seam held and the cocoon was spun. A warmer blue rose then to surround the outer shell and offer reinforcement. A smile fluttered across Llinolae's features, and she acknowledged the tree's shift of intent with a nod; she could do with the aid.

The humidity eased as the temperature rose to a more comfortable level. Llinolae shed her cloak and weapons, making her way carefully across the spongy mulch bed of the so-called floor. With approval she noted Gwyn had not only managed to climb to this haven, but the *Niachero* had stayed coherent enough to bring her pack above as well.

Gwyn lay stretched out awkwardly on a blanket. Her feet had once been propped atop the small pack, though one had since slipped, while her head was gingerly raised by a wooden knob and her rolled-up cloak. Obviously, she had known she was going into shock. But from what?

Llinolae straightened Gwyn's legs gently, propping both feet a bit higher. She threw her own cloak over Gwyn, knowing it would be a while before the clammy chill would recede—even in the rising, toasty warmth of the tree's nest. Fingers made sensitive by Sight and experience found the bruising to Gwyn's shoulder despite the clothes hiding it. The swelling behind Gwyn's ear was even more tender. Llinolae bent low, a hand moving very, very cautiously as she peered closer. She found she had been right not to move Gwyn's head; the woman's wound was bloodless only on a skin level. The pressure—the swelling! The jolt to the skull must have been horrendous. They were lucky nothing had fractured. Llinolae knelt a moment, hands on her thighs and a scowl on her lips as she considered their options. Yet at the edges of her mind, she kept pondering the cause. From the lingering traces of amarin, some sort of log or branch had caused the injury. But she was decidedly suspicious that it had been a simple accident. Maybe the Clan scout had not been anticipating honors for finding signs of their lost apprentice, but for boasting of a Marshal's kill!

With a physical shake, Llinolae pulled herself back to Gwyn's immediate care. There actually was not much to wrestle over. Gwyn'l needed the swelling to go down without blood clots or nasty complications, and her body's natural rhythms to be restored. If Brit were here, Llinolae would have quickly turned the task over to the healer, because though Llinolae's mentor had taught her about off-worlder physiology—'just in case'—Llinolae would be the first to admit she understood healing very poorly.

A great pulse of amarin throbbed and dispersed, rivulets of rainbows dancing along the soft blue glow of her Sight's cocoon. An amazing simulation of a human hug, Llinolae smiled. Again she felt the reassurance of this Ancient's wisdom. Mechanics in amarin were intricately woven, they both admitted. But amarin were not solely physical nor metaphysical; amarin were truth and light, life and death—intermeshed yet distinct. There were many, many ways to intercede through the Life Cycles. Healers knew of the most concrete. With the strength and guidance of this Ancient tree, Llinolae's Sight could mend through less tangible means than splints and medicines. She knew Gwyn's patterns. Her Sight of Gwyn could recreate what once was. The Great Tree would lend her the power to reshape Gwyn's amarin to that inner vision and temper the shifting to match Gwyn's tolerance for rapid body changes.

Llinolae dipped her fingers into the rushing wall of lights that spun their cocoon and brought her the Ancient's Gifts. Using touch that glowed with the rainbow radiance, she began to paint a new pattern of amarin along Gwyn's cheek.

* * *

Ril slipped into the rooted niche, coming to stretch prone next to Ty with a soft bunt from her nose.

Ty flicked her tattered ear towards her.

Ril grunted shortly, understanding her Sister's impatience all too well. The whole trek with Cinder had been a worthless venture. The scouting apprentice was so haphazard in his attentions that he had repeatedly lost their trail. Eventually she had been forced to abandon the attempt. Instead she had taken Cinder back to camp, leaving the mare for Brit and Sparrow to find in the morning. Then she returned to stand watch with Ty. The trail she had purposefully laid from camp to here had been subtle enough that few, save Gwyn or Southerners like Sparrowhawk, could have been expected to follow it. But it was the best she could do by way of a message for help. Anything more obvious and the Clan's patrol might find it first.

And unfortunately, those more experienced scouts were already bringing themselves in this direction. Llinolae was not going to be pleased.

Llinolae stirred. She sat up, rubbing a hand over her eyes to banish the sleep. Immediately her thoughts turned to Gwyn, but the woman's breath was steady and her pale skin was the hue of golden apricot. Gwyn's slumber was just that now and nothing more. She probably wouldn't even wake to a headache.

The warmth and scent of green, living things surrounded them. Llinolae's smile was gentle and appreciative as she gazed around the openness of the tree's chamber. While she slept, the glowing cocoon had drawn more and more from the Ancient's strength, leaving Llinolae to rest more completely. The temperature had risen to that of a balmy summer's day. The light had become tinged with the coolness of lime-mint, easy to the eye but keeping the darkness well at bay. The more usual inhabitants had crept back as well, sliding into the nooks and crannies between the cocoon's wall and the tree's timber. Even the spongy dust and mulch of the carpenter mites had grown more solid beneath the blanketing coat of that amarin cocoon; her nose no longer tickled with a yen for sneezing and her breeches were clean of the stuff again.

There was much she had yet to learn of amarin, Llinolae ruefully reminded herself.

She nearly felt the tree chuckle—or the equivalent of whatever such Ancients did.

A sense of Ril and concern became more acute, and her smile fled. Now she recognized what had awakened her.

With a glance to Gwyn, Llinolae left her to sleep and made her way back across the chamber to the haymoss. The cocooning light parted and sealed behind her as she slipped through. She'd sensed the danger of the approaching scouting party before she descended the short distance to the broad limb.

"Fates Jest!" She swore under her breath. There were nearly a dozen of them. Though still a few leagues out, they were moving with a systematic thoroughness and an undeniable direction. She recognized that spread formation only too well: sweep and corner. Whether they were looking for an injured Marshal or a wayward apprentice, she harbored no doubts they would know Gwyn's signs when they did come across the tracks.

Ty's sudden alertness sent her into a spinning crouch, and her Sight searched to the west.

"This is not good." Lips set with an irritated scowl. She worked her way out further along the tree limb.

Both she and the sandwolves had been so preoccupied with the patrol in the southeast, they had forgotten that meddlesome apprentice who was still nearby.

Fates Cellars! Why hadn't the boy settled in for the night? For that matter, the lot of them should just turn in!

A boot barely scuffed, and Llinolae recognized Gwyn's approach more from a Sense of amarin than noise. The Amazon came out, keeping low, then settled on one knee beside her. Llinolae smiled at that confident pose, Gwyn's elbow braced on the upright knee and her hand dangling loosely; she doubted she herself could have awakened in a strangely lit tree hole, mysteriously freed from pain and concussion, and so calmly gather herself together for duty.

"What is it?" Gwyn nodded into the shadows of the forest before them. The silvery sheen of the Twin Moons shone brightly through the overhead canopy, but the scout was not quite near enough yet for normal vision to help. "Is it that foolish apprentice again?"

"So nice to see you too," Llinolae quipped, sliding a glance Gwyn's way. "And yes, it is our favorite young scout."

Gwyn had the grace to blush. "Sorry."

"Don't be," Llinolae took pity on her and squeezed her hand reassuringly. "He's over that way a bit," Llinolae pointed. "But over there, the patrol is our real problem. They will be here by moonset of the early Twin."

A sigh whispered through the dimness. Gwyn understood: there would still be more than enough light for them to discern tracks and trails. "We could try it on foot—?"

"Not a thrilling idea." Llinolae agreed with the hesitance Gwyn's tone implied. "I would rather be cornered up this tree than caught in a flat-footed race against their horses."

"Where is Cinder? For that matter, where are Ty and Ril?"

"Hush! They're all fine." Llinolae pressed a kiss to the curled fingers still in her grasp. "Ril got Cinder back to camp. She had to give up the attempt to get the lost scout to follow them back around the east canyon side to Sparrow and Brit."

"Not surprising."

"Ty fetched me while they were off trying, though. Neither of them thought you could wait too long for help."

A crooked grin acknowledged the truth in that. "So they are playing sentry somewhere below?"

Llinolae tipped her head, unconsciously adapting a very sandwolf-like manner. "Is your head all right?"

"Yes. Yes, whatever you did, it worked wonders."

"But your packbond isn't working? You can't tell where they are?"

"Oh no—I know they are hereabout someplace. But they are being overly protective." Gwyn grinned broadly. "They have shut me out of their scheming perceptions for a time. They tend to do that when they are adamant about me resting."

"Wise harmons, the both of them," Llinolae approved.

The two of them fell silent. Their gazes drawn again to the forest steps. There were troubles to be dealt with yet.

Wind driven and being herded to the east, the clouds eclipsed one of the Twins, deepening the shadows. Glancing at them, Llinolae dismissed them as the moon reappeared, but then something whispered across the back of her mind.

Gwyn started slightly as Llinolae's hand withdrew from hers. But as Llinolae pressed both palms to the tree limb, Gwyn realized some path of the Sight was being pursued. She waited uneasily, anticipating worse news of the Clan folk or some note of an entirely new danger. Concentration furrowed a crease between Llinolae's brows and Gwyn began to relax; she was beginning to recognize that scowl. White teeth gnawed absently on a lower lip as Gwyn watched. She felt anxiety yield to satisfaction then she prodded, "You've got an idea."

A slow nod answered her. Then for a long silence, there was nothing more. Until finally, Llinolae's clear blue eyes turned to Gwyn. The Amazon grinned again at that measured air of consideration. "You have more than an idea. You have a solution."

"Perhaps—it may work. Are Ty and Ril up to a good drenching?"

"A what?" Gwyn cocked her head in puzzlement then she realized what Llinolae was suggesting! Never—*never!*—had Gwyn even heard of a Blue Sight so great!

For the first time in their acquaintance, Llinolae saw the *Niachero* balk with fear and amazement at her Blue powers. It hurt. Until suddenly, her lover was chuckling in self-derision and fingering the non-existent bruise behind her ear, and Llinolae's pain vanished with the shake of Gwyn's head. Their eyes met. Gwyn's smile broadened and then they were laughing together quietly, warmly.

"I beg patience," Gwyn amended, eyes still bright with mirth. "I am finding I might not be as enlightened as I thought."

"So I See."

Their hands met halfway, fingers entwining strongly.

"I love you," Gwyn murmured.

It was said so simply. But it was so much what Llinolae needed to hear. Her throat tightened. She almost had to blink away tears…how could Gwyn have known that saying more would have belittled the sweet sincerity of her apology? The grasp of their hands strengthened as Llinolae managed to nod. With a swallow, she found her voice, "Heartbound."

"*Soroi,* " Gwyn agreed.

Enough—! Llinolae pulled herself to duties, and both turned toward the forest.

"What now?"

Llinolae gestured in the direction of the apprentice scout. "He will be here before I can bring the rains. But I am not certain of precisely when."

"He is still combing for signs?"

Llinolae nodded.

"Ril and Ty could play basker pack again and hound him into the scouting party. If you just want to be done with him?"

"Tempting idea," Llinolae allowed. She sighed.

"You would rather not toss away the plan quite so soon," Gwyn saw. "Good. Neither would I."

"All right then," Llinolae glanced at her with a impish smile, "We are agreed."

"We are."

"How well do your packmates mimic the baskers?"

"Even Southerners can not always tell the difference."

"Might be helpful."

"Already has been." At Llinolae's raised brow, Gwyn explained. "They chased him off earlier with the trick after I got hurt."

"He presumes you are dead then?"

Gwyn shook her head, "He never saw me. A hunting cat was stalking him—more for mischief than hunger."

"They do seem to have a malicious sense of humor, don't they?"

"Just be thankful they are so stupid."

"So he was nervous because of the cat?"

"I pulled Ril and Ty way back, he was so jittery. Had his fire weapon unsheathed and was striking at shadows every now and again."

"Mother…," Llinolae hissed.

"What I had not realized was that damn cat had worked its way 'round towards Cinder and me. Startled it out of its wits in the tree above me. Thing screeched and he started shooting. Cinder went one way. I went another. Haymoss, smoke, whole tree limbs exploded! Don't know where the cat went. Ril and Ty took off like baskers from the Cellar, and his horse gave him little choice but running. By the time I had worked my way clear of debris and realized I was not going to stay together long enough for Cinder to get me back to camp, I barely had enough sense to get clear of the area before hiding."

"I'm not certain, *Niachero,* " Llinolae drawled, "but it might have been easier to tie yourself to Cinder than climb this tree by hand-over-hand knife stabs."

Gwyn glanced below, not quite understanding the concern. "I don't remember much aside from the last few falls from the saddle. Or maybe...," she scoffed at herself, "...it's only the one tumble that's playing and replaying in my memory!"

Llinolae smiled wryly. She pointed a thumb back at the tree trunk. "You should get inside. It is going to get pretty chilly and damp soon."

"I would rather wait for you. Unless I'll be a distraction?"

"Never an unwanted one, *Soroi*." Pleasure danced warmly across Llinolae's smile, and Gwyn's own answered her. "But don't complain to me if you end up wet."

"Understood. How do you start?"

"I already have." Thunder rolled in on the last of her words.

The wind whipped down with cold vengeance suddenly, and a cacophony of rattling leaves and creatures shrieked loose. Roosts and nests and higher burrows were swiftly sought as thunderous black rumbles cracked in ground-shuddering glee.

Hair tore from its short braid, blinding Gwyn a moment. She gasped at the fury of the gathering elements, then caught her breath at the beauty of the small shea crouched beside her.

Blue eyes fastened outward, unseeing—uncaring of the raging press against them. Gwyn watched, almost feeling the exuberance—the eagerness of Llinolae's harmon as it called those primal forces. Power pairing with power, respect meeting respect—differences binding to mold passions into purpose! All singing! Rejoicing! All things alive in her!

Skin glowed in dark glossy stain, taut stretched over bone. White teeth barred in front of the light. Ice-gem eyes widened. Aggar and daughter elated!

A basker bay from Ril jerked Gwyn from her trance. Her heart froze as she saw the lost scout had spotted them and drawn his bow. His arrow flew, but Llinolae spun in her crouch, hand flinging fingers wide. And a whoosh of flame took the arrow to ash.

Ty's hound voice took up the call.

The Clan boy fumbled for his fire weapon, the mount shining beneath him.

The metallic weapon raised in one hand and sighted on them.

Llinolae stood and fists went skyward.

Lightning crashed.

The weapon disintegrated as the horse reared and the baying echoed near. The beast shattered its bone bit and bolted west. The rains descended in drenching torrents.

"Inside!"

Gwyn blinked, coming slowly from her daze. Llinolae's hands urged her to her feet and steadied her against the rain. "Inside!"

Gwyn moved then, pulling Llinolae along with her. The wind howled, rising to meet the next crack of thunder and lightning. Llinolae's footing slipped, but Gwyn caught her and pushed her into the netting of the haymoss on the trunk. Gwyn felt Llinolae tremble as she climbed—exertion claiming its toll.

The storm pried at them, no longer heeding any mistress or equal. Then Gwyn climbed closer, huddling to protect Llinolae with her strength and body, until the crevice opened and they were falling inwards to the sheltering warmth and light of the Ancient's waiting cocoon.

"What did you do?!" Gwyn gasped, rolling to her back with a great gulp of air.

"It had…" Llinolae's sides heaved as she panted on all fours, and she had to swallow hard before managing, "It had to be strong enough to wipe clean the tracks and…." She swallowed again and shook her head. "And it had to stop them—the patrol—now…not let them wander until the moon set."

"Stop 'em in their tracks, huh?"

Gazes met. Eyes sparkled and laughter bubbled up at the inane word twist. Llinolae collapsed completely as they howled and rolled into one another. It was inane—insane, and absolutely nonsense, but they hugged each other, still laughing anyway.

Then abruptly they stilled, Gwyn looking down at the most incredible woman she had ever beheld—Llinolae gazing up into the blazing copper eyes of the most remarkable woman she had ever imagined…!

Thunder cracked outside and the force of reality—all they'd nearly lost this night!—descended. Giddiness subsided. Passion rose fiercely and they kissed. Winds wailed as mouths devoured each other. Driving, sharing, needing the taste of each other—to claim, to surrender, to glow in the fire of the other as their lives and love stood in testimony against the Fates' Jest!

Flushed skins of gold-brown honeywood and dark glossy polish contrasted. Hair of flame and ebony slipped through greedy fingers. With both hands, Llinolae pulled Gwyn's mouth back to hers as the Amazon fumbled with the ties of tunic and jerkin—unseeing, uncaring—until things finally loosened enough to strip off, bound knots and all, over Llinolae's head.

Llinolae rasped, "Yours too—" as Gwyn's mouth met her breast. Gwyn half rolled away, with Llinolae already tugging and pulling the shirt off.

Skins slick with heat and rainwater, Gwyn found Llinolae's mouth on her breast first, gasping as she arched away but Llinolae came off the ground following mercilessly—hands holding fast to rib and muscle. Gwyn shuddered, cry becoming moan, and her knee fell between Llinolae's thighs in a selfish search for balance.

Breeches rubbed breeches and Llinolae hesitated, teeth nipping Gwyn's breast. But her Love recognized the need and Gwyn's hands splayed wide across the back of her hips, Llinolae lifting her—bringing her tight against that strong thigh. With an arm she wrapped herself nearer, mouth hungry still upon Gwyn's breast as the Amazon knelt there—guiding her—arching yet further with such deep, coaxing moans.

Llinolae fumbled with the waist ties as Gwyn's head tossed. Hands lost hold, then took better grip with Llinolae higher—and she rode faster as her palm slipped between Gwyn's wet thighs. Then together they rode—soared.

Passion…need…lightning!—flashed outside and in. Their lips met with the final crescendo—thunder shaking the tree and their souls.

They fell…lay together still entwined and breath heaving. Kisses gentled against sweat-slicked breasts. A chin nuzzled damp, ebony curls.

"Heartbound...," Gwyn's hoarse murmur struggled out.

Llinolae nodded shakily against Gwyn's chest, her hand trapped warmly in place by their entangled thighs...her body by Gwyn's own arms.

"Heartbound," Gwyn repeated, the wholeness...the completeness of their bond settling warm around her in a tangible way that had not quite been realized before.

"I'm still here, *Soroi.* " Llinolae pressed a kiss against Gwyn's heart. "Passion will not frighten me away. Not ever."

And to *Niachero* —to those held in awe as often as admired, even in Valley Bay—such simple words carried trust further then touch or kiss ever could.

Chapter Thirteen

don't know...," Brit stepped back and eyed the groundstake, modified horse hobbles, and lead rope with skepticism. "It sure doesn't look like it will hold him."

Llinolae smiled tolerantly. "That is the whole point. If I have to shackle a man I'd rather leave him as much dignity as I can. No use making enemies needlessly."

"Huh—think this youngster is going to notice amenities? Hardly likely."

"He will, especially when he wants the privacy."

"Yeah, Clanfolk are peculiar that way. They do tend to get embarrassed about the most natural things. But I still don't know about this, Llinolae. I'd feel better having him away from the jagged overhead, even if it does give a good bit of shade."

"And having any sort of blind spot is just asking for trouble, let alone the size of that root and haymoss mess." Amusement tinged Llinolae's words, but she wrapped an arm around the older woman's shoulders reassuringly. "I have been listening to you, Marshal."

"Still sure about this amarin trick of yours?"

"Quite sure," Llinolae grinned. The cocoon she and the Ancient had spun last night had given her the idea. "He won't be able to pick up a pebble inside that perimeter. The grass won't tear. The cliffside will seem granite hard, yet too slippery to climb. The leather and bone buckles will have the tenacity of Clan steel. He will be comfortable. He will be contained."

"He will be visible and loud!" Brit concluded.

"Well...that too."

"I don't know. I just don't know...."

"Wait until Gwyn and Sparrow bring him back. You'll see. It will hold him."

* * *

And it did, but about as graciously as Brit had foretold.

The wooden bowl clattered and Llinolae winced as she heard him from inside the tent. Midday meal was apparently not much more to his liking than yesterday's eventide had been.

"Stupid old...old, dray-sized hag!"

Llinolae chuckled over her maps, shaking her head. She had certainly heard more imaginative curses in her time. At least he had the courtesy to be screaming his insults in Trade-Tongue. But if he wanted the Amazon to take him seriously, he was going to be disappointed. All he was accomplishing now was proving the continuing need to serve him on wooden platters instead of ceramic—and possibly, that he preferred bread and water to stew and tea.

Llinolae glanced up as Sparrow appeared at her open tent flap. She had a steaming bowl and a plate of fresh bunt bread in hand, saying, "Ril circled in as arranged. The elder Clan scout approaches!" Sparrow wiggled her brow and hips as she spun in a prancing mime of a troubadour.

"The players assemble." She set the food down and danced out again, tossing back over her shoulder, "our show begins!"

Llinolae laughed and reached for a piece of the sweet bread. She grew more somber as she chewed. The woman she was about to meet was not only the Lead scout of the patrol, but she was the older sister of this young scout, and Llinolae was doubly glad the amarin cocoon had worked so well. The young man might be too naive to grasp the courtesy of his prison, but a more experienced scout would quickly notice. Llinolae hoped it would win her some concession of courtesy in return—some listening might be a nice gesture.

If the Lead would listen...if she would only talk with her! Llinolae's fist curled in tense frustration. So much was riding on such a haphazard meeting. So much more than even she had first intended! But in Gwyn's questioning of the man yesterday morning, the amarin had been all too betraying. His sister, Camdora, was Lead of the patrol and undoubtedly concerned about his disappearance—she had been responsible for him since the farming accident that had left them young orphans. Yet aside from their kinbonds, this Lead was more than a patrol sergeant. This woman was the liaison in charge of 'civil defense and welfare; for all practical purposes, she was the Steward of all Clanfolk not in the militia. Steward? No, more the liaison than the ruler. Nonetheless she was respected by the farmers and crafters *and* cognizant of political policies. Within the militia she held less power, certainly, but to the rest of the community, she was trusted and heeded.

Even if Llinolae allowed for a certain amount of sibling pride—or outright adoration!—the apprentice's assessment of his sister's position was undeniable. Gwyn had been watching her, had met with her briefly already to arrange this meeting, and both sandwolves and Gwyn were in unanimous agreement: this Lead was a woman to reckon with.

So many questions needed answers...so many pieces Llinolae could not account for.

Blue eyes looked out into the dusty sunlight, barely seeing Brit or Sparrow as they moved around camp in nervous chores—all of them biding time until Gwyn's arrival with Camdora.

"All of us waiting," Llinolae mused. She held a sinking Sense of out-of-time fear as, outside, the sunny yellow haze flirted with the misty shadows of her dreamspun visions. The damage done from her uncle's meddling...today might well bring answers she would rather not face.

She sighed. It would be worse, if there were no answers to decipher at all.

* * *

The Forest's amarin murmured to her and Llinolae's hand stilled in Ril's ruff. Brows peaked questioningly as Ril's nose lifted, and the woman gave her friend's muzzle an amused, gentle shove. "Don't give me that. You know who comes."

Ril nuzzled her with a grin. She did, in truth, because Gwyn was accompanying their visitor.

Llinolae sighed and gazed a long last moment into the cascading falls. Rainbows flashed and danced in the afternoon light. The cove was warm with summer heat, cooled by the tumbling waters' mist, and peaceful in its seclusion. Beyond the pool's edge, a welcoming spread of foods and cushions had been laid out. Braziers had been placed between torches in a semi-circle, in case of need later. Flagons of tea, mead, and cider-water had been set out on the two low, square tables. Everything had been made ready. Now she could only hope this Clan woman would accept the hospitality graciously.

She would know soon enough.

"Off with you," Llinolae gave Ril a last pat as she stood. The sandwolf scurried away from their sunny rock seat. Llinolae descended more slowly, watching as the other disappeared into the undergrowth lining the cliff's walls; none of the packmates—Llinolae now included—wanted the Clan to know of the sandwolves with them. They had all agreed that some things were better left unshared.

Sparrow had found Llinolae a satin tunic of indigo to wear with the ruddy jerkin, boots, and breeches of a Marshal's dress. The Dracoon had admitted that wearing her district's colors along with Churv's had offered some measure of confidence. She didn't need to conduct this meeting while feeling herself to be in some position of superior power. But it was odd enough to be standing here with short, cropped hair for the first time in her official dealings, and a little familiarity from the cloth and colors was welcome. A point, she had noticed, which Brit and Sparrow had carried over in choosing cushion fabrics and table matting.

"Whereas you, Camdora? What will you make of us all, I wonder?" Llinolae chewed the inside of her lip a moment, then straightened as a woman stepped warily through the curtain of the haymoss with Gwyn close behind her.

The Clan Lead was tall as most of the Clan's women, barely half a head shorter than the Dracoon or Amazon. Her clear gray eyes darted everywhere, noting details of cove and preparations with the skill of an accomplished scout. Her skin was weathered and lined, yet it's light flesh tones seemed quite pale in contrast to her glossy tumble of black curls. Jaw squared yet chin pointed, her innate sense of self kept that chin from thrusting out—arrogance was absent in favor of steady assurance. A level gaze came to Llinolae, and she turned unhurriedly to approach the Dracoon. Her tread was as deliberate as her scrutiny, her weight balanced. Her entire manner was undaunted, merely assessing.

Then Llinolae glanced past their guest to Gwyn, noting Gwyn's amarin was still approving of this woman. Gwyn knew Llinolae had been watching Camdora covertly since their arrival, taking her own measure of this Clan Lead as Gwyn showed Camdora around the camp and allowed her time with her brother.

Aye, Llinolae admitted, this was a woman of honor. The question still remained, however, how much honor and power had come to be equated with the Clan Leads.

* * *

"No!" the Clan Lead whipped around, her patience breaking as she cut Llinolae's words off in mid-sentence. "You haven't heard a thing I've said. Have you? Not one single thing!"

Camdora rose to her feet, coiled fury springing her towards Llinolae in a rush! Gwyn moved forward in alarm, but Llinolae's hand flew out, palm raised in a halting command to the Amazon, and Gwyn checked herself in midstride. Camdora swept past Llinolae to resume her pacing.

Gwyn eased back to stand at the edges of the viney overgrowth, and once again assumed her role as an informal honor guard. In the moons' lit shadows further along the cliff stone, Ril sank down as well. She remained unseen.

The silence among the three women sat heavy on everyone's already thinly stretched nerves. Even the drone of the waterfall seemed hushed tonight. Her skin browned, Llinolae's poise still seemed outwardly calm. Her respect was evident in her patience as she stood waiting.

Abruptly, Camdora turned to Llinolae as her step paused—words hovering on her lips. Then a hand tossed the foolishness of the sheer hope aside. "This is a wasted venture!"

Her pacing began again.

Camdora's long strides switched to-and-fro in a shorter and shorter route. Her fists clenched, opening then grasping at emptiness. "There's nothing more important to the militia than their precious rank, save their weapons! Nothing!"

Llinolae watched the other's walk quicken. The desperation hanging in the night's damp chill grew even worse.

"Yes! The farmers and crafters choose the Clan Leads. Yes! As Leads we appoint the militia's commanders!" Her hand chopped hard on each point. "Yes—you have it right that the tolls in food, in gear and in our numbers— *sheer bleeding death!*—threaten to annihilate us every bit as much as our weapons threaten you!

"But we don't have your resources! We don't have the...*the luxury* ...of losing one single bushel in harvest.

"The Plateau was fine! They said! They still say, 'Or so it was then!' The soil was rich. The prospects good. The Plateau broad. There were chances to expand and grow—become self-sufficient. And whatever we needed—well! We've got all that metal, don't we? Such a precious resource to melt down and barter off as we please. Sounded good way back then, didn't it?

"But after 280 Clan years—we're still trying to find the good!" Camdora swung to face Llinolae full, her stance wide and her breath short as she bit out each syllable with a basker's vehemence. "Our fields have no water. The land erodes without the trees—or with trees!—because the winds that howl across the old spaceport's plain are relentless. And sure! We're metal rich, but that's scant good without some means to gather, melt, and disperse it. Well, if the Council of Ten ever gets 'round to taking down that damned Unseen Wall, maybe we could to try it!"

"They did take it down—for a time."

The Clan Lead shot Gwyn a bitter, piercing glance. "There are no excuses. Neither for my folk or Aggar's—or *yours!*" Her voice dropped low as she addressed Llinolae again. "For one summer that Wall was down—and we abused it. In Clan reckoning, that happened two hundred years ago! A hundred of your seasons, right? Yes, but of course," she rounded back on Gwyn, "when the Council of Ten sets a precedent, it does not change.

"But we live now—today! And the Clan has set a new precedent. Since we have only limited access to the metals or technology, the militia has been given all rights of priority."

Llinolae's gaze met Camdora's steadily, neither imposing nor persuading,

245

merely sad. "I can't undo what was done four generations ago. I can only help fashion us a new treaty—to keep all our children from repeating the folly."

"Still that's the whole problem, isn't it? Our people's heritage of conflicts and betrayals? Because we're dealing with a scrambled mess of ethics found in Council, Clan, and Ramains. And shattered souls don't do very well when you talk to them of trust and opportunity."

"Then talk of food and safety—"

"No!" Camdora wailed, waving with a futile gesture of the impossible. She spun back as suddenly, "Don't you see? There's no time left anymore! In a handspan of harvests, the land we do farm now will be useless. There's rarely been enough to feed us properly, let alone stockpile it for reserves. Then the water table will drop again…. The militia's ambitions are *not* our best hope, Dracoon. They are our only hope!"

"Hope for what?" Llinolae pressed. "For land to farm? I can give you that! For seeds? New water holes? New skills for forest farmsteading?"

Camdora stood there, shaking her head despairing and incredulous. "You would *give* us that? With no questions, no concerns of what we would be doing to ourselves in accepting it? No! You'd be shredding our most fundamental foundations of self-respect. Charity earns debt, not independence!"

"You're wrong," Llinolae countered, stepping near. The flushed brown of her skin deepened in it's rich color as she shook her head with a grim scowl. "There you are so very wrong."

"Yet you do understand? Giving us land will not succeed."

"Taking it will do you no more good in this circumstance," Llinolae warned. "The land that your militia tramples and burns won't do you much better than the Plateau's wastes; the militia destroy your folk's livelihood before they even settle you.

"Hear me, Clan Lead! Both our folk need this truce. Mine because yes, your militia has forced Khirlan to the negotiating table. And yours, because you're right—you have run out of time!"

"When there is nothing left to lose, the impossible suddenly becomes viable…," Camdora stated with a dulled calm.

"What?" Llinolae drew back with startled confusion.

"It is the rally of a desperate people." Camdora admitted. "It's the cry of our militia."

"It's suicidal."

Camdora moved a shoulder in a listless shrug.

"And so *everyone* follows them? No one will dissent? None care for the waste and the pity—that this will only bring a new legacy of hopelessness—of no trade, no trust? If the Clan persists in following the militia's insanity!"

"Follow? Follow the militia?" Camdora scoffed at the idea, until outrage kindled again. "Farmers and crafters do not *follow* militia commanders, Min Llinolae."

No, Llinolae thought sadly. Brit had been right. The Clan folk weren't ready to forge paths through simple talking.

"I may be a Clan Lead," grimaced Camdora. "And I want a better way for my folk…but once the Clan Leads listened carefully to a young woman of the militia. She was persuasive. She was impressive. Many of us found sense in what she could offer." Eyes dull with regret lifted to Llinolae. "We were wrong. Or perhaps we were right, but we—like you—have grown less eager for the bartering in blood and lives. Perhaps my great-grandchildren might be able to answer that question—I no longer try.

"She was placed as commander above the others, until…. We gave her so much desperation to feed upon. Popularity became omniscience, beliefs became dogma. Cooperation—sheer blind obedience! Now, she's got the support and loyalty of the militia, strong with its weaponry, and it's fanatics are among her elite. She is commander to this day and she will remain Clan commander. As for her orders…. Brutal times lead to brutal measures."

"Do only her elite carry fire weapons?"

"Not quite," Camdora's smile held no humor. "Still, close enough. They've first choice of goods."

"Yet some of you are expecting this commander to begin using those weapons against your own?"

"We don't have to anticipate anything, Dracoon. She and hers have been quite willing to demonstrate whenever needed."

"I see."

"Do you?" Camdora paused and glanced about to include Gwyn as well. "Do either of you? Because—it's not simply a matter of her anymore."

"No, it isn't," Gwyn interjected soberly. "The threat to the Clan's survival is very real. She didn't create that—she's only capitalized on it."

"You do understand." Camdora paused and then, "After so many generations, the Clan's prowess and technology has declined, especially because of our isolation. Our farmers have harvested more dirt than crops. Our children know more of drought than metals. All our resources keep pouring into expanding territories. But it is not from greed! That's only what your Council and kings will say.

"Even today, most of our farmers have no sense of mutual dependency among crops and honeywood—nor among grazers and predators. So the land's erosion has forced them to continually pick-up and move on to new plots. Yet as fast as they ready the new farmlands, they lose the old! And now they're running out of plots. We're all running out of land!

"Yes, we've seen it coming. But we were—we are—afraid that if we reach out to the Council or Court they'll disperse us across the two continents. We don't want that. We don't want to lose our sense of belonging, our sense of self—of heritage. We want to leave the Plateau, not each other!"

"So this commander," Llinolae spoke quietly, "she's taken your hopeless and created heroes. She's founded a dream for folk to cling onto—to escape into!"

"*And* she's monopolized our weapons power to prod our folk—to terrorize them—into overcoming any and all opposition."

"But if someone disposes of her," Gwyn elaborated flatly, "she'll become the Founding Martyr of a New Era."

"Yes!" Clan leader paused, then tipped her head in respect. She approved of the understanding she saw in the two women before her. "This leader of ours, she's taken the cause and built a mystique."

A measured glance of agreement passed between Dracoon and Amazon, the faintest of nods prompting Gwyn to continue.

"Tell me, Camdora," the Amazon's voice rang low with the challenge, "even if the woman and her terrorizing were to simply disappear, would the Clan Leads choose to press folk to different path? Or would you prefer to seek another fanatic to fill her place?"

The Clan Lead assessed that question warily. Oaths and duty cautioned her. "I have always preferred a word to a blade. But sometimes—expediency is a necessity."

The woman hesitated again, clearly weighing the risks of her next words. Then a thought sealed her lips in a tight smile.

"Aye—when you have nothing left to lose…," Llinolae left the rest of that militia's rally unsaid.

Her grin widened as her dilemma resolved—Camdora met the Dracoon's gaze again. "You implied the cost of this bloodshed has grown too high for you and Khirlan. Emotionally—ethically? There are many of the Clan outside the militia—and some of us who are enlisted as well—who've found our costs have grown too high."

"I'd not meant to imply you would or wouldn't," Llinolae allowed quickly. "I freely admit, we of Khirlan have had enough of death and pillage. I'd not presume to know you and your people so well that I'd assume anything."

Camdora acknowledged the reassurance politely with a nod. "The Clan Leads and folk are occasionally willing to entertain the possibility that expansionism may not be so very profitable.

"However—" her words slowed in a grim, deliberate emphasis, "the militia is not. If you do truly seek to negotiate with words instead of blood, you will have to force the militia to the table. There will be no other way."

* * *

Brit glanced up as Sparrow came through the vine curtains into the waterfall's canyon. Gwyn entered behind her. Llinolae gestured to the empty two chairs—the camp table had been brought in when Camdora had retired for the evening. The midnight moon had witnessed a weary Llinolae lose her first argument of the new day. Brit had flatly refused any discussion among the four of them until Llinolae had finished something more substantial than tidbits of bread and cheese. So Llinolae had dutifully obeyed, and as Gwyn encouraged her now with a quick smile…she realized the break had done both of them good.

"We're set," Sparrow dropped lightly into the seat across from Brit. "Camdora and brother are bedded down. Ril's still keeping her hidden watch over them, but I don't think he's going to be any trouble now that his sister—and patrol commander—is here."

Gwyn accepted a mug of cider from Llinolae, adding, "Ty's having no problems of any sort with Camdora's scouts either. Apparently, they're veterans with faith in her judgment and some acquaintance with her orders, even if it's no questions, just do it.' I think we can trust them to stay put for the full five days she'd ordered."

"Good, we'll need the time." Llinolae drew a deep breath and looked to each of them. "We knew that this venture, this attempt, has always held incredible risks and serious considerations."

"I know we'd all done a lot of thinking, before we set foot in Khirlan," Sparrow returned. Her usual mischievous humor had vanished. Her somber demeanor underlined their acceptance of the commitment all of them had taken on from the beginning.

Llinolae nodded briefly. These daughters of *dey Sorormin* were brave women. "Let me explain how I see things and then, I've a plan to propose."

At their general murmur of consent, she started. "Given my talk with Camdora, I think there's more hope than was once seen…but it is a dangerous hope. And though our original tack when Camdora agreed to come was to spend the next several days in talking and exploring mutual needs, it's clear at this point that the Clan Leads aren't free to pursue negotiations, unless something is done about the Clan militia and their commander. Still, any solution we might try, must be beneficial for both Clan and Khirlan, or we'll merely be fueling the fires for more trouble later. Although I admit, this makes a difficult task." She glanced around as she sat back in her seat, steadying her nerves with a conscious effort. "Though the driving impetus for the Clan's aggressions is survival, it's clear the militia's commander is a forceful catalyst. So this becomes the part that's the hardest for me—perhaps for you, it's the newest piece. I found it among the amarin webs the other afternoon and recognized it as a haunting piece of Palace treachery that's been teasing me all my life, but…

"I suspect," she held Gwyn's gaze openly and her voice gentled for a bare moment. "No—I know it was Gwyn's strength that finally made it safe enough for me to face the implications of my mother's assassination."

Surprise caused Sparrow a slight gasp, but she made no attempt to interrupt further.

Llinolae went on. "For a great many seasons, I've Seen Taysa's passions. There are immense depths of purpose and commitment which she draws upon to tackle her challenges. I've always drawn my own strength from within, from an absolute *intensity* of need. Father instilled it in me along with a sense of priority to aid and honor, to lead and protect our District folk. Taysa's passions are not so compassionate. Only I hadn't Seen that. Instead, I was blinded by our similarity of extremes. Recently however, even I'd begun to question her ambitions. Since Brit and Sparrow arrived, my assessment of Taysa has decidedly shifted. I've become better able to See and sort the pieces of Taysa's political abuses, and I'd thought her betrayal and motives had become clear…."

"Until your last mediations," Brit pressed softly as Llinolae's pause lengthened, "when you found even worse is true?"

"Yes," Llinolae responded crisply. Self-pity would have to wait, and duty returned the even resolve she required. She needed no more prompting. "Taysa is more than a traitor to Khirlan's cause. It's she who actually leads the Clan against us. She is the militia commander who decided the priority of the Clan should be to usurp Khirlan's entire district. She is the one who enjoys the terror her power has come to wield, with her Swords and Scouts armed with fire weapons.

"As for her reasons? Some of them I can piece together myself, without the Sight's more explicit images."

"I'd be interested in hearing those," Brit muttered, arms folding in a gruff matriarchal shrug of insult. She was suddenly taking this traitor's doings as a very personal insult. Brit had come to think of Llinolae as her own adopted kin—like Gwyn. She didn't like those who hurt her kin.

"I believe," continued Llinolae, "Taysa initially expected to use her relationship with my mother to gain Court confidence. Then she found an ambitious alliance with my uncle to be even more profitable. I suspect—no, the Forest amarin are too clear—I *know* Taysa eventually instigated the deaths of my uncle and, later, of my father.

"Back in the beginning when she left the Clan's settlements, she was one of an organized handful of Clan and Khirla courtiers who plotted to ruin Mha'del. However, as her power in Khirlan grew and her success in silencing blackmailers solidified her station—the problem of food and resources among the Clan was also worsening. Taysa became more and more pivotal to the Clan's survival.

"Eventually," Llinolae concluded with a weary shake of her head, "she convinced the Clan they'd win the whole district, if they'd follow her campaign of pillage and politicking! She's rallied them into a fanatical blind fervor. When she orders the fire weapons to silence even the Clan's own dissidents, the folk accept that it's done for the good of the cause—Taysa has bound the Clan's desperation to a militia's fanaticism. All who aren't enlisted follow her rule because they literally have no other hope, and no other choice."

"Then it's time to dethrone her little delusions," Sparrow snapped bitterly. "The Prince's troops from the northern campaigns would root her and her militia out. Their skill and sheer numbers would destroy her, despite the fire weapons—her cache of them in Khirla and Clantown have already been destroyed by us. But if we don't strike before she gets more weaponry through the Unseen Wall, then she will become invincible!"

"No, Sparrow, I've got to agree with Camdora." Llinolae paused for only a moment, weighing all her thoughts one last time. "If we do what you say, we'd only make Taysa into a martyr and prejudice more of Aggar's people against the Clan—which would force the Clan to be even more wary of Ramains and Council."

"Which would merely force them back into a desperate corner and return them to their pillage and plunder tactics." Brit nodded. "It wouldn't solve their economic and agricultural problems either. Wouldn't solve anything."

"All right then," Sparrow saw the sense in that. "Going to Churv for help won't work. So what would?"

"We do need to contact the Crowned Rule and ask that she send us the Prince with his troops. But it wouldn't work for them to come and take on the Clan's militia. Taysa's Swords make the better target."

Brit put out a hand in puzzlement. "How is that different from targeting the Clan's militia?"

"There are three factors." Llinolae counted them off on her fingers as she went. "First, Taysa and her Swords must be dealt with in Khirla. Her role as Steward and the Swords' position of tyranny must be displaced. Second, Taysa and her power among the Clan's own militia must also be eliminated. Throwing her out of my Palace isn't enough, if she can come running back to the Clan's militia and her stockpile of fire weapons. However, it *would* work if we drove her out, and the Clan's militia weren't ready to back her anymore; then she'd only have a renegade's group behind her, armed with a small batch of fire weapons left over from Khirla."

"But we destroyed those!"

Brit's gentle touch stilled Sparrow, and she reminded her shadowmate, "There would have been individual pieces scattered among the Swords' personal gear."

"But those weapons would be limited in number," Gwyn interjected quietly. "And once their fuel cells were drained, Taysa would have no replacements to draw on."

"Precisely," Llinolae nodded. "She and her renegades would probably refuse to ever compromise. But their numbers would be cut, their access to information from the Palace would be closed, and eventually I could contain them and there'd be peace again."

"That's only," Brit warned again, "if the Clan itself doesn't decide to launch another young hot-head to scavenge land from your district."

"That's the third piece to be considered. If Taysa's power falls, then we have to be ready to offer the Clan Leads another path, and we'll have to do it quickly, while the shock of the crisis can give the Clan Leads the impetus *they'll need* in order to sway the middle ranks of those militia left in Clantown."

"But the Clan folk need a treaty that addresses so much!" Sparrow protested, setting back in her chair. "Enough land for their community? Is that even viable? They've no gist of trade skills, Ramains or Desert Tribunal law—most of 'em don't even speak Trade Tongue!"

"Aye," Llinolae was undaunted. "And if we truly want to take away Taysa's power, our plans must account for the Clan soldiers as well. In any militia there are honorable fighters who only want what is best for their people. Yet after seasons of warfare, they have no other skills and they have pride in their strength as protectors. No one can expect all veterans to contentedly shed a sword and take a plow. Whatever truce the Clan Leads negotiate for, there must be contingencies for everyone. Remember, Taysa's power was built on the Clan's need to survive, and the border scouts such as Camdora joined her cause as soldiers because Taysa said a larger militia was necessary *for the good of the Clan.*"

"Could you see it? A treaty that gives both farmer and soldier a respected Clan place! I can just see Taysa sputtering objections as her veterans all leave her!" Sparrow gloated with a gleeful slap on the table. "She'll be out there in the forests by herself! Just running around, all by her lonesome!"

"*Mae n'Pour!* Sweet Sparrowhawk—you'll be the death of me!" Brit roared half-rising from her chair. "Don't these things get complicated enough without you flinging tangents every which way. Now sit down..."

"So we can get on with it!" Finished Sparrow undauntedly. "Yes, I want to know too, Llinolae, how're we to do all this?"

"Aye." Gwyn's quiet voice cut gently through her Sisters'. Her copper-bright gaze turned to Llinolae, and her calm spoke only of a confidence in what Llinolae would propose. "What is your plan, *Soroi?*"

Llinolae leaned forward. "We resettle the Clan as an entire community, as a new district with lands legally deeded by the Crowned Rule. But we resettle them on lands which already are better matched to their farming skills..."

"Plows and pastures instead of forest plots?" Sparrow prodded.

Brit tossed a scowl at her with a hissed, "Yes!"

"Yes," Llinolae continued, "a treaty of two parts. First, the Royal Family sponsors them to resettle on better land, then the Council sponsors them to bonded status with the Traders' Guild. In these ways the treaty respects the Clan's pride in its community and acknowledges the Clan is a part of Aggar now—not the ruffian cast-away of another world. They have struggled amongst us for enough generations, even the sandwolves acknowledge they live *here.*"

Ril endorsed Llinolae's words with a faint nudge to Gwyn along their pack bond. Gwyn found herself smiling, but for other reasons, as she turned to Brit. "I've just had the most extraordinary realization, n'Minona."

Brit glanced at her wryly. "Yes, I'm a Royal Marshal and a Council representative. I'd already figured that Jes' and my time negotiating with the Changlings had elected me to be the persuasive Diplomat we send into the Clan Leads. I'm just waiting to hear where this marvelous, fertile plain is located."

"I know!" Sparrow pounced upright suddenly, her memory's images of land blooming sweet in the spring—before a battle—and an autumn rain rinsing the late spell of heat from the evening air, cleansing the stained earth by mixing mud and blood into soil for Aggar's growth. For the first time in a season, her mental pictures of the north came to feed hope and not despair. "The Clans wants land that's fertile but empty, district-sized but needing soldiers to protect it? Land that others in Ramains would be too weary to fight for and too frightened to leave as unguarded? Maltar's plains—way up north!"

"The northern ranges?" Brit leaned forward, clutching eagerly at the idea. "Why hadn't I seen...? The Mid-Plains of the old Maltar realm—they border the new Changlings' lands now. They're all those things!"

"Would you agree to negotiate then?" Llinolae pressed.

"Yes! This has the very real advantage of meeting many folks' needs. But I would need to send word quick to Churv and Council that I'm instigating such an enterprise."

"They'll back us," Gwyn said quietly, nodding to those gathered at their table. "Together we four are empowered representatives of Council, Royal Family, and Valley Bay. We've a Dracoon and us Marshals—or apprenticed Marshal. And myself as Bryana's surrogate—she and Jes gave me leave to make decisions as Ring Binder proxy. And Ring Binder as well as you, Brit, have voice for the Council."

"Oh, I'm not worried about that—the damned Seers and Council Masters probably had the thing planned from the start!" Brit scoffed. "But reaching them from here is..."

"Is not a problem," Llinolae reminded them all, with a grin. "I'm a Blue Sight, remember? I can reach Bryana again. I remember well enough what Valley Bay's gardens looked like. Then we can send word to Council and Churv through her."

"That would do...do nicely," Brit agreed.

"Then I'll tend to it."

Their unspoken hesitancy rose suddenly, creating a tense silence. Llinolae glanced about at them, and grinned more broadly. "The need for hiding my Blue Sight is past. The need to use my talents more openly is obvious."

"Then you have our support," Gwyn returned.

"I'd be honored," Sparrow seconded.

"As would I," Brit grinned, still somewhat incredulous at her slowness in adding some of this together. "You know, not only will this help Khirla and Clan...the Changlings' own governing force has trouble managing the Changlings' renegades, and they fear the Treaty will be lost for them all, if the renegades go unchecked by the Prince. But there're so few people left—after the migrations during the wars, after the fears of the renegades—that there's no place nor money to post a Royal Legion along that border."

"Well, the Clan's border scouts are well practiced at roving patrol maneuvers," Gwyn noted.

"And Brit's never lost a delegate or frightened anyone from a difficult barter," Sparrow said with some pride, casting her shadowmate a smile.

"Pretty amazing, isn't it? Considering my temper," Brit admitted. Then her revelry faded, and she turned a level gaze back to Llinolae. "Calling the Prince's troops in deals with Taysa presence in Khirla. Calling the Council and Crowned in, deals with the Clan's survival problems. There's one link left unattended—Taysa's power base was initially sponsored by the Clan's survival needs, but she maintains it by her fire weapons."

"Yes," Llinolae sat back in her chair, tall and calm. They listened attentively to have confirmed what they had all been speculating since the beginning. "The armory must be destroyed. The weapons the militia have among their personal gear, I'd not confiscate, especially if they are to engage renegades once resettled. But the stockpile, their ability to indefinitely resupply any commander—the destruction must stop."

No one protested. Llinolae gave a quick nod, "Then I propose Gwyn and I use these next few days that Camdora is among us to go in search of the armory and leave you and Sparrow with the Clan Lead and her brother."

"With the sandwolves too," Gwyn interjected softly.

Llinolae flashed her a quick smile of agreement. "With my Blue Sight I'll be able to slip our small party past any of the other scouts we might meet. As long as Camdora remains here for the full five days of those standing orders to her scouting party, we shouldn't have difficulty in avoiding Clan scouts once into the Plateau's wastelands."

"Until she tells them to go look for you, no one's going to think you'd get in there so far," Brit agreed.

"But how're you going to find the armory?" Sparrow prompted. "There've been a few attempts in the last generation or so. No one ever succeeds."

"No one's ever had the Sight and used it as I do," Llinolae stated flatly. "The Forest has a sense of rock, crystal, metal. These things aren't particularly alive, I know, but they're recognizable. The other night, when Gwyn and I were caught in the storm and Camdora's brother almost fired at us, his fire weapon was lost and crushed. I wouldn't normally be able to See to search for metal casings or rock formations in and of themselves. But the Forest can, here and on the Plateau's wastelands. Given that I've Seen his weapon up close, I can follow the Forest's amarin and find the armory."

Sparrow eyed Brit worriedly, but the older woman pursed her lips and shook her head in silent denial of a problem. Sparrow held her tongue then, but it sounded like a very risky venture.

"The pack will follow you," Gwyn affirmed, her tone steady.

Llinolae glanced at her, grateful and proud to have their support.

"Then Sparrow and I will occupy Camdora here. If we can get her to trust us any little amount, things will grow immensely easier." Brit liked the idea: a stationary camp, a couple days to chat and eat—either win the Lead's favor with the taste of her best feast, or with swapping bread recipes. She wondered which would be more to the scout's skills? She shook the trivia away for later and cleared her throat. "When Camdora and her brother go, we'll leave with them. If things go well with you and Gwyn, then we ought to be escorted into Clantown about the same time they get word on the armory."

"A dangerous gambit," Gwyn noted in alarm.

"Best place to win trust is in the sandwolves' clutches," Sparrow recited the desert folk's idiom.

"If you want to worry about dangerous," Brit scoffed and leaned forward heavily, "then think on how you're going to destroy that kind of stockpile and not yourselves with it!"

"I've a few ideas on that," Gwyn murmured, glancing covertly to Llinolae.

The Dracoon smiled wryly, "I'm sure we both do." Llinolae glanced back to Brit. "Gwyn and I should be out of camp before Camdora wakes again. She'll not press for an explanation if we don't put her in a position where she has to ask for duty's sake."

"Good thing to know. I'll give a little line about how you were returning to the Palace. Which I assume you eventually will be doing?"

"We'll do fine," Gwyn assured her friend, reaching across the table for a warm clasp.

Then Sparrow leaned in, covering their hands with her own. Llinolae stood and took their four, one of hers atop and one beneath.

"May the Mother's Wind ride with each of us," Llinolae murmured, looking at the Sisters. "For our strengths and our compassion, may we remember why we're pledged to protecting. And I am honored in having had you all near for a time." Her smile fell to Sparrow with an even greater gentleness. "I wish you both care—even if it comes full season again, before we meet."

"Full season or more," Brit mumbled sadly. She knew how long it took to build trusts. The Clan Leads would probably ask for neutral negotiations, and another Shea Hole would most likely be the wisest setting. The Dracoon would not be a welcomed figure in those meetings for a long, long time—if ever. "We'll remember you. Keep pack and hearts sound, yes?"

Llinolae nodded, and Gwyn added, "I'll miss you and Sparrow, *ann!*"

Hands grasped, then loosened. They turned quickly—there was little time to pack them off before the dawn came.

* * *

"And where are you now?"

"We're camped at a Shea Hole in the Great Forest—the Virgin's Nest. It's about five, maybe six days hard riding south of your Council's Keep."

"Not *my* Council nor Keep," griped a lackadaisical drawl.

Both of them glanced at the Mistress n'Athena, but it was such an old argument of semantics that the Mistress n'Shea refused to rise to the bait. Instead she inquired, "Do we have Shea Holes on Aggar yet?"

"No." She grinned, quite undaunted by her Beloved's silent reproach and she turned back to Llinolae with her brown eyes still full of mischief. A slender hand pushed through the short, whitened hair, but the bangs needed trimming and refused to stay back off her tanned forehead. "Mind you, Daughter, we have a number of those aid stations hidden on quite a few other planets. But back in these decrepit times barely anyone on Aggar even knows about the Terran Base, let alone about the Sisterhood! We've got no *reason* to place a Shea Hole in the Great Forest. There's nobody to smuggle out!"

"Not quite," the Mistress n'Shea corrected dryly. "There was me."

"You're the exception."

"You always say that."

"Only because it's true."

Their banter paused as brown eyes met blue, while the Sight bound them in a wordless, cherishing touch, and Llinolae smiled. She didn't need her Blue Gift to decipher the love these two shared. Her heart warmed, making her think of Gwyn and how it might be after a lifetime to look across a garden to find the *Niachero* still loving her...she rather liked the idea.

"You've got better things to do than sit here watching the teachers fawn over one another," the Mistress n'Athena suddenly declared, and Llinolae sighed. The woman was right. "So, where is your Shea Hole? East or West of the Trade Road?"

"West—by two days of careful riding."

"You're among all those winding stream beds and gorges then?" prompted the blue-eyed n'Shea. At Llinolae's nod, the Mistress grew more concerned. "That's awfully close to the Terran Plateau borders, isn't it?"

"Uncomfortably so," Llinolae affirmed. "It's why we're still in camp."

"Sitting tight 'til the scouts get discouraged and ease off their search?" The Mistress n'Athena surmised quickly. Then at her partner's startled glance, she explained, "It's what I'd do in Llinolae's place. Shea Holes are infamously hard to find, well stocked with non-perishable supplies—including weapons—and strategically placed for defense."

"Aye—I see how that makes sense."

"And it's especially good sense, if you're still hoping to make some contacts in Clan Territory who might help you pursue your peace talks."

A raised eyebrow prodded Llinolae to affirm the Mistress n'Athena's speculation, but she could not do so. "An ally may be not quite the right word. I had indeed hoped to find one, and we did make contact. But it seems that Taysa has caused too much unrest—the Clan will not negotiate, unless they have no other choice."

"So it seems, you must fall back on your second plan." the Mistress n'Shea observed quietly.

"Which brings you seeking our council today." The elder Amazon lent Llinolae a supportive, crooked grin. "What do you need, Daughter?"

"From you?" Llinolae very specifically nodded to her Mistress n'Athena. "Information on fire weapons—and on the layout of the Clan's old Base."

"What I know, I'll certainly tell you. But—" she cautioned with an upraised hand, "it may do you little good. The technology and building layouts I'm familiar with will be sorely outdated."

"I know," Llinolae accepted, already having known it would be. "But you'll be giving me something to start with. And that's what I need—a basic grounding in the mechanics of such weaponry as well as what I might expect about the Base."

"That I can give you."

"Which brings you to me and my Sight," the Mistress n'Shea broke in gently. Her blue eyes danced lightly across the shimmering harmon of Llinolae's face.

"Aye—something I did while held in Clantown caused one of their weapons to…to ignite. I know that it happened because of my Sight. But I don't know what I actually did to make it happen."

"Hmm…not so unusual when you're the one in the middle of the crisis…." Her brow knit, and she glanced at her student. "How long ago for you was this?"

"A little more than a ten-day."

"Ah then, I wouldn't worry about understanding it. It's still very soon after the event for you. Your out-of-time Seeing is probably blurred by your own personal reactions…give it a little more time before you go back through the amarin to search the images again. With your unique style of Seeing, you shouldn't need more than a couple of reviews to identify the elements you're missing."

"I can't wait. I can't afford to. You see, the scout who agreed to speak with us, left strict orders with her veteran scouting patrol to wait five days for her. If she's not back by darkfall the fifth day, they'll bring out the entire Clan's border corps to the area they last saw their Clan Lead and her 'abductors'. When our discussions were obviously not going to resolve anybody's problems, she offered an informal, *personal* gesture of good faith; she agreed to stay at the Shea Hole camp for the full five days—no questions asked, no conditions to Marshal or Dracoon staying with her."

"In essence," the Mistress n'Athena mused, "she gave you permission to slip across her patrol's section of Plateau border without hindrance. She's condoned your attack on the armory."

Llinolae nodded. "If I can get in and destroy the stockpile by evening of the fifth day she won't send the patrols after me. But she's not willing to suspend her civic duties completely. She swore to protect her folk and she'll lose any authority to do that within the militia's corps if she's discredited by my actions."

"So she'll give you five days, but then there's no chance that anyone will believe she hadn't glimpsed some inkling of your plan during that time." The Mistress n'Athena saw that clearly enough. "She'd have to send the alarms out or be branded as traitor."

"And probably be executed." Llinolae turned back to the Mistress n'Shea, knowing that the elder's silence was from very real concerns. What Llinolae was about to ask of her Mistress, was not an idle, safe chore.

"You need to know—and soon—how you ignited the fire weapon." The Mistress spoke softly, saving her the pain of actually finding the words. "And you need to know if you can do it again."

Llinolae nodded mutely.

The Mistress n'Shea took another moment to consider their risks. For any other Blue Sight asking her such a question, she wouldn't have hesitated to reassure them. Llinolae, however, had never been much like any other Sighted in the way she embraced her Gift. And in this circumstance there was a very real danger that, in discovering what had happened, Llinolae could inadvertently ignite the two of them in the process. But the cost of life and limb in Khirlan was growing, and she understood that too. In the end, all the Mistress could do was square her shoulders, shrug her long braid of sal t 'n pepper hair behind her, and agree to try.

Chapter Fourteen

Are you sure you are going to be comfortable enough with that tack? I mean...I know Khirla's original tradition shuns stirrups as dishonorable tools of warfare. But do you actually prefer it?"

Llinolae chuckled. "I do."

Gwyn still held her reservations as she eyed the light harness and saddle pad Llinolae had purloined from Sparrow's acrobatic stocks. Calypso protested Gwyn's concern with a snort before reassuringly nosing Llinolae's elbow; regardless of the gear, the sturdy bay had no intentions of allowing her new friend to fall.

Gwyn grimaced. "All right, I concede. It's just...well, this could turn into a ten-day sort of excursion."

"If it does," Llinolae returned sensibly, swinging herself up easily into the stirrup-less saddle, "then we've lost. Camdora's patrol will follow her orders explicitly. Come darkfall of that fifth day, they'll send a runner to Clantown announcing that we're in the vicinity. After that...," Llinolae shrugged.

Gwyn sighed. "After that, every scout—wobbly old veterans and green apprentices—will ride out armed with fire weapons and ambition!"

"No, not ambition—but with fervor. With the zealous, fearful conviction of a cornered animal needing to strike in the face of death."

"Taysa will be informed as well."

Llinolae nodded grimly. She shifted the bow bag a bit further behind her left knee and tightened the tack straps to hold it. A long sword hung to the front of her right leg as well. Light tack had not meant lightly armed. If they were going to get as deep into the Clan's upper territories as she expected, it would be foolish to leave their defenses solely to the powers of her Sight or to the sandwolves.

"Are we ready?" Gwyn prompted, mounting Cinder with a grace that warmed Llinolae's heart.

Abruptly distracted, Llinolae glanced upstream towards the camp. She nodded Gwyn towards that canyon's bend. "Our packmates bring Sparrow."

Cinder stomped, shifting restlessly, and Gwyn calmed her with a murmur. "Can you See if something is wrong in camp?"

"Nothing with Camdora or her brother, at least."

Sparrow appeared quickly, skipping from rock to rock as she crossed the stream bed with Ril following in her footsteps. Ty gave the matter less thought and, tongue lolling happily, splashed through the creek bed undaunted.

"Good—I didn't miss you!" Sparrow reached them. She smiled broadly and extended a small map to Gwyn. "Brit found this in her 'obscure box.' Thought it might do you some good. It's the old boundaries of the original Unseen Wall that the Council had set up around the starcraft port."

Ty bumped Llinolae's foot playfully. The Dracoon grinned, teasing the sandwolf's chin with her booted toe. Since Gwyn's accident, the two of them had gotten to be fairly close.

"I hope we don't have to go in quite that far," Gwyn frowned. She caught

258

Llinolae's attention and tossed her the map tube to store among the sleeping gear on Calypso's packs.

"But Brit is right. It will help anyway," Llinolae allowed. "It will let us estimate how much land and erosion damage has occurred. In short, the more that is outside of that old 'wall,' the worse it is."

"To estimate leagues and timelines…," Gwyn nodded, seeing the value in that. "Aye, it will help both the Council and the Royal Family in evaluating how much land to deed the Clans in the northern ranges."

"Brit's thought exactly," Sparrow echoed. Then she looked to each of them. Ril pushed under her hand for a farewell pat. "May the Mother ride your winds, my Sisters."

Llinolae smiled. Gwyn nodded. They were going to need the Mother's blessings.

* * *

Gwyn straightened from her crouch, tossing aside the handful of pebbly grit she had been studying. Even in the moons' dimmed light, the abandoned fields were a pitiful sight. Rocks the size of cobblestones were littered about. The land was craggy and sparsely grassed. There were scattered bracken hedges and twisted skeletons of nearly dead saplings; poor attempts at windbreaks, Gwyn realized.

She brushed her hands off on her breeches and squinted at the abandoned structures on the northern horizons. The wind stirred up and rushed past her, blowing her hair loose from her short braid. Cinder nosed her shoulder with a grunt, black mane whipping back to mesh with Gwyn's own red silk.

The Amazon leaned into the mare's warmth, pressing their cheeks together as she scratched the ruddy hide behind an ear. It wasn't that she was cold. The wind was dry. It smelt faintly of dust. Despite the recent rains, the countryside had the barren feeling of a wasteland.

"Aye," Ril came to lean into Gwyn's thigh. The curled coat felt reassuringly real beneath Gwyn's hand. "This is a coldness of the soul—not the weather that we're feeling."

The wind rose with another swirl and passed. The utter stillness its absence left was almost as disturbing.

"Come, it's time we rejoined Ty and Llinolae," Gwyn spoke aloud to break the emptiness of the place. "We've seen enough to know Camdora spoke only the truth about this wasted land"

She swung into the saddle and sent Cinder off in a canter, Ril close behind. In truth, they had seen enough.

* * *

The winds mourned of ghosts and loss as they crossed the Plateau and passed the camp. The three canvas walls had been angled and slanted to resemble something of a truncated pyramid, and they deflected the worst of the wailing forces over or around them. The design left the travelers open to a sky of starry velvet. But within, the sloping walls hid the small group and their fire amazingly well.

And tonight the fire was a welcomed light to circle around. The midnight moon had set, and the darkness amidst these winds seemed to linger endlessly with no hint of dawn.

The mares moved restlessly, shifting to stay close for warmth, but avoiding contact with the chilly tarp wall. On the far side of the fire's defiant little circle, the sandwolves nestled in between gear, canvas and women. They lay nose to nose, their furry bodies half-curled around Gwyn and Llinolae who sat murmuring in low voices.

None of the small crew were thinking of sleep yet.

"This isn't working," Gwyn muttered, struggling to rearrange the blanket she shared and yet stay careful not to pinch a stray paw in her squirming.

"Are you stealing the covers already, n'Athena? At least let me get in closer here—"

Gwyn glanced at her partner with a feeble smile and opened an arm obediently to pull Llinolae in beneath a blanket. She waited then, until they were settled to ask. "Your harmon found the village then—what was there?"

"The fear and desperation Camdora spoke of." Weariness sang in her sigh as Llinolae leaned a bit against Gwyn's shoulder. "They have some food and shelter of sorts, but these winds have been as unforgiving to their clay brick and timber structures as it has been to their land. Their milkdeer are the sturdiest stock I have ever seen, with woolly hides wrapped thick from the perpetual chill—"

"Again from these winds," Gwyn saw quickly.

"And they seemed prepared to eat anything short of petrified wood. All of which might bode well for adapting to the north...."

"But—?"

"They had but one house in the whole village—perhaps in this whole district!—which had anything remotely resembling a bookshelf. Gardens are scraps of roots and weeds.... Everywhere eyes were dull with need—or bright with fear if the horizon road to the old Base Port swirled dust for a moment."

"Those Taysa would trust to fetch weapons would probably not be the kindest among the scouts militia," Gwyn noted.

Llinolae shook her head, sadly agreeing. "And these folks struggle so for such a dismal survival. They've a single millstone with bins that store everything from the community's grains to salted meats. But salt seems to be about the only thing they have got plenty of!"

"Nothing's safely accessible."

"As for their farming—I'd always suspected things were bad, Gwyn, but I'd never really grasped the concept of 'barren' before this wasteland. These folks have been losing more and more land, faster and faster as they approach the Plateau's edge."

"More slope to the ground run-off maybe?" Gwyn bleakly recalled Brit's maps and notations. "They've got only worsening exposures to the weather fronts too."

"And the wind factor multiplies with each lost league! It will be worse once they begin to drop over the Plateau's edge." Llinolae sighed and turned her face into Gwyn's shoulder. "If they insist on clearing fields and plowing furrows, nothing will ever change. I don't know if they've realized that. I don't think it much matters if they did...Taysa's dream is the only one available."

"It won't be for much longer," Gwyn observed grimly.

"Aye, not much at all." Blue eyes shifted to glance up at her, and a melancholy little half-smile appeared as Llinolae admitted, "I'm afraid I don't like playing bully, just to force a smaller bully into behaving."

"But this isn't some challenge of who is louder or stronger. Neither of us are doing this to be proud of outwitting Taysa."

"It could easily seem an act of vengeance—in so many ways."

"You're not here for revenge," Gwyn reassured her quietly. "I know that, as does Brit and Camdora. We act to protect both Clan and Khirlan from Taysa—or from any other like her. We're acting on a chance to lessen the pain and misery for hundred of families. *Mae n'Pour*— your hope is to aid the Clan folk as well as Khirlan's!"

"I would not do this, if I didn't believe it could work for both peoples," Llinolae confessed softly, her insides shrinking at the very possibility. "With the Forest's amarin eternally reflecting truths—the elusive wisps of abuses and past pain—I would go mad, caught in a web of my own making, if I acted with bitter, raging ambitions." She huddled into Gwyn, seeking the *Niachero's* strength. Her voice dropped even lower as she shuddered. "Because I See through Aggar's awareness when I use my Blue Gift and not through any single person's perspective—not even my own when using the out-of-time Sight?"

"I understand the difference," Gwyn assured her quietly.

"Because of that I can never hide long from my own ambitions or motives. I can't ever freely ignore the consequences of my actions. If ever I were to do something that caused such harm intentionally—or through negligence allowed circumstances to become abusive, the nightmares would…"

"They'd haunt you for seasons," Gwyn finished for her.

"Yes."

They were quiet for a time, Gwyn's chin atop the soft tousle of those black curls, Llinolae's ear pressed close against the steady rhythms of that beating heart. Until finally, Gwyn stirred to ask, "Are you afraid we toy unjustly with the Clan's future in deciding to destroy these fire weapons, Llinolae? Do you fear tomorrow will begin only nightmares?"

"Fears…doubts? Yes, I have them. Churv may have an alternative; the Council may have anticipated and divined another way…I don't—"

"Stop." Gwyn pressed her fingers to Llinolae's lips, then gently they curled beneath her chin to lift her eyes. The two women shifted to sit and face one another a moment, before Gwyn began. "When I left Valley Bay, I had to think very carefully about the rights of the Clan folk, about my duties to the Ramains. As I am a Daughter of the Stars, am I not also an off-worlder's descendent and hence kin in some sense to the Clan? How can I justify the autonomy of Valley Bay's settlement and the Council's endorsement of our own technology, yet in the same breath say I condemn the rulers and technology from the Clan folk?

"The fact is, I haven't found a clear answer. I don't like what I'm about to do to the Clan, because I am imposing a personal judgment on them and casting them into exile. I have no inherent rights that put me above being wrong, no irrefutable argument that I act with divine knowledge from the Mother. If we are wrong this will destroy the Clan's way of life and many of their lives. Even if we are right, their way of life will still be forced to change and the seasons ahead will be struggle. The only difference offered between the two is hope—hope that the northern ranges will eventually yield better shelter and food...and hope that their children can learn to dream again. But with the Changlings as neighbors...?" Gwyn broke off with a shrug.

"Aye...life may grow worse."

"But I can't stand by and do nothing. Too many people in Khirlan and Clan are being hurt. To live with the certainty that things could *only* grow worse, when I had held the opportunity to maybe change that? To me, that would be unbearable. As with you, I find I'm as responsible for the consequences of both my actions and inactions. No, I'd rather live with doubts than know the suffering could only continue and worsen."

Llinloae sighed in resignation but she nodded. "As Dracoon I am Churv's appointed guardian of the district people, and of those of the Clan who by treaty may ask for shelter beneath the Royal Family's care."

"The Clan militia is not abiding by the treaty."

"But others of the Clan folk once did. And they would again, if the choice was freely theirs to make. Camdora was proof of that."

Gwyn couldn't disagree.

"So ethically I feel some responsibility to protect the Clan folk even as I protect Khirlan's people from the Clan."

"Ethical responsibilities forge difficult paths," Gwyn returned wryly. "But I understand. The principal of lending aid and tolerance first, is fundamental to both *Niachero* and Marshal."

"All of which does what? It only leaves me with an ambivalence, similar to your own." Yet Llinolae's resolve was as unwavering now as it had been the day she vowed to end strife between Clan and Khirlan. She took Gwyn's hand in a strong grasp. "I cannot claim Royal enlightenment to endorse my personal decisions." She smiled without humor. "But people are hurting; that always returns me to the simplest of facts."

"Which is?"

"I must do this, because I am the only one who can."

"As I must," Gwyn affirmed. "Because negligence doesn't excuse responsibility."

* * *

Her head bobbed forward and with a jerk Llinolae pulled herself back to alertness. She had the watch. This was not a time for sleeping.

She rubbed her eyes, set her feet a bit flatter and stiffened her backbone against the stone wall of the ruins. The early moon was high, cloudy fingers veiling some of its light. The wind howled faintly, echoing with a lonesome wail among the old, dilapidated buildings. There was not another human soul for leagues, it seemed. But her Sight had warned them differently.

On the southern edge of the starcraft port, a stone and brick barrack housed three elder Clan folk. Two were obviously well-trained militia, and they worked with a wizened team of basker jackals patrolling the immediate area around the armory. The third was a woman who seemed less occupied with guard duties and more concerned with cooking and household chores. She limped a bit when she walked though, and she always wore a small fire weapon on her hip, so neither Llinolae nor Gwyn harbored any illusions—she obviously could be as lethal an opponent as either of her burly male companions.

Not for the first time, Llinolae Saw only too clearly how invested the Clan's militia had become in hoarding the power of these fire weapons.

Llinolae's eyes began to itch again with that dry, bone-deep fatigue which demanded sleep. She sighed, the breath turning into a yawn. There had been too many nights of too little sleep and too many demands on her inner reserves from using her Sight so frequently.

Ty's head lifted from where she lay next to Gwyn. Llinolae Sensed the movement as well as the sandwolf's concern for her personal well-being. From the flat of the last bit of rooftop above, Llinolae felt Ril's nudge question her as well.

They were right. She was no good to any of them like this. A couple hours of sleep would see her stronger, but right now she was more of a liability than a guardian.

Ty rose, careful not to disturb Gwyn's sleep, and padded quietly across the floor rubble. She nosed Llinolae away from the wall. The sandwolves would take the watch for a while. With bow and quiver in hand, Llinolae conceded to their common sense and went to roll herself in next to Gwyn. The bedding was warm from Ty's weight. Her lover turned without waking and wrapped an arm about her to spoon them close.

Bow notched with an arrow and within easy reach, hunting knife laid even closer at hand, Llinolae snuggled back into Gwyn to sleep.

* * *

A whirling mist of gray paled and slowly dissolved in the white fog of an early, damp morning.

Llinolae shivered as the chill crept through the intangible ghost of her harmon. Then cold turned to a deadlier iciness as she made out the building ahead. The whitewash of the small cottage was well tended. The small barn and plowed garden plot seemed miniature replicas beneath the yawning spread of the ancient Forest beyond. Above the cottage door, a circular plaque of red, white, and deep green was tacked to the wall, and Llinolae recognized the sign of her mother's Clan kin—a simple depiction of bird, fruit, and tree.

Her breath caught, horror rising as other details became visible. Bodies of adults and children lay strewn across the yard. A handful of Clan scouts were rifling through pockets and bags for valuables.

Across the threshold lay a young woman of dark hair and slender build. The Clan Lead bending over her, a woman, was patiently prying an ornate wooden ring off of her finger. Llinolae felt her stomach retch—that ring she knew only too well. It had been the handfasting token Taysa had gifted to her uncle, a twin to the one her own mother had gifted Mha'del with on her parent's own wedding.

A thin male scout with an immaculately trimmed beard pushed his way out past the corpse. His Clan Lead straightened, ring safely in hand and glanced down into the open bag he held out for inspection.

The woman turned with him then, barking orders to the rest of the patrol to burn all of the farm's dead.

Llinolae watched in grim sorrow as that Clan Lead and her favorite scout mounted their horses. She felt cold stone encase her heart while they sat there, satisfaction and confidence in their manner supervising the bonfires.

Looking younger than Llinolae was accustomed to seeing them and dressed as Clan military, she nonetheless recognized the pair—Taysa and her Master at Arms. Taysa glanced at the ring in her hand again, slid it part way down her finger, only to find it too small a fit. She pulled out a small knife to shave the wood a bit thinner, and by the time the rest of the patrol were finished and mounted, the ring was fitting well.

They rode off at a curt word from her, and Llinolae turned back to the ashen smoke of the farmstead, back to the remains of her mother's half-sister's family. The woman she knew as Taysa *was not Taysa*.

Llinolae balked at the realization.

"*Soroi?*" Gwyn's gentle voice called to her through the bleakness of that dreamspun vision. "*Ti Mae, soroi?*"

Llinolae blinked, feeling Gwyn's warm breath against her ear. The solidness of Gwyn's hand lay upon her shoulder as the *Niachero* leaned across her in concern. With a shudder, Llinolae rolled quickly and buried herself in Gwyn's strong arms.

"What have you Seen, Love?" Gwyn pressed, holding her close. "What have you found?"

"She...Taysa...," Llinolae squeezed her eyes shut. Her heart shredded at the near success of that long laid plan—at the deaths of so many. "I knew she lured Uncle into her schemes in order to poison Mother. But I'd not Seen her before! Not for who she really is...isn't!"

"Who she isn't? Do you mean your Mother or Taysa, *Soroi?*"

"Taysa isn't Mother's sister! Not really...Mother would have known her to be an impostor.

"I Saw Taysa in the visions tonight, saw how she'd already killed my aunt—killed the entire family! Mha'del accepted Taysa as blood kin because of the ring she gave Uncle."

"Because he recognized it as your Mother's family mark."

"Aye—a wood seal of their Clan kin. Mother described it as a 'tree of life.' Father wore it always, and when Uncle returned to Khirlan wearing a matching piece, Mha'del pressed until Uncle confessed to a handfasting with a woman of mixed blood."

"After which, Mha'del was quick to welcome his wife's half-sib." Gwyn sighed and hugged Llinolae tighter. "I am sorry, *soroi*, so very, very sorry."

Llinolae nodded, tears rising and she clutched at Gwyn's jerkin. "Just hold me..."

"I'm here. Right here."

And then, she could only cry.

Chapter Fifteen

The armory was a great deal further from the barracks that housed the guards and baskers than most might expect. But her Mistress n'Athena had diligently explained—again and again!—how potentially dangerous this cache was. If there were more than two dozen of the smallest fire weapons housed here, an accident could create an earthquake leaving a crater the size of Khirla's palace. The truth of her statement was attested to by the barren perimeter of twice that size surrounding the little hut and its half-sunken cellar.

When Gwyn had first seen the open width of that distance, she cursed the Fates for their Jest. But Llinolae had been far from displeased. As soon as dawn pushed over the eastern peaks and passed the scattered shadows of the ancient rubble, the Clan scout had left his perimeter patrolling, staked a fresh pair of basker jackals on watch, and retired to the barracks for sleep. It was not such an odd defensive tack to take; after all, with good light and cleared land, their fire weapons could strike at an intruder at nearly any distance once they were seen.

So with the humans safely tucked away for a time, that left only the baskers to deal with—and those were promptly subdued by a trick of the Sight and the sandwolves. Llinolae imposed an illusion that hid the sandwolves approach, and then with no warning at all they appeared nose to nose, teeth bared and growling before the slender bullies. The baskers yelped and fell over themselves in utter terror, straining away to the limits of their tethers. Ril and Ty stared the beasts down into a cowering silence and menacingly settled themselves down as well. The intimidation worked. The sandwolves assumed master status and neither basker challenged with disobedience.

"Don't hurt them," Gwyn reminded her packmates quietly. "They could not choose who raised and trained them."

Ril spared her a disgusted glance. Sometimes Gwyn's assessment of their judgment was insultingly shallow.

"Sorry," Gwyn gulped, suitably chastised. "Keep an eye on the house though." She hurried down the cellar steps after Llinolae.

They paused below as Llinolae examined the metal-reinforced padlock. She frowned at its bulk, then Gwyn was shouldering forward with, "Let me."

One of the stiletto knives popped from it's vambrace, and deftly she pried it into the fist-sized lock. Tumblers clicked and there was a sharp 'snap'—she pulled the padlock open.

"I am impressed," Llinolae lifted a brow and cracked a smile.

"Works just like the old oak ones up north, that's all." But Gwyn was grinning proudly as she pushed the door open and waved Llinolae in ahead of her.

Inside they both froze. The light was dim from the open door behind them, but there was enough to see the unbelievable. Racks and crates, workbenches of half-repaired pieces, and careless piles of spare parts littered the room. A fortune in metals and a horrific potential for destruction lay before them.

"*Mae 'n Pour*—" Gwyn breathed and could do nothing but stare.

"The battling will never be done until the Clan itself is dead, if this is here."

"How could we have left so much behind?" Gwyn gasped in dismay. How could *dey Sorormin* have allowed this sort of danger to survive through all these ages? "How could we have been so...irresponsible?"

"Because...," Llinolae met Gwyn's confusion with a quiet command of truth and strength that stilled the Amazon's very thoughts, "your foremothers came from the stars, *Niachero*. And this was not a powerful danger—not to their eyes, not in their time—not in an age when whole planets were destroyed in single battles. To them, this could never be seen as anything nearly as awful as the trials that had brought them to Aggar in the first place."

Gwyn grasped the sense in that, yet denied the excuse of it. "They still knew what this could do—especially because this is Aggar. Especially because there is no defense against this type of raw technology on all of Aggar."

Llinolae considered that, then conceded it with a faint nod. "Yet my own forebearers are not blameless."

"So..." Gwyn stood taller, drawing her sword from its sheath and holding it out before her, hilt up, "our duty is long overdue, it seems. It is time to restore the balance of continents and power—to remove the inequality those such as Taysa must always pervert."

Llinolae laid a hand to Gwyn's atop the weapon. "I cannot let you sacrifice your lifestone nor your sword for this, *Soroi*. Both have done honorable service for all across too many seasons."

Gwyn tipped her head, puzzled. "I know of no way to destroy this much metal weaponry, save for breaking the stone free of my blade. Even then, the lifestone will still not disintegrate the lot for a day or two?"

"I have a way," Llinolae declared softly. "Now that I have been here, have seen this place in such detail...," Her Blue gaze swept the room with a haunting eerieness of resignation. "I can return here as harmon and I can bring...." She sighed shortly and spun on her heels. "But I must do it soon. Bring the baskers back to the ruins with us. They will not be safe where they are staked now."

"They will be missed?"

"No," Llinolae assured her briskly, "it will not take that long."

* * *

She stood at the edge of the stone-paved groundwork that ringed the ruins of the starcraft port. She stood with her leather-soled boots firmly planted upon the dry crust of Aggar's soil. To Llinolae's left the sun glittered silver along the steel and alloy skeletons of scattered, shapeless ruins. To her right, the very, very distant line of the great Forest guarded the last few leagues to the Plateau's end. Behind her, contented and fed, lulled the basker pair in the shade of the half-crumbled building; Ty and Ril sat near, diligently supervising their new charges.

"Ril and Ty will take them back to Brit and Sparrow when they go tonight. Camdora can reclaim them for the Clans then."

Llinolae nodded absently, Gwyn came to stand beside her, sword unsheathed. She hesitated, following Llinolae's gaze towards that distant blur of near-nothingness which marked the barracks and armory.

"Are we sure the Clan scouts there will be safe from this?"

"I will send the force of it east—back into the ruins," Llinolae murmured.

Gwyn swallowed hard. She took her sword in a two-handed grip and widened her stance. With a grunt she drove the blade straight down, cleaving rock and soil as it went in with a blue flash. She stepped away a bit and dried her palms nervously along her breeches.

"Are you ready?" Llinolae's gaze never turned from the south.

"I think so."

"Wait until it is done, before you fetch me," Llinolae reminded her softly, her quiet tone receding like a hollow ghost's whisper.

"I will wait."

Llinolae felt the cold walls of amarin fold about her. She blinked and Saw the armory's interior again. The blue haze fell between her and the room about her, and she gathered her breath in deep.

The sweet feel and taste of the Life Cycles slipped into her at her bidding, filling her harmon with Aggar's strength. She looked again at the stockpiles of weaponry around her. This time the dusty blue webs of amarin sparked. Tendrils spun out in curious questing, until soon the outline of each shadow and shape glowed in a sheath of amarin sapphire.

Then all went still. For a breath, heart and thoughts stood suspended. Time, for Llinolae and Aggar, stood poised. The solution was questioned for one last moment—and then, fire came.

With a whoosh the blue of harmon and amarin went ablaze.

Llinolae felt the heat rising. The torrent of fiery swirls roared loud in her ears. It ate the air and there was a fluttering instant of near suffocation, but she concentrated—passion and purpose intensifying—and the inferno doubled as the amarin fed it through her very fierceness.

Curtains of flame merged! A pool of liquid flame filled the room from ceiling to floor.

The metal casings began to pop. The core cells among the weaponry began to whine then screech as metal and chemicals boiled together.

"Mother save me!" She prayed in a breath.

The universe around her exploded. She went sailing for that distant, distant sun of the east—

Gwyn gasped at the spiral twisting of fire that broke and shook the ground she stood upon. Winds whipped past her ears, not *from* the torrent but sweeping towards it. And in an angry aching stretch, the fire on that horizon grew into a wave and flew east.

She grabbed the hilt of her sword and clenched tight—eyes tight—and called with every bit of her being to Llinolae's harmon.

The lifestone flared hot beneath her hands within the hilt. Scorchingly hot it burnt, and the *Niachero* held only tighter—soul screaming for her Love.

The lifestone pulsed and reached.

Within her mind's eye the swelling tides of flame and fury swept her into them. She saw the frozen figure of another. She reached forward.

They collapsed to the rock-strewn ground, Gwyn rolling to absorb the impact, putting herself between Llinolae and the 'smack' of the landing. Then she hung on and prayed she had brought harmon and heart together quickly enough. Llinolae's arms went around her, faltered limply, then fastened hard.

"*Mae n'Pour!*" Gwyn rasped and buried her face against the sweating, shivering, dark caramel skin of Llinolae's neck. "Sweet, sweet love, I have you...I have you."

Llinolae's body trembled, near convulsing in muscular fatigue. Ty appeared, dragging a blanket with her, and Gwyn took it gratefully. She had barely rolled Llinolae within it when Ril arrived with another one. Even the baskers seemed to hover nearer with concern.

"Not—not so binding," Llinolae croaked.

Gwyn almost laughed outright at that feeble protest, yet she hurried to comply. Then with Llinolae drawn across her lap, she simply held her and rocked her. Tears and laughter choked her, and Gwyn gave way to both in relief.

"*Soroi,* do not break me in two!"

"No—no," Gwyn eased her grip with an effort. Then for a long while there was nothing but their closeness—and the joy of having each other.

* * *

Calculating grey eyes narrowed in a cold sweep of the eastern city wall and the Great Forest beyond. The height of the Tower room gave the woman a clear view of anyone approaching over that long road through the brushberries and livestock pens. A light breeze wafted by, heavy with the berry scents of hot summer fruit. First harvests would be early this season.

Brushberries! The woman scoffed, tossing back the heavy braid of her dark, graying hair. Even after so many tenmoon seasons, the Khirla's wines still seemed overly dry and downright tart to her palette. Samcin would tease her that she was hopelessly plebeian in her tastes, but then that suited him fine. He too preferred District's mead to wine. Still, the rich, heavy scent of those ripening berries was a sweet one, and she drew a slow, deep breath, enjoying the satisfying memory of her first raid as a commander.

The hoe farmers had been busy with their brushberry crop—they'd grown careless. Despite the old matriarch's preparations for defense, the family had been caught armed only with farming tools and they'd been too far afield for a retreat into their walled enclosures—her timing had been impeccable.

Her scouts had scarcely even needed to resort to their fire weapons. She'd prepared for everything, had deployed her scouts brilliantly! And then there'd been Samcin. He'd stood behind her from the first, bellowing and bullying faithfully in swift execution of any order. Silencing her adversaries, guarding her back, spellbound by her success. She'd almost forgotten their celebration that day, when she'd taken him down to the brushberry field of the hoe farm itself.

It had been a thorny first time for him—in more ways than one, she chuckled. Poor Samcin, he'd been so hopelessly in love with her—nearly as hopeless at pleasing a woman as well. But then she had capitalized upon that advantage too. Ahh—but she had sinced groomed him well in many things, both inside the bed chambers and out.

Aye, the brushberry farmers had marked her beginning. The victory had been so clear, it's formula infallible. Patience, stalking—then finally the strike! Sometimes—even now—it still seemed so absurdly simple, as it had been on that first raid.

The hoe farm had been affluent and the cache a rich one. The Clan leaders had begun to watch her then, admiring her gifts of strategy—succumbing to her passionate, yet always so rational style of persuasion. And she'd always been a step ahead of them—just like she'd been with the hoe farmers' matriarch—befriend the enemy, engender trusts and defenses will fall!

Taysa stretched, nearly purring at the mere thought of that sweet, sweet intoxication. Her lips thinned in a feral curl of pleasure. *Power*—it was the ultimate nectar. It held the beauty to control; it gave pleasure to weave and reweave people, lives and resources until precisely everything fell into place!

Even if the Clan folk had not needed land to expand, she knew she would still be standing here at this window. They still would have followed her in usurping this rich, lush District! It was the tradition—the essence—of being Clan! It was their heritage, and she was only leading them to reclaim their fierce greatness.

Her body snapped rigid at a movement below. A rider broke free of the Forest's edge, horse in full gallop and blue cape flying.

"*Finally!*" Taysa leaned forward eagerly, clutching the crisp gilded edges of her royal mantel. She watched the messenger, growing calmer as he neared the stable's Watch Gate. Waiting sometimes took more of a toll on Taysa than she liked to admit. But now the reports would tell if the Clan scouts had snatched Llinolae back or if that infernal Marshal had found her first!

"We certainly can't have that, can we?" Taysa mused. "Given the devastation she ravaged through our little weapons' horde, any prolonged visit with you, Llinolae, would just about ensure my undoing." Which reminded her—the rider would also have news of the replacements Taysa had summoned from the Clan's central armory.

There'd been far too many accidents lately. She should sit down with Samcin and review some of their duty rosters. They should arrange an inspection of Clantown's resources as well.

Accidents came from oversights. She wasn't about to let either the Clan Scouts or the Steward's Swords grow careless! Especially not now, with a Marshal hiding near!

She scratched a palm nervously.

Initially Llinolae's unexpected resourcefulness in starting the Clantown fire and subsequently escaping had been puzzling. Yet after Taysa had sat herself down and gone over the details of the last few monarcs, she realized she might have grown just a touch careless around the girl lately. Somehow she'd grown tempted to become more complacent about their relationship; a dangerous oversight to make with a girl so bright.

Dangerous—but enticing. There was always that delicious little shiver of pleasure in matching wits with her 'niece.' In an odd way, Taysa reveled in the most mundane of exchanges they shared—she genuinely missed Llinolae when the girl was absent for patrols. The simple fact that Llinolae existed kept life exciting, intriguing.

269

"It will be a pity should I lose you quite so soon, sweet darling," Taysa murmured. "But it would be preferable to the Marshal replacing me."

The rider had reached the city's walls. She spun, the mantel's blue flaring wide behind the ruddy satin of her breeches and boots.

It was time to assess the next gambit.

Taysa composed herself. Samcin would be here shortly, but there were always the odd interruptions and unforeseen little duties cropping up. She had learned never to be surprised.

Llinolae still managed her private trick of an unannounced arrival. But there hadn't been another to catch Taysa unprepared since the day of her husband's unfortunate death...which Taysa hadn't really found as distressing as reputed.

She shrugged the tension from her shoulders, her long braid sliding aside as she leaned back against the heavy desk. It was a burnished, shimmering tone of golden honeywood and ornately carved. Her gaze fell to the great, gaping blackness of the fire hearth. This late in summer, even this interior room of the Palace held no fire, and yet...? Elusive slivers of ceramic gems began to tease her eye in those gaping, black depths. A faint smile curled her lips. She knew the illusion was from the scattered torch light of the room glittering among the odd bits of less-sooty hearth tile. But the subtle dance of emerald and ruby, of sapphire and gold always intrigued her.

The clatter of a distant door echoed in the outer corridors. Taysa watched the door at the end of the Steward's Receiving Room. She knew the majestic banner of the twin sabers hung behind her desk—behind her own tall frame. She knew the daunting, handsome picture she made—but if the one approaching was not Samcin, her wrath would flare soon!

"Enter!" She summoned a half-breath before the heavy knock. But she knew before the door moved that it was Samcin, because there wasn't another fellow in the Palace whose fist could thunder a honeywood door into shaking.

The burly frame of the Sword's Master at Arms could nearly be mistaken for a block of honeywood, his thick beard a rusty-blond and his shoulders wide—usually. But today the tanned skin above the beard was blossom pink with exertion, and the door slammed shut with a heave of his shoulder as he gasped, "Taysa..."

"Yes! Word comes from the east!" She snapped at him, grey eyes flashing. "What of Llinolae? Have they caught her?!! Do they know where she is?"

"Aye...but no! Wait!"

Exasperated at herself, Taysa drew her interrogation to a halt. She knew better than to rattle him with questions when Samcin considered something desperately important. Bide her time a breath or two more, that was it.

"Now tell me," Taysa ordered calmly. "First of our young Dracoon."

"But...aye then. She's not been caught. They say there's been no sign of her or the Marshal, but they suspect the both of them were just on the Plateau."

"Not good. When will our shipment be here? If we're going to stop Llinolae from returning to the city, we're going to have to equip every Sword with new arms. Marshal in tow or not, she'll have the sense to call on the City Guards to stand against us."

"Well," Samcin grunted unsurprised, "wouldn't you, after two blue-cloaked replacements led an ambush against you?"

"They were stupid with that."

"They're dead. There's no need to worry about them now," Samcin ended the matter succinctly. "What you do need to attend to is Llinolae and her Marshal."

He caught Taysa's attention completely this time.

"They're together?"

His broad shoulders seemed to grow a bit squarer and wider as Samcin planted his boots in a solid stance. Taysa felt the rigid ice of caution stiffen her spine. There was very little that threatened Samcin's bulk enough for him to slip into that iron, steady pose.

"They are together," Taysa saw. "Yet there's more. Why should we think they're on the Plateau?"

"*Were* there," Samcin amended flatly. "There was another incident."

"Another store of fire weapons?" Taysa's low voice was edged with disbelief and appalled fury. "They got to another one of our store-rooms?"

"Worse then that. They got to the Base Stockade."

Taysa spun and braced herself on the desk. Time hung suspended for an eternal heartbeat—and then she was breathing again. "How did they get past...? No!" She lifted a hand to forestall any attempt at an answer. "It's no longer important. How bad is it?"

"Everything went up in a firestorm of...of some kind." His voice wavered a little and the big man paused to clear his throat.

"No one got any of the fire weapons out?"

"Out?" He barked quick. "The place blew! The whole sorry tomb went up in flame! There wasn't any warning of it coming, it just blew!"

"Then why do they think it was the girl and Marshal?" Taysa quipped. "No one has ever been able to get that far in past us. What's made everyone so certain these two did it now? Or did something freakish happen to shake a weapon into overdrive?"

Samcin took a short breath, thinking about that.

"It makes a difference, Samcin," Taysa's voice grew lower. He nodded, and she felt the steadfastness of his loyalty. Good—she couldn't afford to lose him now.

"What do you want us to do?" His voice came even and deep.

"First things first. Round up the weapons we have here in the Palace. Everything! I don't want a hand-piece left unaccounted for—"

"Done." The bearded chin lifted with half-a-nod. "We're lucky there, what we do have is pretty well-charged. Just had the turn-in before Feasts. What we've got will last."

"It doesn't have to last forever," Taysa murmured, more to herself than the man. A little judicial rationing of the powerful pieces and a few more scouts in each patrol would keep the raiders just as intimidating with sword and torched arrows. Samcin hadn't spent the better part of his life training sword carriers and bow men without anticipating the very real need that they be effective with or without the Clan's technology.

"But it'll all be for nothing, if we can't silence the Marshal and Dracoon!" Taysa's fingers clenched the desk's edge 'til they were white. "Ahh, sweet

Llinolae, just what exactly are you up to…?"

Samcin said nothing, knowing the mood of these mutterings and knowing that some of Taysa's most brilliant maneuvers came in a crisis.

A rapid pounding at the thick door brought Taysa out of her planning and she turned in alarm.

"Enter!" They both shouted in the same breath.

The Chief Scribe scrambled in past the door jamb. Brown ink marred the lap of his sky-blue satins and blotched his fingers, though with his emotions running fearfully high the stuff on his hands was barely discernible. He shied from Samcin, stumbling on the edges of his robes.

The Master of Arms grunted and palmed the door shut.

"What is it, Geran?" Taysa's measured her voice carefully, instilling just the right balance of boredom and concern for her favored Scribe. She'd thought to keep the armory's destruction a secret from the Swords and Scribes for a little while yet, but if Geran's reaction was anything to go by, she was obviously going to have to reassess who was to be trusted and who was ready to flee.

"There's one of our Swords just in from the border—"

"We know that, Geran," Samcin drawled. "It's no alarm for you."

"Samcin," Taysa interjected quietly, and with one glance to her the man took his cue to ease back for now.

"He came straight into me—not a…not another soul knows. My oath on it!"

Samcin lifted a bushy brow in the Steward's direction. At her glance, he sent her a quick shake of denial; their easterly reports had come only to him.

"The man's one of *ours!*"

"One of our messenger Swords?" Samcin rumbled. "Why don't you speak up, man? What can possibly be so awful comin' out of Churv?"

Taysa's stomach dropped, and she unobtrusively clutched at the desk behind her as knees threatened to buckle. Another little piece slipped into place unexpectedly, as she remembered that old Captain of Mha'del's—Rutkins or something?—had been standing duty at the private little Stable's Gate this morning when she went riding. He had smiled ever so slightly before clearing her way through. Ever so slightly? It had been almost a salute of some kind.

Then quite suddenly and completely, Taysa understood what young Llinolae had been doing! The audacity of it—the improbable, impossible gamble of it! And here it was all about to gloriously succeed!

"But the Pr-prince's troops are coming!"

"His what?" Samcin looked at the skinny, quivering clerk like he was as daft in the head as his appearance endorsed.

"His best and fastest horse troops!"

"Don't you see, Samcin?" Taysa broke in softly. The two men turned to her, waiting. "Churv is sending troops against us!"

"How many?" Samcin rumbled, both hands grabbing Geran by his robe.

"Just the…the one company, the Sword saw!"

"A single company we can handle!" He dropped the shaking Scribe as abruptly as he'd collared him, rounding eagerly to Taysa with sparks rekindling in his eyes. "There's nearly three of us to each of them. We've pick of the place and fighting."

"No!" Taysa was almost laughing at his incomprehension.

"We've got the weaponry!" He snarled. "We can wipe them out! We don't need anything but what our Swords' got in their chests and packs!"

"And then what?!" Taysa challenged in astonishment.

"Then we regroup." Samcin stepped closer, fists clenching in gathering frustration.

"Regroup?" Taysa shook her head again with a shrill hoot of laughter. "Regroup to deal with the Marshal and Dracoon as they have their turn at us?"

"Aye!" He picked her up by the arms and barely kept from shaking her silly. "What is wrong with you, Taysa? I can do this! I can do this for you, I tell you!"

"No!" She spat abruptly, staring at him undaunted by his brutal hold. "Hear me Samcin! We've lost! It's done! It's over, Lover! *We've been found out* ! There's no more for us to do, but get out of here before the noose is tight!"

"The...what...?"

"The Prince brings his finest troops against us, Samcin! Do you think he's sending only this one company? No—but this is his fastest. He'll take what he can by surprise and then bring in more of his veterans behind!"

"But—?" Samcin let her go with a gentleness that nearly made Taysa laugh again. "Who did this?"

"Our fine young lass, of course—Llinolae."

He only looked blank.

"She's got the City Guard behind her too."

"That's not fact!" he roared.

"It is!"

"Oh Mother, dear blessed Mother, what are we going...."

"*Out!*" Samcin's fury spun and dove for the little man. "You're part of this no more, do you hear? Out!"

The Scribe scrambled and ran, leaving the door open behind him as the wordless bellow the giant sent after him echoed through and through the stone.

"Now—!" He swung back to face her with a surprising calm that most would have questioned. But Taysa straightened and smiled. She had seen that release of fury and return to the rational—she trusted it more than any Clan technology.

"We started with a handful of reprobates and weapons," Samcin shrugged his blue cloak into a more comfortable fit. "Guess we're going to end up with the same."

"Only our two central corps," Taysa instructed quickly.

"I'll have them tear through the others' gear kits for what extras we can find."

"But don't shirk the necessities." Taysa lifted a brow with ire, "We can't eat steel or leather."

"Though once we did try!" His grin was crooked, but Taysa had always led them before; she'd see them through. "When do we ride?"

"Tonight at dusk."

* * *

Llinolae shifted stiffly in the bulky stirruped saddle, leather creaking when she moved. Gwyn glanced at her as did the two sandwolves seated beside the horses. She nodded across the rolling stretch of brushberry farms to the rising walls of her city.

"Do you notice the difference?"

Gwyn studied the shape of the twists and curves of the upper galleries. The slender towers of the Palace beyond seemed like pale shadows against the rich blueness of the skies. A steady hum of wagons and people drifted out even to this shady knoll where the Great Forest enclosed their milkdeer trail.

She shook her head, unable to place anything odd in the scene. "What do you see as changed?"

"Taysa's rule is gone. Those banners hung along the upper wall—they are from the days of the old City Guard."

Gwyn looked again, but could not make out any design upon the deep blue of the cloth. There was only a simple border of Churv's ruddy brown-reds.

"Father believed no single person or symbol of Khirlan should be more important than another. He thought there was a time and place for all things in Aggar's Living Cycles." Llinolae smiled as Gwyn grinned at her. "I do not think he would begrudge even the Clan some forgiveness."

"Well—" Gwyn shrugged with a shoulder and a tilt of her head, "there is land for the Clan's resettlement now, only because the Changling Wars ended last season. I can just hear the Archivists of the Council's Keep arguing in a few generations, adamantly declaring that it was merely time for the Wars to cease and for the Clans to find their way into the fabric of Aggar's amarin."

Llinolae groaned.

"Aye—it is still a philosophy I find hard to embrace once in a while."

"As long as you embrace me at least as often!" Llinolae breathed, her heart suddenly pleading from the depths of her blue, blue eyes.

Gwyn's smile softened. She tugged off a glove and reached across to gently pull Llinolae into a kiss. Lips lingered, reassurance rising steady and strong.

They drew apart. Gwyn's hand cradled her cheek for a moment longer, then Llinolae caught it and pressed a kiss to the palm.

She glanced up at Gwyn. "Are you certain this is what you want—for you and your packmates?"

Ty butted Llinolae's booted shin indignantly, and Ril rolled her clear eyes in an annoyed human fashion. Gwyn bit back a laugh, then met her lover's gaze once more. Her voice was level and confident though—all hint of teasing gone as she answered, "We are sure, *Soroi!*"

Llinolae squeezed Gwyn's hand. Then she drew a deep breath and squared her shoulders as Gwyn slipped her glove on again.

"Would I sound completely cowardly if I admit I am not looking forward to this welcome I am riding into?"

Gwyn noted Llinolae's voice held none of the trepidation her words reflected. She gave a crooked grin, "You'll manage."

"I'll have to, won't I?"

"You will." A mischievous glint lit in Gwyn's copper eyes. "At least through eventide."

"At least through...?" Llinolae eyed her suspiciously. "What do you mean by that, *Soroi?*"

"Well, if there is a time and place for everything...? And you should not waste the advantage you have here, since you are heartbound to both a Royal Marshal and a sandwolves' bondmate." Gwyn's gaze traveled tellingly down the length of Llinolae's body and then slowly back to her eyes. "As Marshal I have every right to demand your private attentions, don't I? And no one—but no one!—will get past Ril or Ty to contest it." She kicked her heels and Cinder lunged off.

Llinolae turned in astonishment to the two grinning sandwolves. In unison, their chins bobbed in sneeze-like nods, and then they were trotting off as well. Nia followed on without urging.

For a full moment, the Dracoon simply sat there. Then a shout of gleeful laughter rang through the forests, and she sent Calypso on to catch up with her new family.

amarin: the essence of life; the empathic imprint of animate existence; aura; cumulative pattern of feelings, thoughts and reflexes

basker jackal: a sleek, scavenger canine, native to the Ramains' plains and renowned for its blood lust; semi-domesticated by militia for chase and guard chores

black glass: a ceramic-glass compound of especially durable strength that hones to a sharp edge; commonly used in making knife blades

blackpine: a valuable hardwood conifer with a black, barkless trunk and green-black needles; common to Maltar's lands

bondmate: any eitteh, human, or sandwolf who has been empathically bonded into a sandwolf's familial unit (see pack bond; sandwolf)

Blue Sight: the Sight or Blue Gift, a sixth sense genetically linked to blue eyes; an awareness of and ability to manipulate life auras and amarin; a person possessing the Blue Sight

boko: a food native to the Ramains, a vegetable-meat paste wrapped in boiled leaves

braygoat: a short-horned goat native to Ramians' southern districts

brushberry: an evergreen bush with a sweet-tart berry; a Ramains wine

bunt: a tall stemmed grain yielding red-brown seedlings; husks often used for animal fodder; a greyish flour produced from the seedlings

buntsow: a carnivorous, hooved mammal; a scavenger native to the northern forests; a non-venomous cousin of schefea

"by the Mother's Hand": 'done with the Goddess' blessings' (an idiom)

Changlings: sentient half-human, half-feline beasts native to the Northern Continent; a race of people known for their amoral selling and reselling of information; miners of lifestones

Clan, the: people of the Clan's Plateau; descendents of off-worlders who were stranded on Aggar at the fall of the Galactic Terran Empire; renowned for their weapons technology and raiding activities

Clan Lead: legislative representatives chosen by and from among the Clan folk; (plural)a governing assembly; civil servant

Clantown: the governing settlement and militia corp of the Clan's Plateau; a village in the ancient Terran Quadrant, located at the edge of the eastern plateau adjacent to the Ramains' Great Forests

commons: a Ramains' term for the tavern housed by an inn

Council of Ten: a collection of ten Masters and Mistresses educated in the history and humanity of Aggar; guardians of planet integrity

Crowned Rule: the designated heir of the Ramains' Royal Family; usually chosen for skills of statescraft rather than warfare

cucarii: (singular: cucarae) small, poisonous crustaceans found in the wastelands, usually nested in large groups; scavengers

Desert Peoples: (the Southerners) loosely organized nomadic tribes, native to the Southern Continent; renowned for their distilled liquors and merchant ventures

Diblum: a small Ramains' village southeast of Khirla

dracoon: a governing marshal appointed by the Ramains' King

early moon: the first of the Twin Moons to rise on any given evening eitteh: sentient feline, native to the Northern Continent (see winged-cats; men-cats)

Eldest Prepared: best of the shadow trainees at the Council's Keep; preferred choice for next assignment and lifebonding; instructor of younger recruits

Fates, the: the male deities of evil mischief; mythical rulers of the dark underworld; primary figures refer to Malice and Ambition with numerous secondary figures such as War, Ire, Greed, and others

Fates' Cellar: home of the Fates; the mythical world of a punishing afterlife; place of evil souls; hell

"Fates' Jest": a malicious turn of events attributed to deities, the Fates (an idiom)

Firecaps: intersecting mountain ranges that comprise the northeastern third of the Northern Continent; volcanic and uninhabited; Seer controlled to stabilize continental land masses

grubber: a generic term for ground rodents in the Northern Continent; smallish, nasty tempered mammals

harmon: a soul-spirit; self-image projected by a Blue Sight to another

honeywood: a deciduous hardwood with rough, red bark; yields a golden grain of decorative value; common to the southern Ramains

Jezebet: title given usually to a woman; resident of the Council's Keep; person trained in the arts of lifebonding shadowmates

jumier: a fowl native to the Ramains' northern districts

Khirla: Dracoon's capital in the Ramains' southeasterly district Khirlan

lexion: a domesticated fowl raised for its meat; common to farms of the Northern Continent

lifestone: an opal-like energy stone often found amidst limestone deposits in the Northern Continent; used by the Council in lifebonding shadowmates

mala´: a female slave or bond-servant of the Ramains whose duties are reserved for the household and bedroom

Maltar: the ruling family of the northern half of the Northern Continent; term may refer to both ruler and country of rule

men-cats: male eitteh; cat-like savages of impaired intelligence; isolated inhabitants of mountain ranges on the Northern Continent

mesta: an amber, thick skinned fruit with a tart, meaty pulp; a fruit pod cultivated by farmers in the Northern Continent

midnight moon: the second of the Twin Moons to rise on any given night

Min: a generic title for women in the Ramains; conceptually similar to "ma'am"

milkdeer: middle-sized, long necked mammal native to the Ramains; frequently domesticated for its milk

monarc: a standard division of four ten-days; conceptually equivalent to 'a month'

mumut: a spice leaf grown chiefly in the lower districts of the Ramains

Mother, the: Goddess; omnipotent, nurturing Female Deity; Birthmother of the Universe

pack bond: empathic understanding of personal commitments; empathic bond of sandwolves used to define familial units (see sandwolf)

pripper: a small, tree-dwelling feline; known for its comical antics and bushy coat; frequently found domesticated in Ramains' cities

Royal Marshal: special emissaries of the Ramains' Royal Family; originally banded to protect travelers; duties expanded to provide districts with legal and military resolutions, to supply the Royal Court with information from outlying districts

sandwolf: sentient canine, originally native to the Southern Continent, which instinctively imprints at birth to one or more sentient others to provide an emotional, empathic bond in developing protective behaviors and communication skills (see pack bond)

schefea: a middle-sized, hooved mammal native to the northern mountains; a scavenger with protruding tusks and venomous saliva glands

Seers: those gifted with the Blue Sight who are bound to Aggar's lifecycles and no longer capable of individual thoughts or actions; directed by the Council of Ten, crafters of Aggar's landscapes; mystics

silverwood: (silverpine) a hardwood conifer with smooth, silver-green bark and grey-green needles; common to the Ramains foothills and mountain regions

single moon: synonymous with monarc; the close of each monarc is marked by a night in which only one of the Twin Moons is visible—this night is referred to as "the single moon"

Ramains: a liberal monarchy uniting most of the Northern Continent; borders the Council's lands and the Clan's territory

Tad: generic title for men in the Ramains; conceptually similar to "sir"

tinker-trade: a traveling merchant member of the Traders' Guild

ten-day: standard division of days; conceptually equivalent to "a week"

tenmoon season: (a season or a tenmoon) a standard division of monarcs; roughly equivalent to two Terran years; name arises from the ten single-moon nights experienced within the planet's completion of one orbit around its sun

torin: a broad leafed fern; an edible plant commonly found in the wooded ranges of the Northern Continent

Traders' Guild, the: a merchant union supported by membership dues that promotes the fair exchange of market goods; endorsed by the Desert Peoples, Ramains, Council and Valley Bay the union may provide arbitrators, bonded transport agents, and travel lodging to supplement regional resources

Twin Moons: the two planetoids orbiting Aggar's globe; associated with the Mother's watchful care

Unseen Wall: an unidentified energy field controlled by the Seers; the border of the Terran Base Quadrant, ordered by the Council of Ten

Valley Bay: the settlement of the Sisterhood; located near the White Isles, isolated from the Northern Continent by the Firecaps; governed by the Ring of Valley Bay and bound to the home world through the Blue Sighted gifts of the Ring's Binder.

White Isles of Fire, the: the archipelagos; a group of volcanic islands extending off the eastern Firecaps of the Northern Continent; origin of the Council and Seers

Wine of Decisions: a spiced wine containing a natural drug known to prompt the visions of the Blue Sight

winged-cats: female eitteh; highly intelligent, cat-like flyers; advocates of Ramains' rule, the Council, and Valley Bay cultures

Dictionary of Sororian Terms

Amazon: a Sister choosing to work/settle outside of the Sisterhood's jurisdiction

ann: Take note!; to emphasis thoughts or ideas; a verbal exclamation point

be: far, distant

beasties: a large,wooly mammal with horns, usually copper-orange in color, descended from stock brought to Aggar for Valley Bay's original settlement

bin: between, to (from)

Cee: customs, the ways of a people

cheroan: to make safe, to protect

coraen: to treasure, to find precious

Coramee: daughter

crone: a wise elder among healers n'Shea

dey: article or pronoun inferring respect; "we", "our" or "the"

duen: to do kindly; to act with concern

Dumauz: (plural: —en) a kind-hearted individual; a concerned friend

Feast of Helen: the anniversary celebration of the Sisterhood's first born child; celebration of unity and independence

felan: using, doing, creating (with)

Founding, the: the original planetary colonization of dey Sorormin under the Galactic Terran Empire; settlement of the home world

Helen: red star of dey Sorormin's home solar system; firstborn of the Founding on the home world, leader of n'Sappho during early negotiations to retain independence (see Founding, the)

Houses of dey Sorormin: surnames of Sisters, designating family and/or skills; six of Seven Houses recall ancient goddesses of Terran lore (n'Athena: guardians(Greek), n'Awehai: crafters (Iroquois), n'Hina: agricultural providers (Polynesian), n'Huitaca: artists (Chibcha), n'Minona: historians/teachers (Dahomey), n'Shea: healers (Irish); First House of dey Sorormin (n'Sappho: legislative leaders) recalls a Terran stateswoman of Greece

Kahmee: little daughter; a very young girl

Kahn: dawn, sunrise

kamak: is made, is finished, brought to completion

Kau: you (singular)

ki: yours (possessive)

kumin: to join together

m' : as, of, springing from

m'Sormee: birth mother; (literally) from the woman's life

mae: dear, precious

Maez: dear one, precious loved one

"mae n'Pour": 'give me strength'(an idiom); used in angry cursing or frustrated prayer to the Holy Goddess

Mau: (plural: —en) heart

Mee: life

Minmee: birth; carries a sacred connotation of creating or life-giving

n' : of (possessive)

n'Sormee: parenting mother or guardian; (literally) of the woman's life

Niachero: Daughter of the Stars; descriptive of Sisters who genetically resemble those n'Athena who negotiated the settlement of Valley Bay; Amazons who led the space protectors to save Aggar during the fall of the Galactic Terran Empire

nehna: so-then; then-it-happened-that; a prompt for more information

nor: past; did happen

Pour: strength, stability; virtuous

Quinn: peace, tranquility; absence of violence

quitan: to nurture; to tend with compassion

ret: cruelty, cruelness; harm

sae: please; request

Sak: intelligence; cleverness

shea: a healer of the House n'Shea; a witch, frequently one closely bound to Nature; a mistress of love potions; possessor of the evil eye;

Sheaz: earth, world; components of a nurturing Earthmother Creator

Shekhina: the moon of Helen's second planet; a hi-tech moonbase which once hosted the diplomatic contacts between dey Sorormin and the now dissolved Galactic Empire; recalls a Terran goddess of ancient Judaic lore, a divine image of woman

Sor: woman

Soroe: friend, dear companion

Soroi: loved one; lover; beloved

Sororian: native tongue of dey Sorormin

Sorormin, dey: proper name of The Sisterhood; colonizers of Aggar's Valley Bay; an off-worlder culture of women (see Helen)

suehn: to lose; to misplace

Tau: me

ti: my (possessive)

tizmar: to remain, to settle; to unite or join together

vara: adamant denial, no; refusal; expression of protest

vu: very little, few; a small number

z' : for; with

"Z' ki Sak, Diana!": 'by your wits, goddess!' (an idiom); expression of regret or disbelief

When I was diagnosed with terminal cancer at age thirty, my crusading in community psychology was forced to the wayside. But not so, my writing. Never my writing. I can't imagine not writing. I write simply because I breath. In weaving words...of passion and justice, of love and hope...I try to remind us all of the beauty we can claim.

So—when the days are gloomy, I listen to Jennifer say, "Snap out of it. Stay out of it!" and pick up my pen to court our mistress, Muse. She lends me peace, and in an odd way I discover more freedom than I've ever known. Because I'm dying, I'm free to put my loved ones and my writing first. I am free to make each day a wonder to treasure. Life is incredibly good. It's never been better.

—Chris Anne Wolfe,
writer / psychologist.